KISS & TELL

TRUDI PACTER

Harper Paperbacks

Harper & Row, Publishers, New York
Grand Rapids, Philadelphia, St. Louis, San Francisco
London, Singapore, Sydney, Tokyo, Toronto

Harper Paperbacks a division of Harper & Row, Publishers, Inc.
10 East 53rd Street, New York, N.Y. 10022

This book was first published in 1989 in Great Britain by Grafton Books, a division of the Collins Publishing Group.

It's All Right With Me reproduced by kind permission of Chappell Music Ltd. Copyright © 1953.

First Harper Paperbacks printing: February, 1990

Printed in the United States of America

HARPER PAPERBACKS and colophon are trademarks of Harper & Row, Publishers, Inc.

10 9 8 7 6 5 4 3 2 1

For Nigel, my husband

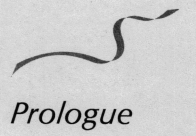

Prologue

The man in the gray suit was in a hurry. Just how much of a hurry became apparent as the plane made its final descent into Heathrow. Before it had even touched down his seat belt was unbuckled. And at the moment of impact he was halfway out of his seat.

Not that this was any guarantee that he would be the first one into the terminal. Like all New Yorkers, Ted believed firmly in making his own luck. So the moment the cabin door was open, he pushed and jostled his way to the front of the line. The resentment he stirred up amongst his fellow passengers made no impression on him at all.

He was a man with a mission. And a destination. Until he got there it was as if he was walking through a dream.

Does she still wear her hair the same way? he wondered, as he stepped onto the moving walkway which would speed his journey to the terminal. Does she still wear those great, horn-rimmed glasses to cover her shyness with strangers?

He remembered the first time he saw her. She was being led toward his table at The Four Seasons and he smiled as the picture of her dumbstruck face swam into his mind. The way she acted on the phone, he assumed she was in the habit of lunching in expensive restaurants. The way she acted when she came in told him otherwise. The kid had come from out-of-town. That was obvious. Her hair was longer than the style the girls were wearing that season. And her skirt was too short.

He knew she realized all this the moment she came into the room. But she got herself together fast. He admired that. He knew, right from the start, you could kick the ground from out under her and she'd pick herself up, give you a nice smile, and send the blow winging all the way back.

Kate, he thought. My Kate. With your terrible clothes and that cheap scent you were wearing, you still had more style than any other woman in the room.

He reached inside his jacket to retrieve the passport and immigration documents he needed for the British customs. And as he did, the picture of her he always carried fell out. It showed a dark, solemn-faced girl, with an air of class that girls from the East Coast always seemed to carry. Ali McGraw had it when she was younger. This girl would have it till the day she died.

He bent down and picked up the Polaroid. Why did she chase him so hard? he marveled. It was not as if he was anything special. He knew he had a strong face. An open face, even. But all the expensive barbering and the Brooks Brothers' suits didn't conceal the fact that he came from the wrong part of town. Manhattan was merely a place he worked in.

What was a well-brought up girl like Kate doing wasting her time with the likes of him? One date should have been enough. One night, if she was really curious. Deep down he knew it. Which was why he was so surprised when she came back for more.

He went along with it, of course. He had to. He was dazzled. And when the newness had worn off and he started to see through the gloss to the real woman underneath he still went along with it. But by then neither of them could help themselves.

We were so convinced we were right, he thought bitterly. We were so sure we were innocent. What crimes we commit in the name of love. What lies we tell. Particularly to ourselves.

He put the photograph back in his pocket and joined the end of the line at passport control. A glance at his watch told him it was nine-thirty. How long, he wondered, was it going to take to get through customs?

The sky over the Hudson river was growing dark. Ruth pulled the long brocade curtains together, shutting out the panorama. "Soon it'll be time to look around the stores for spring fashions," she observed.

"Not before you've bought something for Kate, I hope." Betty McQueen, the editor of *Fashions*, was pouring herself a drink. Rye over ice. A solid drink. An editor's drink.

For Ruth she poured a Coca-Cola. Being friendly with a teetotaler had certain compensations. The bar bill for one.

"I wish you wouldn't keep going on about this present for Kate," Ruth said crossly. "What in God's name am I going to get her? What do you get for someone like Kate?"

"You tell me, darling. She's your friend, not mine."

"Correction. She was my friend. I haven't seen her in three years. She's changed a lot, I've heard. She may not go for the kind of thing she used to like."

Ruth walked across the length of the room, which took some time. It was a big room. Built like a bowling alley. Ruth thought it was flashy and pretentious. But then that was the way she always felt about penthouses. Ruth might have come up in the world, but she was damned if she was going to change her opinions.

Betty handed her the cold drink.

"Don't drive yourself crazy worrying about Kate's present," she said. "A girl who's marrying the kind of money she's marrying isn't going to be too fussy about what she gets. It's not as if she's collecting place settings or anything."

"That's not the point," said Ruth. "I might not have seen her for a few years, but I am her oldest friend. She expects more from me than just another Tiffany's token."

Betty looked at her with admiration. Ruth hadn't seen Kate for three years. The guy she was marrying was reported to be loaded. Yet Ruth still cared how she felt about a wedding present. "I don't know why you bother," she said, "Kate's not going to notice one more bauble in the pile. Baubles are something she's going to have coming out of her ears."

"Do you think she loves him?" asked Ruth.

"What's not to love? He's under fifty. He's got money. He's got clout. If I were younger I'd go crazy for him."

Ruth pouted. "You know what I mean. I'm sure she likes him. But love. That's something else. It's something else with Kate anyway."

"You're talking about Ted Gebler, I suppose," Betty said softly. "What an incurable romantic you are. Kate and Ted said their farewells a long time ago. What they had is dead. Finished. I don't suppose she even remembers his name."

For a moment Ruth looked angry. "I don't think you ever really knew Kate, did you?" she said. "If you had you would have known that what you just said was a load of baloney. Nobody loved a man like Kate loved Ted. Nobody in the world. She would have walked barefoot across burning coals for the guy if she had to.

"What those two had for each other was different from anything I've ever seen before or since. So don't tell me that Kate's forgotten Ted's name. She'll carry it with her for the rest of her days. She'll go to the grave with it."

Betty sat down on the gold brocade sofa, stiffly, precisely like the fashion dictator she was. "I'm touched by your emotion. All your emotions. But answer me one thing. If Ted was so crazy about Kate and vice versa, why in Heaven's name didn't Ted leave his wife?"

*　　*　　*

The customs man stopped him as he strode through the green channel. "Anything to declare?" he asked.

"No," Ted replied, "I don't know if I'm staying long enough to drink two bottles of whisky."

"What about the coat?" the customs man persisted, indicating the camelhair slung across the overnight case he carried.

"I bought it in New York," said Ted, annoyed now. If the joker went on like this, Kate would be married and on her honeymoon before he got to see her.

"Prove you bought it in New York," said the official. "Show me your receipt."

Ted put down his case. "I can do better than that."

He lifted up the coat and turned it inside out, displaying the label. "Look, dummy, it says Brooks Brothers here. I don't think they have a branch in Savile Row. Not yet anyway."

And with that he turned on his heel. If some junior asshole wanted to play games they'd picked the wrong guy. And the wrong day.

Briskly he walked into the terminal. Nobody followed him. He stopped briefly at Barclay's Bank to cash a travelers check. Then he was on his way.

He got a taxi almost immediately and gave the driver her address. Nine Eaton Mews. It sounded very English. Quaint, sort of.

He tried to visualize what kind of house she lived in. But his imagination failed him. The Kate he had known wasn't the kind of girl who kept house. His mind strayed back to the sparse, bachelor-girl apartment she had had in New York. For her it had been a stopping place to sleep, change her clothes, receive her mail. He smiled; when they had finally got together the place had been put to better use, and when they had parted, when she had stopped loving him, he couldn't even get through the door.

He remembered that last evening when the janitor had to stop him from banging it down. "She's not there," he had said. "Miss Kennedy's moved away. She won't be coming back."

He had felt dead when he heard the news. As if someone or something had turned off his feelings. Leaving nothing but numbness.

He'd been walking around like that for three years now. A zombie was what Sandy called him and he winced. He knew he had hurt her. He even suspected how deep the wound had gone. But there was nothing he could do.

The most loving wife in the world couldn't make a man feel something when he was dead inside. In the beginning he had tried. But he was a lousy actor and finally she told him to stop making the effort.

Maybe that was when she started to look for someone else. Or maybe she had a lover all along and simply didn't tell him. In the end it didn't matter. David came along and scooped her up. And that was that. Parting from Sandy had been a formality. A public acknowledgment that they were no longer man and wife.

But Ted had left Sandy long before the world knew about it. Long before Sandy herself knew about it. He turned his back on his wife the day he met Kate. Only he didn't want to admit it. Not even to himself. What a complete fool I was, he fumed. What an idiot. If I'd been straight with Sandy from the start none of this would have happened. Kate would be marrying me, not some stuffed shirt of an Englishman.

He looked at his watch. Half past ten. She was getting married at four-thirty. He willed the taxi to move faster through the traffic.

Sandy was lying on her stomach at the end of the swimming pool. The Los Angeles sun beat down, frying the oil on her back, making the sweat run down to the deep vee of her bikini briefs.

To one side of her a tall, tanned man was sitting under an umbrella playing chess with a computer. "Honey, I think you've had enough time in the sun," he said. "I don't want you dying of heatstroke two days after you got here."

She picked herself up and padded over to where he was sitting. He had anticipated her move. A whitecoated servant was wheeling over a second chaise longue, placing it next to his. She threw herself on to it, like a schoolgirl coming in from gym class. From Sandy the gesture was not out of place.

Despite the fact she was in her early thirties, she had not lost her girlishness. Her face was still plump with youth and the blonde hair which almost touched her bottom suited her style. It made her look like Lolita. And David liked that kind of thing.

"Have you finished packing?" he asked gently when she had settled down and lit a cigarette. "We're leaving at the crack of dawn and I don't want a last minute rush."

Sandy pouted. "Do we have to go to London?"

"Sure we have to go to London. I want to catch

Charlie before he disappears to Barbados on his honeymoon.''

She wouldn't let it go. "Can't you talk to the man on the phone? What's so important about seeing him face to face?''

David sighed. Women! "Honey, when you've had as many agents as I have, you know you have to see the sons-of-bitches face to face. Without that eyeball-to-eyeball contact you never know if they're lying or not. And I can't afford any lies with this new contract. Wiseman's a tough customer. If Charlie hasn't tied the whole thing up tight the film could be the biggest grosser in the world and all I would see is peanuts. The way you spend money, I'm going to need to earn more than peanuts.''

She allowed herself a faint smile. A very faint smile. "OK, I'll buy it. But there's one thing you have to promise me, or I'll stay right here by the pool and let you fly to London alone.''

"OK, sweetheart, what is it?''

"I don't want to see her. Kate, I mean. I need an absolute guarantee that I don't get one glimpse of that scrawny, tight-assed girl. Or I can't be held responsible for my actions.''

"But what if Charlie asks us over for a drink? Hell, he'll have only gotten married the day before. You can't expect him to act as if nothing happened. I dare say he'll want to toast the bride or something. And you can't expect me to refuse him champagne. Charlie and I go back a very long way. Longer than you'll ever know.''

She leaned over, grabbed the top of her bikini and

put it on. If she was going to lose her temper, at least she'd do it looking respectable.

"If we're talking about histories," she said coldly, "then what about my history with Kate? We go back a long way as well, you know. Too damn long."

He looked surprised. "You're not still sore with her?" he said. "I thought all that was over long ago. She stopped seeing your old man years before you split with him. I honestly don't understand why you still blame her. He was probably screwing some other broad by the time you got weary of him."

She inhaled deeply on her cigarette. Then she stood up and threw it into the swimming pool. Without saying another word, she turned on her heel and stormed into the house.

What did he know about Kate? What did any man know?

They were off the highway now and coming into London. In winter, without the green that set it apart, London could have been any other town. Frankfurt maybe. Or Brussels.

Then the cab pulled into Eaton Square and Ted realized he was wrong. The English were grand in a polite way that New York or Brussels could never imitate. Eaton Square, with its clean, expensive buildings, said all there was to say about the town. That and the grassy patch between the buildings. Every ritzy London square has its own little patch of park. The English, if they've got money, never abandon their gardens.

He wondered if Kate had a garden now that she lived here. Somehow he couldn't imagine her pruning the roses. But maybe she'd changed. No, he couldn't accept that. He couldn't let himself.

Kate had to be the same as she was the last time he saw her. Proud. Classy. New York to her fingertips. Women like that never change.

The taxi rattled its way down the cobbled mews and behind Eaton Square pulled to a stop outside a bow-fronted, terraced cottage.

For a moment he considered telling the driver to turn around and go back to the airport. The past was the past. Why couldn't he let it go? Kate had.

Then he got out the photograph of her from his jacket pocket and the memories crowded in on him. Insistent. Demanding. He had to see her again. To tell her he loved her. That he was free at last to be able to love her the way she once wanted.

He put the photograph away and paid off the cab. Then he stood and looked at her front door, like he had looked at the entrance to her home three years ago. This time he knew that Kate lived behind that door. That when he pressed the bell she would come down and answer it.

What would happen next he had no idea. But he had to find out. For both their sakes.

Later he had no recollection of pressing the bell. Or of the door opening. All he could see, all he was aware of, was Kate standing there. They looked across at each other for what seemed like forever. Then she asked him in.

After three years, the past had finally come face to face with the present.

PART

one

1

She was far too bright to be a secretary, but when she graduated from Radcliffe in 1978 Kate Kennedy found they weren't hiring twenty-two-year-old girls for executive positions.

She didn't let it get her down. Kate wasn't the kind of girl you could put down that easily. She had majored in English and journalism at college with the express intention of making her name in newspapers. If it was going to take a bit longer than she anticipated then it was tough. But it wasn't insurmountable.

Kate came from one of those God-fearing Catholic communities in Westchester. Her father was a surgeon at the county hospital. Her mother, when she wasn't being run ragged by Kate's five brothers and sisters, worked for the local church charities.

The whole family lived in one of those white, neat

clapboard houses you find in the well-to-do suburbs of New York. Kate's father had worked his guts out to provide this kind of background for his family. He was a pillar of the community. And he was justly proud of his achievements.

It was a pride he handed down to his children.

Kate was brought up to believe that if you worked hard to get what you wanted, then you got it. God looked after the determined. At least that's how she saw it. So when she signed on at the typing pool of the *New York Post* she had little doubt that before long she would become a crack reporter. After a year she started to wonder if God had forgotten her.

Where did I go wrong? she reproached herself, as she climbed onto the commuter train at Grand Central every night. She had done all the right things. Well, the things she had thought were right, at any rate.

She haunted the city desk, overhearing snippets of conversation from the desk men. Whenever she felt she could contribute to a story with a bright suggestion, she did so. But nobody seemed to listen. It was as if she was invisible. A silent voice in the hum and bustle of the newsroom.

So she tried the bar where the reporters hung out. It was an Irish pub on the block next to the paper. And the hardworking newshounds saw it as a combination of the homes they rarely saw and an extension of the office. The petty injustices of the city editor, the stories they missed, the stories that made the front page. It was all dissected and endlessly discussed over a beer at Donahue's.

Kate loved the busy, ramshackle bar, which always

seemed to be full regardless of the time of day. She made it her business to chat with the bartender, Steven O'Gradey. To buy beer for the boys when they came in late after a punishing day. She wanted to be liked. She wanted to be included in their banter, their problems, their freewheeling camaraderie.

After three weeks of using up her paycheck in Donahue's, Kate realized she was getting the bum's rush. It was not that the boys didn't like her. Several of them asked her out on dates. All of them asked her to go to bed. Sure, they liked her all right. But not in the way she wanted to be liked.

To them she was just another girl. When she joined a group of the guys an embarrassed silence came over them. If they were talking about a story they stopped what they were saying and started talking about something else. The game, the quality of the beer.

Anything but the thing she most wanted to listen to. The babble of newspapers. It was as if they all belonged to some kind of exclusive club and they were deliberately trying to keep her out.

Kate decided to take stock of the situation. She was bright and she was hardworking. Her college grades proved it. But these qualities weren't enough in this hard-edged world she was doing her damnedest to enter.

OK, so what else did she have to offer? Conversation? She was popular enough with her friends, the kids in Westchester she hung out with. But she didn't want applause from a bunch of green kids. She wanted the big boys, the adults with power, to sit up and pay attention. And they didn't even know she existed. Except as a date.

Perhaps that was the way. She knew she wasn't Marilyn Monroe, but she also knew she wasn't altogether un-appealing if you liked tall, skinny, dark girls. With her long, straight, brown hair, which she wore parted in the middle, and her honey-colored skin which was perma-nently suntanned due to a keen interest in outdoor sports, Kate Kennedy was attractive before her time. The girl of the moment in New York that year had curves, fluffy blonde hair and a cute smackable behind. There was nothing cute about Kate and she knew it. She also knew about the laws of supply and demand. When she decided the only way to get ahead was through sex ap-peal, she was careful where she made her pitch.

All the eligible guys, the high flyers with the big by-lines, could take their pick. She'd made a big enough fool out of herself already. She didn't need to set herself up for another turn-down. No, the guy she picked for her passport into newspaper society had to be needy. Which is how Kate came to lose her virginity to Stan Brooks.

Brooks was a worn-out hack of some thirty-five sum-mers who worked on the night desk. Every evening he came into the office with his bag of sandwiches and his air of crumpled cynicism. He was the kind of man on whom the sun rarely shone. So when Kate began to show an interest in him, he was flummoxed.

Though Stan was none too attractive, and, if the truth be told, none too bright, he was streetwise enough to recognize an invitation when he saw one. And he was intrigued. Most of the guys had tried to get into the sack with the thin, pushy kid. And all of them had failed. So why him?

He didn't take too long to ponder the question. Op-portunity was not in the habit of seeking out the likes of Stan Brooks. And his basic cunning told him there was only one thing to do when it came his way. Get in there and grab it.

So on his night off Stan invited Kate out for a hamburger dinner at PJ Clarke's.

PJ's was the jet-set version of all the Irish bars that were Stan's natural habitat. The only difference with this bar was that it was close by Bloomingdale's in the fashionable part of town. And it had cleaned up its act.

The tables sported bright gingham cloths. The restaurant was a place where you could sit down and have a decent meal instead of just a hastily grabbed snack. And they knew how to charge for the privilege. Stan reckoned it was worth it. He saw the price of dinner at PJ's as a down payment on the joys of what was to come.

If Stan had done anything but work in newspapers, Kate would have found him a dead bore. As it was, she hung on every word as he talked about the copy he processed, the petty tyrannies of the night editor. In years to come Kate was to accept and dismiss all this as humdrum routine. But that evening, sitting on a bar stool at PJ's, she felt as if she were being initiated into the heady mysteries of a bright new world. When Stan invited her back to his apartment for a nightcap she accepted readily. She knew that if she wanted to set foot in Stan's world she had to go along with what he wanted. She'd had no other choice.

With a sigh, she glanced at the overweight, pudding-faced man sitting beside her. Then the gritty determination which had always propelled her took over. Grabbing her purse, she smiled brightly. "Lead on, Stan

Brooks," she said. "I've always wanted to see your etchings."

When Kate walked into Stan's bachelor apartment on the Upper West Side, it took every last ounce of will to conceal her distaste. The place looked as if a bomb had hit it. Empty beer cans lay on the floor where they had been thrown. Ashtrays overflowed with cigarette butts from God knew how many weeks. The covers on the chairs and sofa were torn and stained and the whole place reeked of stale cooking.

Kate fought down the urge to ask Stan where he kept his mop and vacuum cleaner. In half an hour she could have restored some semblance of order to the place. Then she remembered she hadn't come here to clean up. The reality of what she was doing suddenly hit her. Panic gripped her insides, making her heart flutter and her mouth go dry.

I can still leave, she thought wildly. It's not too late to get out.

Then she heard another voice inside her head. Pull yourself together, it's a hard world out there, it said. You've got to be a tough nut to crack it.

"Well," she asked. "Where's that nightcap you were talking about?"

"How about we have it in the bedroom?" said Stan. He'd bought the kid dinner, he'd put up with her prattle all evening. Now was the time for a little action.

"Wherever you like," she said with a bravado she didn't feel. "I'd love a bourbon. You do have some, don't you?"

If he offered her a beer she would die. She needed

the anesthetic of a strong drink to blot out the reality of what was about to happen.

Stan walked over to the cupboard where he kept his booze and extracted a half-empty bottle of Bushmill's. "I don't go offering this to every visitor," he said, then he added with a leer, "but I guess this is a special occasion."

Kate gulped the drink. She thought of the beers she had consumed in PJ's, and smiled. I wonder what he'd say if he knew the only alcohol I ever drink is communion wine. The smile grew to a giggle. She felt light-headed and giddy. She raised the glass in a silent toast. Here's to you Mr. Bushmill's, she thought. The ultimate cure for virginity.

For some unknown reason the room started to spin around her. Abruptly she sat down on the bed.

Stan took this as a signal to go. Kneeling beside her he clumsily started to take off her silk print dress. Kate sat there like a rag doll, observing the proceedings but somehow outside of them. Only when he started to pull the dress over her head did she join in the struggle, pulling and tugging at the offending garment. Finally she was free of it. Now all that stood between her and Stan Brooks was her bra and panties.

She leaned back and took a firm hold on her glass of bourbon. As she threw the contents down her throat she was dimly aware of Stan pulling down her panties. Then he was upon her, forcing open her legs with a strength which surprised her.

He was pushing his fingers inside her now, probing, feeling, exploring. For Heaven's sake, she thought, why don't you just do it to me and get it over with? He must have read her mind, for with surprising swiftness he pulled his trousers down to his knees.

Holy Mother, she thought, looking at the length of it. He'll never get that inside me. If he tries, he'll kill me.

Stan didn't kill Kate. It just felt that way. The hammering in her insides seemed to go on for hours. The man was insatiable. He took her lying down, standing up, with her legs around his neck. Finally he even took her from the rear. And when she screamed out in agony, all he did was laugh. "Horny bitch," he said. "Don't you tell me you haven't done this before. You're made for it. I bet every guy in Donahue's has had his fill of this juicy little cunt."

Finally, after what seemed like hours, it was over. Stan pulled up his trousers and collapsed exhausted onto the bed. "I think I'll take a little nap," he said, pleased with himself. "Wake me up when you want a return match."

With that he was asleep. Tears of shame burned her cheeks. There was blood on the grimy bedspread. Her blood. Her thighs and her buttocks were covered in bruises and when she tried to move, her whole body felt as if a truck had run over it.

Jerkily, like a broken doll, she got to her feet. Then, taking care not to wake the snoring man on the bed, she got dressed.

By the time Stan woke up, Kate was on her way to Grand Central in a taxi. With any luck she'd catch the last train home. Whether it was luck or simply the urgent need to reach her own territory that propelled Kate through the barrier as the train moved off, she never knew. Aching in every muscle, she pounded along the platform, grabbing at the door as it sped past her. Then she jumped, twisting the handle as she did so, and half fell into the moving train.

The tall, bluff figure of Brad Jones, a regular commuter, caught her as she hurled herself through the door. "Good God, Kate," he said, as he pulled the bedraggled girl to her feet. "You could have killed yourself."

She shrugged and pushed her way through the connecting door into the compartment. "Yes, Brad," she said. "I could have. And you know what? No one would have given a damn. Least of all me."

It occurred to her to hand in her resignation. After all, she had failed, hadn't she? Those bastards at the newspaper had picked over everything she had. Her charm, the free beers she bought them, even her body. And when they'd had their fill of her, they'd thrown her away as if she were no more than a piece of garbage.

There must be other places where she could succeed. Other professions that were less tough, less all-excluding. But there was something in her that wouldn't give up. She remembered the first time she took her high school SAT's. Her mother had wanted her to excel. Radcliffe was a dream Anne Kennedy had never attained. Instead she had settled for marriage, children and the church committee.

But the dream lived on. And she knew she could make it come true, through her daughter. How Kate studied for the SAT's. Night after night when the other girls in the neighborhood went out on dates, Kate sat up taking the practice tests. And always at around ten-thirty, her mother brought her a cup of hot coffee and a Danish.

"My grade A student," Anne Kennedy would say fondly. "I'm so proud of you."

Kate remembered the days before the exam results came. She couldn't eat, she couldn't sleep. And her mother went around the house on tiptoe, as if Kate had some terminal illness and wasn't to be disturbed.

Then the results came. Kate couldn't believe it. She hadn't excelled. But she hadn't done horribly, either. She was what the guidance counselor called a borderline case.

Her hopes of getting accepted "early decision" at Radcliffe were now impossible. If she wanted she could take the SAT's again next semester. At this stage most students opted out, going instead for less demanding colleges. Kate had the choice of a place in Orange County and another in Washington. She was happy to take either. But she wasn't given the chance. Kate's mother had set her heart on Radcliffe. And if her daughter had to take the exams again, then she would take them. And she would do well. Anne Kennedy would see to that.

She got Kate a tutor. A stern Catholic priest from a teaching order. It meant parting with more money than she could afford from the church funds, but it was worth it. She was determined to see her daughter graduate from Radcliffe. Cum laude.

Kate finally got accepted at Radcliffe, after taking the SAT's a second time. But the late nights studying with the sour-faced priest were worth it when she saw her mother's face.

That night the whole family sat down to a celebration dinner. Not the usual dinner around the kitchen table, but a grown-up dinner. There were candles on the table and Anne had roasted a goose for the occasion. Kate was served with the meat from the breast. The best meat. Her mother gave her first pick of the vegetables. And afterward it was Kate who got the biggest slice of the lemon meringue pie.

For the first time in her life, Kate felt special, loved. She looked at her three older brothers and two younger sisters, their faces shining in the candlelight. She's fond of you, Kate thought. She's fond of all of you because you never failed her. Now she loves me too.

The knowledge of this filled her with contentment. She wanted her mother's approval more than anything else in the world. And she had finally discovered the way to make Anne love her. All she had to do was succeed. All she ever had to do was come out on top. It was an ambition which was to haunt Kate Kennedy for the rest of her life.

Kate put the Stan Brooks episode behind her. Survival was the name of the game from now on. And survival meant going back to her desk in the typing pool at the *New York Post*. It occurred to her to behave as if nothing had happened. Then she thought, the hell with that. Why should I?

What was the point in standing around waiting for hand-outs from a bunch of dead-beat newshounds who behaved as if they were some kind of Hollywood super-stars. Who were they anyway? They didn't come from better homes than she did. They weren't any smarter than she was. They were simply more experienced and luckier. Somewhere, somehow, they'd gotten the breaks and she hadn't.

She discovered to her surprise that she still had her optimism. It was an instinct that refused to be quenched. So, okay, she hadn't had the breaks. But she was still only twenty-two. Her life hadn't ended. And she wasn't going to throw the rest of it away by taking second best from anyone. Least of all Stan Brooks.

Predictably he asked her to have a beer the next time she ran into him on the city desk. She turned him down flat. She wasn't rude. She didn't call him all the names that most accurately described him. She simply wasn't interested. It was as if Stan and all the others didn't exist for her anymore.

She took her lunch breaks alone now. Poring over the latest newspapers and periodicals, with coffee and a Danish in her local Chock Full O'Nuts.

She found to her surprise that she took a growing interest in what was going on around her: the latest reports from Wall Street, the political machinations in Washington, even the to and fro of the movie game in Hollywood.

But more than the stories themselves, the people behind them fascinated her. When one of the big banks crashed she was glued to the *Wall Street Journal* following the fortunes of Abe Heinmann, the president who built the corporation from nothing. In addition to *Time* and *Newsweek,* she started to subscribe to *Forbes* magazine, *The Hollywood Reporter,* even *The New Yorker.* And she developed a mild obsession with the men who pulled the strings. They were the real power in the land in which she lived and payed her taxes. Everyone else—the movie stars, the salesmen who called themselves vice presidents, and the editors whose copy she typed—they were all puppets. People who danced to someone else's tune.

She vowed that wherever life might lead her, whoever she became, she would never join the dance.

Kate's big break came when she least expected it. And because she was not looking for it, she nearly turned it down. The *Post's* showbiz editor had lost his secretary. She was the third girl to walk out of the job that year and there were no volunteers to replace her. Phil Myers had ruled over the movie world like an old Russian Czar for the past twenty years. Unfortunately he ruled over his secretaries in much the same manner.

He was a small, ugly man with a florid complexion and a high-pitched voice which he used a great deal. He was a bully, compensating for his lack of inches by demonstrating his power at every conceivable opportunity. When he couldn't shout at his executives he shouted at his reporters. And when he couldn't shout at them, he shouted at his secretaries.

Kate was fully aware of this when she was offered the job. And there was no way she was going to take it. But she went along to the interview with Myers to please the head of the typing pool. The one thing Kate Kennedy didn't need was to make another enemy.

To her surprise, instead of making an enemy that day, she made a friend. Though friendship was the last thing on her mind when she walked into the large penthouse suite that the showbiz chief liked to call an office. The walls were covered with Myers's interviews with the famous. And just to prove he really knew them, there was a montage of thank-you letters from old movie stars. They must date back to the dawn of time, thought Kate.

Then her attention was arrested by Myers's desk. Strategically placed at the end of the room it was impossible to ignore, for it dominated the landscape. Like the Hollywood moguls who were his stock in trade, Myers liked to make it plain to everyone who entered his office that he was the boss. The man who called the shots. To emphasize his point, the desk was on a raised dais. Anyone who sat on one of the chairs in front of it was automatically gazing up at Myers.

This might make him feel important, thought Kate, but it irritates me no end. She started to figure out ways in her head of turning him down. Then the unexpected happened.

Phil Myers asked her to have a drink. This was unheard of. Myers, as well as being a bully and a bore, was notoriously stingy. His liquor cabinet was always kept securely locked, except at Christmas time when he shared a bottle of champagne with the editor. But that was all. On every other occasion it was someone else's round. And here he was offering Kate a martini. For the second time in her life, she accepted a strong drink. This time nobody raped her.

Instead Phil Myers treated Kate to a demonstration of his considerable interview technique. He had been charming the secrets out of movie stars for the past twenty years and for the first time Kate realized how.

Phil Myers, when he turned on the charm, was irresistible. Everything about her was interesting to him. Her opinions, her ambitions, what she had for lunch. Kate found herself telling Myers the story of her life, carefully skating around the Stan Brooks incident. It might have been common gossip in Donahue's, but she saw no point in giving anyone the satisfaction of hearing her version.

When she had finished Myers looked oddly sympathetic. "You remind me of someone," he told her.

"Who?" she asked.

"Myself at your age. We're outsiders, both of us. You because you're a girl and you look like class—big no-no's on newspapers. Me, because I'm an ugly Jew in a world where only the beautiful succeed." He held up his glass in a toast. "Welcome to the club, Kate."

She looked confused. "I didn't say I was going to join you," she protested.

"So what else are you going to do?" he asked. "Sit like a dummy in the typing pool for the rest of your life. Wait for one of the city reporters to do you a big favor and pass the time of day. Take another dance with Stan Brooks maybe?" He waved away her embarrassment. "Forget about it. We're all entitled to our mistakes. You should hear about some of mine sometime. They make you look like the Virgin Mary. Listen, don't be a schlemiel. Do yourself a favor and take the job. Okay, so I'm a pig. I can't be more of a pig than that Stan Brooks and at least I won't lay a finger on you. All I can do is shout and that don't bruise anything except the ego."

She smiled despite herself. For some unknown reason she found herself warming to the little man. There was something honest about him. Phil Myers seemed to cut through all the bullshit and get to the point. And if it was a point that was unpalatable, well, she figured she'd find a way of handling it.

She swallowed the rest of her warm martini. "OK, Phil," she said, "you just talked me into it."

*　　　*　　　*

She found the job easier than she expected. Myers gave her a desk in the corner of his suite. In a way it was her own little island, for it came complete with two glossy filing cabinets, a dictating machine, a photocopying machine and a large fully automated typewriter.

But most of the expensive gadgets at her disposal were never put to use. For Myers didn't have the patience to dictate letters. Or anything else for that matter.

His business was tying up interviews with the famous. And if he couldn't talk them—or their agents—into it on the phone there was no point in wasting time writing them letters. As for his considerable staff, he saw no point in putting anything at all in writing to them. If he had anything to say to them he'd yell it to their faces.

After she'd listened to some of the abuse she heard bouncing off the walls of Myers's office, Kate thanked her lucky stars she didn't work on his showbiz team.

The only person Phil Myers didn't yell at was Kate. Whether it was because he identified with her in some way or simply because he couldn't afford to lose another secretary, Kate never knew. What she did know was not to question her luck. She had an easy job. The pick of the magazines to read in her increasingly long lunch hours. And she was learning the business.

At first she didn't realize it. Then after Myers had wiped the floor with the fifth feature writer of the day the truth began to dawn. What would happen was this. Myers would call one of his writers into the office and brief them on a story. The writer would go, do the interview and a day or so later hand it to Kate to type up and present to the great man. Then the fun would start.

Myers would take the unfortunate writer through his story, pointing out each and every fault. He wouldn't stop there either. Once he'd pinpointed where the writer had gone wrong the little showbiz tyrant would berate him for his inadequacies.

Because these conversations were usually conducted at the top of Myers's voice the victim would turn off and nothing would be gained. Until Kate came to sit in the office. For of the three of them, the only person to pay any attention to the tirade was Kate. She listened to all Phil's points, considered them, analyzed them and started to understand what he was getting at.

Because of his manner, Kate knew Phil Myers would never succeed in educating any of the writers who worked for him. But she didn't give a damn. Though he didn't know it, Phil was educating her.

Two months later, she got her chance to put her education to practical use. An unknown English actress, Fanny Foxwell, was opening in a new play on Broadway. The *Post* had decided not to cover the event, until the play proved to be a success. As far as Phil Myers was concerned, Fanny Foxwell was a nonentity and his reporters were too busy to waste their valuable time chasing after unknowns.

Nevertheless, Myers didn't want to ignore the play totally. It was being produced by his old friend Jack Katowski and he deserved some display of courtesy. If not for the sake of friendship, then at least for the fact that he might prove to be useful on some future occasion. Phil solved the problem by instructing Kate to go to the opening night party. If she passed herself off as his personal assistant then honor would be satisfied.

Kate accepted the assignment with some reservation. The party, which was to be held at the Plaza, wouldn't start until after eleven at night. And that meant staying overnight in New York with her older brother, Chuck. It was on the tip of her tongue to turn down the Fanny Foxwell party but she thought better of it. Phil Myers was the only human being outside her immediate family who had been remotely kind to her. She knew how important it was to have someone from the *Post* go to the party. So in the end she gave Phil a reluctant yes and made a note to get her good black cocktail dress dry cleaned.

Kate arrived early, and already the flood lights were playing across the front of the grand old hotel at the bottom of Central Park South, making everything look like Christmas Eve. Men in tuxedos, accompanied by their elaborately coiffured wives and girlfriends, were pushing and shoving their way up the stairs and into the vast square hallway which ran around the circumference of the ground floor. The party was being held in the restaurant in the center of the hallway, which normally served as a tea room. But any resemblance to its daytime use had been eradicated. The tiny circular tables had all been cleared out and in their place were long trestles covered with floor-length, white linen tablecloths. Waiters in white dinner jackets hovered with trays of caviar-covered canapés and glasses of champagne. Overhead floated brightly colored, helium-filled balloons.

Kate was dazzled by the glitter and the heady, almost cloying aroma of expensive perfume. She spotted the star, Fanny Foxwell, in the corner, surrounded by bodyguards and public relations men. It crossed her mind to make her way toward the actress. Then she remembered that Fanny Foxwell was of little news value until she had proved herself. Kate grabbed a glass of champagne from a passing waiter, leaned back against one of the trestle tables and took a long, delicious sip. When she looked up she realized she was being observed by a tall, graying, sardonic-looking man.

"And who might you be?" he asked.

"Kate Kennedy," she replied, "from the *Post.*"

"I don't think I've come across you before? Are you new on the staff?"

Kate remembered Phil Myers and his anxiety not to offend the theater management. She also remembered his temper.

"Yes," she lied. "I only joined a week or so ago. I work with Phil Myers . . . as his assistant. They haven't given me a byline as yet, but I'm working on it."

He smiled. "Good to meet you, Kate, I guess we'll be seeing quite a lot of each other in the future. You look like star material to me. Oh, by the way, forgive me for not introducing myself. The name's Katowski. I'm producing the show."

Kate gulped. Jesus, she had rotten luck. All she had intended to do was put in a brief appearance, sign the guest book and disappear before anyone found her out. Now she was standing in front of the producer himself and there seemed to be no escape. Oh well, too late now. She'd just have to go on with the lie.

She started to ask Katowski about the show, but he brushed aside her questions. "If you've seen one Eugene O'Neill play, you've seen them all," he told her. "No, what's remarkable about this production is its leading lady."

When he saw the expression on Kate's face, he held up his hand. "I know what you're going to say. She's a Britisher. An unknown over here. But let me tell you something, tomorrow you won't be able to get near her. This little lady is going to walk away with every award going."

"How did you discover her?" asked Kate, interested despite herself. For the next half hour, Jack Katowski told her about Fanny's success on the London stage. How he brought her to New York for a try-out. Her tears and tantrums. The fights they both had over her interpretation of the role.

Then he gave Kate the clincher. He told her how he fell in love with the British actress.

"Are you saying you're going to marry her?" asked Kate.

"Sure, I'm going to make it legal," said Katowski. "Just as soon as my divorce papers come through."

"How many other people have you told this to?" asked Kate.

"Just you," replied the producer. "Phil Myers is an old friend of mine. If you think the *Post* can use the story, I'll keep it exclusive. The paper's always played fair by me."

"I'll use the story all right," said Kate. "You can depend on that. But let me hold it for a couple of days. That way it'll make a bigger splash, and it's better publicity for the show, if you see what I mean."

"I get your gist," said Katowski. "Don't worry. The

story's all yours. I won't open my mouth about Fanny until I see the whole thing in the *Post.*"

Kate gave him her most demure, most grateful smile. You'll be lucky, she thought.

There was no way she was going to give the story to the *Post.* Not after the treatment she got the last time she offered them something. Kate thought back to Silas Smith and winced at the memory.

Smith was a country and western star in the Johnny Cash tradition. Not Myers's cup of tea at all. And when Smith was due to appear at Madison Square Garden, Kate was sent to attend the concert. The rest of the show-biz team knew better than to waste their time covering the event. It was tough enough doing the stories Phil Myers was interested in. Nobody needed the flops.

So Kate used the ticket and showed the flag for the *Post.* She also had a ball. She had been crazy about country and western ever since her teens. You only had to mention Patsy Cline or Silas Smith and Kate could give you a complete rundown on their music, their lifestyle, even their drug habits.

For Kate the show was a gift, the press party afterward a bonus. Only it turned out to be a bigger bonus than she imagined. For Silas Smith took a shine to her. She had the kind of clean, wholesome look he went for. And she knew about his music. He asked her to join his group for dinner and made sure she sat next to him.

He talked to nobody but her. And how he talked. After they had discussed his music they moved on to his three marriages, his struggle against booze and the way he finally kicked the habit. And when he had got all that out of his system he asked her to spend the night with him. Kate was tempted, but she said no.

She had no ambition to be a camp follower. So she caught the last train home and sat up the rest of the night writing down everything Silas had told her. It was a good story and she knew it. When she showed it to Phil Myers his reaction took her breath away.

"I like it," he said. "It's not my kind of thing, but just because the guy doesn't turn me on is no reason not to use it."

Kate's heart started to hammer. "You don't mean you're going to put it in the paper?" she said.

"Why not? It's a little rough around the edges, but there's nothing the rewrite men can't fix. Stay where you are, Kate, and I'll see what the feature editor has to say about it."

She couldn't believe her luck. Everything she had done so far—the drinks in Donahue's, sordid episode with Stan, sitting in on Myers's endless harangues with his writers—all of it seemed worthwhile because in the end she was going to get what she dreamed of. What she had waited to get. A story in the paper.

The next half hour waiting for Phil to get back was the longest in her life. She went over every line, every comma of the piece in her mind. She agonized whether or not she should have been quite so indiscreet about Silas's sex life. The guy had trusted her, hadn't he? Then she thought, what the hell, he also asked me to go to bed with him. Trust, she was rapidly discovering, was a two-way street.

For the twentieth time that morning she looked at

the clock. Phil had been away just over twenty-five minutes. What was taking him so long?

Five minutes later she had her answer. The little showbiz editor marched stiffly back into the office, threw her story on to his desk and headed for the liquor cabinet.

"What happened?" she asked in a small voice. Myers stood with his back to her. He seemed to be taking a long time fixing the ice in his bourbon. Finally he turned around, but he had a problem meeting her eyes.

"Something went wrong," she said, struggling to keep the tears back. Then she banged her fist down on the desk. "For Christ's sake, Phil, tell me what's going on."

He took a long pull on his drink. "You're not going to like it, Kate."

"Even I can see that, so just give it to me straight. I'm a big girl now. I don't need any fancy lies to make it better."

For the first time since he came in, he looked at her. She saw respect in his face. But there was something else there too. Despair.

"It's Stan Brooks," he said finally. "You shouldn't have had anything to do with him."

She looked bewildered. "What's that got to do with my story?"

He sighed. "Not a lot. Not if you were dealing with sane people. But sane isn't a word you use around our city desk. Okay, Kate, you wanted it straight, so here it is. Jim Bean, the guy who runs my department, seems to think that a girl who sleeps with juniors, his juniors, is not capable of writing English."

"You're kidding."

"I wish I was. It was a damn fine story, Kate. Good enough for this paper. Too good, if you ask me. But today nobody's asking me. Today all they do is tell me. And I don't like what I'm hearing."

Neither did Kate. For in a way it was like listening to her own death knell. She knew now that whatever she did, however hard she worked, there was nothing for her on the *Post*. As far as the paper was concerned she was a bimbo. Fit for only one thing.

She smiled ruefully. It was my own damn fault, she thought. I shouldn't have done it. I shouldn't have slept with Stan. Then she thought, how was I to know? I hung around for nearly a year waiting for somebody to tell me the ground rules, and nobody even gave me the time of day. Despite herself she felt a bitterness toward all the men she had bought beer for. All the men who had taken from her, and judged her for what she gave.

I'll show the bastards, she vowed. One day I'll get even. Now that day had come. Katowski's romance with the British actress was the kind of story the *Post* would have given its eye teeth for. For it had a news value—a scandal value—that put it head and shoulders above any soft showbiz interview. If Kate had learned anything from Phil Myers, she had learned to recognize a hot story when she saw one.

It didn't take her long to put it down on paper. Good stories, really good stories, she realized, have a habit of writing themselves. And when she was satisfied that no one, not even Phil Myers, could fault it she put the manuscript in a brown envelope and sent it to the *Daily News*. The *News* was the *Post*'s closest rival, and because she had learned to write in the style of the *Post* she was pretty sure her material would appeal to the *News.*

She was right. The day her story arrived at the *News* Kate got a phone call. She had put Phil's private line number on the top of her manuscript, knowing she was the only person to answer it.

Ted Gebler of the *Daily News* dialed that number at eleven-thirty, right after the editorial meeting. Having established that he was talking to Kate Kennedy, author of the piece sitting on his desk, he then set out to establish a price for it.

"You're going to use my story?" she asked.

"Well I'm not buying it to wipe my ass. The lady you're writing about seems to have become the hottest property on Broadway. The fact that she's done it overnight and she's marrying Jack Katowski into the bargain makes her a candidate for tomorrow's front page."

Kate was stunned. One minute she couldn't get a single soul in newspapers to recognize her worth. The next minute she was on the front page of the *News* with the hottest story of the day.

"Do I get a byline?" she asked. Suddenly it seemed like the most important issue. More important even than the story. After all, what's the point in slaying dragons, if nobody knows you've done it?

There was a long silence at the other end of the line. Just as Kate thought her heart was going to burst, Ted Gebler spoke.

"Look, lady, I don't know who you are from a hole in the wall. Except that out of the blue you send me in a terrific piece. And you answer Phil Myers's private line. To be honest with you, I'm intrigued. What do you say to meeting me for lunch this afternoon? If you're free of course. For all I know, you could be having lunch with the President.''

She kept her voice steady. "No, I'm not busy for lunch. I'll be near The Four Seasons if that's any use to you.'' Anywhere but Donahue's.

Gebler chuckled. "The Four Seasons, eh? I like your style. In fact I like it so much, you know what I'll do? I'll go crazy and buy you lunch there. Look, I'll see you in the restaurant at twelve-thirty. If you get there first order me a gimlet, straight up, okay?''

Before she could answer he had hung up. Which was probably just as well. Kate had no idea where The Four Seasons was. And she certainly didn't know how expensive it was. All she knew was that Phil Myers lunched there every Monday. She knew that because she made the reservation. Today was Wednesday and she was in the clear.

Kate arrived at the Grill Room exactly on time. It was grander than she had imagined. And busier. As she came in, the brightly lit bar on her right was crowded with advertising men and business executives in their button-down shirts and gray flannel suits.

Beyond the bar was the restaurant. And this time she was really overawed. The carpet was thick underfoot. There seemed to be three waiters to every table. And all the women there looked as if they had walked out of the pages of *Vogue*.

Peering through the gloom, her eyes searched the room for anyone who might remotely resemble a newspaper man. She expected someone in his early fifties.

Someone like Phil Myers. Slightly shabby and a little heavy around the middle.

So when Ted Gebler came up to her and took her by the arm, she thought he was some kind of lounge lizard looking to pick her up. As she started to pull away from him Gebler introduced himself and her heart skipped a beat. For he was simply one of the best looking men she had ever set eyes on.

He was tall and spare with ice-blue eyes and the kind of crooked smile that reminded her of Robert Redford. Like Redford he was blond, but no crew-cut blond. Instead his hair was thick and bushy and tickled the top of his collar.

She allowed him to lead her to the table. Dumbstruck, she let him order gimlets, steak sandwiches and for some unknown reason, Cokes. But at this stage Kate was beyond reason. If King Kong had walked up to the table and asked to join them she would have accepted the request as normal.

"Now let's get down to business," Gebler said as the drinks arrived. "First, who the hell are you? And what do you do to keep yourself busy when you're not writing front-page stories or answering Phil Myers's phone? And how do you manage to do the two things at once? Or is that a rude question?"

Kate took a deep breath and started at the beginning. She told him about Radcliffe, about wanting to be a journalist. And about how she'd failed. She even told him about Stan Brooks. After all, the whole world seemed to know about it. One more person didn't make a whole lot of difference.

When she'd finished Gebler looked at her long and

hard. "I guess I should call you a poor kid and pat you on the fanny and say there there. But I'm not going to do that, because you're not a poor kid. You're a tough kid and you've got guts. After the kind of treatment you got, most other girls would have gone running all the way home to Westchester, or wherever the hell you come from. But not you. You dug your heels in and went to work for that pig Myers. And you managed to learn something from the old bastard too. Which is more than can be said for the rest of his flybitten staff. That story you sent me. It's not bad. Don't get me wrong. The story would work if a chimpanzee wrote it. But it's not the content of the thing I'm talking about. It's the way you tackled it. You structured it like a professional. And you gave it a style of your own. I like it, I like it very much.

"I also like the way you shafted the *Post* by sending it to us. You have the true killer instinct, little lady. One day you'll make a fine reporter."

"But when will that day come?" asked Kate. "I don't have the rest of my life to sit around waiting. When this story appears tomorrow morning I'll be out of the *Post* on my ear."

"I knew you'd say that," said Gebler with a sigh. "Which is why I'm sitting here buying you lunch. The *News* just happens to have a vacancy on its staff for a junior writer. If you're willing to start at the bottom with a salary to match, the job's yours. If you've got bigger ideas than that, forget we even had this conversation. I'll pay you the going rate for the story, and we'll call it quits."

"Oh no," stammered Kate, "I mean yes. I want that job. I want it more than anything I ever wanted before."

He smiled and once more she was reminded of Robert Redford. "Then welcome to the *Daily News*," he said. "But before you hand in your resignation and flounce out of the *Post*, let me give you a word of advice. Don't do it. Turn up tomorrow morning, keep quiet, and give them a chance to look at your story. With any luck they'll be so mad at you they'll sack you on the spot. And if they do that they'll have to pay you two weeks' salary. As you grow up in newspapers you'll get to learn one basic lesson. Never leave a job unless you leave it with money in your pocket. In this game it's the only way to go."

2

Everyone at the *Post* was up in arms. She was a bitch, she was a dirty hustling whore, she bit the hand that fed her. Kate took the insults with a confident smile and said nothing.

If they knew she had another job to go to she might not get her severance pay. It wasn't the money that mattered; her father would have supported her until she got another job. But it was the principle. She wanted to start her career in newspapers like a seasoned trouper. And if leaving her first newspaper with a few hundred dollars was the way to do it, then do it she would.

In the end it was Phil Myers who got Kate her money. In spite of what she had done he had a grudging respect for the solemn, dark-haired girl who had worked for him for the past three months.

In Kate's shoes, Myers would have done the same.

And he marveled at her guts. Without telling her, he paid a visit to the city editor and advised him to give Kate two weeks' salary plus vacation pay. If he was going to kick Kate out, as he was threatening to do, then at least she'd have a little money to tide her over.

At first Jim Bean balked at the idea. "Since when did we start giving secretaries severance pay?" he asked.

"Since never," said Phil. "But you're not kicking this girl out for being a secretary. You're getting rid of her for being a journalist. And if you ask me, a damn good one. If one of us had spotted the potential in the girl, this story wouldn't be all over the front pages of the *News.*"

Jim nodded. "I guess you're right," he said. "But she was so damn pushy, she got our backs up. Hanging around Donahue's. Taking off on her own and writing little showbiz interviews. I mean, maybe if she'd asked politely we might have given her a chance."

"Since when did a good reporter ever ask for anything politely?" said Phil. "In my experience the kids with fire, the real ones, always push and shove their way to the top. Just like Kate. If I were you I'd give her the money. Then when you want to buy her back from the *News* she might just come."

"OK, two weeks and whatever vacation money she's got coming. But I want the bitch out of the building by lunchtime. Who knows what other stories she might try to steal?"

Kate started as a junior writer on the *News* the following day, and she went in with two ambitions. She was going to come out on top. And she was going to make Ted Gebler really notice her.

It took her six months of appearing in the paper regularly before they started running her photograph alongside her stories. By any standards Kate's work was remarkable. Its excellence lay in its originality. While other writers ran after the big star interview, Kate held back. She wasn't interested in some big shot shooting his mouth off. He or she was probably telling a pack of lies to grab some free publicity.

What fascinated Kate was the story behind the story. From her days of reading about the men who pulled the strings she deduced it was the quiet men of power who told the real truth.

She made it her business to seek them out. The agent behind the movie star; the guy who wrote the ads at the Madison Avenue agency rather than the guy who sold the ads; the associate who wrote the brief rather than the hotshot attorney who delivered it.

When Kate had pinpointed the people she sought out, she set out to prize the truth from them. This she did with a mixture of charm, nerve and deep cunning. Her classy, dark looks and her increasingly voluptuous figure didn't hurt, either.

At the end of two years on the *News,* Kate had gotten herself the reputation of being the hottest interviewer in town. A profile by Kate Kennedy was something to be reckoned with. People either pandered to her or gave her a very wide berth. But Kate was long past caring what anyone thought of her. Except Ted Gebler.

Gebler had become a fixation with her. Kate always wanted what she couldn't have. And the one man she couldn't have, out of the dozens who were now crowding around her, was Ted Gebler.

The reason was simple. Ted Gebler was married. Normally this state of affairs didn't preclude him from the occasional fling. Late hours and the loneliness of newspapers occasionally led him into unfamiliar beds. But it was solace he was looking for, not love, which he got plenty of at home. He was not looking to complicate his life by getting close to someone. Even if that someone had long, sexy, dark hair and the kind of class he found hard to live up to.

So Ted kept his distance from Kate outside the office. Not that it fooled her one little bit. She knew he was attracted to her. She also knew that once she managed to get him on his own he wouldn't be able to resist the magnetism which flickered so strongly between them.

Despite the fact that Kate went after Ted for all the wrong reasons, and even in spite of Ted's wife, Sandy, the two of them were irresistibly drawn to each other.

When they met, wherever it happened to be, the roar and hum of the world died down a little. And in the center there was only Ted speaking to Kate, Kate speaking to Ted.

She knew she was playing with fire. She knew that one of them would get burnt, and likely as not it would be her. But she didn't care.

Her burgeoning career had given her a new self-confidence and her family and friends started to notice changes in her. She cut her long, shiny, dark hair into the swinging bob Jane Fonda was beginning to make fashionable. Her ever-increasing salary made it possible for her to buy the kind of fashions she had only dreamed of. She began to frequent expensive boutiques in the

Upper Sixties, searching out the chic, tailored suits and dresses which were all the rage in the late seventies.

She started to look like the person she was becoming. A young woman on her way to the top. As soon as she decently could, Kate moved away from home. She loved her family dearly; they had always surrounded her with support and security. Yet because of this she viewed her home as a launching pad into life. And life beckoned. First tantalizingly, then urgently. The time had come to make a home of her own.

She rented an apartment in Greenwich Village. The Village was still a hang-out for artists and poets when Kate moved there, so accommodation was affordable if a little run-down.

Kate soon fixed up her apartment the way she wanted it. She might have had to plod up five flights of steps to get home, but it was worth the climb. With its white walls, stripped wood floors and potted plants, the place had a homey, yet expensive look to it. The perfect setting for the media's newest rising star. The only thing she needed to complete the picture was a man. There was no shortage of candidates. Rising young bankers, heirs to considerable fortunes, even the odd movie actor, all vied for her attention. But she barely noticed them. For Kate, there was only one man who existed. Ted Gebler. And no matter how hard she tried, she couldn't have him.

It became a kind of game between them. Kate would rush into the office, flushed and triumphant after a successful interview, and she and Ted would go into conference. While they were talking about the story she would have his complete attention. If the story was a big

one and Kate needed more help than usual, Ted would
take her to the local bar for further discussions. But the
moment business was over, so was their time together.

Occasionally, halfway through a snatched meal they
would start to talk as friends. But Ted was wary of this
kind of conversation. He knew only too well where it
would lead and his life was complicated enough already.

Kate started to get desperate. She'd known him for
more than two years now. She dreamed about him in all
her lonely moments. Even in a hectic day he was still with
her. A shadowy presence, beckoning, enticing, yet van-
ishing into thin air every time she got near him.

She started making herself obvious. She'd sit on his
desk, hitching up her already-too-short skirts, swinging
her long legs. She started asking him out to lunch, taking
him to romantic little restaurants tucked away on side
streets. It became obvious that she was using too much
perfume.

In the end, Ted asked her to have dinner with him.
Kate couldn't believe her luck. But when she met him
at seven-thirty at the "21" Club, she began to have
doubts. Ted didn't look his usual relaxed self. He also
didn't look pleased to see her, which dented her confidence. She had taken a great deal of trouble with her appearance that evening, washing her hair, painting her
nails, shaving her legs. She wanted to look her best for
this man. Yet for all the attention he was paying her she
could have been wearing blue jeans instead of the Calvin
Klein original which had cost her three weeks' salary.

"Is anything the matter?" she asked. Ted had been
sipping at his gimlet distractedly from the moment she
arrived.

He looked up, frowning. "Yes, Kate, something is the matter. You're the matter. And what's more you know it."

"So what's the problem?" she asked. "You're male, I'm female. The human race has been coming to grips with the situation ever since Eve."

He didn't smile. "Not funny," he said. "Anyway it's not that simple. If all you wanted from me was a fast fuck during lunch hour, we wouldn't be sitting here now. But it isn't what you want, is it? You want love and affection and babies and commitment. And damn it, why shouldn't you have those things? If there was ever a girl who was entitled to them, you are." He looked sad. "There's one small complication. I already have a woman I've given all those things to. And it's too late to take them back— even if I wanted to."

He'd taken the wind out of her sails. What could she ask from him now? And what could she offer him? She was stumped. So in the end she said the only thing she had left to say. "I love you, Ted. I can't help it. Don't yell at me anymore, please. It's not my fault, honestly."

The words were intended to be a lie. Part of her seduction technique. Only the moment she gave them voice, she knew she wasn't lying. She really did love this tall, sober-suited man she hardly knew. And for a moment she panicked. For to love was to be vulnerable, to be hurt. What if he didn't feel the same way?

He took both her hands in his. "Are you sure?" he asked.

She nodded, afraid of his answer. Then she saw the answer in his eyes. And she stopped worrying.

"What are we going to do about it?" she asked. The

question was not a challenge. For quite suddenly she had
no idea how to cope with this heady new emotion. Chasing a man was one thing, she thought. But catching him
and finding out that you hadn't caught him at all, he'd
caught you, that was totally confusing.

Get a grip, she told herself sternly. Pull yourself together. He's only a man. Then she looked at him and
knew it was no use. There was nothing to be done. Nothing but to go along with it.

For a while he was silent, considering. Then he said,
"We can do one of two things. You can leave me. Now,
while we both still have a chance. Give notice. Start looking for another job. It won't be difficult at all. I know
for a fact that you've already gotten at least two offers
which would pay more than the *News* can afford." He
smiled. "Once you start a new job, you'll forget my ugly
face in seconds. I promise you."

She looked at him hard. "Tell me the other thing
we can do."

"We can go to bed."

There was a silence between them interrupted only
by the hammering of her heart. What happened to discretion? she wondered. What happened to shame? For all
she could think of was his body, Ted's body, without
clothes. Now she wanted him, and so urgent was her
need that it seemed to be written in bright letters across
her face.

Three middle-aged executives standing by the bar
began to stare at her. Ted caught their expressions and
suppressed a smile. "I get the picture," he said. "But if
you can hang on for another twenty minutes we might
manage to solve the problem in private."

*　　　*　　　*

They held hands in the taxi on the way to her apartment in the Village. Neither of them said a word, for they both knew they were embarking on an adventure which could only end in tears. Tears and passion.

The anticipation of passion survived the early evening traffic jam on the way downtown. It even survived the five-floor hike up the stairs to Kate's apartment. But when they walked through the door, into the plant-filled, single-girl room, it began to fade.

Until that moment they had been playing a sophisticated game, the moves made in chic bars and expensive restaurants. Now the game was over, and they were standing in the room where Kate lived, the remains of a hurriedly consumed breakfast still on the kitchen table. For a moment passion put up a struggle against reality. Then, with an almost audible sigh, it finally died.

Kate rummaged in her bag for a cigarette. And when she found the pack, she spent a long time fiddling with the cellophane, tearing open the top, finally extracting the cigarette she needed more than anything else in the world.

She flicked open her lighter, cupping her hand around it as she held it to her cigarette. Nothing happened. She tried a second and a third time with the desperation of a boy scout trying to light a damp campfire.

Ted started to smile. "So this is the girl who wanted to screw my ass at all costs. I'm disappointed. Aren't you supposed to take your clothes off or something?"

She threw down her lighter in exasperation.

"Maybe you should try talking dirty," he suggested.

"Anything's better than standing there with a cigarette in your mouth. You look like Bogart on a bad day."

She started to laugh, the giggles coming first in gulps, then in waves, washing away the tension. She felt relieved. As if a great responsibility had been lifted from her shoulders. "I would have made a terrible Mata Hari," she gasped. "Thank God that's all over."

She suddenly noticed he wasn't smiling anymore. There was a new tension now, but she was in control of it. He touched her face, her hair, her neck, his fingers confirming what his eyes had been doing all evening. Finally there was his mouth, retracing the same path.

And then she couldn't stand it any more. She wanted him again. But this time she wanted Ted. The real Ted. Not the fantasy man of her imagination. She found his mouth. Then his tongue, communicating a rehearsal for what was to follow.

It followed quicker than she could have imagined. Quicker than it had ever happened in her dreams. She was lying on the bare boards of her living room, somewhere between the hearth and her coffee table. Her dress was unbuttoned down the front and her panties were halfway down to her knees.

He started to please her with his fingers, tracing the lines of her breasts. Moving slowly down her body to her navel and beyond.

She was aware of her hands on his back and she moved them up to the nape of his neck until she had the ends of his springy blond curls firmly in her grasp. Swiftly, without warning, she jerked his head back.

"Can we skip this part?" she demanded through

clenched teeth. "I want you inside me. Right now. I can't wait anymore."

He eased himself into her, gently, as if he was afraid he might hurt her. Then they fit together and he stopped worrying about hurting her.

Kate had not come to this encounter as a virgin. Yet in a way she had. With other boyfriends her body had been out of it. Because she had known nothing different, she had thought this was as it should be. Until now. Now she would never again allow the polite after-dinner sex she had previously accepted as part of being single.

The ecstasy she was experiencing touched her soul, and when the climax came it enveloped them both, fusing them together as one being.

She lay where she was for a long time afterward, exhausted by happiness. "I love you, Ted," she said for the second time that day. This time she meant it.

Love, like any other obsession, develops a pattern of its own. Kate would wake up every morning with the taste of Ted on her lips and the smell of him in her mind.

And that's where she kept him. In her mind. Their lives dictated it.

Ted was true to his marriage, if only in appearance. He still caught the commuter train to Stamford every night. He ate his meals with his family. He took his sons to the ball game on the weekends. He was in every detail the devoted, caring husband. And he felt nothing.

The only moments that had any meaning at all were his moments with Kate. Any lunch hour when they could both get away they spent together. They didn't waste time in restaurants or bars. There was no point. They went back to Kate's apartment where they made love and ate sandwiches. Or just made love.

Then there were the times when there was no space for love. After work, when all they could do was snatch a quick drink at Grand Central while he was waiting for his train to come in. Those were the times when Kate discovered the flip side of love.

Before she loved she never felt lonely. Now she felt lonely all the time. Without realizing it she had made a space for him in her heart. And when he wasn't with her, filling that space, she felt incomplete. As if she was surrounded by music but had no ears to hear it.

In her saner moments—which were rapidly getting fewer—Kate saw the situation for the cliché it was. She had worked with girls with married lovers and the puritan in her despised them. What was wrong with them that they had to share a man with another woman? Now she was the one who was doing the sharing and for the first time in her life she understood why all those other girls before her put up with it. They loved. And love somehow dignified the stolen half hours in dimly lit bars and the showers taken in the middle of the day to remove the traces of lunchtime sex.

As the weeks of love multiplied into months, Kate felt she was living not one, but two lives. There was her busy, everyday life of stories and socializing with her colleagues after work. And there was her life with Ted. Enchanted and secret.

At least that's what she told herself. Thinking that anyone could keep a secret in a busy newspaper office was her only piece of self-delusion. Kate truly believed that nobody at the *News* had the slightest idea that she and Ted were lovers. After all, she hardly looked at him now. She no longer sat on the edge of his desk, provocatively dangling her legs. She didn't even wear perfume any more.

And that was what gave her away. Many girls before Kate had chased Ted Gebler and made no secret of it. And when they found they couldn't catch him, they either got bored or they found somebody else.

What they didn't do was change their style. What they certainly didn't do was behave as if Gebler no longer existed. Something had to be going on.

Life on a newspaper is a mixture of excitement and boredom. And during the dull stretches between stories, the usual ways of passing the time are filling out expense reports, drinking and talking about other people's sex lives. Ted and Kate's affair was the main topic of conversation in most of the bars near the office that season.

Ruth Bloom did not hear about it in a bar. As the fashion editor, she rarely went to bars. Not because she was afraid of not being welcome there. She was as much a part of the paper as anyone else. No, Ruth found bars grubby and boring. Besides, she didn't drink.

Ruth was one of those New York women, somewhere in her early thirties, who had opted for a career instead of marriage and kids. A casual acquaintance could easily jump to the wrong conclusion and assume that no man could possibly have wanted her. For Ruth wasn't just a big girl, or a plump one. Ruth was fat.

But her fatness wasn't a turn-off. For sitting on top of her generous frame was the pretty all-American face of a cheerleader. Ruth knew she was pretty, so unlike other fat women she didn't hunch around making excuses for her appearance. Instead she dressed like any other successful, modern career woman only several sizes larger. She also wisely didn't go in for short skirts or anything tight over the hips. Because of her job she understood clothes and how to make them work for her.

The reason Ruth was sitting in a photographer's studio supervising the spring fashion feature instead of cooking supper at home for a husband was not her fatness. The reason was her mother.

Ruth had one of those mothers who laid down the law as soon as she was old enough to understand the meaning of the word. She had Ruth's future all planned out.

She was going to be the sleekest, most beautiful girl in New Jersey. And she was going to capture the heart of a doctor. So when Ruth started eating, her mother was naturally put out. When Ruth changed from a chubby child into an overweight teenager, Phyllis Bloom decided to take action.

Ruth went on her first diet at the age of thirteen. For the first week the regime had amused her. After that she just felt hungry. So when Phyllis wasn't looking, she went back to eating.

No matter how loudly her mother yelled, no matter how many bribes and incentives she offered, Ruth went on with her life the way she started it. Fat.

Apart from her mother, it was not a problem for her. None of the boys she knew seemed to care about her size. A number of them found it rather sexy, and sex was the other thing Ruth and Phyllis disagreed about.

According to Phyllis Bloom, there were two kinds

of girls. Girls who went out with boys. And girls who got married.

"Do you mean to say," Ruth demanded of her mother, "that if you want to get married, you don't go out with anyone else but your husband-to-be?"

Phyllis told her that was the rule. Not only was it golden. It was inviolate.

"OK," said Ruth. "In that case I'm not getting married. But you have to realize it has nothing to do with you. It has to do with men. I like them too much to settle for just one."

Then, seeing the look on her mother's face, she softened. "Well, that's how I feel right now. Maybe it'll change when I've had some experience."

"Maybe pigs will fly," said Phyllis. And so they agreed to disagree. It was an armed truce. But it was a truce. And it allowed Ruth to move away from home when she had finished college and find something to do that didn't involve cooking and having babies.

She found fashion. Ruth started out by helping her uncle, who had a manufacturing business on Seventh Avenue. Uncle Reuben made suits and dresses for stores like Bloomingdale's and Saks. And from the start, Ruth was fascinated by the whole process of design, manufacture and selling.

Ruth, who could never be accused of being silent about her enthusiasm, longed to communicate the way she felt about the fashion business. When her family got sick of hearing about it and her friends started to drop her, Ruth realized she needed a different audience.

She found it by writing for a trade magazine, *Trends.* Every week *Trends* ran Ruth's page on what was new, what was hot on the streets of New York. She started to develop a following in the rag trade.

A year after she started her page Ruth got her first offer from a fashion magazine. It came from a reasonably influential glossy based in Los Angeles. Ruth turned it down flat. As far as she was concerned, the American fashion center was New York. She saw no point in moving to an outpost, even a glamorous one.

News of Ruth's refusal buzzed around the fashion editor's desks. The kid was either nuts, or she had something special.

Betty McQueen on the *News* believed that Ruth Bloom had something special. And she backed up her belief with the offer of a job as one of her three assistants. By the time Betty left the paper eight years later it had become crystal clear to everyone that Ruth was the only choice for the job.

Now, due to Ruth's boundless energy, the *News* was the clear leader in the fashion field. And much of that had to do with the fact that she spent her time in photographer's studios rather than bars.

She relished office gossip as much as she relished strong drink. Which was not at all. So when her assistant relayed the juicy item about Ted and Kate, Ruth was unmoved.

"I don't understand you," said Tracy. Fresh out of design school, she seemed to be in a permanent state of awe about the comings and goings of her colleagues. Ruth wished her new assistant would get as worked up about the spring suits they were preparing for that afternoon's session.

"What's not to understand?" said Ruth peevishly.

"You mean I'm a mystery because I'm not stunned by the fact that Ted Gebler's fucking Kate Kennedy? Believe me, I don't think it's wonderful and I don't think it's terrible. I think it's normal and a bit sad for Ted's wife, Sandy, if you want to know the truth. But I guess they'll work it out for themselves. They always do, you know."

"But what about Kate? She's a big name on the *News* now. It can't be doing her reputation any good. I mean, Ted is her boss."

Tracy, Ruth's assistant, was a pale, thin girl with dark auburn hair which twisted in unruly curls about her face. If she had paid attention to her appearance she would have been pretty. The basics were there. Porcelain-white skin, blue saucers for eyes, turned-up little nose.

But Tracy didn't seem to care how she looked in the office. And with her sullen expression and the jeans she seemed to live in she looked like a perennial student.

Ruth looked at the girl with something approaching distain. Why couldn't she just mind her own business?

"Listen," said Ruth, "and listen carefully. Ted was Kate's boss before she got into bed with him and the sex act doesn't seem to have changed her as a writer. Or do you know something I don't?"

Tracy felt her cheeks burn. All morning she'd felt like a faithful retriever, ferreting out a tasty morsel of information to lay at her mistress's feet. And what happened when she brought it in? She made a mental note to tell Ruth nothing in the future. Let the bitch get her own news items.

Oh dear, thought Ruth, I've upset her. But before

she could do anything to remedy the situation, the model arrived. Like all New York girls who earned their living by posing for the cameras, Jade was bone-thin. A bleached blonde with a mobile face, she reminded Ruth of a Barbie doll.

You could put her into any outfit, drape a leg here, lift an arm there and she'd take on its personality. Girls like Jade didn't come along very often. And when they did, they were in heavy demand. It paid to be nice to them.

"How's the diet going?" asked Ruth.

Jade made a thumbs-down sign. "Terrible. I drink this revolting guck from the health food store three times a day and before I go to bed. And nothing happens. Thank God I'm not losing any more weight. But I'm not gaining either. I just hope you don't have any low necklines for me today."

"Is this your way of telling me you haven't got any cleavage anymore?"

"I haven't got any bosom," she pouted. "How can I have any cleavage without a bosom? You pay me to model the clothes, not perform miracles."

"Okay, okay, calm down," said Ruth. "It's not the end of the world. If worse comes to worst I can paint in some cleavage. We're working in black and white, so with the right bra and decent lighting nobody will know the difference."

Mollified, Jade walked over to the brightly lit cubicle at the end of the studio and allowed the make-up man to get to work on her face.

The session went well. Tracy's spirits picked up and Jade didn't make a fuss when Ruth painted in a line of dark make-up between two non-existent breasts to give a voluptuous illusion.

I'm home free, thought Ruth, as Jade slid out of the last dress. With any luck I'll be home in time for the Merv Griffin show.

As she turned to leave Jade stopped her. "I've been meaning to ask you all afternoon, what do you know about Kate Kennedy? The word is she's having a hot affair with one of your editors."

Ruth looked blank. "Why don't you ask Tracy about it?" she said sweetly. "She's closer to the situation than I am."

Then before anyone could say another word Ruth was out the door. Damn gossips, she thought. You couldn't fart in this town without somebody spreading the story around.

Stan Brooks of the *Post* was buying a drink in Donahue's for Bill Gerhaghty of the *News.* For years the two had held the same position on the rival papers. Because of this they would meet regularly once a week to exchange news and gossip. It paid to have a foot in the enemy's camp.

That night Stan was buying the beer. Bill had just been promoted to assistant editor. As such he had ceased to be just a useful drinking companion. Now he was a valuable contact. Someone to be fed information in exchange for future favors.

They made an incongruous pair. Stan, shambling and pudgy with his going-nowhere eyes. Bill, whippet-thin, with a sharp, ferrety little face and eyes which seemed to dart around corners. It was only a week since his promotion and already he was beginning to look as if he'd had the job for years. Instead of his habitual blue jeans he was wearing a dark, sharply cut suit. His shoes were polished and he was wearing a tie.

"How's tricks over at the *Post?*" he asked.

Stan looked gloomy. "Tricky. Phil Myers is stirring up the team on the showbiz beat. I don't think he ever got over losing that cute little piece of ass, Kate Kennedy, to your boys."

"As far as I'm concerned he's welcome to take her back. She's a headache I can do without. Every time I try to put one of my reporters on a big interview, the answer's always the same. Kennedy's doing it. She knows the score. She knows how to get them to talk. She can write it like it's never been written before. I'd like to know something that stuck-up broad can't do."

A smile flickered across the pudding that passed for Brooks's face. He looked crafty. "I know something Kate Kennedy can't do," he said.

"What's that?" said Gerhaghty, putting down his beer.

"No matter how hard she tries," said Stan, "no matter how many times she fucks him, Kate can't get Ted Gebler to leave his wife."

"I didn't know she and Ted were doing it," said Gerhaghty, interested now. "It never occurred to me she'd be that dumb. Doesn't she know old man Henkel comes from the Bible Belt? Every time an editor joins the *News* he gets handed a chastity belt along with his contract. We may write about sex, sin and adultery in the paper but we're not supposed to put it into practice." He chuckled. "I wonder if Kramer, our revered editor-in-chief, knows?"

"I wouldn't think so," said Stan. "From what I hear about him, he likes to keep away from office gossip. Maybe he's got problems of his own."

"Maybe," said Gerhaghty. "And maybe not. Anyway, it doesn't matter. What matters is Kate. She's the one with the real problem. Only she doesn't know it yet."

Stan signaled the bartender for another round of drinks. "I imagine you'll find a way of letting her know," he said.

I t was one of those mornings when you knew that spring was just around the corner. The city was throwing off its snowy winter coat and the glass buildings were starting to sparkle with the first tentative rays of sunlight.

Kate welcomed the change in the season. It had been a long dark winter. Now with the coming of spring she felt a new optimism.

Something good was going to happen soon, she told herself as she hurried up Fifth Avenue.

She had good reason to believe in her fortune. For she was on her way to the annual editors' lunch. She had been on the paper for four years and this was the first time she had been invited to the gathering. The people who normally attended Kramer's lunches were the decision-makers. And Kate felt honored. The invitation was an acknowledgment of the contribution she had made and, more importantly, the contribution she was going to make.

Kate was wearing a bright green wool suit to celebrate the occasion and to echo her mood. Her straight brown hair, which just tipped her shoulders, was freshly washed. And her smile told you that today she was going to win.

She slowed down to a halt outside Il Gattopardo and checked her reflection in the window. Then, satisfied that all was well, she pushed her way through the doors.

Ruth Bloom had arrived before her and Kate made her way over to the fashion editor. "Hi," she shouted in greeting. "How many are there of us today?"

Ruth made a face. "About a dozen, I'd say. Kramer likes to keep his lunches cozy and informal. I hate these things. I get indigestion the day before. I'm tongue-tied while it's going on. And I spend the rest of the day drinking seltzers, trying to recover from it."

"Surely it can't be as bad as that?" Kate was surprised.

"You wanna bet? It's always as bad as that. What in God's name can twelve people and one editor achieve over lunch in a fancy restaurant, apart from indigestion? When you see them in there you'll know what I mean. Every last one of them is trying to score points with Kramer by trotting out as many antique ideas as they can think of. And if they can't think of anything that day then they spend their time shooting down somebody else that can. It's pointless carnage. It's boys playing at being men. It's . . . oh, shit, I think I'm going to have to go to the bathroom. Wait for me here. I'm not going into that restaurant alone."

Kate's good mood started to deflate like a punctured balloon as she watched Ruth disappear into the crowd. It was four years since her first expensive publishing lunch, at The Four Seasons. Since she sold her first story. Since she first met Ted.

Was I ever that young? she thought. Was there ever a time when all I could think of was getting my name in print and lusting after Ted? She smiled. She still lusted after Ted. More than that. She loved him.

But she knew that their affair wasn't the reason she got her name in the paper. Her name was as big as it was because she produced the goods. Week after week she produced the kind of stories the paper wanted. When she stopped doing that, all the love in the world wouldn't get her a byline.

She knew her enemies believed differently. In the bars and locker rooms of Third Avenue, hungry men on the way up and worn-out men drinking their way down spread the legend that when you saw a woman making a name for herself, you looked for the man behind her. It was often true. Too many ambitious girls believed the passport to success was sleeping in the right executive's bed. Kate had known girls like that on other papers. Girls who had made it work for them, for a time. She had seen their names and faces appearing above badly crafted stories and non-interviews. Those names and faces went on appearing as long as the men they were sleeping with favored them. Or as long as those men stayed in favor themselves.

And when the game was over they sank without a

trace. Kate suppressed a shudder. Wouldn't people say she was doing that herself? No, she was being neurotic. This whole lunch scene was getting to her. With an effort she pulled herself together.

The sight of Ruth approaching, hair brushed, freshly lipsticked, made her feel better. Here at least was an ally. Maybe she wasn't a friend, but Kate knew the generously proportioned Ruth wouldn't go out of her way to knife her.

Which is more than you can say about Bill Gerhaghty, she thought, as she observed the sharp-eyed assistant editor in his too-tight dark suit come in with the team from the city desk. The three men were in close conversation and she wondered what plot they were hatching. They converged on her and Ruth at the entrance to the restaurant. And as they made their way toward Kramer's table Kate found herself praying she would not be sitting next to Gerhaghty. She couldn't stand the man. And what was worse, she was too inexperienced to conceal the fact.

Gerhaghty had caught the whiff of Kate's distaste from the moment of their first meeting. And without hesitation he had returned the feeling. Enemies on newspapers were not made out of disagreements or hard words. They came from shared antipathy.

When they got to the table, Kate found to her relief that she was sitting next to Bernard Glen, the political editor. Glen was an elderly queen who liked rose-pink shirts and silk cravats. He was a cozy, rather harmless man, who was invariably wrong about almost everything. She wondered, not for the first time, how he ever survived. Then she took a peek at the place card on the other side of her and found to her surprise that she would be sitting next to Ed Kramer himself.

As yet the great man was absent from the proceedings. And the other executives who were drifting into the restaurant in groups of twos and threes reflected this in their conversation. A casual observer listening in might think he had stumbled on a convention of door-to-door salesmen. For none of them talked about newspapers. In fact they didn't talk about work at all. Kate detected three separate conversations about baseball. Gerhaghty was talking about a party he and his wife were planning. And Ruth was sounding off about the weather.

Jesus, they were a devious lot. None of them was going to give anything away until Kramer arrived. It was as if they were a theater audience waiting for the curtain to go up. Kramer operated the curtain and until he sat down at the table, the play couldn't begin.

They didn't have long to wait. At the stroke of twelve-thirty, the tall, slick-suited editor arrived accompanied by his deputy and Ted Gebler. Kate noticed that Ted was wearing the tiepin from Tiffany's she had given him that Christmas. And the fact that he was wearing her token reassured her. Quickly, when she thought no one was looking, she met his eyes. And for a split second he returned the glance and warmth surged through her. Her enemies didn't stand a chance. No one stood a chance against her. She was ready to take on the world.

Ed Kramer's table was in the corner of the peach-colored restaurant. There was an austerity about it. Today, this was a workbench where people met each other to discuss business. And now that the editor-in-chief was present the air hummed with the topics of the day.

Ben Franks, the sports editor, was sounding off about the success of his last week's supplement. It had attracted advertising away from the *Post* and he was making the most of his triumph. The sports desk, although a necessary part of the paper, was often out on a limb. Baseball wasn't going to affect the way the country, or even the city, was being run. And its stars didn't make the kind of headlines the products from Hollywood did. So in the general scheme of things sports were largely ignored. Now Ben Franks, at the editors' lunch, was restoring the balance. And nobody resented the fact.

Bernard Glen was a different story. The old political editor had everyone gunning for him on all sides. Ted Gebler and Bill Gerhaghty both wanted a younger man in the job. Ted wanted a writer, Bill wanted a news man. But whether the incumbent could write or gather stories was largely irrelevant. What both Ted and Bill wanted was a man of their own in the political arena. A man they could control. A man who they could claim credit for. There could only be one political correspondent and it looked inevitable that there would be a fight over which department and which man he answered to.

But the fight couldn't start until Bernard Glen had been destroyed. And it was on his destruction that Ted and Bill were temporarily united. If Glen was aware he had a problem he didn't show it.

In fact, of all the people there, he was the one who appeared to be enjoying lunch. "Had a little drink with Carl Bernstein," he said to Kramer. "You've no idea what naughty things he had to say about Teddy Kennedy and his nice wife, Joan.''

"Like what?" asked Gerhaghty nastily.

"Like mind your own business, you nosy boy. Carl baby and I are friends from way back. When he's got the goods on the Kennedy marriage, yours truly will get a tiny tip-off.''

"Like hell you will," said Gebler. "Bernstein's not famous for his charitable works. When he's tied the whole thing up—if he ties it up—the *Washington Post* gets the whole caboodle. You don't really think he's going to share a hot number like that with an old pal, do you? Even a pal as old as you," he added darkly.

"Don't be a bitch, darling. It doesn't suit you." And dismissing Gebler like a naughty schoolboy Bernard Glen went on fluttering and flirting with Kramer like an aged courtesan with a new admirer.

Kate marveled at the sheer audacity of the man. He had a hide like a rhinoceros. It was a familiar joke in Donahue's that nobody had to bother stabbing Bernard in the back. Such was his disregard for his competitors that you could stab the man in the front and still hardly make a dent in his ego.

She wondered if she would ever be as tough as Glen. With only the smallest of talents the man had managed to stay the course. Despite the efforts of Bill and Ted, she thought wryly, I bet he makes it through to his retirement. If I had to back any of these three, I'd back Bernard every day.

She stole a look at Kramer. The well-tailored patriarch was quizzing Ruth on what she planned to do about the Paris fashions that year. She knew it would be her turn next. And she dreaded it. Before they went into lunch Ruth had warned her not to talk about anything she was working on, unless it was tied up and watertight. "If it isn't a hundred percent," said the fashion editor, "somebody's bound to steal it from you. That, or destroy it."

Nothing Kate had on her agenda was foolproof. She sighed. And not for the first time that day she found it hard to believe they were all really working for the same paper.

"I was thinking of taking a Christie Brinkley looka-like to Paris with me this year," Ruth was saying.

Kate pricked up her ears. This sounded interesting.

"That bunch of high-class dressmakers in France always seem to put their clothes on way-out-looking models. You know, skinny, ten-foot-tall broads. They make the merchandise look great on the catwalk. But nobody else in the world, and I'm talking about the women who are going to have to wear the gear, has any idea what it really looks like. Now, if we do it my way, if we bring along an all-American-looking girl and photograph her in a couple of the outfits, the girls over here will get a better idea of what Paris had in mind."

Kate looked at Ruth with something approaching respect. That was one hell of an idea. But what did she think she was doing? This was just the kind of thing Ruth had warned her to keep quiet about.

Then she heard Kramer and his deputy discussing Ruth's brainwave and she suppressed a grin. Both men had clearly talked about it before. Almost every detail of the trip, including the choice of photographer, had been worked out. Today was merely the first time the scheme had been talked about in public.

So that was what Ruth meant about watertight. She made a mental note to watch her in the future.

Ted started to say something, and Kate jerked to attention when she realized her name was being mentioned.

"I think it would be a great idea if we sent Kate along to Paris with Ruth," he said. "She could do a series of interviews with the top designers. The kind of thing she does best. The real story behind the fashion story."

Kate started to feel excited. She had never been farther afield than Los Angeles in her whole life. Now they were talking about sending her to Europe, to France. It was the chance she had been waiting for.

She noticed Bill Gerhaghty making furious notes on the other side of the table. And she felt a prickle of fear. What the hell did a fashion feature have to do with him?

He started to speak and the room fell silent. "Won't the delightful Miss Kennedy feel a bit lonely in Paris?" said Gerhaghty softly. "I mean there won't be anyone there to protect her, will there?"

"And just what exactly do you mean by that?" shouted Kate angrily. Too late she bit her lip. Gerhaghty had laid a trap for her and she'd risen to it.

"Why don't you ask Ted Gebler what I mean?" he replied, smiling, moving in for the kill. "My friend Ted's become something of an expert on protection during the past few months. If you ask me . . ."

But nobody got the chance to ask Gerhaghty anything.

The cut-crystal water pitcher standing at the head

of the table suddenly toppled over and came crashing down amongst them. Most of the ice cubes seemed to find their way into Ed Kramer's lap. At least six people sitting on either side of him got soaked to the skin. And shards of glass flew in every direction.

At the center of the pandemonium was Ruth, flushed and embarrassed. "Oh my God," she screamed. "I didn't mean to do it. Honest I didn't. It's just I'm so damn clumsy I never know where my elbows are going until it's too late. Tell me, what can I do? Shall I call the head waiter?"

But the unobtrusive staff in the dining room of Il Gattopardo were already dealing with the disaster. Towels were produced to mop up the worst off in the group as an army of waiters converged on them. The *maître d'* offered to move them all to another table. But the damage was done. Kramer had finished his main course and he was in no mood for dessert.

He had also had quite enough of his executives for one day. He called for the bill and having signed it with a flourish, informed everyone the meeting was at an end. Then he walked out of the restaurant.

In the hush that followed Kate caught Ruth's eye. The fashion editor winked broadly. It was then that Kate realized that her reputation and probably her career on the *News* had been saved by Ruth Bloom.

"You're not really going to have lunch with Kate Kennedy, are you?" asked Tracy.

"Why not?" said Ruth. "I've been slaving away for hours on this layout. It'll be a nice break."

Sitting in front of her was a pile of contacts from the

session on spring fashions. Grabbing a magnifying glass, Ruth squinted at Jade doing her best to look voluptuous in a low-cut party dress. Ruth shook her head. You could pad her bra and paint her breasts as much as you liked, the model was just too skinny to have any sex appeal.

"Why are you bothering?" persisted Tracy. "It's not as if Kate was a friend of yours. I mean, what possible good can come of it?"

"Not everyone was put on this earth just to be of use to the fashion department. Who knows, we might just have a fun lunch."

Ruth wasn't sticking strictly to the truth. Ever since Kramer's disastrous lunch party, the Kate affair had intrigued her. Why did a girl of Kate's class and talent risk everything she had worked for on such an unlikely affair? It was like putting your life savings on the wrong horse.

The feminist in her resented the situation. Stopping Gerhaghty's blabbing she knew was merely a temporary measure. In the end he'd find a way of getting the message through to Kramer. And then all hell would break loose. No, Kate had to be made to see reason. It was definitely not going to be a fun lunch.

Pursing her lips, she returned her attention to the set of pictures in front of her. It was beginning to look as if they were going to have to be re-done. With another model. She looked up. "Tracy love, did you get Jade to sign her model release form?"

Tracy looked stricken. She ran a hand distractedly through her dark red curls. "Jesus, I'm sorry Ruth, I forgot. There were so many things to do that day it must have slipped my mind. I'll run over to the agency when you go out and get her to sign a copy."

"That makes us look very efficient," said Ruth sarcastically. "What if she isn't there? What if she's on some exotic location in China? You know as well as I do, if she hasn't signed the form we can't pay her for the session. I can't see Elite being too anxious to supply us with any more models after this."

"Come on Ruth, it was a mistake. It could have happened to anyone."

The older woman looked pained. "It couldn't have happened to anyone. The only person this brand of fucking disaster happens to is you. You're a dingbat, Tracy, with a sieve for a memory. I wouldn't mind if this was the first time it happened. But it isn't, is it? You're always getting the department involved in some screw-up or other. Well, it isn't good enough. If you don't start concentrating on the job at hand I'll have to have a talk with Kramer."

She threw the pile of contact sheets over to Tracy. "Take these over to Ed Dixon in photography and tell him we won't need to have any prints made. Oh, and while I'm out, start calling around the studios. I want a reshoot organized by tomorrow at the latest."

"What model do you want to use?" Tracy put on her ingratiating voice. The one she always used to get out of trouble.

"Don't bother your empty little head about models. It's not exactly your best subject. I'll set something up when I get back this afternoon." And she grabbed her bag, brushed her hair off her shoulders and walked out of the office.

Tracy stared despondently at the chaos of her desk. If she admitted the truth to herself, she would have known she wasn't up to the job. But it wasn't a truth that Tracy wanted to face. So instead she blamed Ruth.

Fat cow, she fumed. Laying down the law like a goddamn Jewish princess. The woman needed to get laid. Not that anyone would be interested when they saw the state of her.

Such was her fury that the phone on Ruth's desk rang for a full three minutes before she even noticed it.

"Hi," she yelled into the mouthpiece. "Tracy Reeves here. Can I help?"

The voice on the other end asked for Ruth.

"Sorry, she's out to lunch. Can I take a message?"

"Yes, you can." The voice was young, male and not very sure of itself. "Would you tell Ruth that I'll meet her at the theater on Thursday night at seven? I can't tell her myself. I'm on location and I won't be anywhere near a phone for the next three days."

"Who shall I say is calling?" asked Tracy, interested now.

"Dale Keller."

"Not Dale Keller, the model. I saw your spread in *Men-in-Vogue.* It was terrific." It was hard to believe: Fat Ruth dating a dreamboat like Dale Keller. He had to be at least ten years younger than her.

"Hello . . . are you still there?"

"Yes," said Tracy, not bothering to conceal her excitement. Wait till she told the gang about this.

"Look, I'd like to change my message. If it's not too much trouble."

"No problem. Fire away."

"Okay. Tell Ruth I won't see her at the theater, we're bound to lose each other in the crowd. I'll meet her at The Box Tree at six-thirty instead. Oh, and tell her not to be late. The show starts at seven-thirty sharp. We don't want to miss any of it.''

"Don't worry about a thing," said Tracy smoothly. "I'll see that she gets the message."

She put down the phone and looked at the scribbled piece of paper in front of her. Then she picked it up, screwed it into a ball and tossed it into the nearest waste basket.

I'll see that Ruth gets the message, she thought savagely. But it won't be your message.

Serendipity, just around the corner from Bloomingdale's, was one of those restaurants where women met other women for lunch. On the outside it looked like any other artsy boutique, selling pottery ashtrays and ginseng. The inside was a different story.

On both its levels art deco reigned supreme. Giant, multi-colored lanterns swung over circular tables. And an abundance of ferns gave the whole place an atmosphere of expensive camp.

The menu was mostly salads and ice-cream sundaes. Ruth had both. Watching her eat, Kate marveled at the fashion editor's appetite. On her arrival she had started to pick her way through a whole loaf of bread. Now she was starting on her second and Kate wondered if she was genuinely hungry or whether eating was just a neurotic habit.

"The coleslaw here is to die for," said Ruth. And picking up a fork, she thrust it into one of the many dishes in front of her and offered it to Kate.

"Thank you, no," said Kate, wondering if this lunch

had been such a good idea after all. She had invited Ruth as a thank you for her salvation from Gerhaghty. Now she wondered if they had anything in common. What the hell were they going to find to talk about? Ruth's extreme Jewishness made her feel conscious of her Catholic Westchester background. This won't do, she told herself. She examined the prejudices of her forefathers and made a hasty readjustment. Ruth Bloom might be gross, she thought, but without her I'd be heading straight back to the typing pool.

Finally she said: "That was a kind thing you did yesterday. I've got a lot to thank you for."

"Don't mention it," said Ruth. And just as Kate thought the fat girl was going to dismiss the whole incident, she seemed to think again.

"Look," said Ruth, "I know it's none of my business, but just what the hell is going on with you and Ted? Everywhere I go I find people whispering in corners about this hot affair you're supposed to be having. Even the bimbo who calls herself my assistant has started yapping about it."

Kate was shaken. "I had no idea," she said, reaching for her pack of cigarettes. "We were so discreet." She took out a cigarette and started fumbling around wildly for matches. "How could it have happened?" She was close to tears now. "We were so careful not to let anything show."

Ruth stopped eating. "Hey, calm down a minute, will you? You sound like the end of the world has come. It's just a silly rumor. Newspaper offices are full of this kind of story. Next week it'll be somebody else's turn. You'll see."

"Silly or not," Kate said, "at least thanks to you Ed Kramer didn't get to hear it."

"Bill Gerhaghty fights dirty," muttered Ruth. "There was no way I was going to let him get away with a shitty trick like that. Even if it did mean covering half the party in broken glass."

Kate drew on her cigarette. "So you did it to stop Bill?"

"Not entirely. I did it as a kind of favor to you as well. Listen, Kate, you're a class act. Some of the stuff you've been turning out recently, it's good. I mean, really good. You don't need to get involved with Ted Gebler to help you in that department."

"You've got to be kidding," breathed Kate. "Let me get this straight. You think I'm having an affair with Ted to help me get ahead." She smiled and blew cigarette smoke into the gilded room. "That's the stupidest thing I ever heard."

"So why *are* you fucking Ted?"

Kate stared at her lunch guest. How did I get into this? she asked herself. Here I was saying thank-you nicely, and all of a sudden it turns into the Spanish Inquisition. Despite herself she felt defeated.

"I guess I must be in love with him . . ." Her voice trailed off.

Ruth smiled. "Why don't you try talking about it? It might make you feel better."

For a moment Kate hesitated, then she let go. And all the pain, all the frustration she had felt in the past months came pouring out of her. Kate was not close enough to any of her sisters to confide in them. Her girlfriends had problems of their own. So in the end it was

Ruth who listened to her story. When she had finished, Kate looked at her companion. She had expected judgment, even criticism. None came.

Ruth simply looked at her levelly across the table and said, "I guess I'd better tell you what I know about Ted. Though I can't promise it's going to be much help."

For the first time since they sat down together, Kate was interested in what Ruth had to say. "When did you first meet him?" she asked.

"When I was about sixteen, in junior high. Yes," she said, noting Kate's reaction, "Ted isn't just an office acquaintance, I virtually grew up with the guy. Not that it did me any good."

"I'm not following you."

"Okay, I'll spell it out. If you think Ted Gebler's gorgeous now, you should have seen him eighteen years ago. Robert Redford wouldn't have held a candle to him. We were all crazy about him in Fleetwood. I knew girls who would actually ask him out on dates. But it was all pointless. He wasn't interested in a nice Jewish girl from New Jersey. Ted had his sights set higher."

She leaned back, remembering the Ted she knew. The Ted who wanted more out of life than a safe job and a place in the Jewish community. His father had had that back in Germany and look where it got him.

Joseph and Sophie Gebler managed to avoid the concentration camps. Just barely. Three years before the Holocaust, Joe, a lecturer at the University of Hanover, suffered a severe beating at the hands of the emerging Hitler Youth movement. He needed no other warning. He wrote to his cousins in Philadelphia and told them to expect him on the next boat. Then with Sophie and little Walter, who was only eight, he left his house, his job and his country behind him.

By the time he had arrived in America all he had was his dignity. It was something he clung on to for the rest of his life. It was his dignity that prevented him learning to speak English. His pride that stopped him from taking a menial job—the only one he could get speaking German and Yiddish.

So they lived on his savings and handouts from his cousins . . . until Ted was born several years later. Then it wasn't enough. So Walter went out to work. He delivered groceries. He worked in a deli. He did the menial jobs his father should have done to keep the family going.

Ted grew up in the shadow of his father. And he idolized him. Other people might have called him a freeloader, but Ted knew better. For Joe Gebler brought his second son up to read Goethe and play chess like a master. With Ted, Joe discussed world politics, the crash on Wall Street and the painters of the nineteenth century.

Walter watched all this happening and said nothing. Let his little brother keep his illusions while he could. Soon he would be old enough to go to work. Then he'd learn what life was really about.

Ted learned about life, but not in the vegetable market. Joe Gebler played chess with Hymie Cohen, the editor of the local rag. It wasn't much of a paper—little more than a round-up of local events. But Joe knew that if he could get his youngest son a foothold there, he would be on his way to a real profession.

So Ted started as a copy boy for the *Fleetwood Enquirer.* It paid five bucks a week—ten less than he could have earned in the market. And Walter threatened to leave home. It was bad enough carrying two people without having to take on another. In the end it was Sophie who made the peace.

"Give the boy a year," she begged. "Just a year. If it doesn't work out, I'll send him down with you to the markets."

It worked out because it had to work out. Ted knew that. By the end of the year he was pulling down twenty bucks a week as a cub reporter. And there was no stopping him. He loved newspapers, even crummy local rags. But more than that, he loved the power working on a paper gave him. That and the entrée.

You could go up to anyone, anyone in the world, and ask them the sort of questions you wouldn't dare to even ask your friends.

As he worked his way up through the business, first in Philadelphia then in New York City, the power and the entrée became a kind of drug for Ted. His father might have failed in America. His brother might be a blue-collar worker. But he, Ted Gebler, would save the family fortune.

One day, he vowed, he would be the man who called the shots. No wonder, Ruth thought, Ted didn't want to meet a nice Jewish girl and settle down. He didn't have time for that.

Kate interrupted her thoughts. "How did Ted get involved with Sandy?" she asked. "I thought you said she wasn't exactly his cup of tea."

Ruth smiled. "Put it down to sex. In those days Sandy looked like every man's dream of a Swedish au pair. You know, blonde, all the right equipment in the right places. And boy, did she know how to show it off. When she started turning up at the local tennis club all the guys' eyes popped out."

Kate pulled a face. "I take it Ted was a good tennis player."

"You got it. And yes, when he saw Sandy Goldberg, as she was called in those days, he got even better. It turned out our golden girl came from California—her father was some big-shot producer in L.A. And Sandy was in Fleetwood visiting some elderly relation.

"This made her even more attractive to Ted. If she wasn't going to be staying long, there was no way they could get serious about each other. Then things heated up and he didn't notice that Sandy had actually been in Fleetwood for three months and showed no signs of going home. The inevitable happened, of course. Sandy got pregnant. And instead of going off quietly and having an abortion, she decided to tell her mother. If Sandy hadn't come from a rich Jewish family, things might have been different. As it was, Sandy's parents got together with Ted's parents and a marriage was arranged. It wasn't exactly a shotgun wedding, but it was close. Ted had to give up his fancy ideas about being a man of power. His family needed him now. So he put his savings into a down payment on a rambling house in Stamford and settled for a safe desk job. It was a good thing he did. Five months after the wedding Sandy gave birth to twin boys."

"Tell me about Sandy," said Kate.

"What's to tell? She's blonde and dainty. She had her nose fixed as soon as she was old enough and she likes to look expensive. Everyone knows she buys her clothes at Loehmann's, but she goes on pretending they come from Bergdorf's. And who knows, maybe when the kids get through school, she'll actually be able to afford to shop there."

"I thought you said her folks were loaded?"

"They are, but Ted wouldn't take a penny of their money. He was the man of the house. His wife and kids were his responsibility. So Sandy just had to go along with it and do the best she could. To be fair to her, she doesn't do badly. After she got over the shock of having to do without, she grit her teeth and made the marriage work. At least she made it look like it was working. She got the house together with pieces of furniture she imported from her parents' house in L.A. She did a lot of the decorating herself. And of course all the other wives rallied around and helped out. The most surprising thing was the cooking. Sandy, who had never lifted a pan in her life, suddenly got involved in cordon bleu."

Kate felt depressed. There was no way she could compete with this. In her mind's eye she could see Sandy, blonde, petite, perfect, serving up home-baked casseroles. Fussing around her children.

"What's the matter with you? You look like you just saw an enemy."

"I think I did. An undefeatable one."

"I suppose you're talking about Sandy. Well, let me tell you, you're wrong. Sandy's defeatable. Too defeatable if you ask me. She's got no imagination, no style. She's not in your class, Kate. All Sandy ever wanted in her life was a husband and kids to take care of. And now it doesn't look as if the husband situation is too stable."

"I suppose you think I'm the reason for that."

"Actually I don't. If Ted had loved Sandy in the first place he wouldn't have given you the time of day. But I don't think he did love her. Sure he felt something for her or he wouldn't have got involved in the first place. But he didn't love her enough to marry her. That part just happened. Look, he's made the best of the situation. Until he met you there weren't any girlfriends. The occasional fling here and there but nothing serious."

"Are you saying this is serious?"

"You know damn well it is. You might think you're risking your career by taking on Ted. But he's got just as much to lose. Don't think Kramer isn't capable of firing Ted for this little involvement. And then who would pay the mortgage on the house in Stamford? No, Ted's up shit's creek and he knows it. What bothers me is he doesn't seem to care. Neither of you seems to give a damn."

Then she looked across at Kate and regretted the harsh words. Her food was virtually untouched. The only thing she seemed to have consumed during the entire lunch hour was a pack of cigarettes. She looked drawn and somehow older than her twenty-seven years.

"You're telling me I should give him up, aren't you?"

There was a small silence.

"I came here today to tell you that. Yes. Now I'm not so sure. I like you, Kate. I think you've got guts. I like Ted too. And I don't think he deserved to be tricked into a marriage he didn't want."

"So what are you saying?"

Ruth smiled. At least she attempted to smile. But the smile didn't quite make it up to her eyes. "I suppose

I'm saying you should fight for what you believe in and to hell with the consequences. If worse comes to worst, both of you will find other jobs."

"And what about Sandy?"

Ruth looked thoughtful. "Look, I'm not a surburban wife with two kids and a washing machine to look after. But if you want my opinion, I'd say Sandy will weather the storm. What other choice does she have? She hasn't got a glamorous job like you. She's not all that scintillating at parties. And no other man is going to fall over himself to take her on. Especially with two young kids. So what can she do except hang on and hope Ted will come to his senses."

"And if he doesn't?"

"Hell, I don't know. Sandy will come up with something."

She gave Kate a sharp look. "Never underestimate the power of the truly desperate. Sandy may not be the brainiest woman in New York State, but she's got nothing to lose by fighting."

In the middle of the overheated restaurant Kate felt suddenly cold. She remembered a time, not so long ago, when she'd had nothing to lose. And for a brief moment she felt she could see into Sandy Gebler's mind. It was not a pleasant sight. And it worried her.

Ruth was on edge. She had checked her message service a dozen times that day, but nobody had called. The story was the same at the office. Although the phone rang constantly, there were no personal calls for Ruth. There was nothing doing from Dale Keller.

By seven-thirty, when she got home, she began to

get seriously worried. It was unlike Dale not to call. For the past twelve months, ever since she started seeing him, they had spoken every day. Sometimes twice a day.

Now he wasn't calling her. And when she called him, all she got was his service. Mixed in with the worry was a feeling of intense irritation. They had a date tomorrow. Not just any old date. A hot date. Thursday the fifteenth was the anniversary of the day they first met. To mark the occasion Ruth had gotten tickets for the first night of Noel Coward's *Private Lives*. It starred the British actor, David O'Neill, and it was already sold out for months to come.

The first night was going to be glamorous, that was for sure. She had even managed to finagle an invitation to the on-stage party afterward. And here was her jerk of a boyfriend not even bothering to confirm the arrangements.

Nervously she paced around the roof terrace which ran around the perimeter of her living room. The climbing creepers on her trellises were beginning to sprout new shoots. In every pot along the long thin terrace there were the beginnings of life. Ruth went inside to get her watering can. Tending her garden in the sky always calmed her.

Perhaps when she was in the middle of watering, the phone would ring. She took the portable phone off the hook and shoved it in the front pocket of her apron. Please God, let the phone ring.

Ruth's apartment was in a co-op block on First Avenue down by the East river. On a fine day she could see the Hudson River from her roof on the twenty-fourth floor. She had saved up for two years to buy her apartment and it had proved to be well worth the effort. The apartment was in the Forties, which wasn't a neighborhood which housed the very rich, but was respectable nonetheless.

Actors lived there. So did ad men on their way up. And the inhabitants gave the streets a cosmopolitan artiness. Trendy little restaurants jostled cheek-by-jowl with vegetable shops spilling their contents onto the street.

The apartment itself was much like the neighborhood that surrounded it. There was a big living room with windows on two sides overlooking the terrace. Ruth had kept it stark and uncluttered, because by the time she bought the apartment she couldn't afford to do anything else. But underneath the bentwood furniture and over the stripped floorboards there was one extravagance. An exotic Persian carpet.

Ruth had bought it on sale, and even then she was sure she had been ripped off. Not that she cared. The carpet made all the difference to her apartment. It no longer looked like the setting for a hardworking career girl. It was the backdrop for a prima donna or a princess. Tonight nobody was treating Ruth like a princess.

By nine-thirty there had been two phone calls. One from her mother chiding her about a bar mitzvah in the Catskills she refused to attend. The other was from a girlfriend who wanted to moan about her men problems. Ruth cut the second call short. She had enough trouble with her own love life. She didn't need to hear about anyone else's.

At ten o'clock Dale still hadn't called. And by then Ruth had had enough. There were plenty of other Dale Kellers in the sea. Ambitious young men were not exactly a shrinking commodity. She would go out and find herself another.

If nothing else, Ruth Bloom was realistic about herself. A teenager she wasn't. Beautiful she wasn't. Thin she certainly wasn't.

But she had one thing all the bimbos in the world could never possess. She had connections. If a young man wanted an introduction to a powerful rag-trade merchant, Ruth could arrange it. If he wanted to model in *Men-in-Vogue* or *Women's Wear Daily,* Ruth could arrange that too. As long as he was pretty . . . and very young.

Young men, unless they were heirs to large fortunes, needed help to make their way in the world. And there were certain young men who actually enjoyed getting a helping hand from an older woman. The world was a lonely place when you'd just started to struggle your way through it. Comfort and support were frequently as important as sex. Until you learned to stand on your own two feet.

Maybe, thought Ruth, Dale had found he didn't need her anymore. After all, with her help he had become one of the most popular male models in New York. She sighed. The time had come to find a new model.

The unintended pun amused her. And with a wry smile on her lips she re-did her face, passed a brush through the tangled mane of her hair and, satisfied with the way she looked, stepped out into the night.

Ruth arrived at Sweats jazz cellar at eleven o'clock. From the outside it looked just like any other bar in the Village. But when you climbed down the winding, cramped little staircase into the basement, you knew this was no ordinary neighborhood watering hole.

A long bar ran the length of the room. But that wasn't the focus of the action. What grabbed the attention was a combo of four who were remorselessly belting out old Fats Domino numbers.

Somebody had been smoking dope and the air smelled like it. That and the peculiar musty smell you found in cellars in that part of town.

The moment Ruth hit the room she felt good. The place was jammed full of men. Men in groups. Men on their own. Men with women.

She ordered herself a beer to look sociable and a glass of Pepsi to drink and waited for the action to start. Nothing happened for forty minutes. The guys in the club were mostly in their thirties and forties and, apart from a few friendly words about the band, they displayed no interest in Ruth. It didn't bother her. She knew the score by now. She might be sexually invisible to ninety percent of the male population. But to the magic ten percent who needed her, she stood out in neon lights.

It was getting on toward midnight and she was starting to feel bored. Wearily she ordered another Pepsi and, just to keep herself going, she asked for a burger as well. Her mind was made up. She would eat the burger, finish the Pepsi and head for home. There were plenty of other nights.

Then she saw him and she stopped thinking about home. He was tall and pale with white-blond hair, the color of flax. If the boy was out of his teens it would be a miracle. Ruth figured he was probably eighteen. But there was a streetwise air about him that made her think he was eighteen going on forty.

Her feeling was confirmed when he caught sight of

her and, with all the confidence of a door-to-door sales-man, ambled over.

"Lonely?" he asked, offering her a cigarette. When she declined he leaned over the bar and ordered her another Pepsi.

"I like to see a woman who doesn't drink. It's healthy. It's also cheap." He grinned.

Ruth grinned back. "You live in town?"

"Sure." Once more the confident grin. "I share a loft over in Soho. There's a gang of us. We take turns using the bed."

"What do you do when you're not lining up to use the bed?"

"Hang around here. Walk the streets. Peddle a little dope if I can raise the ante. Why are you so interested anyway? You're not a plain-clothes cop are you?"

"No, I'm a journalist. An off-duty journalist," she added.

"So, off-duty journalist, you're not going to do an exposé on me then?"

She leaned back and brushed the hair off her shoulders. She felt better now. This was territory she understood. The brash come-on. The testing exploratory banter. Establishing who was poor and who had money. Who needed and who was in need. For Ruth, sex was a negotiation. She wanted to get the best terms.

With the blond, who turned out to be called Rocky, the terms came easy. He needed a bed for the night. A comfortable bed. And if there were a couple of extras that came with it, then that was all right by him.

As they made their way out of the club Ruth felt relieved. This was the way she liked her male company.

Simple and uncomplicated. She didn't have to hustle to get him an introduction to the right agent. Or the right casting director. All he wanted were the comforts of home. And those she had in abundance.

She had underestimated him. She knew he would be a good lover. Men that young never had any problems getting a hard-on. But in her wildest imagination she couldn't have anticipated what else he had in store for her.

As soon as they got to her apartment he made it clear that he wanted her. Not for him the preliminary cup of coffee or glass of beer. Instead he took her hand and led her to the bedroom.

"Take your dress off," he commanded.

And when she reached for the light switch he put a restraining hand on hers. "It's okay," he said. "I like big girls." He meant it.

Some people have a talent for playing the piano or painting pictures. Others, like Ruth, are good at their jobs. Rocky excelled at making love. Gently, carefully attending to every detail, Rocky brought Ruth to climax after climax. Yet while her body abandoned itself to sensation there was a part of her that remained detached. As if she was an onlooker gazing at a scene which was happening to somebody else.

What's the matter with me? she thought helplessly. I wanted this, didn't I? And as she began to question what she was doing, the marvelous things that were happening inside her started to slow down. It was if she had been turned into marble. A Botticelli Venus, all curves and soft places on the outside. But on the inside there was nothing. No life at all.

She lay back on the bed, feigning exhaustion. "Rocky, you're marvelous, you're the best . . . but even the best can be, well, overwhelming." Then, seeing his crestfallen face, she relented.

"There's beer and Pepsi in the fridge, Superman," she said. "Why don't you go and get us some?"

He was as eager to please as a puppy. Pulling on his faded blue jeans, he scampered into the kitchen.

Ruth pulled the bedclothes tightly around her. What she wanted more than anything else was to take a shower. Or maybe to soak in a hot tub. But she wanted to do these things alone. She didn't need this callow teenager. This artful lover in blue jeans.

She glanced at her watch and discovered with a start that it was nearly two o'clock in the morning. The boy must have been gone for twenty minutes now. What the hell was he doing?

She padded through to her living room. And there she found him, surrounded by her furniture. Everything had been moved out of position, even the Persian carpet. And Rocky, a strange look of concentration on his face, was busily redirecting her possessions to new locations.

"What's going on?" she asked, mystified.

"I'm straightening out the room," he replied, as if it was the most natural thing in the world to rearrange someone's home at two o'clock in the morning. He looked pleading. "You told me I could stay," he said. "You still mean it, don't you?" His self-confidence was rapidly returning. "Things were great between us in the sack. I know how to make you want me. There are other things too. Things I haven't even showed you yet."

The walls started to close in on her. She was seized with an unfamiliar panic. "I thought you had a home," she said. "What about the loft in Soho you share with your friends?"

"That's not a home. That's a flophouse." He looked scornful.

For the first time that evening Ruth realized that she might be in trouble. Swiftly she returned to the bedroom. Then, as quietly as she could, she pulled on a jogging suit.

"Hey, Ruth, where are you going?" he called, as she made her way to the front door.

"I want to leave a note with the doorman about getting an extra key," she said.

Then, before he could say anything else she was out the front door and on her way down the elevator.

To her relief she found the night doorman right away. Skipping the details, Ruth told him she had an unwelcome visitor. A visitor who wouldn't leave. The doorman was not paid to judge situations but to protect the interests of the people who lived in the building, and five minutes later a protesting, disheveled Rocky was being carried by the scruff of his neck down the hall which led to the street. With one final shove the doorman propelled him through the tall glass doors which formed the entrance to the building.

"And don't bother coming back," he yelled, wiping his hands on the seat of his trousers. How did a nice woman like Ruth Bloom get involved with scum like that?

Back in her apartment Ruth poured herself a glass of wine. Normally she didn't touch alcohol, but this evening she felt she needed it. The episode had shaken her. Not because she was worried that the young man she had found that night might become violent. It went deeper than that.

Ruth had been in the habit of using men and being used by them for three or four years now. But she had never really stopped to think seriously about what she was doing. It had all been a glorious game full of instant sex and not too much worrying about tomorrow.

That night she had come face to face with the future and she didn't like what she saw. She was thirty-four years old and a strange young man was offering her his sexual services on a permanent rental basis. What really chilled her was his confidence. He really believed that she was so desperate for a man that she was willing to pay. She shuddered and took a long gulp of her wine. What happened to youth? What happened to friendship? What happened to love?

She felt empty. Not just in her stomach, but in her heart. And with the emptiness came a familiar hunger. Slowly she made her way to the fridge. Inside there was a cooked chicken, some salad, some fruit and a whole cheesecake. She knew she was going to eat all of it. And she knew that when she had finished eating the contents of her refrigerator, she would feel just as hungry as she had before she started.

She came in as dusk was falling. Even in the half light the room looked beautiful, but then Sandy was prejudiced. The room had always looked beautiful to her, even when they were living out of packing cases and bare boards.

It had taken her a long time to find the rambling house on Acorn Avenue. All my life, she thought, laughing at herself a little as she ran her hand over the oak paneling in the downstairs den.

The place gave her such pleasure she literally had to touch the walls from time to time to remind herself she really lived here. She was home.

She noticed with delight that the fire she had lit before she went out to collect the twins from school was still burning steadily in the hearth.

"Lionel, Thomas!" she yelled through the open front door. "Hurry up inside, you'll catch your deaths."

There was no answer. Instead she heard squeals of delight, punctuated with loud woofing. The golden retriever who lived next door had come out to play.

"Okay, boys," she said, resigned. "You can bring him in just this once. But don't let him stay too long. You know it bothers the cat."

Two identical small boys, with Ted's blond hair and Sandy's pale blue eyes came trooping through the door. Hot on their heels was a large, muddy retriever.

"He's called Yop," Lionel, her eldest by two minutes, informed her. "The people next door are Dutch."

"I don't care if they come from Timbuktu. That animal is not staying longer than ten minutes. Do you hear me? I want him out of here by the time Joanna comes."

She sighed. With any luck Joanna would be there by half past four. And the kids would be off her hands for the evening.

It was a rare treat for Sandy to spend an evening without her children. Not that she didn't love them. The kids were the center of her life. The reason for her life. But it was nice to be rid of them occasionally, so that she could go out on the town with Ted. The way they did before they were married. An excursion like tonight reminded her that she was still only twenty-nine. Still young enough to set the world on its heels.

She made her way up the wide curving staircase, which had taken her two months to strip and polish. Her high heels tap-tapped along the landing, which was still waiting for carpet, until finally she was in her bedroom.

Sandy examined herself critically in the mirror

above her dressing table. Then she smiled. You'll do, she told herself.

Sandy Gebler didn't overestimate her beauty. If the truth be known, she rarely found the time to take a good look at herself. But when she did, she wasn't usually disappointed.

She was one of those baby-faced blondes who could eat anything and not put on an ounce. Her body, firm from summers spent playing tennis, was still the body of a girl. She cupped her hands under her breasts and made a face. Her breasts were the only things she hated about herself. Simply because they hardly existed. In her dreams she longed for a voluptuous figure, like Sophia Loren's. Instead what did I get? she asked herself. Woody Allen.

Shaking her head she went into the bathroom and started running a tub, throwing in bath crystals and scented oil with the abandon of a teenager.

Tonight she was going to the theater. Not just any old show, either. Ted was taking her to *Private Lives*. And on the first night.

In her mind's eye she riffled through her wardrobe. There was her mother's black lace. No, too old-fashioned. There was the Ralph Lauren she bought from Loehmann's last winter. No, not dressy enough. Finally she settled for the Oscar de la Renta her sister had given her. It had taken Sandy two evenings to alter it to fit her. But it was worth the effort. The dress clung to her like a second skin, its simplicity relieved by one ruffle which ran all the way down the length of it. It instantly told the world the identity of the designer. It also told any interested parties that its owner was stylish enough to choose it. And rich enough to afford it.

An Oscar de la Renta was instant status. And for Sandy, who had no accomplishments and no identity outside her husband, status was very important. She thought about the evening ahead of her. Ted had told her a month ago, when he got the tickets, that David O'Neill was starring in the show.

She had met the actor, just once, at her parents' house in Beverly Hills. Her father was an independent producer and from time to time, when he could raise the ante, big fish like O'Neill would swim into his fishpond. Ironically it was Sandy's father, rather than O'Neill, who had decided he shouldn't take the starring part in the forthcoming production. The Irishman had a reputation as a heavy drinker. And to Cy Goldberg that meant one thing. He was unreliable, a sure sign that they would go over budget.

So, as the big studios could afford that kind of luxury and Cy Goldberg with his tight budget and anxious investors couldn't, David O'Neill had disappeared from Sandy's life. Until now. Tonight she would meet him again. She looked forward to the prospect.

Yes, tonight she was definitely going to set the world on its heels.

Kate was surprised when Ruth invited her to the first night of *Private Lives*. Particularly when she waited till the day the show opened to do so. She imagined the older woman had been let down by someone at the last moment, but she didn't ask any questions.

As far as she was concerned she had been asked to

see the hottest show in town. She wasn't doing anything else that night. So why look a gift horse in the mouth?

She picked out her most invisible black dress to wear that night. Every girl she knew had something like it. Expensive, demure, guaranteed to disappear into the crowd. There was a private party after the theater and she had no intention of being noticed. There was only one man she wanted to attract, and he was spending the evening with his wife.

She met up with Ruth at the box office of the theater. The fat girl wasn't difficult to miss, particularly as she had chosen to drape herself from head to toe in crimson silk. On anyone else the ensemble would have looked cheap and flashy. On Ruth it looked majestic, as if the designer had known all along that only someone with a substantial height and girth could possibly get away with it.

As there were twenty minutes to go until the curtain went up, they decided to stop for a drink in the lobby. As Kate delved into her bag for some loose change, she noticed a tall, spare, impossibly handsome young man pushing his way through the crowd.

As he reached them he stopped, grabbed hold of Ruth's arm and swung her around. Kate saw a flash of fury in her eyes and wondered what was going on. She didn't have long to wait.

"What the fuck are you doing here?" Ruth exploded.

"And just what the fuck is that meant to mean? I've been waiting around for you at The Box Tree for forty minutes. When you didn't show, I figured you'd got caught up in something, so I ran all the way over to the theater."

Kate thought Ruth was going to burst into tears.

"Of all the lying, two-faced excuses, that one takes the prize. If you think for one minute, Dale Keller, that you can sweet-talk your way back into my life, you've got another thing coming."

"Hey, calm down a minute, lady. Don't lose your shirt. I called you two days ago to tell you I'd be away on location and I'd meet you at The Box Tree before the show. I know I didn't imagine it. And I certainly didn't make it up. So how come your secretary didn't give you the message? Or are they all as bananas as you on the *News*?"

For a moment Ruth was confused. He could be telling the truth. On the other hand he could have dreamed the whole story up. Young men like Dale Keller frequently made elaborate plans which had a nasty habit of crashing down at the last moment. She suspected the girl he was planning on seeing that evening had dumped him and he had fallen back on the easiest option. Ruth. Good old dependable, good old forgiving Ruth.

Well, since last night, the whole ball game had changed. Ruth was in no mood for fickle young men, no matter how handsome they were. If the truth be known, Ruth was in no mood for men at all. In the last few days she had been forced to face a bitter truth about herself. The realization had left her bruised and unsure about the future.

Until she healed, she had no idea how she was going to cope with her life. But of one thing she was sure. She wasn't willing to trade favors for love any longer. Dale Keller had had too many favors from her. And given too little love in return. Innocent or guilty, Dale was no longer an item. He was finished, kaput, over.

She turned on her heel. "Go tell your story to someone else," she said. "My friend and I have a show to see."

A disconcerted Kate found herself literally propelled into the auditorium. "What was all that about?" she asked.

"Just a case of mistaken identity," said Ruth. "A young man on a bad trip who had a vision his mother had come back to him. They do it all the time, those kids. When he comes down to earth he'll forget it ever happened. I've forgotten it already." And she refused to say anything more about it. Instead she opened her program and started reading about David O'Neill.

Kate had seen *Private Lives* before, yet the fragile, mannered piece still amused her. Its charm for Kate lay in the fact that it had little to do with the tough reality that was her life.

Here on the Broadway stage love was a trifle. Nothing to be taken seriously. Marriage was something people did on a whim. And when David O'Neill left the actress who was playing his wife on their honeymoon night, nobody in the audience spared a thought for her.

The play could only have been written by a homosexual, thought Kate cynically. Somebody who didn't give a damn about commitment. Or love, for that matter.

When the final curtain came down Ruth motioned her to stay in her seat. It is a Broadway tradition that the first-night party is always held onstage. And those who had been invited sat and waited for the rest of the audience to disperse.

In keeping with theatrical tradition, the stagehands

had left the scenery for Act Three exactly as it was when the curtain came down. And Amanda and Elliot's love nest in Paris was not a bad backdrop for a party. It was as if you had been invited to drinks in somebody's living room—except the bar was better stocked.

The cast had already assembled on the set and were busy handing out drinks. Kate accepted a glass of champagne from a tall, distinguished-looking man in a dinner jacket and was about to make her way over to David O'Neill when she saw them.

For a moment she thought that her heart had stopped beating. There was Ted and a petite blonde woman who had to be his wife. She felt hollow—as if in a dream—and she groped behind her for somewhere to sit down.

The gray-haired man who had handed her her drink was by her elbow. "Are you all right?" He sounded concerned. "Look, there's a sofa, I think you should sit on it."

Gratefully she accepted his invitation. She tried to look interested as he explained who he was and why he was there. In actual fact she didn't hear a word. Her whole attention was concentrated on the blonde who had her arm so possessively on Ted's shoulder. Her lover's shoulder.

Her first emotion was one of surprise. Somehow she hadn't expected Sandy to be so, well, girlish-looking. There was a dewy-eyed innocence about her which didn't quite go with her image of suburban motherhood. She had always imagined Sandy Gebler as a frumpy woman somewhere in her early middle age. The sort of woman who drove a station wagon and wore sensible shoes.

Instead here was this pretty blonde with a cute snub nose and hair as long as a mermaid's. She felt betrayed. This was not the kind of woman who went in for twin beds or separate rooms. She slept with her husband. If that shiny red mouth was anything to go by, she slept with her husband every night.

She took a long swig of her champagne. And the irony of the situation hit her. Here she was sitting in a demure little black dress, raging with jealousy because the man she loved was arm in arm with a blond bombshell. Noel Coward would have had a field day with this, she thought. The mistress swapping places with the wife.

Her thoughts were interrupted by the man sitting next to her. "You haven't listened to a word I've been saying, have you?" The accent was cultivated. Very English.

She was irritated. "Of course I have," she said.

"Okay, what's my name then?"

"Um, er," she floundered. Why didn't this pushy bore let her alone?

"Shall we start again? My name's Charlie Hamilton. I act as agent for David O'Neill. Now it's your turn. What's your name? And who are you?"

Clearly he wasn't going to let her off the hook. She decided to humor him. Anything was better than being left on her own at this party. With any luck she might be able to avoid talking to the Geblers at all. She turned on the charm. "I'm Kate Kennedy from the *News*. I specialize in in-depth profiles. You probably saw the one I did last week on Nixon."

"I'm sorry but I don't think I did. I only flew in from London last night."

The wind was taken out of her sails. As a well-known columnist she was used to being read. She had been all set to tell him about her interview with the former President. And she expected him to be fascinated. Instead the jerk hadn't even heard of her.

He caught her injured expression. "Oh, dear," he said. "The very instant I have your attention I go and put my foot in it. Do accept my sincerest apologies. I'd no idea you were such a big star."

He was laughing at her. Injury turned to fury. How dare he make such a fool out of her?

"Hey, calm down. I didn't mean to upset you. You're far too pretty for that. Look, stay there and I'll go and get you another glass of champagne."

"No," she said, with something like panic. "I'll come with you and get it. I'm feeling better now."

As if to emphasize her point she took his arm and walked him over to the makeshift bar on the side of the stage. Out of the corner of her eye she could see Sandy Gebler, her blond hair almost touching her bottom, flirting and laughing with a group of men. One of them was David O'Neill. He looked as mesmerized as everyone else around her.

Kate felt the stirrings of competition. The dress might be invisible but she sure as hell wasn't. For the first time that evening she took a good look at the tall, courteous man at her side.

He was broader than she had at first imagined, with a physique that looked as if he played squash a lot, or worked out in a gym. And the cut of his suit was expensive. She guessed he had his clothes custom-made and it occurred to her that the tailor could be found in London's Savile Row.

Coyly, from under her eyelashes, she cast a glance at his face and wasn't disappointed with what she saw. It was a patrician face. Hard and cleanly cut. Yet for all of that, he had humor. As if its owner had lived in it too long to take it seriously.

It's funny, she thought, I've been standing next to the best-looking man in the room, and if I hadn't been forced to look at him, I would never have known it.

She drew herself up to her full height and tossed her hair back. Two can play at your game, Sandy Gebler, she thought.

She had no idea how much champagne she consumed in the next half hour. But one thing was for sure—she was feeling no pain. So when Ted came over, dragging Ruth behind him, she no longer felt like running away.

"Did you enjoy the play?" she asked sweetly, too sweetly. "By the way, I don't think you've met my friend. Charlie Hamilton, David O'Neill's agent. Ted Gebler, a colleague of mine on the *News*."

The two men shook hands and exchanged platitudes. They were both masters of the art of small talk and Kate felt suddenly stranded. What am I doing here? she thought. How did I get into this? Then, because she loved him, she looked with concern at Ted, formal in his formal suit. Behind the glossy façade, she knew he was uncomfortable. As if he was an actor in a very bad play and he wished he hadn't taken the part.

A lock of her hair fell across her face. Without thinking, almost as a reflex action, Ted leaned across and brushed it out of her eyes. It was a curiously intimate gesture. A lover's gesture.

Ruth looked horrified. Charlie Hamilton stopped what he was saying. But Kate didn't give a damn. Ted loves me, she thought. The hell with his wife.

But Sandy, it seemed, had no intention of going to hell. Disengaging herself from David O'Neill she chose that moment to make her way across the room to where her husband was standing.

"You've got to be the famous Kate Kennedy," she said. "I don't think we've met."

No, Kate thought savagely, and I have no intention of repeating the mistake. But she held her hand out pleasantly enough. And she turned her lips up into a smile. When you came from Kate's background the world could come crashing around your ears, but you never forgot your manners. In Westchester, politeness was an art form.

Close up, Sandy Gebler was even prettier than Kate had supposed. She wasn't dumb either. Her conversation revealed she had a surprising knowledge of the theater. Something she owed to her father who was a Hollywood producer. Kate envied the ease with which she talked to strangers.

Because of the way she looked, Sandy Gebler seemed to accept that any opinion she might have was an interesting opinion. It never occurred to her that most of what she had to say had already been said a thousand times in the color supplements. Kate suspected that Sandy owed her knowledge of the arts more to the *New*

York Times, than she ever did to her father. But she didn't say anything. She didn't trust herself.

Instead she reached for another glass of champagne. To her surprise, Charlie Hamilton took it out of her hand.

"Why don't you wait until we have dinner before you drink any more? You'll only lose your appetite."

Before she could say anything, he had led her away from the group. "What was all that about?" she asked.

He raised his eyebrows. "You do eat dinner, don't you? I have a table booked at Sardi's and I think it might be wise if you joined me there. You don't really want to go on being shown up in public by your lover's wife, do you?"

She was speechless. Then after a few minutes she said in a small voice, "Was it that obvious?"

"Only to an experienced eye," he said gently. Then, picking up her wrap, he led her out of the theater.

When was it, Sandy wondered, when was the precise moment when the affection between the two of them disappeared?

Nowadays Ted made love to her as if it was a duty. Like cleaning his teeth or filling out his tax returns. And she didn't say anything. What could she say?

But there was another reason why she kept silent. She was frightened. If she drew attention to the hollowness of their lovemaking it might stop altogether. And she didn't know if she could take that.

Only now she had no choice. After this evening, after she had seen him making cow's eyes at that skinny journalist, she could no longer remain silent. For now she knew the truth. The reason for Ted's indifference. It had dark eyes and brown hair and talked in the plummy accent you heard mostly in the Hamptons. Its name was Kate Kennedy and you didn't ignore girls like that. They were too dangerous.

Ted was taking the babysitter back home and Sandy had used the time to assemble a snack and brew up some coffee. She wondered if she was going to find the appetite to eat anything. In the seven years they had been married, she had never had cause to question their happiness. They had wonderful children. A home they had built together. Shared memories. Why now would he want something different? Someone different?

She felt sick. Maybe she had imagined the whole thing. Maybe when Ted came home, he would be his old loving self and everything would be all right. But she knew in her heart that she was deluding herself. And when Ted came back, white-faced and somehow apologetic looking, the truth was there like a third presence in the room. She could no longer avoid it.

She set the coffee down on the table. "How long has the thing with Kate been going on?" she asked quietly.

There was a silence between them, and for a moment she thought he was going to try to deny it. Then he changed his mind.

"Six months," he said. It was a lie, but what could he do? The truth would have wiped her out. Seeing her face, he added, "Sorry, it wasn't something I was looking for."

"Oh, you mean you had an open invitation. The

classy Miss Kennedy walked into your office one day, took off her panties and told you to help yourself."

She had said it before she could stop herself. The anger and the humiliation she had felt that evening poured out of her in a flood of venom.

"It wasn't like that," he said. His voice was flat, without emotion. It was almost as if he were talking to a stranger. Or one of his junior reporters who had to be placated.

Well, she was damned if he was going to get away with it. There were seven years of marriage and two children between them. She wasn't going to let him erase them from his life. They weren't a paragraph in a story the editor didn't find desirable. They were human beings with flesh and blood and feelings. And they had been there a long time before Kate Kennedy had come on the scene.

"What are you going to do?" she asked.

"What do you want me to do?"

"What do you think I want you to do? Give her up. Throw her out. Stop wanting her. It's me you should want. Me and the children. Not some . . . outsider."

"Sandy." He was pleading now. "It's not as simple as that."

"What's not simple? I don't understand."

"I love her," he said. The force of his words made her sit down. It was as if someone had kicked her in the stomach, leaving her with no breath in her body.

But even if there had been breath, she wouldn't have known what to say. Nothing she had ever done in her life had prepared her for the fact that her husband, the man she loved, would one day love someone else.

When the first shock of his words had worn off, the reality of the situation came rushing in at her. And with reality came pain. And finally grief.

The tears which had been hiding behind her eyes all evening could no longer be contained. She didn't sob. She had too much pride for that. Instead she simply wept, the tears coursing down her cheeks in two silent rivers.

If only I'd gone through with that abortion. If only I hadn't listened to other people, she thought. How different things might have been.

She cast her mind back seven years to the time when she had first discovered she was pregnant with Ted's child. She hadn't wanted babies then. Or marriage.

She had only just gotten accepted to acting school and there were many things she wanted to do with her life before she settled down. So she arranged an abortion and kept quiet about her pregnancy. Then one day, just before she was supposed to go into the clinic, she got frightened. She was still going to go through with it. She'd made her mind up about that. But she needed reassurance. So she told her sister, Natalie.

Sandy and Natalie, younger than her by two years, had been sharing secrets since they shared a room together when they were tiny. Natalie was probably the only person Sandy really trusted. Which was a mistake. For Natalie at nineteen was too young to be trusted with a secret as scary as a baby. What if her sister died on the operating table? It was too big a worry to carry all on her own. She had to share the burden of responsibility. And she shared it with her mother.

After that all hell broke loose. Suddenly an abortion was no longer the issue. Nice Jewish girls didn't have abortions. Not if the father was a nice Jewish boy. They got married instead and raised the child.

So said Sandy's family. So said Ted's family. But Sandy wasn't having any of it. It was her body, it was her pregnancy, she'd decided what to do about it. Then Ted came to see her and all her brave resolve crumpled. It crumpled on the one word which was sticking in her throat that evening. The word was love.

"I love you," Ted had said. "I love you and I want to marry you. I always did, only now it's going to have to be sooner than I planned."

And she had agreed. Not because she wanted a baby. But because she wanted love. Ted's love.

I married for love, she thought bitterly. And looking at her husband with a new clarity now, she wondered what he had married for. Was it love too? Or had he lied to her? Had his parents exerted some pressure she never knew about?

She wiped her eyes. It was too late to cry now. She was twenty-nine years old and life's other chances had passed her by. All she had was Lionel, Thomas and Ted. At least she had Ted for the time being. Though how long that would last she didn't dare think.

Ted interrupted her reverie by getting up and clearing the plates and coffee cups away. "It's getting late," he said. "I'm going to turn in." Then seeing her expression he added, "Don't worry about me getting in your hair. I'll use the spare room tonight."

The nightmare she had been dreading had finally taken shape. Ted was sleeping in the spare room. There would be no more making love. No more love at all.

*　　　*　　　*

Sardi's always had a special buzz after a successful opening. The leading actors, the show's backers, even the producers seemed to have a table there that night. And everyone in the theatrical fraternity came by those tables to whisper their congratulations. Charlie, as the star's agent, got his share of the attention.

"What happens if the opening turns out to be a flop?" asked Kate. "I mean does everyone cancel their table and go home?"

"On the contrary. If the company has a flop on their hands, you'll see exactly the same scene. The same people would come up and offer the same congratulations. They wouldn't mean a word they said, of course. And the actors would know it. But they'd all play the game and accept the compliments gracefully. The theater is a very phony place, full of very phony people, all frightened of being found out. You may be down to your last dollar. Or you may be on your way home to quietly cut your wrists. But on no account do you ever let on. 'The show must go on,' they all cry. Frankly I think it's a crock of shit."

Kate was amused. She always liked to listen to someone who knew more about things than she did. Talking to Charlie was like taking a privileged look into another world. It was a world that fascinated her.

"That's a very basic American expression," she observed, looking at him sideways. "Crock of shit, I mean. How does an English gentleman come to be talking like that?"

"When he has clients who work on the West Coast." Charlie smiled. "One or two of my up-and-coming talents seem to be abandoning an honest living in the theater in favor of Hollywood. These kids like the glitz of the movies. If you ask me, I think it's a load of plastic. But they don't seem to care."

"So you have to dash over there and negotiate the million-dollar contracts?"

He raised his glass. "Here's hoping you're right. About the million dollars I mean. So far my embryo stars are growing very slowly."

Kate started to relax. Charlie Hamilton was easy to be with. Normally with strangers Kate found she had to do all the talking. Think of interesting things to say. Draw them out about their pet loves or hates. But as far as this evening was concerned, Charlie very clearly had the reins in his hands. He had invited her to dinner and the invitation didn't mean he had simply elected to pay for the food and drink. He had taken it upon himself to entertain her. And he took his responsibilities seriously.

By the time the coffee came, Kate was thoroughly enjoying herself. And she could almost forget the disastrous party earlier on. The one where she had come face to face with Sandy Gebler.

Charlie called for the bill. Then as casually as if he was offering her another cup of coffee, he asked her the one question she had been dreading. "How did you manage to get yourself involved with a married man?"

"Why do you ask?" she said more sharply than she intended.

"Because I'm genuinely curious. It's not as if you're a desperate old maid on the shelf or anything. Quite the contrary. You're young, you're bright, you have an exciting career. Men must be falling over themselves to pay court to you."

"That's not the point," she said. "I don't happen to be in love with any of those courtiers."

For a moment he looked serious. "Forgive me. I didn't know you were in love. I thought it was one of those convenient little habits you modern career girls seem to go in for nowadays."

She started to get angry. "I really don't know any of these modern career girls you run around with," she said. "But if you're getting any fancy ideas, you can forget it. I sleep alone. Unless I'm in love. In which case I sleep with my lover. And nobody else. Are you with me?"

He held his hand up. "Sorry, I didn't mean to offend. And by the way I wasn't making a pass at you. I don't go to bed with strangers either. And even if I did, I don't think my wife would be exactly impressed."

For a reason that was totally beyond her, she felt disappointed. "I didn't know you were married," she said. "Now it's my turn to apologize."

"Don't," he replied. "You weren't to know. My kind of Englishman considers it vulgar to wear a wedding ring."

"And what kind of Englishman are you exactly?" She was intrigued.

"A very boring, old-fashioned type," he laughed. "Not the kind of thing you would be interested in at all."

"Try me?"

"Okay, where do you want me to start? I know, I'll start with my father. Sir Cecil Hamilton. Note the handle. It was very important to men like my father. It means he was a baronet—the eleventh baronet, to be precise."

"What does that make you?"

"A bloody successful agent with an office in St. Martin's Lane and a stuffy family who despise me for it."

"That doesn't sound like America at all," observed Kate. "Over here anyone who's successful has nothing to be ashamed of. It doesn't make you automatically classy. But people don't despise you for it either."

"Kate, you and I live in different worlds. But much as I admire the freedom of your brave new system I wouldn't swap my cobwebby old heritage for anything. The past, going back for generations, gives me a security you couldn't even begin to understand. I love America, but it is always with intense relief that I get on the plane to go back home."

She wondered if he looked forward to going home to his wife. Then she strangled the thought at birth. What was she interested in other people's wives for? Wasn't Sandy Gebler enough? She stood up to leave and the captain hurried over with their coats. As they went down the stairs Charlie put his arm around her. "I have a car and a chauffeur waiting for me outside. Would you feel offended if I offered you a lift home?"

She grinned. "I'd feel offended if you didn't. I hate the idea of going home alone after such a glamorous evening. And by the way, I don't find you stuffy or boring. I had a wonderful time. Your wife's a very lucky woman."

"Next time I'm over here I hope you'll be able to tell her that yourself. Fiona promised she'd come back with me in September."

"I'd love that."

They climbed into the car. And all the way to the Village they talked about London, and the English stage.

The following morning an armful of red roses arrived. They were from Charlie, who sent his love. Kate wondered whether Fiona knew her husband was in the habit of sending red roses to strange American girls he picked up at parties.

Kate wasn't the only one who got red roses. That afternoon, just as Sandy was thinking of defrosting a chicken for dinner, the front doorbell rang. It was the man from the local flower shop.

The blooms he delivered were huge, expensive and filled the hall with their exotic scent. There were about three dozen of them.

"Who's the admirer?" asked the delivery man.

"Mind your own business," said Sandy. It was an automatic reply. She hadn't the faintest idea who could have sent them. Nobody sent Sandy Gebler flowers. Not even her husband. Especially not her husband, she thought bitterly.

When the man had gone, she tore the wrapping off the huge bouquet, delving around the thorny stems for any kind of card. After five minutes of tearing her hands to shreds she finally found it buried inside the rose bush.

The message was simple. It said: To the most beautiful woman at the party. All my love. David.

She was astonished. A few minutes earlier she had been all washed up. The discarded wife, rapidly approaching thirty. Unloved, unwanted. Now she was a beautiful woman again. Her heart soared with joy. "I'm beautiful" she told the cat, who was rooting through the wrapping paper with his usual curiosity.

"I'm beautiful," she said, picking him up and swinging him around and around. "A famous movie star says I'm beautiful." The cat did not share her enthusiasm. Instead he reacted like all cats who find themselves in a less than comfortable position. He dug his claws in and screamed.

"Okay, buster," she said, putting him down and smoothing him out. "It's not the greatest news in the world, but it's a start."

And indeed it was. Flowers from David O'Neill weren't exactly going to solve her marital problems. She knew that. But they revived her. Rather like a strong drink revives a shock victim. She felt better.

She went on feeling better as she arranged the scented velvety flowers in her collection of cut-glass vases. She had inherited them from her grandmother, yet although she had had them for three years they had been rarely used. Struggling young couples with children to bring up don't go in for expensive cut flowers. So the vases had stayed in the cupboard. Until now.

She was standing back admiring her efforts when the kitchen door burst open and Thomas and Lionel hurtled in, closely followed by Martha Ward, whose turn it was to do the car pool.

"Did somebody die," Martha asked, "or is it fiesta time at Acorn Avenue?"

"I think it's fiesta time," said Sandy. "Have you got time for a cup of coffee or are there more deliveries to make?"

"No, all the brats are safely home for one day. I'd love a cup."

Martha Ward was a tall, rather toothy woman who was married to the local gynecologist. If Sandy had lived a different kind of life she and Martha would never have crossed paths. And even if they had, they would most certainly never have become friends.

But in the suburbs you don't get the big choices you get in the city. Martha Ward may not have been the most scintillating companion. And an intellect she wasn't. But she had kids the same age as Sandy's. She was good-hearted. And, most important of all, she was there.

This vital fact provided the touchstone of their relationship. Being there meant you could pop into each other's houses and gossip. You could borrow things from each other. You could share things too. And if you were having a barbecue or people over for lunch on Sunday, the Wards were in the neighborhood.

Such were the friendships that grew up in the suburbs. And as Sandy watched Martha and the boys giggling and wondering about the roses she felt warm for the first time since her husband told her he loved somebody else.

"Tell," said Martha, as she helped herself to a cup of coffee. "Where did all this come from?"

Sandy smiled. "If I tell you, you're never going to believe me. I mean, never."

"So give it a try. The worst I can do is call you a liar."

So Sandy told her. And from the quality of Martha's silence she knew she'd gone up at least ten notches in her friend's estimation. By that night, she could have celebrity status in Stamford.

"That's incredible," said Martha, for whom movie stars had the same kind of reality as the moon. "I mean what's going to happen next?"

"What do you mean, what's going to happen next? What can happen next? He knows I'm a happily married mother of two. He's hardly going to fly over to Stamford by private helicopter."

Martha looked unconvinced. "You don't know movie stars," she said. "I was reading only the other day in *Event* magazine how Barbra Streisand got together with her hairdresser. They didn't care about happily married." She lowered her voice in case the children heard. "All they cared about was getting into the sack. Happily married never stood in the way of passion. Not for movie stars at any rate."

"Martha Ward, aren't you forgetting something? Just one small something? I might have nearly been to acting school but that's as close as I ever got to being a movie star. Barbra Streisand was overcome by excitement, perhaps, but I don't distract that easily. Anyway"—she looked through the kitchen window—"I don't see any helicopters coming in to land."

"They will, you mark my words. There are times when I think you underestimate yourself, Sandy Gebler. Men go crazy for your type."

Sandy pulled a face. "I wish I could believe you. More than that, I wish Ted could believe you."

"Why, there isn't anything wrong, is there?"

For a moment Sandy was tempted to tell her everything. The effort of covering up the wounds her husband had inflicted had worn her out. But something told her to be quiet. The time for grief and confidences would surely come. But that time was not yet. Right now all she could do was sit on her haunches and wait for the next move. She had no idea whether it would come from her husband or her husband's mistress. But she did know that the way she played that move would be crucial to her survival. And the survival of her children. She wasn't about to blow it by blabbing her troubles to Martha.

"No, there's nothing wrong," she said. "But there will be if I don't do something about that chicken in the freezer. If there's one thing that drives Ted crazy, it's not having dinner ready when he comes home."

Dinner was the last thing on Ted's mind when Sandy picked him up at the station that evening. He'd been feeling guilty all day about the things he'd said the night before. Sure, he meant them. But there were kinder ways of breaking the truth. He vowed to be gentler with his wife that evening. At least he owed her that.

"Hey," he said as he opened the front door. "What's with all the flowers? Did somebody die or something?"

"You're the second person who asked me that. No, somebody didn't die. Somebody lived. And because I helped them enjoy the experience, they sent me flowers."

"I'm not with you? What's so special that you should get a hundred dollars' worth of roses?"

She was exasperated. "I'm special, that's what. You might not think so right now. But there are other people in the world who do."

"What people?" He looked suspicious. "Who's the creep who's sending you flowers?"

"Why should it be that anyone who sends me flowers has to be a creep? Couldn't they be a passionate admirer? Or a movie star maybe?"

"Do me a favor, Sandy, come down off cloud nine.

Admirers only happen in the crappy novels you read. Movie stars? In a minute you'll be saying David O'Neill came sniffing around."

She stopped what she was about to say. The next move had come. And from all people, it had come from some actor acquaintance she had run into by chance.

Sandy walked into the kitchen and started preparing supper. She was back in the game. Now she would have to be very careful how she played it.

Ted followed her into the kitchen and grabbed her by the arm. "I asked who sent the flowers," he said quietly. "I didn't ask for any lip about movie stars."

"You're not getting any," she said. And she took the card she had been keeping out of her apron pocket and handed it over. He read it with disbelief. Half an hour ago he had been making plans to be gentle with the little wife who couldn't defend herself. Now he could cheerfully strangle her. What had she promised to O'Neill that he should send roses? He looked at Sandy with something approaching curiosity. "That dress you were wearing last night," he said. "Where did you get it?"

"My sister. Why?"

"It's a bit horny for your sister, isn't it? Are you sure you didn't go out and buy it?"

She sighed. "How could I do that? You don't give me enough to cover the groceries, let alone to buy designer dresses. Of course my sister gave it to me. Who else?"

"I was just asking, that's all. I think it's the dress that caused the problem."

"I wasn't aware that I had a problem. Since when has getting flowers been a problem?"

"Since you got married. And just you remember that the next time you go to a party. Coming on to actors, for God's sake. Who do you think you are? Some groupie?"

"Bullshit," she said, grabbing the chicken out of the oven and flinging it on to the plate she had waiting. "You're screwing some bimbo at the office and I'm supposed to sit at home pretending to be happily married. Well, you can take that idea and shove it."

"Just you leave Kate out of this." He was yelling at the top of his voice and Sandy worried about the children sleeping upstairs. But he seemed to be unstoppable. "And don't call her a bimbo, do you hear? She's a serious woman doing a serious job. You wouldn't catch Kate wearing a whore's dress like the thing you had on last night."

"Then perhaps I should lend it to her," said Sandy sweetly. "It might suit her."

Ted got up from the table. "I don't have to listen to this," he said.

"Where are you going?"

"Out. And don't bother waiting up for me. I'll use the spare room when I get in. If I get in."

Sandy stared at the uneaten dinner sitting in front of her. Either I've completely blown it, she thought, or I'm winning. For a moment she felt scared. Then she poured herself a glass of wine and reconsidered.

If she went on playing the cards which had fallen so accidentally into her hands she could lose badly. On the other hand she stood a chance of winning. If she did nothing, all that could happen was that she could lose.

She took a sip of her wine and stared at the roses, lush and expensive in their cut-glass vases. They reassured her and the fear started to recede. She was going to go on playing her game. She had no other option.

If Sandy had been having an illicit affair, somebody would have noticed. At least that's what her mother had always told her. "It's little things that give you away," said Freda Goldberg.

Sandy counted them off on her fingers. The guilty party, if she's a woman, takes more trouble with her appearance. She changes her hairdo. Uses more make-up. She becomes obsessive about the telephone, spending all her time waiting for it to ring. Then when it does, she jumps out of her skin running to answer it.

Sandy had been doing all of these things for the past few weeks. Religiously. Not that she was cheating on her husband. She didn't want to. Anyway David O'Neill hadn't been in touch. What she did want was to look as if she was.

Ted didn't turn a hair. Ever since he started falling in love with Kate his wife had become invisible to him. Sandy could have danced the cancan on the dining room table and gone unnoticed. At the end of a month, she realized this and reconsidered.

Aside from actually having an affair, there was very little she could do to attract her husband's attention. It was then that she made up her mind. The next day she called David O'Neill at the theater to thank him for the flowers. He responded by asking her to have lunch with him. With married women it was perfectly appropriate to make the first move. But then they have to show an interest, otherwise you risk making a fool out of yourself. And David O'Neill wasn't in the habit of appearing foolish in front of women.

Sandy's phone call was, for him, like the starter's pistol for a racehorse. He went into action. He asked her to meet him for lunch at The Four Seasons on Thursday. It was a day when he didn't have a matinee. If things were going to develop, he wanted to have the afternoon free to take advantage of the situation.

Sandy dressed for The Four Seasons with a certain determination. She wore a closely fitting black suit with black lace stockings and the highest heels she could find in her wardrobe. She then piled her long blond hair on top of her head, generously applied red lipstick and set off for the city. If she wanted an affair, she had to communicate the fact.

She began to regret the high heels the moment she started to make her way up the wide, curving staircase leading to the main restaurant. When her mother had bought them for her twenty-fifth birthday she had called them sitting-down shoes. And she had been right. Shoes this high you only wore when you were entertaining in your own home. At least there you could sit down when your feet began to hurt.

The Four Seasons was the kind of place the chairman of the board had a working lunch when he didn't want to work too hard. For it had a frivolous, theatrical air that some called glamor.

There were two rooms to eat in. The first, the Grill Room, was high-ceilinged, dark and full of wood paneling. That room was for the chairman of the board to play hookey.

The other room was something else entirely. For the center of it was dominated by an azure-blue swimming pool. It was a pool that saw sunlight, for on all sides were tall windows giving the place a brightness. It was a perfect setting for having fun and Sandy was reassured to see that David O'Neill had decided to make it his choice for lunch.

Her feet were killing her as the waiter led her over to David's table right by the side of the pool. Then when she caught sight of the matinee idol she forgot about her feet entirely.

Some movie stars, when you take them off a stage or a film set, seem to shrink before your eyes. She remembered feeling disappointed when she met her father's actor friends. If they weren't tall, then they were losing their hair. Or they were shy.

David O'Neill was none of those things. His blond hair was slightly ruffled, as if someone—some woman perhaps—had been running her fingers through it. His eyes were as blue as the pool he sat beside. And he was smiling. More than that he was laughing. "Jesus Christ," he said, standing up to greet her. "You look just like a French tart. We'd better have a bottle of champagne."

Without further ado he summoned the waiter and ordered a bottle of Crystal.

"It's the classic courtesan's drink," he explained when it arrived five minutes later. "It should make you feel comfortable."

Things were getting out of hand.

Two bottles of Crystal later, things were definitely

out of hand. The actor proved a marvelous host. He flattered her outrageously and made her laugh with inside gossip about the theater. He even asked after her father whom he remembered from his Hollywood days.

By the time they got to the main course, a perfect poached salmon ordered just for the occasion, Sandy was feeling mellow. She had approached the whole enterprise with a mixture of determination and dread. The idea of teaching her husband a lesson had metaphorically set her jaw. Now the pressure was off. O'Neill was doing all the running and she felt deliciously relaxed. The coming ordeal could just turn out to be fun.

David poured out the vintage Chablis and raised his glass in a toast. "Here's to you," he said. "By the way, how is that nice husband of yours?"

The question floored her. The gaiety of the occasion had stopped her thinking about Ted and the impending end of her marriage. Now it all came flooding back. Desolation hit her like a tidal wave.

Tears started to form in the corners of her eyes. O'Neill looked concerned. "What's the matter?" he asked. "You look like the roof's fallen in."

"You shouldn't have asked about my husband," she sobbed. "If only you hadn't mentioned him everything would have been all right."

"Oh, lord," said the actor, taking out a white linen handkerchief and dabbing at her face. "It can't be that bad. He didn't die or anything, did he?"

"No, worse than that."

He relaxed and leaned back in his seat. "Don't tell me, let me guess. Your old man, who you're more attached to than you care to admit, is having an affair with another woman. So you turn up here decked out like the whore of Babylon and decide to get your own back." He grinned. "I'm right, aren't I? Well go on, say something."

She was speechless.

"Well at least the shock of the truth has dried up your tears. Which is just as well. I've a reputation to maintain. O'Neill, womanizer, and roaring boy. If you go on looking like a wet Wednesday, you'll disappoint my public. They'll think I'm getting to be a boring old fart, depressing the ladies instead of giving them a thrill."

Despite herself, she smiled. The man really was a charmer. "I'm sorry I tried to use you," she said. "It was a rotten thing to try. Anyway, I didn't pull it off."

"And more's the pity. There's nothing I would have enjoyed more. Even in that ridiculous get-up you look good enough to eat."

"I wish Ted agreed with you," she said mournfully. "Nowadays he doesn't even look at me."

"Well, we're going to have to change that, aren't we?"

"You silly, romantic Irishman, how could we possibly do that? My husband's fallen for some tight-assed bitch from Westchester. She's everything I'm not. Serious, hard-working, snotty. And she sees him every day. I don't stand a chance."

O'Neill signaled the waiter and ordered a round of cognac. Taking a brandy balloon in both hands, he signaled Sandy to do the same.

"First you swirl it around. Then you inhale the bouquet. And finally you sip it, slowly. After you've done that, we'll discuss how you're going to stop being a silly goose. Pull yourself together, girl. With eyes like yours and that body, you stand more than a chance. Stop doubting yourself. You pulled me, didn't you, and I'll tell you, I can have my pick. If I can want you, so can your husband. You're just not handling him right."

"What do you suggest I do?"

"Nothing for the moment. Just go on looking the way you do and try putting a smile on for him occasionally. Don't let him see you're rattled. You can do that much, can't you?"

She nodded.

"Okay, if I can rely on you to put on a good face, you can leave the rest to me."

She was intrigued. "What do you have in mind?"

"Nothing I'm prepared to discuss with you. But I have a little plan and I think it'll do the trick. Just promise me two things, will you? Leave this Sunday free. Don't go planning anything. And if something out of the ordinary happens that day, don't look surprised. Go along with it." He paused. "Have you got that?"

"Yes, but you might give me some warning about what you're planning to do."

"What, and spoil the fun? Not on your life. Now drink that brandy down, it'll do you good."

Sandy had no idea how she got home that day. She vaguely remembered being put on the train at Grand Central. Then she fell fast asleep. If the conductor, who recognized her, hadn't remembered she lived in Stamford, she could have ended up in Boston.

As it was, she staggered from the station into a taxi and managed to get home in time to say good night to her children, who were being sent off to bed by the ever-capable Martha.

"You smell like a brewery. What on earth have you been up to in the city?" she asked.

"Nothing I planned," Sandy replied. And with that she kissed her children, pushed Martha out the door and staggered up to her bedroom. The only remedy for a boozy lunch was to lie down and forget about it. She was still asleep when Ted came home at nine-thirty. He didn't wake her.

Sunday was bright and perfect. The sort of day that brings the promise of a beautiful summer. And from the moment they got out of bed the boys wanted to go on a picnic.

Ted joined in their enthusiasm. They could take the car and drive out to the lake. It wasn't warm enough yet to go swimming, but they could rent a boat and maybe get in some fishing. The prospect filled them with excitement.

On any other day it would have filled Sandy with the same enthusiasm. Today it filled her with dread. She knew that at all costs they had to remain at home. If they didn't, all her careful planning would be for nothing.

She racked her brains to find a suitable reason not to go to the lake. She had invited the Wards over in the afternoon, she told them. Cancel it then, said her family. Wasn't it still too chilly this time of the year for such an expedition? she protested. Nonsense, said the boys, we'll pack extra sweaters.

Finally she got exasperated. "I defrosted a huge hunk of beef for lunch," she told them. "I can't cook it in time to take it with us. And I can't refreeze it now that I've put it in the oven. Ted," she said, pleading now. "We're not made of money. If we go out today, we can kiss goodbye twenty-five dollars' worth of meat. Why don't we plan to go next week? At least I'll have some notice. That way I can get together a real picnic, a picnic you'll enjoy."

Wearily he gave in to her. It was a minor skirmish and they had too many major battles to fight to waste their energy on trivia.

At twelve she started to set the table. She was wearing tight blue jeans and a huge mohair sweater she'd bought last time she'd been in Los Angeles. With her hair tied back and her face clean of any make-up except for a little eyeliner around the eyes, she could have passed for a much younger woman.

It's not fair, she thought, here I am donating the rest of my life to these three spoiled wretches. And not one of them could give a damn.

The front doorbell rang and Ted, who was in the middle of the Sunday *Times,* put down the paper and went to answer it. Sandy heard a voice asking for her and hurried out to see who was there. The scene that confronted her made her smile.

There was David, his eyes even bluer than she remembered, standing in her driveway. Behind him was a stretch Cadillac which seemed to go on forever.

He shot Ted a winning smile. "I've come to take your wife out for some lunch," he said. "The lake's perfect at this time of year, so I thought she'd enjoy that."

Sandy thought Ted would have a heart attack.

"You've got a hell of a nerve," he spluttered. "Turning up on a family day and trying to drag my wife off."

"What's wrong with that?" asked the actor. "From what Sandy tells me you're not much of a family anymore. I bet she'd enjoy being away from you for a change. It'll cheer her up."

"Sandy," said Ted, turning around. "Will you tell this joker to go away, or should I?"

Sandy smiled. It was her social hostess smile. "Wouldn't that be a little rude, darling? After all, the man has driven all the way out here. The least we can do is offer him a drink."

"Hold it a minute, what's going on here? First you send my wife flowers. Now you turn up on the doorstep. What kind of dirty trick are you trying to pull?"

"Don't be childish, darling," said Sandy, who was beginning to enjoy things. "This is my old buddy, David. He's only trying to be friendly."

And with that she took his arm and led him into the paneled den. Through the windows she could see her sons playing with the dog next door. They'd be out there until someone bothered to call them in.

She went over to the liquor cabinet. "Can I make you a martini, David?" she asked. "Or would you prefer some wine?"

He grinned. "If you're having a martini, I'll join you. What about you, Ted?"

"I'm going to have a beer," he said sourly. "But you go ahead. Help yourself to anything you want. You seem to be doing that anyway."

"Now what exactly do you mean by that?" said the Irishman.

"For God's sake don't pretend you don't know what I mean," growled Ted. "Anyone can see you're making a play for Sandy."

"And does that bother you? I thought your interests lay elsewhere."

Ted set his mouth into a thin line. There were troubles in his marriage, he knew that. But they were his troubles. Only he could sort them out. He had no intention of letting a matinee idol interfere in them.

"Do me a favor and get lost," he said. "Sandy's my wife. She's the mother of my children. And yes, it does bother me that some clown should be chasing after her. As for my so-called other interests, that's none of your fucking business. People like you thrive on gossip and rumor. Well, if I'm so interested in somebody else, why aren't I with her now? Instead of at home with my wife and children."

David poured the martini down his throat in one gulp and held out his glass for another. Sandy handed him the pitcher.

"You sound to me as if you're a little jealous," he said, helping himself to another glass.

"Jealous? Why should I be jealous of my wife? She's my wife, isn't she?"

"I wouldn't count on it for too long, if I were you, my boy. There aren't too many ladies that look like Sandy. If she belonged to me, I'd keep a better eye on her."

"Well, she doesn't belong to you. And if I have anything to do with it, she never will."

O'Neill put down his glass slowly and deliberately. "We'll see about that," he said.

But before he could move into position, Ted landed the first punch. It smacked into his chin with a sickening thud. The actor went down like a felled oak.

"For Heaven's sake, David, what's he done to you?" said Sandy, moving quickly over to where he lay. Before she could reach him Ted was in front of her. "Keep out of this," he told her. "I'll deal with it."

And so saying, he heaved O'Neill to his feet and half-carried, half-pulled him to the door. With no ceremony, he shoved him into the driveway. "If you want to stay in one piece, I'd get into that snazzy car of yours and start driving back to New York," he shouted. Then he slammed the door.

The actor did his best to hide a smile as he climbed into the Cadillac. He could have taken Ted with one hand tied behind his back and left him for dead. Instead he had chosen to go down like a hero. The things he did for women.

Sandy needed a drink. David O'Neill had promised a solution to her problems, and he had delivered. Right on the money. Now all she needed to know was how her husband was taking it.

She made her way toward the pitcher of martinis.

"I'll have one of those," said Ted quietly, as she filled her own glass. "I think the occasion merits something stronger than beer."

The children were still outside in the garden, playing happily with the neighbors' dog. So she filled both drinks and brought them over to where Ted was sitting.

"Cheers," she said. Then she threw the drink back.

Fast. Getting to her feet, she went over to the cabinet and poured herself another.

Ted started to look worried. "Hey, take it easy. I only knocked your boyfriend down. I didn't kill him."

Sandy took a long swig from her second martini. Then she said, "He wasn't my boyfriend, you know. He never even got near me."

"So what was he? A distant cousin come to tell you news about the family?"

Sandy emptied her glass and observed with a certain surprise that the room was revolving slowly around her. Abruptly she sat down.

"Look," she said with an effort, "I know you're jealous. And that's what I wanted. At least I thought I did . . . now I don't know."

Ted got to his feet. "I'm going to make us some hot coffee," he said. "Then you're going to tell me what's been going on in this house. Right from the beginning. And don't spare me any of the details. I want to know the whole story, do you hear?"

Sandy heard only too well. For a moment she was tempted to go along with David O'Neill's elaborate lie. After all, it was having the desired effect. Why stop now?

Then she faltered. She had already told him half the truth, she couldn't deny him the rest. I'm going to lose, she thought to herself. I know it and for the life of me, I can't do a thing about it. In her mind's eye she had a vision of Kate. Expensive, sophisticated. More knowing than she could ever be. Take him, she thought. He's all yours. I've had enough.

With shaking hands she took hold of the coffee Ted held out to her. Then slowly and in a very small voice she told him the whole story. Right from the moment David O'Neill sent her the big, vulgar bunch of red roses.

Ted stared at his wife, appalled. Finally he said, "You poor thing, I had no idea."

"No idea about what?"

"No idea of what I'd done to you. What I'd done to us. Why in God's name didn't you tell me how you felt?"

She made a wry face. "I seem to remember that at the time you weren't very interested in what I had to say. I mean, you had other things to think about."

There was a silence. Then he said, "Do you mind very much if we don't talk about Kate right now? That's something I have to work out for myself."

He went over to where she was sitting and pulled her to her feet. Then he kissed her. Slowly, experimentally, as if the taste of her mouth was something new to him. "I love you, Sandy, you know that."

There were tears in her eyes. "No I didn't. I didn't know any of it. I thought when I told you the truth about David you'd walk straight out the door."

He took her in his arms and rocked her gently back and forth. "Then you really don't know anything about men, do you? I'll be honest, I was jealous as hell when I thought you were getting your own back with that horny actor. And if you had been telling the truth, then I might have walked out of your life. But now? Don't be silly. You're my wife, Sandy. We have a family together. I can't just turn my back on the years we've had. It would be like denying they ever existed."

She took a step away from him. Then she pulled a

grubby handkerchief out of the pocket of her jeans and wiped her eyes. I really should tell him to get lost, she thought. He hasn't told me he'll never see her again. Then she looked at him and the helplessness she had felt earlier washed over her.

"I'm crazy about you," she said, "I wish I wasn't but I am."

He took her hand and looked at her seriously. "Well, Mrs. Gebler, if that's the way you feel, it's about time you put your money where your mouth is."

She looked past him into the garden where Lionel and Thomas were still playing. He caught the question in her eyes and pulled her toward the stairway.

"They can wait for their lunch," he said evenly. "It won't do them any harm. What I have on my mind isn't going to keep much longer."

Slowly she followed him up the stairs to their bedroom. I've won, I've won, sang a voice in her head. Yet underneath it another voice whispered to her. "It's only the first round," it murmured, threatening and insistent. Don't count your chickens.

Dear God, how I hate Sundays, thought Ruth as she cleared the remains of breakfast from her scrubbed pine kitchen table. It's the one day of the week when New York has no charm whatsoever.

She remembered when Sunday mornings were full of Dale Keller. They would lie in bed all morning and read the papers. Then they'd take a walk, maybe in Central Park, or they'd go down to the river. And then there was brunch. Lovely, mouthwatering brunch with lox and bagels, coleslaw and corned beef. Her stomach ached at the memory.

Now who do I see? she thought bitterly. Tourists and out-of-towners and poor black kids with their shirts hanging out of their trousers. Sunday in New York. If it wasn't for Kate I think I'd commit suicide.

For Kate had been her salvation. Having turned her back resolutely on casual sex Ruth had to find some other channel for her abundant energies. And Kate had come to the rescue. For she didn't have anything to do on Sunday either. Not since Ted had come on the scene and put an end to her party days. But there was a life after dating and Kate had shown it to Ruth. She took her to the street fair in Greenwich Village where the city's struggling artists showed their work once a week. She dragged her around Macy's which stayed open for the tourist trade. And on a rainy day, she even talked her into having her cards read for a couple of dollars by a Puerto Rican gypsy in a booth on 54th Street.

But the weekend always ended up the same way. The two women would have dinner at PJ Clarke's. There was something special about the Irish bar. And it was nothing to do with the way it looked. There must have been a hundred other restaurant bars in the city with wooden floors covered in sawdust. And the checkered cloths on the tables weren't so unusual either. What was different about PJ's was its ambience.

It was darker, more Irish, somehow racier than any other establishment. Visiting movie stars haunted the long curving bar. Jackie Onassis was rumored to eat the odd hamburger there. Even when the place was quiet and half-empty, as it was when the two women drifted in at five-thirty, Ruth somehow expected to see the ghost of Hemingway getting drunk in the corner.

As they always did on Sunday nights they ordered a bottle of wine. And Ruth drank her one toast of the week.

"Here's to getting through," she said, raising her

glass. The liquor tasted strong and acrid and she knew she would never acquire the taste for it. But she also knew that Kate was as lonely as she was and didn't like drinking alone. So Ruth struggled through her glass and pretended to enjoy it. It was her way of saying thank you.

Kate looked at her with a certain curiosity. "I don't understand you," she said. "Every Sunday night you're always so thankful for getting through, but you don't have to spend it this way."

Ruth shook her head. "Sorry, I'm not with you."

"I think you are," said Kate. "Only you don't want to admit it. Look, I spend every weekend on my own for one very good reason. Ted. I'm not interested in parties or dating, because I know very well where all that ends up. But that doesn't apply to you. When I first joined the paper, you were the original girl on the town. Even before Dale came on the scene you always had a date or a party to go to. What happened?"

Ruth grimaced. "Maybe I lost interest in guys. It happens."

"Baloney. It happens, sure it happens. To my mother it happened. It doesn't happen to healthy young women in their thirties. You'll have to think of something better than that."

"Okay, Kate, if you want the truth, I'll tell you. But you might not like me for it."

"I'm willing to take the chance."

Ruth poured herself a second glass of wine. She needed to blur the edges for this kind of confession. Then she said, "I have a taste for young men."

"So? Who doesn't?"

"I don't mean ordinary young. I mean very young."

"You mean, like teenagers?"

"You're getting close."

"But why? There are plenty of single guys in their thirties and forties. With the present divorce rate, they'll soon be outnumbering us. So what's this obsession with the junior league?"

Ruth looked thoughtful. "It's difficult to pin down. I guess you could say I don't like to make an effort. I mean, I can't get it together to go after a guy. All the women I know who date the complicated divorcees, they tell me they're working at their relationships. They cook. They run around after the ex-wife's kids. They handle his problems and their own. Look at you and Ted. I know he's married, but you put up with that. You understand when he can't see you. You believe every excuse he gives you."

For a moment Kate felt vulnerable. Was Ted giving her lies and excuses? Was she being used like some convenient mistress? Some diversion during the working week?

Then she remembered how it had been between them on Friday, the day they said goodbye for the weekend, and she smiled. Men lie with words. Sometimes if they are skillful they lie with their faces. But they don't lie with their bodies. When you're that close to somebody it's impossible to fake it. The memory of their lovemaking left its warmth. And despite that fact that she was alone that Sunday, she felt safe.

Ruth's voice, strident, demanding to be heard, cut into her thoughts. "I'm not made like you, Kate," she said. "When I see a guy, I like it to be easy and fun. Like it was when I was a teenager. I just had a good time then.

Sex was no big deal. Relationships were nothing to be serious about. You stayed with each other for as long as it was fun. And when it wasn't, you split up and found somebody else. You both did. And you sometimes stayed friends afterward, too.''

"I still don't get it," said Kate. "If young guys are such a barrel of laughs, how come you're not with one now?"

"I kinda hoped you weren't going to ask me that." She sighed and took another slug of her wine. "Okay, I promised you the truth. You know all that stuff I told you about kids being easy and fun. Well, they are, as long as you're a kid yourself. When you're not, the game changes. You're not equal any more. And believe me, there is a kind of equality in having nothing but hopes and dreams. When one of you has gone further in life, when one of you has actually achieved something, and that someone is you, then you have to contribute.''

Kate looked worried. "What kinds of things are you expected to give these young boys?"

Ruth laughed. "Don't worry. I don't pay them. I'm not that old. No, I help them. Take Dale for instance. When I first met him he'd just come out of college and was doing a training program with Elite. I only ran into him because the photographer I was using that day was doing some test shots of Dale after the session.

"The minute I saw him, I knew he was for me. I also knew that with a little encouragement I could be for him. He was ambitious, even then."

"So what did you do?"

"Easy. I asked him to bring his test shots over to my office when he got the prints and I'd see if I could use him on something." She smiled, remembering. "He never did come up to the *News*. He was too bright for that. He rang me and asked if he could show me his pictures over a drink. He thought it would be more friendly. Well, it was more friendly. Dale, you might say, has a talent for friendship."

"And you have a talent for helping friendly young men, is that it?"

"Sure," said Ruth. "That's it. And at the time it suited both of us perfectly."

"And now?"

"Now Dale doesn't need help anymore. Mine or anyone else's. So he can screw for the pleasure of it, rather than for anything it might get him. And I'm suddenly a little weary of being used."

"Don't you think you're being hard on yourself? Dale's been a pretty big name for at least six months now. By your calculations it should have ended before Christmas, rather than two months ago."

"I hear you. For a while he had me convinced he liked to be with me. For me, I mean. Then came the night of the Noel Coward play. Our anniversary. I was stupid enough to buy tickets, and plan dinner back at the apartment. The whole schmear. And he didn't show. He didn't even call me to tell me he wasn't going to make it. There was nothing. Silence. Zilch. So then I knew."

"Hang on. That's not the way I remember it. Dale did show. I was with you that night at the theater and he came running in late saying he'd gotten hung up waiting for you. I never could understand why you brushed him off like that."

"Because he hadn't called for nearly a week." Ruth

was in tears now. "And he always called me. Every day he called me. Then when I called him and all I got was his service, I knew there was something wrong."

"I'm not arguing with that. Of course something was wrong. But didn't it occur to you that whatever was wrong had nothing to do with you? Maybe you just got your messages screwed up."

"Why did you say that?" said Ruth, more sharply than she intended. "The part about the messages, I mean."

"Because when he caught up with you at the theater he clearly said he'd been away on location and had called the office to tell you so."

"So why didn't I ever hear about it? I don't have half-wits working in my office, you know. If anything, my secretary is too good at wasting my time with all the garbage that comes in from outside."

"Did you ever ask her if she spoke to Dale that week?"

"No, I couldn't. She was away on vacation."

Ruth sat bolt upright. The truth was starting to swim into focus and she didn't like the look of the picture it was forming. "When Brett goes away," she said, half to herself, "either I answer the phone, or Tracy does."

She shook her head. "No, I'm being neurotic now. Tracy might be the original dingbat, but she does know how to take a message. My in-box is full of little scraps of paper covered with her scrawl."

Kate signaled the waiter for another glass of wine. Then she lit a cigarette.

"Is there any reason," she said slowly, "why Tracy wouldn't pass on a message from Dale? Does she like him herself? Did you have a falling out? Think hard, Ruth, it's important."

"Now that I think of it, I did yell at her about some model we'd used in a session. But it wasn't anything important. It certainly wasn't anything I don't do ten times a day when Tracy's being slow. Look, a brain she isn't. But she's a good kid, a willing kid. And I'd be a bitch if I thought otherwise."

Ruth leaned back in her chair and shook the mass of dark, crinkly hair off her shoulders.

It was then that she saw him. Across the smokey, rapidly filling restaurant, half-hidden in one of the booths was Dale Keller. The man they had been talking about. Her former lover. He was better-looking than she remembered. He'd let his hair grow and now it curled around the collar of his denim jacket. It made him look stronger somehow. And wilder.

Rather unsteadily, Ruth got to her feet. Sure she was weary of being used by young men. But just lately the nights alone had become intolerable. She wanted to feel Dale's arm around her again. She remembered the smell of his body when he was aroused and the ache she felt for him was physical.

She put her glass down. Maybe I misjudged him, she thought. Maybe, just this once, I'll give him the benefit of the doubt.

It wasn't until Ruth was halfway across the restaurant that she saw that Dale Keller wasn't alone. Sitting with him in the leather-lined booth was a slender redhead with curly hair. Ruth recognized her instantly. It would have been hard not to.

The girl with her hand resting possessively on Dale

Keller's thigh was none other than her assistant, Tracy Reeves.

"Why do you suddenly want to fire the kid?" Ed Kramer was using his reasonable voice. The one he used with difficult women. "You knew when we took her on as a trainee she was green. But you said then you'd give it eighteen months. Damn it, Ruth, I committed to the school on your say-so. You can't go changing your mind after a year. It doesn't make sense."

Standing in the editor's office with its walnut-paneled walls and barrier of a desk piled high with the day's proofs, Ruth felt as if she were back at school. She was the rebellious child again. And Kramer was the principal.

She had been in there for over half an hour and during that time she had gone over Tracy's faults and shortcomings with the accuracy of someone who keeps a diary. If Ruth wanted to get rid of Tracy, she had to have concrete evidence of her inability to do the job.

Through the blur of pain and rage following their dinner at PJ's the only thing which made sense to Ruth, which restored her sanity, was the idea of eliminating Tracy from her office. She and Kate had talked the prospect through into the night, Kate forcing her to go through her files and records, making her dredge up from memory every time her assistant had made a mistake.

There were many examples and now Ruth, with deadly accuracy, was retelling them chapter and verse. Yet the tall, blond editor with his Hamptons tan seemed unmoved. It was as if she was arguing about her expense report rather than trying to fire a colleague.

"Listen, honey," said Kramer, "why don't you give young Tracy another chance? Think back to the days when you were an assistant. Can you honestly say, with your hand on your heart, that you were a hundred percent perfect? Of course you weren't. None of us are when we start. Journalism, the craft of newspapers, has to be learned on the job. You can't get it out of books. And Ruth, I'm looking to you to pass on your valuable knowledge. Knock that kid into shape. You can do it. I know you can."

He's bullshitting me, thought Ruth. He's snowing me and he knows he is. She began to feel distinctly uncomfortable. I wonder what he's up to?

If Ruth had known, she would have felt more than uncomfortable. For Kramer had plans for Tracy. Plans which if they worked, would lead to Ruth's dismissal.

Every editor has his style. His quirks and his preferences. And Kramer, who had been editing newspapers for the past twenty years, had very definite ideas about how he liked things run. In a way his management style was an echo of his own personality. To look at, Kramer was neat to the point of fastidiousness. His full head of dark blond hair was slicked back and barbered within an inch of its life. He imported his suits from England's Savile Row. A shoeshine boy came in every day after the editorial meeting to make sure the gloss was intact on his handmade loafers.

But Kramer's polish went below the surface. He was a careful man who took pains to be in control, always. He never drank too much in the company of his col-

leagues. Even when a hot story came in at deadline time
he never showed emotion. His enemies said that it was
because he had no emotion to show. But this was nonsense. Kramer had emotion all right, but he made sure
he directed it into safe channels. Sailing on the Sound.
Playing a round of golf. This he could get excited about.
Pursuing his ultimate goal, power, was something he
only did when his head was clear.

Everything about Kramer was lethal, quiet and controlled. Which was why he couldn't stand Ruth. From
the moment she joined the paper, before she had even
spoken two words to him, the woman offended him.

What business did she have to be so fat? She worked
on fashion, so why didn't that give her an idea of how
a woman should look? Kramer, who had spent years
manicuring his appearance, firmly believed that if you
did a job, you should look the part. Ruth didn't look like
a member of the fashion department, let alone its head.
And when the retiring fashion editor had suggested Ruth
as her successor he had turned the idea down flat. She's
sloppy, he said. Anyone can see that.

There was of course a huge battle among his executives, who for once didn't agree with him. Ruth wasn't
just a worthy successor to Betty McQueen, she was a brilliant one. Like the seasoned professional he was, Kramer
called for Ruth's clips. And after half an hour he was convinced. Betty and all the others were right. Ruth Bloom
had something. If he didn't promote her some other
paper would grab her. No, he was saddled with Ruth,
fat and all.

But nothing on newspapers lasts forever, he mused,
as he pushed Ruth's salary up several notches. Sooner or

later he would find his chance to get rid of her. Now, in the lissome shape of Tracy Reeves, that chance had come.

Like everything else he did with his staff Kramer looked first and decided later. And when Kramer looked at Tracy, neat and spare in her designer jeans, he saw the future fashion editor. The fact that she couldn't write or lay out a spread bothered him not at all. She was apprenticed to Ruth, wasn't she? She was ambitious, wasn't she? So she could learn like he'd had to. Not everyone is born with talent.

But all this was in the future. Right now, listening to Ruth, the kid had her work cut out just toeing the line. And keeping her job. He'd have to have a word with her. But first things first. There was Ruth to take care of.

He turned to the intercom system at the far side of his desk and pressed the buzzer. "Ask Gerhaghty to step in," he said to his secretary. "Oh, and while you're at it, tell Ted Gebler to stop by my office too."

Then he swiveled around in his chair to face Ruth. "I've decided to kick that problem of yours around a little," he told her. "See what the other boys think."

Ruth's feeling of discomfort began to turn to distress. Newspapers had the habit of turning your best friends into enemies. The frozen silence which had fallen between Ruth and Kramer was suddenly shattered as the door swung open, admitting Bill and Ted. Both men were hastily buttoning their jackets and adjusting their ties. Preparing themselves for a meeting. Though what the hell this get-together was all about, neither of them had a clue. Fashion was Ruth's area. Unless it threatened to encroach on their territory they tended to leave it strictly alone. There were more interesting things to stick their noses into.

Then Kramer told them about Ruth's plans for Tracy. And suddenly they sat up and took notice. A fashion story was neither here nor there. But blood on the carpet, a colleague's blood. Well, that was another matter. How each man handled this meeting could have an effect on his future. For hiring and firing were the life's blood of newspaper politics. And it was crucial to be on the right side. Kramer knew this. He also knew that in this matter there was only one side to be on. His.

"I'm surprised at some of the things Ruth's saying," he said gently, deceptively gently. "I always figured she was a good kid."

With this one mild statement Kramer had determined the outcome of the meeting. Ruth cursed inwardly. Overnight Tracy had been transformed from an awkward college graduate to some kind of newborn golden girl.

Her suspicions were borne out when she listened to Gerhaghty. "I kinda like her approach," he was saying. "When Ruth was in Los Angeles, I came up against her in the meeting a couple of times. She's got a stack of fresh ideas in that little red head. I'd say she's definitely worth watching."

"Did you use any of these fresh ideas?" Ruth inquired acidly. "I mean, were you moved to give this embryo talent space on your pages?"

"Give me a break," groaned Gerhaghty. "You're the fashion supremo around here. If I started backing Tracy's brainwaves you'd give me hell. And rightly so.

No, all I'm saying is the kid's better than you think she is, Ruth. I think you've misjudged her."

Ruth turned to Ted. "What do you think, superman?"

He looked at the floor. Then he looked at Kramer. He was smiling. Christ, that was a bad sign. One of the legends surrounding the editor was that the man never stabbed you in the back, he smiled you in the back. Ted suppressed a shudder. He had no choice but to play it safe. There would be time later to make it up to Ruth. "I'm not saying anything for or against Tracy Reeves," he said cautiously, "what I'm worried about is you, Ruth. I think you've made this decision a bit too fast."

She was about to interrupt, when he waved her down. "Look, I had a writer fresh out of college wished on me five years ago. Compared to Tracy, he was a deadbeat. He couldn't write his name, let alone a story. I admit, I was tempted to march in here and demand his resignation, just like you. Several times I nearly said, 'The hell with it,' and went ahead. But I didn't. Something held me back, call it instinct if you like.

"Anyway, I'm glad I listened to myself. Two years after he joined the paper I sent the guy to cover a Democratic Convention. And he came back with the best damned political analysis I've ever seen outside of the *Washington Post*.

"Before I sent him on that story I'd been making him cover beauty contests and interview TV personalities. And when he gave me garbage I put it down to lack of talent. In fact the person at fault wasn't him. It was me. I hadn't figured out what he was good at.

"The whole experience taught me a big lesson.

You've got to listen to the new kids sometimes. Find out what makes them tick. This Tracy could be a mine of untapped talent for all you know. You've just got to find out what turns the kid on."

"I have," muttered Ruth, half to herself. "That's why I want her out."

"Sorry, Ruth, I didn't catch what you were saying," said Kramer from the other side of his desk.

Ruth didn't repeat it. She knew when she was licked. For some reason, totally unknown to her, Ed Kramer was opposing her on a matter which should have been settled in ten minutes. A routine dismissal. Experience told her something was going on that she didn't know about. It also told her to keep her mouth shut and her opinions to herself. She liked her job and she wasn't about to move into shaky ground over a dispute with her junior. She'd find her own way to take care of Tracy! Right now it was time to shore up her own position.

She smiled. Then she set her jaw. "What I was saying, Ed, was that perhaps Bill and Ted are right. Maybe I have misjudged Tracy. I'll listen to her harder in the future. Maybe she's got something I haven't caught on to yet."

"That's my girl," said Kramer. "I knew you'd see reason in the end. All of us get too close to a problem from time to time. But once you give it an airing, listen to a couple of independent opinions, you get the thing straight in your head. Next time you have a problem, just come and talk it over with Uncle Ed Kramer. He'll straighten it out for you."

Ruth got up to leave. You'll be lucky, she thought bitterly. With friends like you, who needs enemies.

Because it was her birthday Kate bought a bottle of champagne. Because it was the school sports day for Ted's twin boys, she drank it alone. Yet she bore Ted no malice for going home early. She had gone into the affair with her eyes open. She knew her lover had a wife and children. He made no attempt to disguise it. On the contrary, he'd been upfront about it right from the start. And she'd accepted it like the cool, clear-headed grown-up woman of twenty-eight she had just become.

So why did it hurt so much? The anger which she should have vented on her lover she vented on herself.

So he forgot my birthday, she said to herself bitterly as she rummaged in the refrigerator for the champagne. So he's running home to some cockamamie sports day.

So he loves his kids more than he loves me. So who's to blame?

She put the bottle of champagne on the draining board and started to struggle with the cork. It popped, spilling some of the fizzy wine, and the noise in the empty apartment sounded out of place. Champagne was the currency of parties. Or lovers. It was wasted on single women. After all, what did they have to celebrate?

She carried the champagne and a single, tall, crystal glass to the coffee table. Then she threw herself into an easy chair, poured herself a generous measure and gazed gloomily into the gathering dusk. What the hell am I doing sitting here like an old spinster woman? she thought. Then she considered the alternatives.

She could have bought the boys a drink in Donahue's. No, too many uncomfortable memories. She could have spent the evening with Ruth. She deleted that one too. Ever since Ruth had told her she knew Sandy, Kate had been shy about discussing the ups and downs of her love affair. Ruth knew the facts. And she knew how Kate felt. That was enough.

If there were tears she preferred to shed them alone. She supposed she could have called an old lover and taken in a movie. But what if the old lover misread the signs? The idea of sharing herself with anyone but Ted made her feel cold.

No, she was better off alone. She poured herself another glass of champagne. It was going to be a long night.

By half past ten she was feeling no pain. The wine had blurred the edges. She decided to take a hot shower, a couple of Mogadon, and call it a night.

Then she heard her doorbell. It was getting close to eleven. Who on earth would come calling at this hour?

She struggled into her terry-cloth robe and made it to her intercom. "Who is it?" She felt scared. By day the Village was a friendly, almost cozy neighborhood. At night things changed.

"It's Ted, let me in."

She felt confused, almost disoriented. Ted belonged to the day and this was after hours. What did he think he was doing. She stood there, slightly woozy from the wine, wondering at this new turn of events.

It wasn't until Ted's voice came crackling over the intercom for a second time that elation finally hit her. She pressed the buzzer and when he finally arrived on her doorstep, she threw herself into his arms. Then she burst into tears. "I thought you'd forgotten," she said over and over again. "I thought you didn't give a damn."

He took out the large linen handkerchief he always carried and wiped her face. Then as if she was a small child, he smoothed her hair and led her over to the sofa.

"How could I have done that?" he asked, concerned. "I love you. I don't go around forgetting people I love. Not on their birthday."

But there was no stopping the tears. They poured down her face as if a well had been opened. All the grief and need that her pride had made her keep private was finally on display. And with her tears Kate declared herself. For she showed that she needed Ted. As much as his wife needed him. As much as his children did.

She should have been horrified at what she had done. Instead she felt relieved. I'm in this right up to my neck, she thought. The hell with the consequences.

Hours later, drowsy with love she woke him. "I want to ask you something," she said.

"Now . . . in the middle of the night?"

"Now."

"Okay," he said wearily. "Let's have it."

"What did you say to Sandy? I mean about being away."

There was a silence. Then he said, "I told her I had to see a man about a story. In Washington."

Kate was tempted to inquire if Sandy believed him. Then she changed her mind. Fate had been kind to her. Ted had been kind to her. She knew better than to look a gift horse in the mouth.

It had been a bad week for Tracy Reeves. Ever since she came face to face with Ruth in PJ's on Sunday, things had gone sour for her. It was Dale Keller who started it.

When he had seen the fashion editor he looked as if someone had struck him down. Before Tracy could protest that she hadn't finished her drink, Dale had hustled her out of the booth and was propelling her toward the door.

"Hey, wait a minute," she yelled. "Where the hell do you think you're taking us? I thought we were going to eat or something."

But Dale had suddenly lost his appetite. When they hit the street he hailed a yellow cab and gave the driver Tracy's address on the West Side. The evening ended on the sidewalk outside her apartment. Dale had been silent on the ride home. And when he paid off the cab he showed no signs of wanting to come inside with her.

"I don't understand you," Tracy was whining now.

"Last night you couldn't get enough of me. Now you're acting like I got some kind of disease. What is it with you?"

If Dale had a problem he was unwilling to share it. Instead he shrugged himself deeper into his faded denim jacket, muttering something about an urgent appointment. Then he was off and running down the subway.

Damn him, thought Tracy. Him and all men. Her temper did not improve when she saw the state of the living room. The three students she shared with had had some kind of a party at lunch and the evidence of it was all too apparent. Empty beer cans littered every available surface, including the floor. The remains of a takeout Chinese meal lay congealing in its cardboard containers. And every ashtray and most of the paper plates were piled high with cigarette butts.

Yecch. She'd get them when they got back. She retreated to her room, an island of neatness in a sea of pandemonium. Her clothes were pressed and hanging neatly in the closet. The row of freshly polished shoes. These things reminded her of her identity. Or the identity she wished to acquire.

For Tracy had no intention of remaining a nobody. In the poor district of Minneapolis where she came from you were lucky if you had one pair of shoes. Already she had six. But her sights were set on being able to buy the whole store.

Which is why she had made a play for Dale in the first place. Dale belonged to Ruth Bloom. He was her property. And right from the start, Tracy wanted everything Ruth had. Her prestige, her talent, her chic little apartment in the Forties, her lover. But more than anything else she wanted Ruth's job.

Tracy figured if she hung around Ruth long enough maybe some of the polish, some of the success would rub off. None of it had. It had been a year and she still didn't have a piece in the paper with her name on it. Nobody on the paper even thought of her as a journalist. She was just a gofer, Ruth's gofer.

Well, if Ruth's abundant gifts didn't rub off on her naturally, then she would have to help herself. And the easiest thing to steal from Ruth was her lover. How pathetically easy that had been.

A broken date, broken by her. A chance meeting at a fashion show. And Dale was hers. For the night at least.

And what a night it had been. She could understand why the fat Jewish princess had gone crazy for him. To put it mildly, Dale Keller was a ram. And he was built like one. Tentatively she felt between her legs. She was still sore from what he had done to her.

For a moment she was sad that it all had to end so quickly. Then she thought, so what? She had enjoyed what Ruth had enjoyed. And it wouldn't end with Dale. Soon she would start to encroach on her authority. Then perhaps a little corner of her page. Not much. Not at first, anyway. No, a corner would do. It would give her a toehold, which was all she needed. Her ambition would do the rest. David had conquered Goliath with less.

Now it was not to be. Ruth had chosen PJ Clarke's of all the joints in New York for Sunday dinner. And the game was up. She had little doubt that Ruth would have her out on her ear by the end of the week. The thought did not please her. She slept uneasily that night.

The atmosphere in the office the next day was worse than she had feared. Ruth behaved as if she wasn't even in the room. Then she got a message from Kramer. He wanted to see her in his office that afternoon.

So this is it, she thought. The ax. Nervously she ran a hand through her fluffy red hair as she approached the forbidding mahogany door which led to the editor's inner sanctum.

She knocked twice. Soft, frightened little taps. Kramer's voice yelled at her to come in. And when she sidled through the door she felt a sudden, urgent need to go to the bathroom. She sat down hard on the chair he offered and squeezed her thighs together. Soon the ordeal would be over.

She noticed there was a bottle of wine on the desk. And two glasses. Kramer noticed her noticing and started to pour the dry white Chianti.

He handed her a glass. "You look like you could do with a drink," was all he said.

As she took it, some of her confidence returned. If the guy is going to fire me, she reasoned, he wouldn't be wasting a glass of wine on me. I'm not senior enough.

She took a sip and some of the color returned to her cheeks. She smiled her nicest smile, the one with the dimples. Then she watched to see which way the wind blew.

It blew warmer than she thought.

"You know I've always thought a lot of you," said Kramer.

Her eyes were huge with surprise. Twin blue saucers. "I didn't think you even knew I existed."

"Don't underestimate yourself. You're a great-looking kid. Lots of style. I had an instinct deep down when I first saw you in the office that you could be a winner."

"But why didn't you tell me? I mean, all I've done for a year is run around for Ruth. Make the coffee, write the photo captions if I'm lucky. To be honest I thought that's all I'd ever be doing."

While she was talking in breathy little gasps, her mind was ticking away. This was the last thing she expected. She knew she had no natural talent. She also knew she could never win, unless of course the dice were loaded in her favor. Now it looked as if they were.

She took another look at Kramer. The guy was fifty-five if he was a day. He obviously worked out. And from the way he dressed, he was putting in a lot of effort to look young.

Did he want a fast fuck in the office? She dismissed the thought. Guys like Kramer, guys with power, could get all the sex they wanted. No, there was something else. She hung in and listened. Hard.

"If I were you," said Kramer softly, "I wouldn't worry about what's happening to you right now. You have a big future with the paper. I can guarantee it. But if I make sure of your career with the *News,* you have to do something for me in return."

"What would that be?"

"Be very nice to Ruth Bloom."

If he had asked her to stand on the desk and take all her clothes off she couldn't have been more surprised. She smirked. The latter wouldn't have surprised her at all. But this? The guy must have lost his mind. Didn't he know Ruth couldn't stand the sight of her?

It was as if Kramer saw into her head. "I know things are difficult for you in that office," he said. "But they will get better. That I can promise you. What I want you to do now is be a good girl and pay a great deal of attention to what Ruth is doing. More than that. Watch how she writes her stories. Ask her advice if you're not sure how she's doing things. She won't bite your head off. She'll be flattered. Then when you start to get the hang of it I want you to come up with a couple of ideas. But don't tell Ruth about them. Don't tell anybody about them. Just come to me and we'll talk them through."

Tracy was mesmerized. "What happens then?" she asked.

The old war horse took the glass out of her hand and motioned her to get up.

"What happens then, my dear child, will remain a mystery for now. Go back to your desk. Work hard. Try not to get on the wrong side of your department head. Oh, and keep your trap shut. If you tell anybody about this little conversation I'll deny it ever happened. Then the scenario you thought was going to develop when you first came through the door could all come true."

He opened the door and ushered her into the outer office. Tracy walked through the newsroom as if in a dream. The whole world had turned upside down and gone out of focus.

As she approached the fashion department she started to pull herself together. And as she did she realized there was an ache in her left buttock. As if a wasp had stung her. Then she burst out laughing. When she had walked out of the editor's door the horny old goat had pinched her ass.

It was Ruth who first noticed the difference. During the past year she had gotten used to seeing her assistant in the office in jeans and an assortment of sweat shirts. Her image was the image of a trendy kid. And it was the way she wore the street fashions of the day that had persuaded Ruth to give her the job.

The fashion editor believed in keeping in touch with what was going on before it got into the shops. And Tracy, if she did nothing else, performed that service.

Now everything had changed. The wavy red hair, which she normally wore screwed back in a ponytail, now fell sleekly to her shoulders. She had taken to wearing a full array of make-up instead of her usual hastily applied lipgloss. And the jeans had totally disappeared.

In their place were neat little suits and demure blouses. What had happened to the girl? wondered Ruth. Had she ditched Dale and found herself a middle-aged lover?

And then, because Ruth was always honest with herself, she took a closer look at Tracy. She observed how the girl was making a fresh effort to cope with her work load, sometimes staying late in the evening to make sure she had left nothing unattended. She noticed the new interest Tracy was taking in the fashion department. An almost unnatural interest. And because Ruth had lived and breathed newspapers for nearly ten years she started to get worried.

Dingbats who thrived on office gossip and spent more time in bars than they did at their desks didn't change overnight. Unless something had happened. Someone had said something to Tracy that they weren't saying to her.

She confided her worry to Kate. "It's not the fact that she's cleaned up her act that makes me suspicious," she told her over a drink after work. "When she knew I was on to her it was natural she should be contrite. But there's contrite and contrite. The way she's behaving she'll be applying for sainthood next."

"Or your job, maybe," said Kate.

Ruth roared with laughter. "Give me a break. For my job you need to know how to lay out a spread, write it, and get the idea for the goddamned thing in the first place. So far I haven't noticed Tracy displaying any aptitude for any of those things."

"She could learn. Or she could try."

Ruth picked up her Coke and jiggled the ice around in the bottom of the glass. "It's not about learning," she said. "If it was, any bright college graduate could walk into my job tomorrow. What it's about is instinct. Gut feeling. I know a wonderful set of pictures when I see them. They could look quite ordinary to anyone else. But I can visualize them when they're cropped into the right shape. You know, I can actually see them sitting on the page most times. Nobody can learn to do that. You're born with it."

"I agree," said Kate. "But how many bad fashion editors do you know? Powerful women who got their jobs and kept them with something other than talent."

Ruth jiggled the ice some more. It helped her think. "There's Dexter Clark on the *Post.* Her uncle sits on the main board of the paper. Oh, and Rose Castle on *Vanity*

Fair. But she's having a thing with the chairman, everyone knows that.''

Kate gave Ruth what passed for an old-fashioned look. "I think you're getting my drift. If my hunches are right, and they usually are, then somebody up there likes Tracy. For sure as God made little apples, somebody must have given her the incentive to turn over this bright new leaf. Based on her past record, Tracy didn't strike me as a stayer. Or a trier. If she could find a short cut or an easy way to do things, then she would. No, someone's put her up to this. I only wish I knew who it was. What do you think about Bill Gerhaghty? He has a thing about skinny redheads. Maybe it's him promising her the earth in exchange for a few sweet moments.''

"Can't be," said Ruth. "Gerhaghty doesn't have any power as far as my department's concerned. The best he could do for her, would be to give her a column on a news page. And that's not worth revamping your wardrobe for. No, there has to be someone else.''

"Well, it's not Ted," Kate laughed. Such was the security of her love, she couldn't imagine the object of it giving anyone else a second glance.

"Well, I give up," said Ruth. "Maybe there's an aged relative upstairs none of us know about.''

"Whoever it is," said Kate. "I think it's time you put a crimp in her style.''

"How do you mean?''

"Just what I said. Stop the bitch. Thwart her in some way. You can't just have her walking into your department and helping herself to your job. Well, not without a fight anyway.''

Ruth, who still saw the situation as something of a

joke, gave her friend a broad grin. "Okay, Popeye. So I'll take on this Tracy broad. I'll fight her in the offices, I'll fight her in the bar. I'll even stick a knife into her in the boardroom. And I won't stop until I see the whites of her eyes. How's that?"

"Not good enough. What you need is a plan. Something that will put her on the shelf for a couple of months. At least that way you get a little breathing room. And with any luck you can settle the bastard who's trying to screw up your department before she gets back."

"You naturally have such a plan."

"Actually I do."

Ruth shook her head. "Look, this whole thing is getting out of hand. This is the kind of conversation Bill Gerhaghty has in bars. It's paranoid and if you take it too seriously it makes you crazy in the end. What we're talking about is an inexperienced college girl, for Chrissakes. Sure, she gets on my nerves. She'd get on anybody's. But she's not planning to hijack the department. She's not smart enough for that."

"Okay, hold it there. She gets on your nerves. Isn't that enough of a reason to get her out of the way for a while?"

"Yes, but how do I do that, aside from keeping her under heavy sedation?"

"You send her out into the field."

"What field exactly did you have in mind?"

"Washington, San Francisco, Houston, New Mexico. Anywhere really where there is an up-and-coming street style. You told me when you took her on that Tracy had an eye for what was new and young on the fashion scene. Well, put that ability to use. A weekly bulletin from Siberia is exactly the job you need for Tracy right now. She can report on what's new, what's exciting, what's really happening on the streets of Houston.''

''I think I get the picture,'' said Ruth. ''And actually it's not such a terrible idea. But how on earth do I sell it to Tracy? I can tell her to do it, sure I can. But if it doesn't appeal to her then she can kick up a hell of a fuss. And maybe run to this rich uncle of hers on the Board.''

Kate smiled. ''I never thought I'd see the day when I had to show an old hand like you how to put a plan into operation. In fact I'm not going to show you anything. I'm going to set up the whole thing myself. Then I'll come and tell you about it.''

Before Ruth could stop her Kate had picked up her bag and was pushing her way out of the bar.

The following afternoon a stack of airline tickets arrived on Tracy's desk. Meekly, obediently, she picked them up and put them in the large tote bag she carried everywhere with her. Despite herself she felt a thrill of excitement. Ed Kramer sure knew how to make things happen fast. This latest assignment on street fashions could be the start of everything. It was the toehold she had been looking for for the past year.

She felt in her bones her chance had come when Ted Gebler had called her into his private office. When he briefed her on what he wanted her to do and where she was supposed to go she had ventured a demure question. ''Does Ruth know anything about this new job of mine? I mean, I don't want her to make a fuss or anything.''

Ted was puzzled. ''Why should Ruth make a fuss?''

''Well, you know what she's like,'' said Tracy conspiratorially. "She probably thinks I'm planning to grab the limelight from her."

Ted shook his head. Ruth had told him many times that the kid wasn't all there. But this delusion that she could be any competition to the talented fashion editor struck him as ridiculous.

He put his arm around her in what he hoped was a fatherly way. "Don't you worry about Ruth," he said. "I've talked to her about the idea and she seems perfectly happy about it."

Then seeing the doubtful look on the girl's face he added: "Look, if Ruth starts being difficult, and I don't think she will, then just come along to me and we'll try to work it out. But honestly I can't see any problem. Really I can't."

Women, he thought, as Tracy walked out of his office, were something he would never comprehend as long as he lived.

"Hello," said the doorman of the "21" Club as Kate spilled out of her cab and on to the pavement. "Have a nice day."

"Have a nice lunch," echoed the *maître d'* as she climbed the red-carpeted stairs to the restaurant. Normally these commercial courtesies managed to make her feel good. Today they had no effect. She was meeting Ed Kramer today and the whole world could have stood to attention and applauded and she still would have felt uneasy.

As she pushed her way through the crowded room she wondered why he should give her the jitters. She interviewed tougher characters than him every day of the week, and they didn't faze her. Then she caught sight of Kramer, immaculate, alone, surrounded by glittering glass and white linen. And she thought, sure, I've run into tougher than Kramer. But they weren't this cold. And they weren't paying my salary.

She took her seat and he rose politely in greeting. Then he smiled and Kate knew she was in trouble. Kramer smiling was even more dangerous than Kramer in repose.

He waved to a waiter and Kate ordered a Gibson straight up. She didn't normally go in for hard liquor at lunchtime. But on this occasion she felt she needed it.

The preliminaries were pleasant enough. Kramer congratulated Kate on the interviews she had lined up for the Paris collections. Karl Lagerfeld of Chanel, Marc Bohan of Dior and the legendary Yves Saint Laurent were an impressive list. Kate sent up a prayer of thanks to Ruth who had pulled every string she could to arrange it.

She never failed to be surprised at her friendship with Ruth. It wasn't the unlikeliness of the alliance that made her wonder. It was the alliance itself, for Kate had always been too busy to have many friends. You needed time to get close to people and Kate spent her time getting ahead, not getting close.

Her attention was distracted by the waiter, who presented her with a large leather-bound menu. It was typical of the "21" Club that the menu should look more like the minutes of an annual board meeting than a list of things to eat. But then the "21" Club specialized in treating people as if they came from old money. And many of the customers did. Most of the prominent East

Coast families had memberships here. Chairmen of public companies took their wives to dine here. Ari and Jackie Onassis even had a regular table.

If you have arrived, the "21" Club was the place to be seen at. If you merely traveled in the hope of arriving, like Kate, then it intimidated you.

There were pages of things to eat. Solid, expensive things like lobster, prime rib and caviar. Kate was dazzled with the choice. Kramer, sensing her indecision, made a suggestion. "The best thing to eat here," he said, "is the corned beef hash. They make it better than anywhere else."

Kate was momentarily knocked off balance. Corned beef hash? Had the man gone out of his mind? Truck drivers ate hash. Sunday leftovers ended up as corned beef hash. It was hardly the stuff sophisticated lunches were made of.

Then she regained her perspective. How silly she was. Men like Ed Kramer lunched at the "21" Club every day of the week. Eating here was for him like eating in the deli was for her. She wouldn't dream of stuffing herself full of heavy, rich food in the middle of the day. So why should Kramer, just because it was offered.

She settled for the hash and made a mental note not to underestimate the hard-faced man sitting opposite her.

"By the way, I think I owe you one more congratulation," he said.

"What's that?" said Kate, intrigued. She knew she tried hard, but this was becoming ridiculous.

"That trip for Tracy Reeves. Ted tells me it was your idea to send her out to the provinces."

Oh Christ, she thought. I hope the kid hasn't already

screwed up. I only wanted to get her out of the way, not make a fool of her. "How is she doing?" she asked warily.

"Doing? The kid's doing fine. Some of the stuff she's sending back is first class. Lifts the whole tone of the fashion page."

Now Kate knew Kramer had lost his mind. Corned beef hash was one thing. But Tracy breaking records for street fashion? That was something else.

She started to feel uneasy. She'd seen the copy Tracy had sent and it was ordinary to say the least. Just as the idea to send her in the first place was ordinary. She remembered what a tough time she had had selling the plan to Ted.

"Tell me," said Kramer, his face full of concern. "How long did you envisage keeping Tracy out of town? I mean, we can't have half the staff of the fashion department running around America when there's work to be done back at the ranch."

"I would think that would be up to Ruth," said Kate. "It might have been my idea, but she's taken the whole thing on now."

"Good," he said, pursing his lips. "I'll have a word with Miss Bloom. We can't keep talented young staff away from the center of things for too long. I think you'd agree with that, wouldn't you? I know Ted would."

He had laid a trap for her and her inexperience led her right into it. "What's Ted got to do with Tracy coming back to the city?" she asked.

"Come on," he said softly. "I wasn't born yesterday. You talked Ted into sending Tracy on that wild goose chase. And he went along with it because he doesn't know how to say no to you."

She took a sip of her ice water. It didn't stop her mouth from feeling. "I'm sorry, I don't think I quite know what you're getting at."

Kramer leaned forward so that both his arms were resting on the table. Close-up and in a bad temper there was something menacing about him. This was a man who would commit murder in cold blood if he felt like it.

"Why don't you try dropping the polite Westchester lady act?" he said pleasantly, evenly. "Everyone on my staff knows what you and Ted are up to outside the office. And it isn't playing dominoes."

Bill Gerhaghty, she thought. So the bastard finally got to Kramer. Her terror turned to anger. Of all the lousy tricks. She'd get even with the Irishman if it was the last thing she did.

Aloud she said, "I take it your sources are impeccable." He allowed himself a chilly smile. A back-stabbing smile.

"Of course, my dear. You don't think I would have gone to the trouble of taking you out to lunch without being sure of my facts. I'm not here to discuss gossip and rumor. I'm here to talk about a very real scenario which is going on in my office, behind my back and which by the end of this meeting I will take some action on."

It was worse than she thought. She had been tried and judged. All that remained was to sentence her. So this was what lunch was all about.

"What do you want to do?" she asked.

"That very much depends on you and how you react

to the suggestion I'm about to put forward. You do value your career on the *News,* don't you Kate?'' he asked.

"You know I do."

"Fine. Then I take it you wouldn't be averse to a promotion."

"That depends what it is." Her years in newspapers had taught her never to accept anything unless she knew precisely what it was. Many journalists she knew had been offered blind alleys in the guise of advancements. She knew to look before she grabbed.

"It's nothing sinister," he said, guessing what was going through her mind. "In fact I think you'll be pleased with what I'm about to offer you. You've wanted it for long enough."

Her sense of reality was suspended. A moment ago she'd been prepared for the ax. Now he was offering to make her dreams come true. What was the catch? "You're not talking about the special investigations unit?" she asked. The man who ran it had just left to edit a paper in San Francisco.

Kramer ran a hand over his sleek hair. "You've hit the nail on the head," he said. "Well, will you take it?"

"Why, of course." She was momentarily dazzled, then she remembered the earlier conversation. "Does this offer have anything to do with Ted?"

"Ahh, so she's got brains as well as good looks." Despite the last few years of equal opportunity, Kramer remained at heart an old-fashioned chauvinist.

"My dear child," he said, "the new job has everything to do with Ted. Ted, if you like, is a condition of the appointment."

"How do you mean?"

"Okay, I'll spell it out for you. If you want the job, if you decide to take it, then the thing between you and Ted has to end."

She frowned. "I might have guessed it. You're not offering me a promotion at all. You're offering me a bribe. What would have happened if I hadn't been involved with Ted? Would somebody else have been offered the special investigations desk?"

Kramer signaled the waiter to take away their plates. Kate's food had hardly been touched. Then he lifted the half-finished bottle of wine and refilled their glasses. It was something the wine waiter would have fallen over himself to do. But Kramer took the task upon himself because it suited his game. By prolonging the silence between them he had Kate at a disadvantage.

Finally he said, "Aren't you taking all this rather personally? I could name at least a dozen of my executives who would have jumped at the opportunity I'm offering you. Strings or no strings.

"Grow up, Kate. If you want an affair with a married man, have one. I don't give a shit about it. The only time I worry is when it's in the office. Keep your private life out of the company's business and you can run a bordello for all I care."

"This is ludicrous," said Kate. "What Ted and I do in private has nothing to do with what we do in the office. It's a completely separate issue."

He looked deep into the mists of his expensive claret. "The reason I employ people of your age," he said half to himself, "is for your energy and enthusiasm. It's at times like this I have to keep reminding myself of it. If I didn't I'd have all of you out on your asses.

"For God's sake, girl, try to develop some sophistication, will you? When the star columnist climbs into bed with the guy who runs the desk, it becomes a hot news item. Now I know it's nobody's business, but with a hot news item people make it their business. You of all people should know about that.

"So what am I supposed to do? Close my ears when I hear a group of my colleagues talking about it in a bar? Ignore it when an executive drops it into conversation over lunch? Kate, believe me, I'd like to. But with Henkel's morality policy I can't. Like it or not our proprietor is a born-again Christian. He doesn't approve of married men cheating on their wives. Now he can't impose his will on the entire American population. But he can sure dictate what happens among the individuals he employs. And it's my job to see that you guys behave like the God-fearing Christians you aren't.

"So, let me say it again. You want the investigations desk? It's all yours, Kate. But that business with Ted. It's got to stop. And by that I mean, right now."

She felt anger spill over. "You're in danger of sounding like my father," she said. "Only my old man wouldn't dare say some of the things you have just now."

"Then he lacks courage."

"And you lack taste. What makes you think that just because you pay my salary, you can poke your nose into my private life? It's my talent you're buying. The way I write my copy. What I do with my body is my concern."

He took a cigar out of his top pocket. "If only that were true. If only I could share your lofty idealism. But I can't, and furthermore I'm not going to."

The waiter came forward, silently, expertly putting a light to the end of his cigar.

"My offer, dear Kate, stands . . . the way I said it. You want the investigation unit, it's yours. But you stop seeing Ted. In fact you stop talking to Ted; investigations comes under the city desk and he's got nothing to do with that."

"What if I don't want to stop talking to Ted?"

"I take it you mean outside the office. The sex business."

"Yes that's exactly what I mean." And she shuddered. When men like Kramer talked about love they reduced it to the basics. Sex instead of sentiment. She wondered how he talked about his wife.

"Then it's very simple." His voice was neutral and quiet. Disturbingly quiet. "You're fired."

The words took the wind out of her. "You mean everything. The job I have now, as well as the investigations unit?"

"That's what I mean."

She felt herself floundering. She'd been fired before. The *Post* had thrown her out of Phil Myers's office. But she had been a secretary then and the job had little value to her. Now it was different. She'd worked her guts out to get to where she was. Her job was her life. Or was it?

She thought about Ted and despite herself she faltered.

"How long do I have to think about it?" she asked.

He considered. "I'll give you two weeks. Most of that time you'll be in Paris so you won't get the chance to cause any more disruption in the office. But when you get back I'll want your answer. I don't have the time to wait any longer."

She thought quickly. There were five days to go before the Paris trip. In five days she could touch base with Phil Myers at the *Post* and a couple of news magazines. It was cutting it close but that couldn't be helped. Her profession went in for tight deadlines.

She looked at Kramer. "We'll talk after Paris then." Lifting her glass she said, "Thank you for lunch. It's been an experience."

She checked out the news magazines first. With both of them she drew a blank. Sure there were vacancies, but not at her level. As in all businesses, the bottom rungs of the ladder were interchangeable. A junior editor could trade places with any number of other junior editors all over town. But the moment you became a major columnist or headed up your own department the jobs were scarcer.

Two days before she left for France Kate called her old boss, Phil Myers.

"Hi, doll," he yelled into the receiver. "To what do I owe this unexpected honor?"

She felt embarrassed. In the old days she would have leveled with him. I'm in trouble, Phil, I'm looking for a job. The words would have come naturally. Now it was more difficult. She wasn't a little secretary anymore. She was a big-time columnist. And big-time columnists didn't talk about their troubles. So she asked about his family.

"How's Frances? And the kids? Are they well?"

"Do me a favor and cut the crap," he said. "If you wanted to know how Frances was you could have asked her yourself. You always used to. No, something tells me there are things you want to tell me you can't tell me on the phone. Am I right?''

"Always," she said, delighted. "When can we meet?''

"Can you wait longer than ten minutes?" he asked.

"Yes but not much."

"OK, tiger, I hear you. Look, it's four o'clock now. I have to check a page for the last edition. These days I can never be sure what creeps onto the proof when I'm not looking. You should see the dreck they try to pass off as reporters, Kate. You wouldn't believe it."

She laughed. "You haven't changed. What time are you thinking of giving the poor bastards a break and calling it a day?''

"I guess five-thirty's late enough. Tell you what, I'll meet you at Friday's around six and buy you a beer. Will that do?''

She hesitated. "Friday's is a little too public for what I have to talk about. What about the Oak Room bar in the Plaza? Can you get there in time?''

"No problem," he said. "I'll see you there just after the hour. If you get there before me, mine's a bourbon straight up.''

And he hung up. For the next five minutes he stood in front of his desk, thinking. So Kate Kennedy was ready to leave the *News*. It didn't surprise him. Highly strung writers like her didn't last long anywhere. The pressures were too great, the fashions too fickle. He wondered who her enemies were, and what they had done to her.

Then he turned his mind to more practical matters.

A loss for the *News* could be a gain for the *Post*. He made a mental note to call in and see Hartmann before he left the office. As editor-in-chief, Hartmann knew where the holes were or where they could be created. And he was sure Hartmann would put his mind to creating one. A star like Kate didn't come on the market every day of the week.

The Oak Room bar, paneled in oak and smelling of cigars, was rather like the reading room of a gentleman's club. And that's the way the gentlemen who drank there liked it. It was intimidating to women, and it kept them out. This meant that the well-heeled Wall Street types could drink and do their deals without the distraction of cocktail chatter.

When Kate arrived she was glad of that. Phil had not yet arrived and she needed the silence to formulate her thoughts. She also needed a drink. As soon as she could catch the waiter's eye she got herself a bourbon on the rocks. Then she stared into the future.

The *Post* was the only place she hadn't checked out. If there was anything coming up there Phil would know about it. If she drew a blank with him then it was time to start looking at Washington or the West Coast.

She had rejected the idea of calling it off with Ted. She knew she would find a job if she looked hard enough. Love was less replaceable. She clinked the ice cubes against the side of her glass, thinking of how she was going to tell Ted she was leaving the paper. She wondered if she could get away without telling him why.

When she looked up Myers was already sitting down on the other side of the small circular table. It was three years since she had last seen him and the years had made little difference. Like all truly ugly men, Myers had appeared to be the same age for the last twenty years. He was still small, still florid, with a huge nose that made him look like a Jewish Pinnochio.

Kate regarded him with pleasure. He was the first man, outside her immediate family, who had ever shown her kindness. To her he would always look good.

"So what's the big problem?" asked Myers, taking a sip of his bourbon. Then seeing her face, he smiled. "Well, there has to be a problem, hasn't there? I don't see you for three years and suddenly it's cocktails at the Oak Room. You can't be announcing your engagement."

"Hardly," she said. And then she smiled, too. "Hell, Phil, there's no point in shitting you. You'd find out soon enough anyhow."

Then having justified herself she settled back in her chair and told him everything. She remembered all those years ago, when she had discovered he knew about her grubby adventure with Stan Brooks. He hadn't judged her then. And when she told him about Ted there were no reproaches. To Phil Myers, Kate was an adult. An equal. All equals reserved the right to go to hell in their own fashion as far as he was concerned.

"Am I to understand you're looking for another job?" he asked.

"Yes," said Kate shortly.

"And where have you been looking?"

When she told him, he smiled. "Why didn't you come to me first? I could have told you there was nothing doing on *Time* and *Newsweek*. They both had their major reshuffles a year ago. There won't be any movement in that neck of the woods for some time—unless somebody ups and leaves. And at those salaries most guys would think twice before making a move."

"I guess you're right. So what about the *Post*? Am I wasting my time talking to you, too?"

He put down his drink. "No, you're not wasting your time," he said. "We do have something. Though whether you want it after what you've been telling me is a different matter."

"I'm not following you. Why shouldn't I want a job on the *Post*?"

"Because of where it's located. If I read you right, the reason you're leaving the *News* is because you don't want to be parted from lover boy. If you join us, I can guarantee an instant separation."

"So I'll commute," she said. "National airlines still run a shuttle service."

"I'm not talking national," he replied. "I'm talking Europe. Our big vacancy starts this fall in the London office. Chuck Holders who runs the European bureau is up for retirement then. We need someone to replace him."

Kate looked stunned. "But that's a huge job," she said. "You mean you were really going to offer it to me? I thought you'd have wanted someone more experienced."

"These days experienced means old, jaded, yellow around the edges. What we are looking for is someone young and hot who could beat the shit out of the opposition. The minute I got the hunch you were looking around, I called in to see Hughes Hartmann and told him about it. That's when he came up with the London office.

The way he saw it, you've been giving us a run for our money for the past five years. He figured if you could frighten the tough men on our desks then you could frighten anybody. He wanted you on our side. I don't think he's ever forgiven himself for letting you go to the *News* in the first place. In the light of the past few years, I certainly haven't forgiven him."

"Phil," she said, "I think you'd better order me another drink."

Then she buried her face in her hands. "Why did this have to happen now? Any other time I'd have jumped at a chance like this. My own bureau. All of Europe for my beat. I'd have killed for this."

He took hold of her shoulders and shook her gently. "Cut out the dramatics," he said. "All my life I have to look at theater people going through this routine. And I have to hold my tongue and say, 'There there.' Because I get paid to say it. Well, you're a friend and I'm not being paid to watch you kvetching. So can it."

She sat up straight and took a long pull on her drink. Myers signaled the waiter and called for another. Then he concentrated on Kate.

"Listen," he said. "I'm not asking you for a split-second decision. Go home, think about it. Discuss it with your boyfriend even. Then when you've considered it like a rational human being, come back to see me.

"We're not going to give the job to anybody else until we've had your answer. Old Chuck can hang on until the fall if he has to. So do me a favor and stop being a silly girl, will you?"

Kate nodded, and did her best to look suitably grateful. She knew there was no way she could leave Ted to take a job in London. But she didn't want to hear herself say it. She didn't want to hear herself turn down the biggest opportunity she was ever likely to get as long as she lived.

Love extracted a high price. And she was paying every cent of it.

Bernard Glen was in a snit. The old political editor's column had been getting less and less space as the weeks went on, and he suspected a plot. Glen with his pastel-colored shirts and foppish manner might have looked a fool but it was all part of the act. Beneath the simper was the tough hide of a born survivor.

He knew that Ted Gebler and Bill Gerhaghty were trying to squeeze him. He'd known for some months now. And he wasn't having it. First he tackled Gerhaghty. Striding into the glass cubicle which was the nerve center of the city desk, he sat himself down on the edge of Gerhaghty's desk.

"Shove off," said Gerhaghty irritably. "Can't you see I'm busy?"

And indeed he looked it. Two telex machines on either side of him were clacking out the national and international news as it came in. A constant stream of reporters and desk men came running in and out of the office with news bulletins of their own. And every telephone call had a question attached to it.

It was four o'clock in the afternoon. The most frenzied time for any newspaper and Bernard Glen knew it. "No, I will not shove off," he said waspishly. "I'm sitting here until you inform me just what's going on with my column."

"Oh for Christ's sake, Bernard, can't we talk about it another time? We're coming up to first edition time. I can't even think about your column right now."

"Well, you'd better concentrate your mind," said Bernard. "Otherwise I'll just sit here and go on moaning until you answer my question."

Gerhaghty knew when he was beaten. He couldn't cope with the impending first edition and a siege from Bernard Glen. So he got right to the point. "The column gets the space it deserves. If you come up with something big, I'll give you all the space you want. I'll give you the page if the story's hot. But there haven't been many hot stories lately, have there, Bernard? All I seem to be getting is White House gossip—hardly the stuff banner headlines are made of. Now why don't you go away and come back with something really good and I promise you I'll do it justice."

Glen pouted. It was an unattractive sight. "Since when did you have the say-so on how my column is presented? My contract clearly states that I stay in half a page unless the editor decides to change it. We all know what an ambitious boy you are, darling, but you're not the editor. Not yet at any rate."

"Look, why don't you fuck off and take it up with Kramer, if that's how you feel?" yelled Gerhaghty, exasperated. Then he paused for breath and thought better of it. The last thing he wanted was trouble with the chief. Particularly since he knew Kramer had a soft spot for the old faggot. So he swallowed his pride and, putting on his most persuasive face, he passed the buck.

"Look, I'm sorry for yelling. But four in the afternoon isn't my best time, you know that. Why don't you go and sort it out with Ted? Strictly speaking, your column comes under features. If you and Ted can come to an agreement, I'll go along with anything you decide to do."

I bet you will, thought Bernard. You and Ted are in this right up to your necks. If I try talking to Ted about it my column will remain a floating item. And if I'm not careful it'll float right out of the paper.

Then he had an idea. Under pressure Bill had revealed that he was making decisions on the political column. They were decisions that were not his to make. If he could put a little pressure on Ted he might learn more about the plot they were hatching. And once he had the whole picture, he could lay it at Kramer's feet. If he had a valid case he knew he could count on the editor's support. Bernard had known Kramer since the old days. He was probably the only member of the staff who knew about the skeletons in his closet. Both of them had a vested interest in not letting them rattle.

When Bernard sauntered into Ted's office it was five o'clock and the features man was hoping to get out early to meet Kate. He was out of luck. Bernard Glen was on the warpath. Bill had warned him he might pay him a visit. And here he was, flashing his capped teeth in a smile that made him look like a piranha.

Ted settled down behind his desk. This was going to take at least half an hour. He wondered if Kate had started making the Bloody Marys.

"I hope I'm not keeping you from anything," said Bernard.

Ted said nothing. And taking that as a sign of assent, Glen went to the fridge by the door and poured himself a generous measure of vodka. Before he started on the ice cubes he turned to Ted. "What will you have?" he asked.

It was pointless to argue. "Make mine a bourbon on the rocks. But I warn you, I have to be out of here at five-thirty sharp, so keep your hand steady when you pour it."

Bernard arched an eyebrow. "Rushing home to Sandy, are we? It's a bit early for that, isn't it?"

"No, I'm not going straight home. I have to meet a friend first."

"The talented Kate, I presume. It surprises me how you two have managed to get away with it for so long."

Ted sighed and formed his lips into a thin, bloodless line. "What exactly are you saying to me, Bernard?"

"I'm saying, darling, that if you and that nice Catholic girl are going to continue to carry on, then I think you should be more discreet about it."

Ted's expression told Bernard he had scored a direct hit. "Look, I can live without your bar room gossip. I can also live without you poking your nose into my private life. And leave Kate out of this, will you? She's a good kid, and you have no business dirtying her name."

"I thought you were the one who was doing that."

"Listen, what is this all about? I thought you'd come in to talk about your column. If you want to dish the dirt you can go elsewhere."

"Okay, okay, don't get excited. As a matter of fact I did come to discuss my column. My ever-shrinking column."

Ted relaxed. "Yes, your column," he said. "I hear you're worried about the way it changes size. Well, that's the way it works on newspapers. We only give things the space they deserve."

"And who decides how much space I deserve?"

"That's a very difficult question." Ted was playing for time and Bernard knew it. He decided to pin him down.

"You've got all the time in the world to answer it. Just who is it who decides on the size of my column? You or Bill Gerhaghty?"

"Neither of us. I mean both of us. Sorry, Bernard, what I meant to say was, whichever of us was on the desk when you filed your copy."

Bernard passed a hand over his thinning, dyed-blond hair. He had Ted in a corner and he knew it. "So it's either you or Bill who carves my column up. I thought so. That's a very interesting piece of information, darling. Very interesting. It gives me a certain amount of food for thought."

"Great," said Ted. "Then you just go on home and think about it."

"I'll do that, dear boy. Oh, and while we're exchanging chitchat I've got a little news item that might interest you. Did you hear that your beautiful lady friend was casting around for another job?''

He paused. "No, of course you didn't. Well for your information, a little bird at *Newsweek* told me that Kate had been sniffing around in that direction. He's a very canny little bird, my friend. Always gets his facts right.''

He turned and gave Ted a jaunty wave before sashaying through the door. "Bye for now, dear boy. Give Kate a big kiss from me when you see her.''

Why didn't she tell me? thought Ted. I had no idea she was unhappy at the *News*. What could have gotten into her?

His taxi was at a standstill in the early evening traffic heading downtown. The traffic jam was composed almost entirely of yellow cabs, their noses bumper to bumper like a vast army of killer bees.

Ever since he started this affair with Kate, Ted calculated, he was spending an ever-increasing portion of his day sitting in traffic. Either to or from a rendezvous. He didn't begrudge the waste of time. He loved her too much to begrudge her anything. But there were times when he wished they could quit sneaking around like conspirators. He cast his mind forward to the evening ahead of him. It was to be their last night together before Kate went off to the Paris collections, and because they wouldn't be seeing each other for a while, Ted planned on staying late.

He had told Sandy not to expect him for dinner that night. He didn't bother to tell her why. These days it seemed pointless to make excuses for the time he spent away from her. She knew about Kate and for the time being she seemed to accept the situation.

Ted accepted the fact that they were all living on borrowed time. He also knew that the moment would come when he had to make up his mind between his marriage and his mistress. But as neither woman was pressing him for a decision, he was content to let things go on as they were. It wasn't ideal, but then what was?

He stopped by the liquor store before going up to Kate's apartment. And when he arrived on her doorstep he was clutching two bottles of champagne.

"If you insist on deserting me for two weeks, then at least you deserve a good send off," he said, kissing her.

Then he deposited the bottles in the refridgerator and poured himself a Bloody Mary from a pitcher which looked badly in need of fresh ice cubes. Kate made no excuse for it. Instead she said, "You're late. I expected you nearly an hour ago. I was beginning to wonder if you were coming at all."

She was slicing cucumber by the sink, hacking at it savagely as if it was responsible for her frustration. Ted came up behind her, circling her with his arms. "You're beginning to sound like a wife," he said, kissing the nape of her neck. "Next thing I know, you'll be asking what kept me."

"Well, what did keep you? You're not usually this late without calling. It must have been pretty important."

"Not really. Just Bernard Glen complaining about his column. Bill got an earful of it earlier on in the day, so I thought it was only fair to shoulder my share of the burden."

Kate disentangled herself and started washing the lettuce. "I don't know what you and Bill are up to with Bernard. And I don't think I want to know. Why can't you just leave him alone? He's not doing you any harm."

"That's not the point. Anyway I wouldn't call Mr. Glen exactly harmless. He spreads more malicious gossip than anyone alive in newspapers today. He also hears his fair share. Which reminds me, is it true you're looking around for another job? Glen told me this evening that you were. I admit I find it hard to believe."

Kate was thrown. Damn, she thought, I was going to tell him in my own time. After we'd finished the champagne. Maybe after we'd been to bed. But before dinner, when it wasn't even dark yet, was hardly the moment.

But there was no alternative. So she dried her hands, moved over to the sofa where the drinks were waiting, and proceeded to fill him in on the events of the past few days.

Ted was visibly shaken. "I don't believe that bastard Kramer," he said. "Why didn't he say anything about it to me? After all, I am involved. You're not having an affair all on your own. So why should you be the one who gets the short end of the stick?"

She shrugged. "Maybe it's easier to replace me. Also, let's face it, I'm less responsibility. I'm not married, I don't have a wife and kids and a mortgage. I guess Kramer thought there would be less suffering all around if he got rid of me."

"What's all this about getting rid of you?" Ted asked. "The way you told it, Kramer wasn't firing you, he was warning you."

"Maybe I didn't make myself clear. Kramer told me

that if I didn't stop sleeping with you then I was out. And as I have no intention of foregoing the pleasures of your flesh, then it's goodbye and good luck. All I need now is another job."

"Which you don't appear to have found."

She poured herself another drink. Maybe she should tell Ted about the *Post*'s offer. Then she thought, what's the point? I'm going to turn it down anyway. "Don't worry," she said, "I'll find something."

He felt like a heel. He knew as well as she did that there was nothing for her in New York. When she came back from Paris she'd have to start trekking around the provinces looking for employment. And that would do nothing for the big career she'd worked so hard to carve out.

"Do you know something?" he said, putting an arm around her waist and drawing her to him. "I was thinking about us in the taxi coming over here."

She laid her head on his shoulder. When she was this close she could smell his skin and she marveled at it. Love heightensed her senses and this personal smell of Ted's, a mixture of aftershave and sex, was as precious to her as any of the promises they had made. "What were you thinking in the taxi coming over?" she murmured.

"I was thinking the time had come to call it a day with Sandy. How do you feel about getting married?"

She sat bolt upright. She had expected an invitation to bed, not an invitation for life.

"What made you decide that so suddenly?" she asked.

"It wasn't exactly sudden, you know that as well as I do. It's been a lovely game, playing at brief encounters.

You don't care. I don't care. Let's live for the moment and all that crap. But it's a game, Kate, and we're both too old to play games." He smiled. "At least I am. Contrary to popular gossip, I'm not the sort of man who goes in for affairs. Before you came along I was more or less faithful to Sandy. I never loved her the way I love you, but I was true to her because I preferred it that way.

"One woman at a time is quite enough for me to handle. I've got a job to worry about. I like to play squash at lunch. All this running from bed to bed is killing me."

He ducked as she aimed a punch at him. "Seriously, Kate, I mean it when I say I want to settle down with you. It won't be easy, I warn you. I'll probably have to live here for a while before I sort out my finances. And knowing Sandy, she'll take me for every cent she can. But we'll manage. If you want me, that is."

She was surprised to find she was crying. Was it relief? "Of course I want you. You're all I want. Kramer can take his job and shove it for all I care."

"Not so fast," he laughed. "You're a woman with responsibilities now. If I'm going to go through with this upheaval, we're going to need both our paychecks to keep us in food and booze. Not to mention the rent."

"But Kramer clearly said, if I go on sleeping with you it's all over. There's no job. I'm out on my ass."

"That was because I was a respectably married man, you idiot. When I'm a respectably separated, soon-to-be divorced man the whole picture changes. Suddenly you're on the right side of the fence, as far as Kramer's concerned. We'll even give him an invitation to the wedding—that should satisfy his puritan streak."

She sighed. "You make it all sound so easy."

"Easy," he told her, "is something it won't be. Sandy may look like a frail Norse maiden, but underneath that innocent blonde exterior lives a calculating machine. She'll want her pound of flesh plus my head on a plate if I know her. And her father's lawyers will make damn sure she gets it. No, my darling, it's not going to be easy. But it's going to be worth it. I love you very much, or haven't I told you that before?"

She grinned. "You told me. Now before we go to pieces we need to sort things out. You might not have noticed, but I'm going away to France for two weeks, as of tomorrow morning. Do I give you the keys to my apartment now, or do I wait until I get home?"

"Kate, darling, have some faith in me. I told you I'm leaving home. And that means tomorrow, not in two weeks time. I don't need you here to show me where you keep the sheets and towels."

And she finally relaxed. Ted really did mean what he was saying. It wasn't some married man's promise that she'd seen a hundred times in the movies.—"Wait for me darling, I'll leave my wife someday." Ted didn't deal in "someday." Although that would have been good enough for her. Ted dealt in the present.

She went over to her bag where she kept her front door keys. Then she opened her purse, took them out and handed them to him. "I won't be needing these for a couple of weeks. You, on the other hand, could find them very useful. Especially since you intend to make your home in New York City."

He put the keys in his pocket and she felt her heart shudder. For she was giving him a part of herself, her most important part. She was giving him her trust.

* * *

Kate arrived late at the check-in desk at Kennedy airport. And when she finally made it through immigration she saw that her flight was being called.

Damn, she thought, I'll miss the duty free. She had been promising herself a bottle of her favorite Van Cleef and Arpels perfume but now it looked as if she was going to have to skip it.

Never mind, I'll buy perfume in Paris, she decided. French perfume. But the prospect didn't cheer her. Paris, which had seemed so exciting, so full of adventure, had turned into a chore. A two-week tour of duty before she could return to New York and Ted.

Before she could replay the events of the previous night she was distracted by the sight of Ruth. The fashion editor was treating herself to a Pepsi and her entourage to champagne in the bar of the departure lounge.

"You never change," said Kate, as she made her way over to the group. "Champagne at eleven o'clock in the morning. Where do you think you are? The Plaza?"

"Pay no attention," said Ruth to a plump, scruffy-looking man. "My colleague here isn't used to international travel. Don't you know," she said to Kate, "that every journalist cracks a bottle of champagne before a foreign trip? It's a long-standing custom of the business. And if you want to belong to my party, you'll drop the snotty act and join us."

She poured the rest of the bottle into one of the plastic cups the airport provided. Warm champagne and plastic, thought Kate, ughh! But she took a sip to humor her friend, and introduced herself to her fellow travelers.

Sitting next to Ruth was a bloated-looking man with a boyish face. The blue jeans and the designer stubble told the world that he was young. His expression—jaded, world-weary—told a different story.

Kate figured he must be in his late thirties, and just as she was wondering who the hell he was, he took a steel comb out of the back pocket of his jeans and carefully ran it through his blow-dried hair. Of course, she thought, how silly of me. It's Howie Danvers. Who else but a hairdresser would make such a performance of a simple act like that?

Next to Danvers, almost like his extension, was the make-up girl, Jerry Gould. The two usually worked in tandem on these long trips and Kate could understand why. Jerry was a plain, rather matter-of-fact woman, who supported her husband and three children on the money she made from painting other women's faces. She wasn't a bimbo. She was there to work. And that suited both her and Howie down to the ground.

Looking across at the girl she'd be working on, Kate knew Jerry wouldn't be all that pressed on this trip. For the model they were taking along was the famous Martini, the latest face to take New York by storm. Martini was one of those overnight miracles. One day she was a waitress from Denver. The next day she was a household name.

Nobody really knew how she had made the transition, and Martini refused to shed any light on her sudden transformation. Which gave rise to rumors. One school of thought had it that she was the girlfriend of a prominent Mafia boss. Another that she was the love child of a senator. Yet another that she was reaping the rewards of her somewhat lax morals. For Martini got her name from the aperitif that boasted "Anytime, anyplace, anywhere." The joke had been making the rounds of the photographers' studios and trendy bars for the past few months.

But jokes and rumors were not what got Martini her success as the reigning fashion queen of New York. It was far more prosaic than that. Martini got where she was by sheer hard work. First as a runway model for a Seventh Avenue rag-trade merchant. Then as a photographer's model for small time out-of-town publications.

Eileen Ford had spotted her in a Los Angeles teen magazine. And the moment she saw her face she knew the girl was worth a million. Ford summoned her, the way royalty summons a lowly subject. And that's the way Martini was made to feel while Ford put her through her paces. Only when she was quite satisfied that she knew all the tricks of the trade did Ford deign to launch the model girl.

Her success took them both by surprise. For to look at, Martini was no prettier than any other professional girl who earns her living wearing clothes for the camera. She had the scrubbed-clean look that was currently in vogue. And with her silky blonde hair and innocent face she could have convinced anyone that she was a high school virgin.

That was until you looked into her eyes. For Martini's eyes suggested the jaded experience of a Berlin brothel keeper. It was this contrast of innocence and experience that gave Martini her special magic. That and her reputation, of course.

The moment the rumors about her started, Eileen

Ford summoned her once again. If the truth be known, Martini thought she was about to be given the ax. She knew she loved sex. She also knew there was no way she was going to stop loving it. It was too much fun. No, she would simply have to find another agent.

So she was astounded when Eileen Ford informed her that there was no need for that. She was prepared to live with Martini's predilections. All she wanted from her was silence. All good mysteries start with silence. And if Martini refused to discuss her past and her eyebrow-raising present then people would have to use their imaginations.

So the fantasy that was Martini was born. The high-school virgin with the reputation of a Times Square whore. It made them both a bundle.

Kate's eyes did a quick circle of the bar and then fixed themselves on Ruth. "Where's the photographer?" she asked.

"Didn't I tell you?" said Ruth. "We're meeting him in Paris. Ted and I decided to take a chance on the new, wild English guy, Mike Stone. You know, the one who did *Jet-Set Girls*."

Kate was impressed. "But that's fantastic. The book's been on the *New York Times* bestseller list for weeks now. How did you manage to get him?"

"It wasn't me at all. It was Ted. Apparently Stone's agent is an old drinking buddy of his. Ted heard Mike Stone was covering the collections for *Paris Match* and he asked his friend if there was any chance Mike could double up for us. This agent friend of Ted's said he'd try to talk him into it and two days later he called to tell us we were on.

"It's going to cost the *News* a fortune, but they seem happy enough to pay it. Mike's photo coverage will give us the edge over everyone else in town—including *Vogue*."

The final call for the Paris flight came and everyone started gathering up carry-on luggage. As they went through the departure gate, Kate turned to Ruth. "Have you met this Mike Stone?" she asked. "I'd love to know what he's like."

"No," replied Ruth, handing over her boarding pass to the flight attendant. "I've never set eyes on the guy, but if he's anything like some of the stories I've heard about him, he's either a barrel of laughs or the biggest asshole in the world."

When Mike Stone was called in to photograph the Countess of Cornwall for *Tatler* magazine three top photographers before him had failed miserably. Not even one of the royal photographers could make her look anything other than the old trout that she was. Clever lighting did nothing to relieve the sagging heaviness of her jowls. The lines under her eyes needed a facelift rather than a re-toucher to ease their cragginess.

The fashion editor of the glossy magazine was close to tears when she called Stone. "Mike," she wailed, "our editor's crazy about the Cornwall interview. He's even talking about putting her ladyship on the cover. And I haven't got one picture of her I can show him. *Do something!*"

Stone refused to commit himself. A tall, bony man with a wild mop of black hair and the air of an eccentric academic, he didn't like to embark on any project unless there was a fair chance of succeeding. And when he heard about Bailey and company's efforts coming to nothing he was wary. Then he had a brainstorm. He put in a call to the *Tatler*.

"Lynne, love, is that you? Good, it's Mike Stone here. Listen, I've decided to take on the Cornwall job. I think I've found a way of guaranteeing results.

"Do I have a make-up man in mind? No, I don't think so. Just get your stylist to use her regular guy and leave the rest to me. I promise I won't disappoint you. Or her ladyship."

On the day of the shoot Stone arrived at the magazine's studio accompanied by a huge cardboard box. While his two assistants set up the lights, Stone proceeded to unpack the contents of the box. This turned out to be a giant wind machine, the kind film studios use to create tornadoes. He positioned it in front of Lady Cornwall and plugged it in.

"What on earth is that contraption?" boomed her ladyship. "And why are you putting it so close to me?"

Stone spelled it out. "It's a wind machine, Countess," he said. "When I turn it on it's going to blow directly into your face."

He placed his hands on either side of her cheeks and gently pulled the skin upward and backward. She looked twenty years younger. "What the machine will do," he explained, "is exactly the same as my hands. In the trade we call it lifting the contours." He was improvising now. "I think you'll be satisfied with the result."

There was a sudden silence in the studio. All eyes turned to Lady Cornwall. A slow smile spread over her weathered features.

"My boy," she said, looking at Stone, "I know I'm

an old trout, my husband knows I'm an old trout, and it's never bothered either of us before. Now suddenly this periodical wants to make me look like Marlene Dietrich. I'm not sure it's such a good idea."

Mike was stumped. For the first time in his life he had come face to face with a woman who had no trace of vanity. How could he appeal to her? Then he had his second brainstorm of the week.

"I think you should consider the Queen," he said seriously.

"Consider the Queen?" snapped the countess. "I don't understand."

"Look," he said patiently, "you and the Queen are both heads of two of the finest families in England. If you'll excuse me saying this, you are virtually an ambassador for the aristocracy. How can you allow yourself to represent them without looking your best? It would be like the Queen opening parliament without her crown."

Her ladyship pursed her lips and considered. "You're right," she said finally. "It would be rather letting down the side." She waved an impatient hand at Stone. "Very well, young man, do your worst. Turn the bloody thing on. But I'm warning you, I'm not going to put up with it for long."

Countess Cornwall faced the raging tornado Stone's machine created for precisely three minutes. During that time he had managed to get through half a roll of film. Ten of his shots were good. Three of them were remarkable. The one the *Tatler* used on its cover won him the Photographer of the Year award.

A month later Lady Cornwall booked into the London Clinic for a facelift.

The fashion industry's second favorite Mike Stone story concerned a calendar shoot he went on in Bali. More than anything else, Stone loved location work. It brought out the boy scout in him. And when he was asked to do a girlie calendar on the exotic Indonesian island he accepted the job joyfully.

The models and the crew he took were all, like him, seasoned travelers. But none of them was prepared to go to the lengths Stone did to blend in with the local scene. He rented three thatch-roofed villas high up in the hills. They were local houses and none of them had water purification facilities or even electricity. At night the Balinese servants lit kerosene lamps. They also provided bottled water for the guests. The natives knew their local water upset foreigners and they warned Stone about its effects.

"Bloody nonsense," he roared. "Treating us like a bunch of tourists. We're all pros here," he declared, indicating the crew and the models. "We drink the local water, we also drink the local booze. And you can stop fussing around with that insect spray. The flies won't bother any of use. We're too well-seasoned for that."

The next day all the model girls and most of the crew were confined to bed with diarrhea. Those who weren't suffering from the runs were covered in insect bites. Stone carried on as if nothing had happened.

"Bloody fools," he muttered, as he strode up and down the canyons and gorges that made up Bali, squinting through his light meter. "If the staff hadn't told them they'd get the runs they'd all be perfectly okay."

Stone's tummy didn't rumble once. No insect dared to come within inches of him. The rest of the troupe got progressively worse. Three days later they all wound up in the local hospital. Three days after that, by common consent, they all checked out of the hospital and into the airport. Everyone had had enough.

Stone ended up shooting the calendar in Arizona. With a different set of models. All the original girls refused to work with him again.

Mike Stone paid little attention to any of the things they said about him. A cockney boy from Southend-on-Sea, he cared about one thing only. The pictures. They were how he measured his worth. If people said he was a bastard and the pictures were great, it was fine by him. They could call him anything they wanted.

It was with precisely this attitude that he arrived at Le Royale to meet Ruth.

Le Royale, like all international hotels in capital cities, had about it an aura of expense accounts. The hotel management knew the people staying there were spending somebody else's money and adjusted their prices and services accordingly.

Everything on offer was *de luxe.* All rooms had their own mini-bar. The suites had their own drawing rooms done not in Hilton plastic and foam rubber, but in imitation Louis Quinze. The atmosphere was sufficiently opulent to give the paying customers the impression they were getting value for money. The fact that they had been ripped off only made itself clear when the bill was presented at the end of their stay. And by then it was too late.

Ruth had arranged to meet Mike Stone in the downstairs bar of the hotel. At six o'clock in the evening it was starting to fill up with tourists having a pre-dinner drink, businessmen on their way home from the office, and the usual array of rue de Rivoli hookers.

Ruth had chosen a table by the window, not because of its view, but because it backed on to a banquette seat. The small gilt chairs in French hotel bars did not suit a woman of Ruth's size. Experience had taught her never to venture near them.

It was Ruth's size that made a first and lasting impression on Mike. He thought she was the most wonderful creature he had set eyes on in some years. Stone did not like thin girls. He put everything he had into photographing them, it was true. But that was his job. He was paid to make them appear appetizing to a public which consisted mainly of gay fashion designers and middle-aged women who were either private customers or buyers for large stores.

For them the tall, skeletal creatures who were the world's top models were the ultimate clothes hangers. And professionally Stone agreed with them. That didn't mean he had to have them in his bed. In that private area of his life, the women who turned him on were products of a Rubens fantasy.

So instead of sitting on the tiny gilt chair on the opposite side of Ruth's table, he sat beside her on the banquette. "Welcome to Paris," he said, waving vigorously to the waiter on the other side of the bar. "It looks like I'm the first person to say that to you tonight. The lazy bastard who calls himself a bartender hasn't even bothered to get you a drink."

Before Ruth could protest that she didn't want one, the lanky, leather-jacketed Englishman had summoned a bottle of champagne seemingly out of thin air. Seconds later a white-jacketed waiter had popped the cork. After that it seemed pointless to argue.

Instead she concentrated her attention on this business of the day, which was Martini. Or rather the absence of Martini. For the waif-like American model had disappeared the moment they had arrived at De Gaulle airport. Once through customs she had sighted a group of girls she had worked with at the Milan collections and that was the last anyone had seen of her.

"Didn't she even check into the hotel?" asked Mike disbelievingly.

"No," said Ruth, "I called all my contacts in the press offices and not one girl in one design house has seen her. I'm at my wits' end. The collections haven't even started and I'm in trouble. In two days' time I'll be slitting my wrists."

"Calm yourself," said Mike, splashing champagne into her glass. "At this time of the year the Parisians wouldn't notice if you cut your throat."

"So what do you suggest I do?" yelled Ruth.

Mike yelled right back at her. "Find her, you silly woman," he roared. Three American businessmen standing at the bar turned around in surprise.

Ruth took a gulp of her champagne and turned bright red. "Listen, smartass, I don't need you to tell me how to do my job. What do you think I've been doing anyway? Sitting on my fanny? Like hell I have. I've been running around this town since noon looking for the flaky little bitch. And everywhere I go, I come up with a giant zero. If she doesn't turn up soon I'll have to start calling around the agencies."

Mike shrugged. "Better you than me, bright eyes.

You've got as much chance of finding an out-of-work model in Paris right now as you'd have finding an out-of-work hooker the day the Allies walked into town."

"Very clever," said Ruth. "I knew I could rely on you to solve all my problems. Well, try this one on for size. If I don't find Martini by noon tomorrow, I'm folding my tent and going home. I'll use agency pictures for the Paris collections. I've done it before and I'll do it again."

"Hey, keep your shirt on, lady. If this Martini is so important to you, I'll go find the silly girl myself."

Ruth allowed herself a smile. "So you do want the job."

"No, love, it's not the job I want. I could get ten that would pay me more than this by tomorrow morning. What I want is for you to be happy."

"You're putting me on."

"Why should I put you on? You're a lovely woman, Ruth. It's not right that you should be upset."

Ruth didn't know whether to be flattered or insulted, so she took a closer look at the photographer before making up her mind. What she saw was a tall, bony man of around forty with a day's growth of stubble on his chin and an untidy mop of black hair. But it was his eyes that redeemed him. Gray, slightly narrowed, they looked out on the world with cynical amusement. They took nothing seriously, nothing for granted. And this she understood. For Mike Stone's eyes accurately reflected Ruth's own view of the world. She decided to be flattered.

"Is that last remark some kind of British thing?"

"Sorry, I'm not with you."

"The fancy compliments," she said, a bit flustered.

He grinned. "Only to the women I fancy."

Then before she could react, Mike was on his feet, hefting the heavy camera bag over his shoulder.

"I think it's time I went off in search of Martini. I've got a fair idea of where she might be. And if she is where I think she is, you can expect me back within the hour."

Ruth was intrigued. "You mean she's somewhere nearby?"

"Don't ask questions. Just be a good girl and go up to your room and wait for me to call."

Under normal circumstances Ruth would have told him to get lost. Despite the promise in his eyes, she wasn't used to being patronized and pushed around like some helpless bimbo. But these were not normal circumstances. She was far from home in a country where they didn't speak her language. The girl she had hired to model the couture clothes which were lined up and waiting was missing. And her expenses were racking up.

Collecting the last shreds of her dignity, Ruth stood up and followed Mike out of the bar. With any luck, Kate and the rest of the team had slept off their jet lag and had thought up some kind of solution to the Martini problem. Even if they didn't have a solution it wouldn't hurt to kick the problem around. And if everything else failed, there was always room service.

Impatiently she pressed the call button for the elevator. She could absolutely kill for a chicken sandwich with French fries on the side.

Nobody came up with a single helpful idea. And what was worse, they all had their minds on something else.

Kate was thinking about the time difference between Paris and New York and wondering when it would be safe to call Ted. Howie Danvers was trying to remember the location of a bistro he had been told about in Saint Germain. And Jerry Gould was wondering if she could escape with Howie to the Left Bank and leave the others to sort out their problem. This was her first time in Paris and she was determined to make the most of it.

They were all sitting in the large drawing room of the suite that Ruth and Kate shared between them. In typical French style the hotel had skimped on the bedrooms, which were Hilton ordinary. Instead they had lavished everything on the large reception room. Running down the length of one wall was what looked like a Regency bookcase. Whether the expensively bound editions in it were real or not nobody had the chance to find out, for they were encased in glass.

Opposite the bookcase were floor-to-ceiling windows overlooking the rooftops of Paris. Silver brocade curtains draped and looped their way around them, and the same brocade covered the squashy sofas and easy chairs. The only chairs in the room that weren't easy at all were the fake Louis Quinze antiques with their elegant, uncomfortable-looking gilt backs. But they weren't intended for sitting on.

The whole room with its well-trodden Oriental carpet and crystal chandeliers had an air of faded grandeur. Despite the hopelessness of her situation Ruth started to feel excited. Rooms full of expensive clutter, the musty smell of old ground coffee, showers that never seemed to work. All these things meant Paris and she loved it.

She had been coming here for nearly ten years and every time she felt the same.

She went over to the fridge, which was artfully disguised as a bookcase, and fished out two bottles of champagne. "The way I see it," she said, "things can't get any worse. So we might as well enjoy ourselves before the shit hits the fan."

"Aren't you being a bit rash?" said Kate. "Why don't you let me call Ted and tell him what's happened? He might come up with some other way of handling the collections."

Ruth looked irritated. "Look, I'm the one who decides how the collections are handled. And I do that without any helpful suggestions from the features department. I'm not saying that Ted isn't cute and I know you love him. But can you limit your phone calls to coochy coo and leave me to do the business around here? That's what I'm paid for, you know."

"Listen, I'm the last one who wants a fight," said Kate, "especially tonight after the trip we just had. Go ahead and open the champagne, Ruth. And while we're at it we might drink to Mike Stone. Who knows, he could even find our precious Martini."

"But where?" said Howie Danvers. "That's what intrigues me. I mean, we all know the girl has a taste for the low life."

"She's probably found herself a nice brothel where they made her feel at home," chimed in Jerry. "I can see the headlines now, 'American *poule de luxe* takes Paris by storm.' "

"For God's sake, cut it out, you two," said Ruth. "Listen, I know you're both dying to go and explore the

Left Bank. So why don't you get up and do that, and we'll see you in the morning? And by the morning, I mean seven-thirty, sharp, so don't stay out all night. You never know when Martini might show. And if she does it's business as usual. We're due at Dior at ten."

Jerry and Howie looked visibly relieved. On every trip, journalistic teams tended to split off into splinter groups. The hairdresser and the make-up girl formed the first group. From that moment on they would gossip together, drink together, find other friends like them and do the town together.

Ruth wondered how the rest of them would divide up. She couldn't see herself exchanging confidences with Martini, though she and Kate could do things together. That left Mike Stone. Would he want to join her and Kate? Or would he go with Martini?

She put him out of her mind. As far as Ruth was concerned she was taking a long vacation from the opposite sex. Anyway, the Englishman was showing distinct signs of being a chauvinist. Patronizing her. Giving out orders. It wasn't her style at all.

Half an hour later, when Kate was considering opening the second bottle of champagne, the phone rang. It was Mike Stone. He was in the lobby with Martini and was bringing her up to the suite.

"That settles it," said Kate, slamming the phone down. "I will open another bottle."

"What's happening?" inquired Ruth from the sofa.

"Everything," said Kate, undoing the wire cradle surrounding the champagne cork. "That was Mike Stone bearing gifts."

"You don't mean a gift in the shape of a blonde

model who answers to the name of Martini, by any chance?"

"You got it in one. I do have your permission to open the champagne, don't I?"

"As far as I'm concerned, you can empty the entire fridge. All the fridges. That shyster Stone has just saved our asses."

The buzzer went and Ruth opened the door to Mike Stone who was trailing behind him a rather bedraggled-looking Martini.

"Where on earth have you been?" said Ruth, clutching on to the girl as if at any moment she might slip through her fingers again and go rushing off into the night. "We've been going crazy trying to find you."

"For Christ's sake," said the girl, "since when was it a federal offense to go for a cup of coffee?"

"A cup of coffee? Don't tell me you've been sitting in some sidewalk cafe shooting the breeze over a pot of Cona, because I'm simply not going to buy it."

Mike put his arm around Martini and led her over to the sofa. "Give the girl a break," he said to Ruth. "For once she's telling the truth. Have you ever heard of La Coupole?"

"Sure, it's some brasserie on the Left Bank somewhere. I always planned to go there, but during collection time it's kind of silly to move any further than the Eiffel Tower."

"If you had taken the time and the trouble to visit this Left Bank brasserie, as you call it," said Mike with sarcasm, "you would have known instinctively that it was probably the only place you might have found her. Or any other model girl come to that. They use it as their unofficial headquarters, these chicks. During collection time the place is bursting with them, all rabbiting on about shoes and hairdos and the latest way to tape up their tits.

"It was obvious, at least to me it was, that Martini would make a beeline for La Coupole. The dear little thing wanted to see all her old mates. If I hadn't gone to fetch her she would have found her way back to the hotel before bedtime."

Martini turned her pale-blue eyes on Ruth. "I would have, you know. There's no way I was going to let you down." Then she added like a small child, "I'm sorry if I made you worry. Honest I am."

Ruth sat down heavily. "I believe you," she said. Then she got down to the practical details. Had Martini unpacked? Did she need a bath? What was she doing about dinner?

The crisis was over. Now it was time to move into gear. Martini felt the same way. As far as she was concerned the rest of the evening was to be devoted to cleaning up her act.

Aside from unpacking she wanted to wash her hair, paint her nails and do her exercises. Her sole equipment for the job in hand was her body. She wanted to make sure it was in working order. Dinner, she said, would be a sandwich in her room. Or perhaps a quick visit to the hotel coffee shop. And Ruth believed her. The girl was a pro. If she looked anything less than perfect in Mike's pictures, it would hurt her reputation, which would hurt her bank balance.

When Ruth left the hotel with Mike and Kate she felt happy for the first time that day. Mike had managed to get a table at Fouquets at the top of the Champs Ely-sées. Aside from being one of the best restaurants in town, Fouquets served the kind of food the fashion editor most enjoyed. Seafood, pâtés and plain grills. It was simple, it was ridiculously expensive, and unlike many brasseries in Paris, the portions were generous. It beat room service any day of the week.

As dawn was coming up over Paris, touching the streets with rosy-colored sunlight, Martini was sitting in the small cubicle the Intercontinental called a room, being made ready for the day ahead. Jerry had spent the best part of an hour covering her face with paint and shimmer and gloss and now the model looked like a Western version of a geisha.

But it was Howie Danvers who supplied the final piece of fakery. Swirling her fine blonde hair into a pleat, he popped an artificial chignon on top of her head. Now she was ready for inspection by Mike and Ruth. She failed miserably.

"What have you done to her hair?" demanded Mike. "It's horrible, she looks like a dummy in a shop window, not a real girl at all."

"Yes, take the hair down," said Ruth. "Let it swing around her shoulders."

Howie snorted, "Swing, she says. You'll be lucky. All this hair's capable of doing is hang. Why do you think I decided to put it up in the first place?"

"Howie, honey, don't give me an argument. I want Martini to look like a natural all-American girl. Not a glossy courtesan. I'm going to get plenty of that look from the catwalk pictures. The whole point of this feature is how the clothes are going to look back home.''

Howie stuck a cigarette in the corner of his mouth, and started taking down Martini's hair. ''Okay, have it your own way. You want Raggedy Ann, Raggedy Ann is what you're going to get.''

''When you've finished throwing hairpins all over the shop,'' said Mike, ''you can sit her down and get Jerry to wipe off the red lipstick. Pale pink is more the color I had in mind.''

Half an hour later Ruth, Mike, Kate and Martini left the hotel in one taxi. Jerry and Howie followed in another. It was going to take a while for the team to work smoothly, thought Ruth. She guessed that nobody would be talking until they sat down to lunch, and she was pleased that the first stop was Dior. The couture house's PR girl, Chantal, was known for her efficiency. She was going to need it with this crew.

Dior was opposite the exclusive Plaza Athenée hotel on the Avenue Montaigne. Like most top couturiers it didn't give itself away from the outside. The legendary House of Dior, inventors of the post-war ''New Look,'' could have been any expensive boutique. With its plate-glass windows and subdued display you might have mistakenly imagined it was put there for the convenience of the American tourists staying at the Plaza.

It was only when you walked around the side of the building that you discovered the little hidden courtyard which was the real entrance to the couture house. It was here that the team assembled before passing through the wrought-iron gates and climbing the winding staircase which led to Dior's inner sanctum.

The session was planned to take place in the main salon overlooking the street. Mike needed the strong north light provided by the room's huge windows. And the moment they arrived at the top of the stairs Martini was led away by Chantal to the tiny model's room where she would be fitted into the long evening gown she had ready.

While Martini was being zipped and buttoned into the creation, Mike started setting up his equipment. The mirrors which virtually lined the room bothered him. He tried bouncing spotlights off them. All he got was glare. Then Martini walked in dressed from top to toe in black chiffon and he lost it.

"Chantal," he shouted, "what the hell do you think you're trying to pull?"

The French girl looked confused. "I don't understand," she stammered.

"Well, you bloody well should after all the years you've been in the business. I'm working for a newspaper, dummy. Newspapers publish in black and white. What the fuck do you think a long, black dress is going to look like on newsprint? I'll tell you how it's going to look. A big black lump of nothing. And after that I don't give you tuppence for Dior's image with the American public."

Chantal burst into tears, something she did frequently when faced with a difficult situation. "It's impossible, completely impossible. That's the only dress there for photography. Monsieur Bohan gave strict instructions to take everything away for the show. There's nothing I can do."

Mike screwed on his lens cap. "Then that's it," he

said. "We're snookered. There's no way I'm taking pictures of a girl in a black dress in front of a row of mirrors. Not for a newspaper. Not for anyone. It won't work."

Kate stepped forward. "Maybe if we did the session in the courtyard?" she suggested.

Mike looked as if he was about to strangle her. Then Ruth interceded. Taking Chantal's arm, she walked her over to the corner of the room, out of earshot from everyone else. "Look, this is the first day of the session. Everyone's wound up and no one's making sense. Would you be an angel and take a raincheck on this one? I'll make it up to you with runway pictures later on." Then she turned to the assembled group. "Okay gang," she said "this one's off. Martini, go and get changed. Kate, will you go with her and help her out of the dress? Howie and Jerry, you can go on ahead and grab a table at the Brasserie Lipp. We're taking a coffee break followed by an early lunch. We're not due at Chanel till two-thirty."

Then when everyone had left to do her bidding, she turned to Mike Stone. Her tone was implacable. "If you ever do that to me again, buster," she said, "I'll take your balls off. Understand?"

Then she turned on her heel and walked into Chantal's office.

Lunch was a silent affair. Jerry and Howie spoke only to each other. And nobody at all spoke to Mike Stone. By the time they arrived at Chanel at the Avenue Kleber the situation was critical. With the team in this mood Ruth knew she needed a miracle to get any decent work down.

The miracle happened when she saw the clothes. Ruth and Chanel's publicist had abandoned everyone in one of the large downstairs salons and climbed the circular staircase to the topmost rooms. In contrast to the deep-carpeted luxury of the showrooms the place where the clothes were kept was stark and unwelcoming. Rack upon rack of jackets, skirts and dresses stood at random on bare boards. Glittering costume jewelry, the hallmark of Chanel, lay on the floor in carefully labeled boxes. Every outfit had its own earrings, necklaces and bracelets. And as the junior designers matched outfits to glitter, Ruth's spirits rose. The clothes had the touch of magic she was searching for every time she came to the Paris collections.

The last time she had been this turned on was when Saint Laurent cropped his jackets and raised his hemlines. Now it was Karl Lagerfeld's turn. The suits and dresses she was seeing were his first collection for Chanel. And she knew that this season they would be the talk of Paris. The eccentric German with his ponytail and baggy suits had put the life back into this grand but slightly fading house.

If this doesn't give my little group a much-needed kick in the ass, thought Ruth, nothing will. She was right. When Martini stepped out in the first suit, its swingy jacket covered in glittery buttons, everyone started to pay attention.

Howie was the first to react, sweeping Martini's thin veil of blonde hair into a club at the nape of her neck and finishing it off with a big velvet Chanel bow. As Jerry started touching up the lipstick Ruth realized that at long last they were in business. For suddenly, as if someone had put an electrode through him, Mike sprang into action. Grabbing hold of his small Polaroid camera he started to take a series of fast shots which were to set the mood for the session.

Each picture showed a beautiful girl celebrating her femaleness. Reveling in her sexuality. Yet there was nothing tacky about them. For Lagerfeld had remembered that above everything else, the House of Chanel had class. And it was this elegance that underpinned his sexual statement.

The combination of class and sex was a heady one. And as Martini spun around the pale salon with its tiny gilt chairs, the team started to relax. They were on to a good thing and their talk and laughter reflected the fact. It was six o'clock when Ruth instructed everyone to pack up.

When she saw the time she was startled. They had spent nearly four hours in Chanel's gilded salon, yet none of them had been aware of time passing.

Back on the street, the excitement that had started up that afternoon didn't desert them. It was Mike who decided to prolong the party. "I don't see any point looking for a taxi," he said. "Not yet, at any rate. Nothing comes free in this town till at least seven-thirty. So what do you lot say to a drink?" He didn't wait for a reply. He already knew the answer.

For Howie and Jerry, having a good time meant gossiping about all their mutual acquaintances. So when Mike had found a suitable bar Howie bought a round of drinks and went into a huddle with Jerry. Kate wondered if anyone in the fashion business would have a reputation left by the end of the evening.

For her part, she found there was a measure of joy to be gained from listening to Martini. Like all models,

Martini's favorite subject was the upkeep and maintenance of physical appearance. Kate had always been mildly obsessed with this herself and until now had always felt guilty about it. Her strict Catholic upbringing had taught her that vanity was a sin. Now that she was in Paris, she realized that far from being a sin it was actually a way of life. So she immersed herself in Martini's prattle and found she enjoyed it.

Mike Stone was also enjoying himself. With Ruth. She was the toughest woman he had ever met. But it wasn't a pig-headed toughness. She was tough because she knew what she wanted. And he admired that. He had lived by the same set of rules for longer than he could remember.

At around eight, Howie and Jerry drifted off for dinner and Mike suggested to Ruth that they do the same. She was tempted. Then she started to think.

A veteran of the sexual encounter, she knew Mike must want something from her. But what? All she could give him was work and he had as much of that as he could get.

Because she had no experience of love, it didn't occur to her that any man could possibly want her for herself. And she was confused. She didn't know the rules of the game they were playing, so she refused to recognize Mike's desire for her. Or hers for him. In other words she froze. As she did so, something else happened. A pain, the likes of which she had never felt before, hit her in the stomach. She doubled up, gasping for breath.

"What the hell's going on?" said Mike, grabbing her arm. Then he half-dragged, half-carried her over to the nearest chair. Ruth didn't answer. She couldn't. She was in too much agony.

Five minutes later Mike, Kate and Martini were grouped around Ruth who was still in the same position.

"I'm going to get her to a doctor," said Mike. "I don't like the look of this at all."

"How?" asked Kate. "We're in Paris, not New Jersey. You can't just snap your fingers and hope some obliging doctor will turn up."

"Look, dummy, the hotel must have someone on call. I'll fetch a taxi and we'll get her over there."

Both Kate and Martini looked doubtful. Ruth's face was now pale gray and her breath was coming in shallow gasps. She also looked immovable. Before Kate could draw Mike's attention to this, Ruth herself solved the problem. Closing her eyes, she slumped forward, unconscious. And it was at that moment that the owner of the bar summoned both transport and medical attention. He called an ambulance. It was an act of self-preservation, rather than charity. Rich American ladies collapsing on his premises were bad for business. The sooner she was out of there the better.

Ruth arrived at the Medici clinic on the rue du Pont in the second arrondissement at eight forty-five. By nine-thirty Kate and the others, who were sitting nervously in the hospital waiting room, were informed of her condition.

Ruth was suffering from acute food poisoning. Her stomach had been pumped and she had been tranquilized. If she was well enough she could receive visitors by tomorrow noon at the earliest. If she wasn't, then they suggested her next of kin be contacted.

"That will teach her," said Mike in the stunned silence that followed. "I told her she shouldn't have had that second portion of *escargots* at lunch."

It was time to call New York. Three major fashion spreads all emanating from Paris were scheduled to appear over the next three days. It had become clear that although they might indeed emanate from Paris, it was doubtful that they would emanate from Ruth.

"You'll just have to cover for her, Kate," said Mike crossly. "You're a newspaper woman, aren't you?"

"Sure, I'm a newspaper woman. But fashion's not exactly my bag. I've never been near a runway in my life. I wouldn't know how to start."

"Look," said Mike. "Talk to young Martini here, she'll explain it to you. And I'll come in when I can and fill in any gaps."

"But what about my interviews? I'm booked to see Karl Lagerfeld today and Marc Bohan tomorrow. I can't see them and cover the shows. Then there's the office. Maybe they won't want me reporting on the collections."

"For God's sake, grow up, woman, will you? During fashion week nothing is more important than the shows. *Nothing.* You could have an interview with de Gaulle and they'd can it in favor of the frocks. That's what Paris is about. Pictures of the clothes and a few words describing the details my camera doesn't catch."

"You think a hell of a lot of yourself, don't you? Well, I'm going to get hold of the office and see if they agree with your inflated opinions."

They did. As far as Ted was concerned, getting Mike Stone's pictures was a major coup. The paper was depending on them. Kate would just have to cover as best she could.

"Don't worry, darling," he said. "Just send over all the details you can get your hands on. If we need to fill in the fashion background we have it on file back here. Tracy can also lend a hand."

"Tracy!" she screamed over the airwaves. "Since when did a junior get to interfere with my copy? Listen, I'm standing here in the middle of the fashion capital. I've already visited two couture houses and had a preview of their stuff. I'm also doing this job with Mike Stone who knows the business like nobody else. If I can't get it together without the help of Tracy and your precious files, then I will personally hand in my resignation when I get back to the city."

Then she slammed down the phone. Both Mike and Martini were grinning broadly. "You certainly told him," said Mike. "Ted hasn't had a blast like that since the day he cut back on the housekeeping. I reckon he's sitting there right now counting his lucky stars he isn't married to you."

It was at that moment that Kate realized she hadn't asked Ted if he had moved into her apartment.

Golda Lewis, the head *vendeuse* at Loehmann's discount house in Brooklyn, sat down and took off her shoes.

"Oy vey," she moaned, massaging her toes. "What a day! I'll be glad to get home tonight. You'd think we were shvartzes the way they work us."

Any more uncharitable words about her black brethren died in her throat when she spied a petite blonde walking out of the elevator at the end of the showroom.

"Sandy, doll," she yelled from where she was sitting. "Come over here and give Golda a kiss. Where have you been all this time? I've missed you. We've all missed you."

She indicated the group of elderly Jewish matrons who helped her serve in the vast, shabby warehouse. But as Sandy pushed her way through rack upon rack of dresses and suits and jackets and jumpers, she did so with joy. Sure it wasn't Bergdorf's or some snotty boutique in the Seventies. But here, just over the Brooklyn Bridge, you could buy the same merchandise at a fraction of the price.

Loehmann's was one of the well-kept secrets of women who liked to look rich but didn't have the money. For it was here and in Loehmann's other branches in Queens and the Bronx that the high fashion stores in Manhattan dropped off the goods that didn't move fast enough. Either the sizes were too large or too small. Or the line failed to satisfy that week's fad. Or the weather slowed the sales. The end result was that Bloomingdale's loss was Loehmann's gain. And mine as well, thought Sandy, as she embraced Golda Lewis the way she would an affectionate aunt.

Loehmann's might have worked on smaller margins than anyone else, but they weren't in business for their health.

"You picked a good day to come and see me," said Golda, putting her shoes back on. "We just got a big delivery in. Stuff you would kill for and all the names you like, too. Calvin Klein, Ralph Lauren, Oscar de la Renta. We've even got a couple of French designers on the racks. Do you want me to go and get a selection?"

"Thanks, Golda, I'll do it myself," said Sandy, hurrying into the warehouse. Golda meant well, but her idea of style didn't quite match with Sandy's. She tended to go for tassels, hot colors and anything in lamé. To Golda, glitz added value to a garment. Sandy on the other hand went for style and the absence of extra adornment.

Right at the beginning of their long relationship the two women had argued bitterly over what was worth having and what wasn't. Finally Sandy chose what she wanted to wear. And although Golda wasn't crazy about her choice she didn't criticize either. Sandy was, after all, a customer, not a daughter.

At the end of half an hour, Sandy walked into the vast communal changing room staggering under a pile of clothes. Half of them she knew she would never buy. The other half she would probably put to one side, then change her mind about before she left. But she didn't care. The point of Loehmann's was that it was fun. You could go on trying clothes for hours at a time and nobody pressed you to buy. Not if they knew you, anyway.

Golda left Sandy alone for the best part of an hour. She knew when to give space and when to interfere. When the time came to interfere she did it gently.

"What are you looking for, doll?" she asked.

"A dress," said Sandy with a faraway look in her eyes. "A dress to wear to a fancy restaurant in New York City."

"Well . . . did you find anything you liked?"

Sandy was tempted to lie. If she said she hadn't then she could spend another hour sliding into creations she had no use for. Then she thought, what the hell? The kids would be home from school soon. She was only wasting time. "Golda," she said, "I found something I love."

And she produced a black silk jersey number and held it up against herself. Although the dress was simple, the simplicity was deceptive. For the secret of its line lay in the seaming, which was intricate and artful.

"I don't recognize this designer," said Sandy. "I know you have to cut the labels out to protect the names, but between you and me tell me who made the dress."

Golda looked confused. "It's some British dressmaker," she said, "some guy who goes by the name of Bruce something or other. We don't normally carry his stuff, so I don't know too much about him."

"Well, whoever he is," said Sandy, "he makes one hell of a dress. I'm going to enjoy wearing it."

"Got anything special planned?" asked Golda. "I mean is the dress for an occasion?"

"It sure is," said Sandy, "but not the sort of occasion you think it is. Ted isn't taking me to some trendy cocktail thing or anything. Just a quiet dinner after work."

"So what's all the fuss about?"

"If I tell you, will you promise to keep it to yourself? At least until tomorrow."

"You got it," said Golda, who enjoyed hearing confidences. "So shoot. What's the big secret?"

Sandy smiled and folded her arms around her middle. "I'm pregnant," she said, "and next to my doctor you're the only person who knows. I plan to tell Ted tonight over dinner. After that I announce it to the world."

Sandy was sitting in one of the booths at The Palm waiting for her husband.

All around her, decorating the walls of this long, thin restaurant, were signed sketches of New York's prominent media stars, past and present. Jimmy Breslin looking every inch a newspaperman was there, as was glamorous Josh Owen, the advertising creative genius. There was also a smattering of prominent baseball stars, the only kind of celebrity the cynical men of the communication business actually admired.

It was a masculine restaurant, The Palm. The booths were surfaced in tough, shiny leather. There was sawdust covering the bare floorboards. And the effusive greetings of the regulars and air of camaraderie put Sandy in mind of a locker room. Or what she imagined a locker room would be like.

While she was waiting for Ted, Sandy ordered herself a spritzer and had a good look at the menu. The Palm didn't go in for gourmet cooking. The journalists and ad men who frequented the joint wouldn't have understood it. Instead it went in for Surf 'n Turf, big salads and baked potatoes. Normally Sandy would have been put off by this abundance of food. Tonight she was starving. Pregnancy made her hungry and she started planning a jumbo-sized dinner.

She looked up from the menu ten minutes later in time to see her husband come in through the door. He looked gaunt, harassed somehow. And she wondered if he had a particularly tough day.

It took Ted a good five minutes to get to their table. For on every side there were hands to be shaken, colleagues to be congratulated, enemies to be smiled at. And Ted began to wonder if arranging to meet Sandy at The Palm had been such a good idea after all.

The news he had to tell her was the sort of thing you told your wife in private. But he had resisted that. There were bound to be tears and accusations. Voices would be raised and the whole thing would get out of hand. No, a restaurant was the best idea. He could depend on Sandy coming in all dolled up. And she wouldn't want to spoil the impression she was making by bursting into tears.

A quick glance at his wife told him he had been right. Sandy had really gone to town tonight. That little black dress she was wearing looked like a million. The way she was wearing her hair, swept up into a chignon, only added to the effect.

Just for a moment, a small doubt filtered through his mind. Was he doing the right thing? Sandy was decorative. She had a sweet temper, well, most of the time anyway. Then there were the kids to think about.

He swept the doubts out of his head. He had given Kate his word. He couldn't let her down. Not now. And certainly not because his wife was looking like a reincarnation of Carole Lombard.

Hardening his heart, he pecked Sandy on the cheek and sat down opposite her. "How're you doing?" he said, signaling the waiter for a drink. "You look like you pulled out all the stops tonight. Is this a special occasion or something? I thought we were just having a quiet snack after the office."

Sandy smiled, the way women smile when they're hiding some special happiness. She was tempted to tell Ted her news right away, but then she resisted, wanting in some way to prolong the moment.

She put her hand over his. "You'll find out how special this evening is," she said, "but not till after the broiled lobster."

If Ted had been more in touch with his wife he would have heard the alarm bells, but he was thinking about the Paris collections and whether Kate was coping as well as she said she would. So he didn't notice Sandy's secret smile. Or the fact that she had anything to communicate, other than the price of the new dress she was wearing.

He ordered a highball and swallowed it down in two gulps. Then he ordered another.

"Is something bothering you?" asked Sandy, looking concerned. "You don't usually drink this way. It's the office, isn't it? Why don't you tell me about it? Who knows, I might be able to help."

"I don't think I'm in a situation where you could help me. In fact I don't think anybody could help me right now. And stop looking so worried," he said crossly. "What's on my mind has nothing to do with the office."

Sandy placed a hand on the back of her chignon and tested its security. Satisfied everything was in place she leaned forward and patted Ted's cheek. "So tell me what's on your mind," she said. "You have my complete attention."

He braced himself, the time had come to tell her what he felt for Kate. And how it was going to put an end to their marriage. Then he remembered how Sandy had made love to him the previous night. How wild it had been. And how sweet. He felt like a heel. But what had to be done, had to be done. His mind was made up.

He took a deep breath, the words forming in his head. It's over. We've both known it for a long time. The situation is impossible for you. For Kate. For all of us. This is the only sane way to work it out.

As he was about to give them voice, Ted felt a strong hand clapping his back and heard Ed Kramer offering greetings. "Glad I caught you before you left town," he said, squeezing next to Ted on the banquette seat. "Your secretary told me I'd find you down here."

"What's the problem?" asked Ted. He felt oddly relieved, though for the life of him he didn't know why.

"No problem at all," said Kramer genially, taking hold of the drink which magically appeared before him. Men like Kramer didn't have to order their bourbon on the rocks. The waiters at The Palm knew what he wanted and gave it to him the moment he sat down.

"So why are you here?" asked Ted.

"To congratulate you about Kate."

A cold feeling came over Ted. The whole situation was getting out of control.

"What did Kate do that was so special?" asked Sandy, looking interested.

"You'll find out tomorrow morning, when you see the paper." Then he turned to Ted. "Your protégée just turned in about the best report I've ever seen on a fashion spread. I had no idea she understood Paris so well. In fact I had no idea she knew about fashion at all. And the photos—" Now there was no stopping him. For the next quarter of an hour Kramer raved on about Mike Stone's impressions of the great couturiers. And Ted relaxed. The moment he most dreaded had passed. Now, as Kramer droned on about Paris, it was receding.

He looked over at Sandy, bright-eyed and slightly flushed, drinking in the details of the latest fashions. How easily she was pleased, he thought. Dinner in New York, a sneak preview of the Paris collections and she was as sparked up as a Catherine wheel. Then he started trying to figure out how he was going to tell her about Kate and their plans together. And he felt weary. More than weary. He felt sad. He and Sandy hadn't had a bad life together. Sure, it wasn't what he was looking for when he started his career. But she hadn't made him miserable. In fact, she had done quite the reverse. Until he met Kate he had been content. As content as any guy could be with a mortgage and kids around his neck.

He pulled himself together. This was no time for second thoughts. He knew what he had to do and he vowed that by the end of the evening he and Sandy would have everything straightened out. Like two civilized human beings.

A bottle of champagne appeared on the table accompanied by three of the restaurant's best glasses.

"Hey," laughed Ted, "I know Kate did a terrific job, but you didn't have to order champagne."

"Forget Kate," said Kramer shortly. "We're drinking to your future, not your past."

Now Ted was really confused. "I'm sorry, I'm not with you."

Sandy put her hand over his. Protectively, as if she were soothing a wayward child. "Darling, you've been miles away. I swear you haven't heard a word we've been saying."

As long as she lived, she would never understand why her husband got so wound up with the problems of his office. But he was the father of her unborn child, after all. So she gave his hand a squeeze and poured out the champagne. "This is to toast a new arrival," she said steadily. "My new arrival, our new arrival. Darling, we're having a baby."

Ruth lay propped up in
her hospital bed looking the worse for wear. A rubber
tube firmly taped to her wrist attached her to a drip feed.
And her long dark hair lay across the starched pillows
in an unruly mess of snarls and tangles. She reminded
Kate of an ailing Medusa.

"For pity's sake," she said, her East Coast upbringing coming to the fore, "if I can't make you feel any better, at least I can do something about the way you look."

And fishing a hairbrush out of her bag she went to
work. After twenty minutes of screams and protestations
Ruth began to look as if she belonged to the human race.

"You didn't allow Mike to see you like this?" asked
Kate, concerned.

"Allow isn't a word Mike knows. When that guy

wants something, he goes ahead and gets it. It doesn't occur to him to ask anyone's permission.

"The minute I opened my eyes, the first thing I saw was his dopey, unshaven mug. I can't seem to get rid of him. He sits and clucks over me like he's my mother or something. I tell you, I can't even take a leak without him coming along to see if I do it properly."

Kate looked shocked. "You don't mean he . . ."

"No," Ruth laughed, genuinely amused by the idea, "but he virtually carries me to the door, then waits outside in case I get into trouble. 'Ruthie,' he says, 'you're not getting any pain are you? If you want a hand I'll call the nurse.' "

"How do you feel about all this . . . attention?"

Ruth made a face. "If you want to know the truth, I'm enjoying it. All my life, I've been the Schlepper. Somebody wants something, Ruth goes and gets it. Somebody's got a problem, you can rely on good old Ruthie to solve it. Now everything's turned upside down. I lie here like La Traviata while another human being does the running around. It never happened before and I could get used to it."

"It's all very odd," said Kate. "The man you're describing, the gentle gofer, doesn't sound a bit like the Mike Stone I've been working with for the last couple of days." And she cast her mind back to that first morning when she had arrived, sick with nerves, at the Place de Versailles behind the Louvre. Here, in a vast canvas marquee, was where the shows were held, the fashion parades that Kate had come to cover.

Her first problem had been getting within range of the marquee. For in its forecourt, the size of a small paddock, milled and thronged the representatives of the world's press corps. And what a menacing bunch they were, thought Kate. The women grim-faced in their dung-colored Burberrys. The men built like professional wrestlers, weighted down on all sides by camera bags.

Then Mike had arrived on the scene and suddenly the opposition looked less threatening. Where everybody else had two camera bags, Mike had five. Where other people asked, Mike demanded. And when he wasn't demanding his rights he took them, literally pushing and shoving his way through the mass of bodies and into the tent. Kate trailed behind him clutching her ticket, praying that everything would go according to plan.

It didn't. The moment she had found her seat she knew she was doomed. For sitting on the hard wooden bench that bore the same number as her ticket was a thin, dark whippet of a man.

"Excuse me," said Kate, "but you're in the wrong place." She waved her ticket. "This is my seat. Number 109, it's written down here."

He looked at her blankly. So she waved her ticket again and pointed to the seat number. She was greeted by a torrent of abuse in Italian. She didn't have to understand the language to know that her opponent was saying something very unpleasant indeed.

She looked at her watch. She had four minutes before Montana started showing his autumn collection. Four minutes to regain possession of her seat or get thrown out of the tent. The Italian raised his hand, placed it firmly in the middle of her chest and pushed. As Kate stumbled backward she felt the heel of her shoe give away. And then she fell, sprawling over the muddy boards.

As two Dutch journalists ran to pick her up Kate had caught sight of Mike Stone. He was bearing down on the foul-mouthed Italian and what happened next would be imprinted on Kate's memory for the rest of her life. For Mike picked up the wiry little man by the scruff of his neck the way somebody else would have lifted a trouble-some puppy. The Italian was too stunned to protest. And by the time he had found his voice, Mike had carried him to the entrance and hurled him through it.

He looked over his shoulder to make sure Kate was safely in her seat, then he waved and disappeared, only to re-emerge seconds later at the foot of the runway.

The best photographers, that is to say the toughest and the most resourceful, always took their pictures from a position literally under the feet of the models. The rest scattered around the perimeters of the marquee, behind where Kate was sitting. Until he rescued Kate from the Italian, Mike had never been anywhere near the perime-ters.

Kate had stared at him with fascination. Earlier he had told Kate that when he was learning his profession he used to cover soccer matches. And she could see that the experience came in handy. For Mike moved with his elbows, using them the way a medieval knight would use his shield, to clear a space for himself. So that when the models came swaying and dancing down the runway Mike was able to swing his camera in a wide arc, catching every angle.

The show had knocked her out. As a spectacle it rated alongside a Broadway musical. And the similarity didn't end with the raucous soundtrack. The dramatic lighting effects and the sheer energy and showmanship of the models themselves put her in mind of Sondheim's *Follies*.

Then there were the clothes. Where Chanel was the mistress of the glitzy cardigan and Kenzo the king of the drooping layers, Montana was a leather fetishist. With a difference. For the diminutive Frenchman wasn't into bondage, he was into sculpture chic. He used leather the way a tailor uses cloth. Bending it, seaming it, molding it into some of the most desirable clothes Kate had ever seen.

At the end of the show, in keeping with tradition, the tiny couturier was hauled on to the stage by two of his most statuesque models. And Kate, like everyone else in the tent, had gotten to her feet and applauded until her hands were sore.

When she dictated her story to New York, half an hour later, the words didn't come out of her notebook. They came out of her head. As long as she worked she would never again recapture the sheer excitement of her first Paris show. And it was this excitement, distilled into paragraphs and sentences, that found its way on to the pages of the New York *Daily News*.

Mike's pictures added the crowning touch. And as Ted had predicted, they gave the *News* the edge over every other paper in the city.

Ted, the man she loved. The thought of him jerked her back into the present. Tomorrow she would see him. On Sunday afternoon when she got off the plane, Ted would be waiting for her back at the apartment. Or would he?

For ever since she had blasted him over the phone about her suitability to report on the Paris fashions she hadn't spoken to him. The six-hour time difference hadn't helped. When he was just arriving at his desk, she was sitting in the marquee. And when she finally managed to struggle to a phone, he had already gone out to lunch.

The only opportunity to speak to him at all was at about nine o'clock her time. Then she was having dinner. She managed to get through to him just once from the hotel restaurant. But when she did, he was in a meeting with Kramer and couldn't come to the phone. In the end she gave up. She'd finished her work in Paris and she was coming home. Once she was in New York, there would be time enough to talk to Ted.

"What are you looking so worried about?" asked Ruth. "Anyone would think you were just starting the job, not winding it up. Cheer up, bubola, you did magnificently. Mike told me so. He also brought me copies of yesterday's editions so I could see for myself. Listen, I'm the one who should be worried. If I don't pull myself together and get out of this place, Kramer will be offering you my job."

"When are you getting out of here?" asked Kate, grateful to be off the hook. If she wasn't careful Ruth would ask her what was bugging her. And she was reluctant to talk about the latest development in her affair. There had been enough gossip already. All she wanted was for her life with Ted to settle down into a comfortable rut. A domestic rut. Then there would be time for talking.

"The doctors here tell me they're keeping me in for

another week," said Ruth. "And there's no way I can talk them out of it, even if my French was good enough. So you and the rest of the guys are going to have to fly home on your own. Miss Otis regrets, etcetera."

"We'll manage." Kate grinned. "But what about you? How are you going to cope on your own?"

"I won't be on my own. Mike has to do a job for *Paris Match* that will keep him here till the end of the month. And judging from his past performance, I guess he'll spend some of that time hanging around me."

"Most of the time," said Mike, pushing his way through the double doors to Ruth's room. "So you'd better watch yourself." Then he sat down and ran his fingers over the fresh growth of stubble on his chin. It was a nervous mannerism. People who worked with Mike always knew he was worried when he did that.

Finally he said what was on his mind. "Ruth, I've been having a session with the doctors here. I hope you don't think I was being pushy, but my French is good. And I was worried about all this time they've been keeping you in here. If it was just a bad *escargot,* you would have been on your feet and feeling lively in a couple of days. But you've been lying here a long time now. So I thought I'd find out what the problem was."

"And what did they say?" asked Ruth.

Again he touched the side of his face. Then he looked at Kate. She got up and prepared to leave.

"No, sit down, Kate," said Ruth. "If I'm dying of the pox, the world will know soon enough. Anyhow, you're not the world, you're a friend. And something tells me I could just be in need of a friend right now."

"You could be right," said Mike. "The quacks tell

me you're a sicker lady than they first thought. It's your kidneys, Ruth. Apparently they've been bad news for some time. Did you know that?"

Ruth looked blank. Like a lot of people who hear something they don't want to, she refused to take it in. "I had no idea. Look, they must have gotten it wrong. I've always been one hundred percent. Anyhow, what do they know? If I start believing everything this bunch of frogs tells me, I might as well lay down and give up."

"Hang on a minute, girl," said Mike. "Who said anything about giving up? You're not at death's door you know. You've got a dicky kidney, that's all. Oh, and I wouldn't start casting aspersions on the French medical system. Remember you're at their mercy at this moment."

"Maybe I am and maybe I'm not," she said grumpily. "One thing's for sure. As soon as I can get up, I'm putting myself back on the first plane to New York. If my kidneys are going to give out I'd rather they did so with Dr. Stein looking over me. At least we talk the same language."

Mike took her hand. "I'm not arguing, my old love. I think you should get back home for treatment. The experts here say the same thing. But will you leave the details to me? You're looking at the man who moves gangs of technicians across continents, not to mention the odd covey of model girls. I think you can trust me to see you safely onto the plane back to New York."

Kate looked embarrassed. "Look, do you want me to stay in Paris and wait for you? Then we can both go back together."

"What," said Mike, "and deprive me of a few days

on my own with the glorious Ruth? Not on your life. No, Kate, you get moving with the rest of the team and leave her to me. I give you my word, if she looks dodgy I'll get on the plane with her myself."

"He means it," said Ruth. "Mike's missed his vocation. In another life he must have been a nurse."

"Well, if you're sure," said Kate. "I'm not all that happy about leaving you."

"I've never been surer," said Ruth.

And from the way she looked at Mike, Kate suspected that Ruth wasn't just talking about getting back safely to New York. They'd known each other just a few days, but already Mike and Ruth had a permanent look about them.

The minute the Puerto Rican office driver picked her up at Kennedy, Kate knew something was wrong. Alvin had been collecting her from airports for nearly four years now. And whenever he caught sight of her at the barrier he was pleased to see her. Now he was finding difficulty meeting her eye.

He knows something, she thought. Drivers always knew everything about the goings on in the lives of the people they worked for. Alvin was no exception.

Her suspicions were confirmed when the driver handed her a heavy brown-paper envelope. "Ted told me to give this to you," he said. "He said you'd need them when you got home."

She opened the package and stared in disbelief at the keys to her apartment. It was Sunday evening. Ted should be in the apartment waiting to welcome her. She'd half-expected he would be there to meet her at the airport. But failing that she knew he'd be at home in the Village. So why did she need her keys?

On the highway back into town, Kate's mind started to race. Maybe Ted had had to go out of town. Once a year Kramer sent a group of his senior executives on a fact-finding tour across America. He needed to be kept informed about other printing operations if he was to keep his competitive edge.

But why didn't Ted tell her if he was going away? It wasn't like him to just take off out of the blue. Then she thought, I'm being silly. Ted's probably in the office. The features editor normally worked one Sunday out of three. He's just being considerate, thought Kate. After all, how am I supposed to get through my front door without any keys?

But there was a nagging doubt in the back of her mind. And it refused to go away. Ted knew she was coming back today. It was an important day for both of them. For when she arrived home, today would be the first day, the official first day of their living together. So why didn't he arrange to have it off? He had had enough time to maneuver it, and he had two deputies to stand in for him. What the hell was the matter?

The moment she walked through her front door Kate knew her fears were justified. For the room looked exactly the same as it had when she left it two weeks ago. The daffodils in the glass jar on the window ledge were still there. But they had long since died. The glasses she and Ted had drunk their celebration champagne from were still on the table where they had left them. The bottle was there too, with a few drops of champagne still in the bottom. They had a sad look about them, those dirty glasses. Like a nightclub the morning after a party. Or a wake.

Putting her suitcases down, Kate walked through into the bedroom. Then she opened her closets, and she knew Ted had never lived there. For there was nothing of his to be found. Even the spare suit he normally kept in her apartment had disappeared, along with the two or three ties he hung over her belt rack.

The story was the same in the bathroom. His razor had gone. So had the terrycloth bathrobe from the hook on the door. He hadn't even left his toothbrush.

She had left New York expecting the man she loved to be waiting with his possessions around him. Instead, Ted had moved out.

She was propelled by hysteria, which afterward she realized was a mixture of jet lag and despair. And because she felt she was losing her mind she picked up the telephone and called him. First at the office. And when she found he wasn't there, she called him at home.

Sandy answered the phone. With an effort, Kate kept her voice steady and asked if Ted was there.

"Sure, honey," drawled Sandy. She sounded smug and contented. "He's in the yard playing with the kids. I'll go and get him. Who shall I say is calling?"

You bitch, Kate thought, you know damn well who's calling. Why do you have to make me go through this? Aloud she said, "It's Kate Kennedy. I just got in from Paris."

"Kate," said Sandy, "how're you doing? I read all the stuff on the fashions and I've got to tell you it was great. Just terrific. I almost felt like I was there myself. Hang on a minute, will you? I'll go and get the old man."

And then Kate knew it was all over. The woman who had just spoken to her was not someone who was about to lose her husband. She was too friendly, too happy. "I'll go and get the old man." There was a settled sound to that. The old man. Old Ted, my Ted. The Ted who's going to stay with me for the rest of my life.

And suddenly she couldn't bear to hear any more. She didn't want to talk to Ted because she knew what he was going to say. Silently, with deliberation, she put the phone down.

She'd hear the whole story from him tomorrow. Without his wife listening in. Losing your man was one thing, but a girl didn't have to throw her dignity out along with the rest of her life. An East Coast upbringing left you with certain things to cling on to.

She didn't go to the office the following day. Jet lag was a legitimate excuse for a couple of days' rest. And Kate felt she needed them. Maybe I'll make that a couple of years, she thought, staring at the coffee she'd brewed for herself.

Ted called at ten-thirty. They had to talk. Could she meet him for lunch?

"You don't have to take me anywhere. I'll get something together here."

"No, you'll be tired after your trip. I'll meet you at Murphy's at twelve-thirty. My secretary's already reserved the table in the window." Then he hung up before she could argue.

Kate looked around at the neat bachelor-girl apartment with its scrubbed pine and trailing ferns. For the past three years, Ted had never wanted to eat anywhere else. There was privacy here. Privacy for talking, for touching, for loving. It was their own secret garden. Only now the secret was out.

She remembered the bare closets when she arrived home. The bathroom which looked as if no man had ever stayed there. And she knew why Ted was giving her lunch in a restaurant. Goodbyes were better said on neutral ground.

She felt angry. Who the fuck did he think she was? Some temperamental mistress about to throw a grand scene? It crossed her mind to do that. Just for the hell of it. Then she remembered where she came from, and she set her face. She never cried at funerals, it simply wasn't done. Even if that funeral was your own.

She dressed in black. One of Kate's minor foibles was that she always matched her clothes to her mood. The black Dior that she had acquired in Paris, with its tailored uncompromising lines, picked up exactly on the way she felt.

She arrived late at the restaurant. This was one occasion where she wanted to look laid back. For Kate, this would be the one time in her life when jet lag worked in her favor. If she had been in touch with her true feelings, she would never have survived the meeting with Ted. As it was, the only emotion she felt was anger. And it carried her through the day.

When Kate got to the table, Ted had a drink waiting for her. And from the look of him she was at least two drinks behind. There was a hangdog appearance about him. A guilty look, slightly fuddled by one drink too many.

For the first time since she had started loving him

Kate didn't feel any sympathy. He was no longer hers to feel for.

She took up her drink and placed it in front of him. He looked like he needed it more than she did. Then she grabbed hold of the pitcher of ice water and poured herself a glass. For this, her last scene, she wanted to be sober.

"What stopped you, Ted?" she asked, keeping her voice pleasant. "Did a small nuclear war happen when I was away in Paris? Did Kramer finally threaten to sack you? No, don't tell me, that beautiful wife of yours is dying of a terrible disease and you simply couldn't leave home."

He sighed. "Don't be bitter, Kate. It doesn't suit you. Anyhow, I don't think I'm worth it."

"Too damn right you're not," she said. "But I still want to know what happened. I'm not saying you owe me anything. But an explanation would be nice."

"Okay, Kate, you asked for it. So I'll give it to you straight. Sandy, my wife, is pregnant. The kid's due next spring. I couldn't run out on her, not even for you."

Kate absorbed the news and the misery that went with it like a sponge. It was a fact to be noted and filed away. She would have plenty of time to cry about it later.

"What you're telling me," she said coldly, "is that all the time you were swearing eternal love to me you were going home and saying exactly the same thing to Sandy."

"I wasn't," he said. "It's not the way it looks."

"Then how does it look? You tell me."

He looked miserable. "I know it's rotten, but there

wasn't any feeling with her. No deep love. Not the way it was for us."

"For a guy who had no feelings you sure did a lot of fucking. It takes more than a one-night stand to make a baby when your wife's nearly thirty."

"Cut it out, Kate. If I want locker-room talk, I'll go to the gym. I came here to settle things. To do the proper thing. A shouting match isn't going to solve anything."

"What's there to solve? You've gone back to your wife. What do you want me to do? Start knitting baby booties?"

"I'll tell you what I want you to do. I want you to show a little understanding. I love you, you know that. I'll always love you. You know that too. But I can't just abandon Sandy. The twins are still in elementary school. And now with another baby on the way, how's she going to cope on her own?"

"So you're going to stand on the sidelines and play doting father, are you? Doting father with a nice tidy mistress in the city who he sees every once in a while when he can tear himself away from all that cozy domesticity. Well, forget it, buster. Masochism isn't my line. Nor is playing second fiddle. From now on, I want a man of my own. Someone I can be seen with at the office party and not feel ashamed. I'm sick to death of hiding in corners. And I've had it up to here with men like Kramer making me feel like some cheap floozie."

She put down her glass of water with enough force to make the table shudder. He looked up sharply, and for the first time she noticed the worry lines etched into his face. There was something tormented about him, like a man at an execution.

For he knew it was the end. They both did. But only she had accepted it. Something in the back of her mind made her wonder if he would ever come to terms with what had happened. What was going to happen.

Like a drowning man grasping at anything that might save him, he started to plead with her. "Kate, you're not yourself," he said softly. "It's been a tough trip, I know. Why don't you go home and put your head down? By tomorrow you'll feel differently about the whole thing."

If he was on his knees he couldn't have sounded more wretched. "Please, please, Kate, don't say anything you'll regret now. Anything we'll both regret."

She stood up and picked up her bag. "Maybe you're right. There's nothing to be gained from talking about the situation any more. Tell Murphy I'm sorry to miss out on his charbroiled steak. But I seem to have lost my appetite."

Then she walked away from the table. Quickly. Without saying goodbye.

When she got back to the apartment Kate called Phil Myers at the *Post* and told him she was free to accept the job he had offered her in London.

She had only one condition. She wanted a signed contract in twenty-four hours and she wanted to be out of New York and on her way by the end of the week. She was more or less packed already. All that remained to do was to say goodbye to her family.

Myers called her back half an hour later. The *Post* had agreed to her terms. The editor wanted to meet her first thing the next morning and hand her the contract personally.

Wearily Kate sat down and wrote her last words for the *News*. It was her letter of resignation.

For Ted there was no letter. Ending a job was a simple matter. Ending a love affair was outside her experience.

PART

two

The European bureau of the New York *Post* was located in the Condé Nast building in Hanover Square. As well as being smack in the middle of London's most expensive shopping area, the offices had an added charm. The building was the headquarters of *Vogue* magazine. This meant that Chuck Holders, Kate's predecessor, got an eyeful of some of the best-looking models in the business every time he went up in the elevator. Many of them on their way to the *Vogue* studios didn't bother with anything but the most basic of leotards, and the journey up to the New York *Post* was like traversing the back stage of a Broadway show.

The glamor stopped abruptly the moment Kate got inside her new office. The reception area consisted of a functional metal desk behind which sat a dull-eyed girl who answered to the name of Kathleen. No wonder she looks depressed, thought Kate, if I was her, I'd be suffering from claustrophobia. For all around the desk, jostling for space in the cramped room, were telex machines, fax machines and overflowing filing cabinets.

Kate fought her way through to what she presumed was the main office and Chuck Holders's domain. She was right. And the moment she got there, she realized why all the office equipment had been bundled in with the receptionist. For the room that confronted her was not the kind of place where you would find a typewriter. No self-respecting typewriter would dare to inhabit a place like this.

The best way to describe Chuck Holders's office would be to say it resembled a turn-of-the-century bordello. The room was dominated by a vast walnut desk covered in gilt moldings. It had to be French Empire, Kate marveled, as she took a step forward to get a closer look. She ran her hand over the silky surface of the polished wood and took in the rest of the furnishings. In the corner was an imposing Louis Quinze bookcase. The tiny gilt and brocade chairs grouped around the desk were of the same period. Though for the life of her she couldn't identify the giant, padded leather monstrosity which towered behind the desk. All she did know was that it would probably be worth a fortune in a West End auction room.

What the hell was Holders playing at? she wondered. This wasn't a newspaper office at all. It belonged to a diplomat. Somebody who was in the habit of giving lavish receptions for visiting dignitaries. No wonder they pensioned him off, thought Kate grimly. The old man was clearly having delusions. In which case, she wondered, who did the work around the place? For there had been output from the London office. Every week the *Post* carried a London bulletin. From what she remembered of it, it was competent and reasonably well-informed. No, it was more than that. There were times when she had admired it for its slickness. Confused, she made her way back to the receptionist. Holders must have had an assistant. No doubt Kathleen would be able to locate him. But she didn't have to. For there, sitting at a second desk in the pokey little office, was the man she was looking for.

At first sight he looked like an elf. Or maybe a pixie out of a fairy tale. For when he got to his feet at Kate's approach, she noticed with a start that he was just a shade shorter than she was.

She suppressed a shudder. There was something about this man that gave her the creeps. He had one of those thin, intense faces and long, rather lank, blond hair. He looks as if he could do with a good bath, thought Kate. And that one judgment summed up the reason for her distaste. In Manhattan everyone showered. Sometimes more than once a day. Clean fingernails, shining hair, collars with not a speck of dandruff. These were the outward signs that a person was okay. You could go ahead and do business with them.

The man standing in front of her had none of these attributes, and it was with a certain caution that Kate took hold of the hand he proffered.

"I'm Kate Kennedy," she said. "I guess you've been expecting me."

"I certainly have," he said warmly. "Let me introduce myself. The name's Boyle. Jeremy Boyle. I daresay you've gathered by now I'm the workhouse around here."

Kate couldn't resist smiling. "It wasn't that difficult to figure out," she said. "It doesn't look as if there was too much in the way of hard work coming out of there." She gestured toward Holders's office.

"Why should Chuck have to do any work," Jeremy said, "when he'd got me to do it for him? That's what I was paid for."

Kate drew in her breath. Clearly the time had come to set a few ground rules. "Look," she said, "I don't know what Chuck Holders did for the bureau. And frankly I don't care. It was before my time and anyway it's none of my business. What I intend to do is another story."

Jeremy's eyes narrowed. "And what exactly do you intend to do?"

Oh Christ, Kate thought. I've stepped on his toes. He thinks he'll be out of a job. Aloud she said, "Relax, will you? I'm not going to do anything that will alter your life dramatically. I'm very happy with the stuff you've been producing. I just don't think you should be producing it singlehandedly. I've come here to add to your efforts, not to replace you."

Jeremy looked unconvinced. "But what more can you get out of Europe? My weekly bulletin covers just about everything that goes on in the territory. Why don't you just leave me alone to get on with it?"

Kate sighed. She'd been in her new office for just over an hour and already she had problems. If she'd known Jeremy Boyle better she would have realized just how serious they were.

Jeremy was a product of the English aristocracy gone wildly wrong. The youngest child of a wealthy landowner, he had had the benefit of an education at Eton followed by the discipline of the brigrade.

All it did for him was give him a taste for strong drink and spending his father's money. His father didn't give up on him. Not at first, anyway. A job was found for him at a reputable merchant bank, and while he learned his profession he was given a generous allowance. The whole exercise was doomed to failure. For Jeremy wasn't in the least interested in the City. To him it was a boring, joyless place. He was far more interested in racetracks and casinos and gossiping in nightclubs. It didn't take his employers long to detect this. It didn't take them long to fire him either, despite the entreaties of his well-connected father.

Jeremy Boyle found his own level when the man who ran the William Hickey gossip column on the *Daily Express* picked him up in Annabel's. Jeremy was high at the time. High and drunk and full of gossip. He managed to trash half a dozen of his close acquaintances and two members of his family that night. The contents of the conversation filled Hickey for the next three days. After that Martin Sykes, who ran the column, had little choice but to take young Jeremy on the staff.

It was an inspired choice. Jeremy might have been consistently late. Some days he didn't bother to appear in the office. But when he did, he contributed more than the entire staff put together.

For Jeremy it was an amusing enough diversion. He couldn't say he enjoyed working. He was too fundamentally idle for that. But he was beginning to acquire expensive habits. Champagne cocktails at noon. Whisky and water at sundown. And after that a snort or two of cocaine to give the night an added brightness. Lately he had discovered he was needing more and more of the white powder to put him in the right frame of mind. And the stuff cost so much. He considered asking his father to increase his allowance and rejected the idea. Cocaine was not an expense Father would understand.

So to the despair of his family, Jeremy went on with his Fleet Street career. He might have gone on being indiscreet about his friends for the rest of his life if he hadn't run into Chuck Holders in El Vino's. Holders had just lost his assistant and was loudly bemoaning the fact that he was going to have to buckle down and do some hard work. Had he not been drinking Bollinger Jeremy would have ignored the whining old American. As it was, he wormed his way into Holders's group and was halfway through his third glass when he heard something which caught his attention. He heard how much Holders was prepared to pay his new assistant. It was half as much again as Jeremy was earning.

By the time he left the Fleet Street wine bar he had set up lunch with Holders. Two weeks later he handed in his resignation to the *Express*. He had a job on an American newspaper and as far as he was concerned he had arrived. The hours were short. The pay was high. And there was only one sleepy old boss to fool, instead of a whole battery of suspicious executives.

Until Kate Kennedy came on the scene. He took a dislike to her the moment he set eyes on her. There was something sharp about her. And it wasn't just the cut of her vulgar American clothes either. The woman had brains. Worse that that, she was streetwise, he could tell that just by talking to her. Who did she think she was fooling with that line about adding to his efforts? It was as plain as the nose on his face that she'd come here to replace him.

All she wanted was for him to stay in position until she had learned her way around the town. Then it would be goodbye and good luck.

Well, we'll see about that, he thought, looking at her from under his eyelashes. But nobody gets rid of Jeremy Boyle without paying a price.

Over the next few days, Kate learned her way around the office. Most of the stuff in the files was badly out of date and she made her first decision. She threw everything out and registered with the Press Association library. Most of the national newspapers used it to double-check their own services. And Kate felt a whole lot better once she'd done it.

Such was her mounting confidence that she finally made up her mind to do something about her new office. Holders's old room reminded her increasingly of a mausoleum. The stiff, dark brocade curtains, magnificent though they were, cut out most of the daylight. And she felt uncomfortable working on a desk that probably cost more than her apartment in New York. She summoned Jeremy Boyle, who came shuffling in, looking decidedly the worse for wear. Standing there, rubbing the sleep out of his eyes, he resembled a small, quivering rodent. Stifling her distaste, Kate arranged her features into an expression of welcome.

"Jeremy," she said pleasantly. "What are we going to do about this furniture of Chuck's?"

He looked surprised. "Why, don't you like it?"

"I like it all right. I just don't think it's right in an office." She smiled. "It doesn't exactly encourage a girl to do any hard work. Well, not any hard newspaper work, anyway!"

Jeremy sat himself down on one of the tiny gilt chairs and started to look pleased. "I think I've got some good news for you," he said. "By the early part of the afternoon you won't be seeing any of it any more."

She looked puzzled. "I'm not with you."

"Didn't anyone tell you?" he said absently. "The removal men are coming around to the office at lunchtime to take it all away."

"On whose orders?" she said suspiciously.

"Chuck's. He was very attached to his little bits and pieces. The powers-that-be in New York are letting him have them as a condition of his retirement. The whole thing was settled months ago. I'm surprised Hartmann didn't tell you about it."

"I think we had enough to talk about without discussing the office furniture," said Kate.

Nevertheless she felt uneasy about the situation. She wondered if Hartmann or anyone else from the American office had set eyes on Chuck Holders's antiques. If they had, they might not have been so eager to give them away, she thought.

Then she thought, the hell with it. Who am I to look a gift horse in the mouth? With this stuff out of the way, this office can finally clean up its act.

In her mind's eye, she saw a solid, clean desk of pine

or maybe teak. On one side she would put a large electric typewriter. On the other would go the telex machines. It was high time she was sitting next to them, not Jeremy Boyle.

Her eyes wandered through to the outer office to see if there was anything else she could rearrange. The first thing her eyes fell upon were piles of out-of-date news magazines and old editions of the *Post* stacked untidily on the floor. Her optimism started to collapse. It would take months, rather than days, to come to grips with the chaos. And she was running out of time.

New York had given her just three weeks to clear the decks and start filing good stories from Europe. Her heart skipped a beat. Europe, she thought, I don't even know London yet. The first stirring of panic started to prickle under her skin. Boyle must have caught her mood for he moved in. Fast.

"What you need," he said soothingly, "is a drink. A nice, strong drink with lots of ice." He looked at his watch. "It's nearly lunchtime. Why don't I take you across town to the American bar at the Savoy? We can drown our sorrows there and if you're in the mood I can fill you in a bit more about the job."

Kate was sorely tempted. Once the moving men got in, the place would be uninhabitable. Why don't you face it, she told herself. Love him or hate him there's still an awful lot to be learned from Jeremy.

So she picked her bag up, put on her best smile and told Jeremy it was a date. "While you're at it," she said, "why don't we stay at the Savoy for lunch? It will give us a chance to get to know each other."

*　　　*　　　*

At that lunch Kate made several new discoveries about her deputy. All of them worried her. The first thing she realized was that Jeremy knew his way around. His suggestion that they lunch at the Savoy had not been the random choice of a bored lackey. Jeremy had chosen to take her there because he knew they stood a chance of bumping into some of the prime movers in Fleet Street. For this was their lunchtime watering hole.

When editors talked to editors they did so at the Savoy Grill room. This grand, rather austere, dining area with its huge circular tables set well apart from each other was the perfect place to entertain a cabinet minister or talk turkey with the chairman of the board. It was a serious restaurant, a masculine restaurant, and Jeremy knew better than to push his luck by lunching there.

Instead he took Kate into the hotel's main restaurant—a graceful, elaborate room overlooking the river. The Savoy restaurant was every bit as impressive as the Grill, but like the swimming pool room in The Four Seasons it had overtones of show business. The movers and shakers still came here, but it was to enjoy themselves rather than to plan the next edition of tomorrow's newspaper. As they walked through to their table, Jeremy waved hello to Sir David English, the editor of the *Mail,* who was lunching with his star columnist, Lynda Lee-Potter. Lynda, who was unfailingly polite, returned the greeting as Jeremy knew she would. Sir David smiled distantly, but it was enough to establish an acquaintance. Jeremy also gave the big hello to Bob Edwards, who currently edited the *Sunday Mirror* but in his time had edited more newspapers in Britain than anyone else.

Bob also acknowledged Jeremy. The hard man of

the popular press had a notoriously bad memory for both names and faces and always returned a greeting just in case. By the time they had gotten to their table, Jeremy had waved and smiled to a prominent diplomat, a TV announcer and a member of parliament. Kate was beginning to feel irritated. She wondered if Jeremy hadn't stage-managed his entrance to put her down in some way. No, that was ridiculous. The little rat wasn't here to score points. He was here to make sure he still had a job. At least that's what she thought. Yet as lunch progressed, she began to wonder.

Jeremy, who seemed to be on first-name terms with the head waiter, decided to choose the meal for them. Asparagus in cheese sauce. Rare roast beef from the trolley. Sherry trifle. It was a traditional meal meant for a lavish expense account. Kate, who normally avoided a heavy meal in the middle of the day, was appalled. The presumption of the man took her breath away.

She was attempted to cut in and put a stop to the whole charade, but something inside her, some instinct, told her not to. Jeremy was putting on a show for her. There had to be some reason why he was doing it. If she stopped the game now, she'd never find out what he was up to. So she let him call the wine waiter and demonstrate his knowledge of rare clarets.

Finally they got down to business. Boyle gave a good enough account of the running of the bureau. Primarily the *Post* relied on its network of correspondents. The paper had a reporter in every major European capital and each of them called in once or sometimes twice a day with the main news events in their territory.

London was Jeremy's responsibility and Kate was

surprised to discover just how well-connected he was. His experience on the *Express* had stood him in good stead. The man had tentacles in every field of influence. Politics, the City, show business, even the world of fashion. Kate suspected he gathered most of his material in Annabel's or at the racetrack, but then she thought, so what? The guy comes through with the goods, who cares where he gets them so long as he keeps them coming?

When the beef arrived, looking rare and somehow indecently overindulgent, Kate decided it was time to switch the conversation to her role in the running of things. For the moment, she told Jeremy, she was happy for him to go on masterminding the column. What she wanted to do was increase the paper's in-depth coverage of European events. Jeff Peterson, the New York *News*'s bureau chief, had done a revealing profile of Ken Livingstone, the controversial leader of London's GLC. The piece revealed Livingstone's ambitions to enter parliament and showed his dangerous determination to swing the Labor party further to the left.

"That's the kind of thing we should be doing," said Kate. "It's hard-hitting and it makes the way the British run their country look highly suspect. There are stories like that all over Europe. Not just in politics, either. If you look at any area and just keep on digging, you're bound to come up with something worth printing."

Jeremy tucked into his food and tried to look interested. He had heard the spiel before. Every visiting fireman was convinced that there was more to Europe than met the eye. They were probably right, though he hadn't met one who had succeeded in getting the in-depth features they kept spouting on about. When it came down to it, it was so much easier, so much more comfortable to file a snappy, newsy column from London. All the correspondents he ever met settled for just that. He suspected Kate would be the same and told her so.

She was stunned. What was the matter with the guy? Wasn't he trying to keep his job? "Look," she said, doing her best to be patient. "I know a lot of the foreign boys go in for the quiet life. But I can name you one who doesn't—Jeff Peterson at the *News*. Why do you think Hartmann sent me over here in the first place? The material coming out of London hasn't been enough to compete with his operation. Peterson's office comes through with the in-depth stories in addition to covering the news headlines. And that's what we're going to do."

A movie actress with candy-floss hair and a forty-inch bustline pushed her way past their table. Once more, Jeremy's social smile flashed to attention. The actress blew kisses. Kate blew her top. "For God's sake, will you try to pay attention to what I'm trying to tell you!"

He looked contrite. "I'm sorry, Kate. It's just that you make the whole thing sound like so much hard work. It was never like this in Chuck Holders's time."

Then he took a look at her face and realized he had gone too far. Quickly he put his smile back on again. "Okay, Kate, for you I'll work harder. Scout's honor." Then he added, "This Jeff Peterson's putting up a pretty impressive show. I hear he's quite a character, though I've never run into him myself."

Kate smiled. "Yes, you could say Jeff Peterson was a character."

She thought back to the first time she had met him.

She had been working for the *News* for over a year when Ted sent her to Washington to profile the new senator for international affairs. She'd been green in those days and the idea of a political story terrified her. "I've never interviewed a senator before," she had protested. "How do I start?"

Ted just grinned. "Try looking up the guy who runs our Washington office. He'll fill you in on what makes senators tick. If you're nice to him, he might even take you to dinner."

Those were the days when she was in love with Ted. And she wasn't all that interested in cozy dinners in Washington. No matter what the guy was like.

The guy turned out to be Jeff Peterson. And from the moment she first met him she was enchanted. It wasn't a physical attraction that drew her to him. He was pudgy with thick spectacles and crazy hair that seemed to stand permanently on end. But the guy had charm and the warmth of someone who wanted to share. And share he did. In her two short days in Washington she learned about the way her country was run. And by whom. Jeff Peterson personally made it his business that she knew all there was to know about the subject.

During her years on the *News*, Kate went back to Washington time and time again. And when she was there, Jeff Peterson made it his business to watch over her. She suspected he had found her attractive. But he never pushed it. Like everyone else on the paper he had heard the rumors about her and Ted.

Kate came to rely on her friendship with the Washington chief. For her, Jeff Peterson was a kind of refuge. A cozy retreat from the harshness of her life in New York

City. She looked forward to her visits to America's political center. Then one day it all came to an end. Jeff Peterson got sent to London to head up the paper's European operation. Kate was pleased for him. This was the promotion he had been waiting for. She wished him all the luck in the world.

That was over a year ago. Now it was a different story. The business which had pushed them together, which had cemented their friendship, was now hell bent on tearing them apart. Jeff Peterson, the warmest friend she had ever known, was now her most deadly rival. She sighed and wished it were otherwise. The way this lunch was shaping up, her rivals were looking a damn sight more appetizing than her allies.

With an effort she concentrated her attention on Jeremy. This shallow little socialite was all she had to pull the bureau into line with Jeff's operation on the *News*. She devoted the rest of lunch to getting her house in order.

By the time coffee arrived Kate was exhausted. It wasn't that Jeremy was unwilling to help. His track record was living proof that he was more than equal to the job. It was just that he was so damn uninterested. Oh, he tried to sound involved. He made all the right noises, but they had a hollow ring to them.

As she signed the bill Kate wondered for the hundredth time what exactly Jeremy Boyle was up to. He was curiously silent in the taxi going back to the office. Something was on his mind and it was worrying him. When she caught Jeremy looking at his watch, Kate took the initiative. "If you tell me what the problem is," she said, "maybe I can help."

He looked shifty. "It's nothing." He paused. "No, actually there is something. I said I'd look in at a photocall at the Shaftesbury this afternoon. Tim Rice is putting on a new show and he wants to talk to the Press about it."

"Shouldn't you be there?"

"Well yes, but we were having lunch. I thought what you had to say to me was more important than some bloody press call. The PR can always fill me in about it afterward."

Kate looked concerned. "When did it start?"

"Now you ask, about five minutes ago. I can still make it if I hurry."

There was more to this new assistant of hers than she had thought. Maybe he was interested in working at the job after all and it had just been his manner that misled her. Kate realized it was going to take her time to get used to the English. Gathering her wits about her she took charge of the situation. She leaned forward in her seat and instructed the cab driver to make a detour. They would be going to the Shaftesbury Theater before Hanover Square.

Jeremy looked pathetically grateful. "Are you sure it's not going to make you late?" he said. "I can always hop out and grab another cab. It won't take me five minutes."

"Relax," she said. "I haven't got anything too urgent for this afternoon . . . except maybe cleaning up after the movers and making arrangements for some new office furniture."

The bright social smile she had seen at the Savoy flashed across his face, lighting it up like a beacon. "Yes, you will need some new things for the office. Quite a lot of things, I would say."

Then before she could ask him exactly what he meant, the taxi drew up outside the theater and Jeremy was out in the street. "Toodeloo," he called, "see you in a bit." Then he was gone.

When Kate finally arrived back at Vogue House it was nearly four. Ploughing past the reception desk, she made straight for her office and the phone. She was supposed to have checked in with New York half an hour ago. She hoped the foreign editor hadn't disappeared into a meeting.

However, when she reached her phone, all concern for the foreign editor flew out of the window. For the office was not only devoid of Chuck Holders's treasures. It had been stripped completely bare. Every scrap of furniture, including the desk, had gone. There were no pictures on the walls and, she remembered with the beginnings of alarm, there had been a couple of important oil paintings among them. She looked down, and panic set in. The lush Persian carpet which must have cost thousands had been rolled up and taken away.

Chuck Holders might have been a faithful servant to the company, but this kind of retirement present only happened to the chairman of the board. She ran into the outer office. "Kathleen," she said, "get me the Shaftesbury Theater on the phone. And do it quickly. I want to speak to Jeremy."

Five minutes later the box office was on the line. They were even more confused than Kate. There was no press conference scheduled for today. Nobody from the New York *Post* had turned up. And what did she mean, a new Tim Rice show? *The Revenge* had just started its run and they were taking box office bookings for the following year.

Kate slammed the phone down, and turned to Kathleen. "Have you any idea where Jeremy might be?" she demanded. "Does he keep a schedule of his appointments?"

Kathleen looked blank. It was her usual expression and did nothing for Kate's temper.

"Well, say something," she screamed, "even if it's only that you don't know."

"I don't know," the girl wailed. "I'm only temping here. It's not my business to know anything."

"I suppose you're going to tell me," said Kate through clenched teeth, "that you don't know about the moving men either."

Kathleen's expression told her everything she needed to know.

"God give me strength! On every side I'm surrounded by halfwits. Look, get me New York on the line. Now. I want to speak to Hughes Hartmann. And if you get through and he's not available, I want you to try again and again and again until he comes to the phone. Do I make myself clear?"

The receptionist nodded. Five minutes later Hartmann was on the phone. "What's the matter?" he said. "Where's the fire? I just had some hysterical English broad ranting in my ear that you had to speak to me or else the world would fall apart. Have you all gone crazy over there?"

"Maybe," said Kate grimly, "but before I tell you

my problems, there are a couple of questions I want to ask you."

"Fire away."

"Okay, first, how much did Chuck Holder spend on fixing up his office with all those antiques and stuff?"

The answer took her breath away. The old foreign correspondent had spent close to half a million dollars. "Why so much?" she asked. "He didn't need all that stuff. It's not as if he was a diplomat or anything."

Hartmann's sigh crackled over the connection. "I know, I know," he said, "it all happened twenty years ago, before I was in the Chair. The powers that be at the time wanted to invest some money in Europe. What better investment than English antiques?"

Kate felt a pulse throbbing at the base of her neck. She took a deep breath. "Did you have any arrangement with Chuck Holders over the antiques? I mean, did you promise to give him any of the stuff as a kind of retirement present?"

Hartmann roared with laughter. "Good God, no. The *Post* might be making fat profits, but we're not in the business of giving them away to charity. Anyway Chuck doesn't need any bonuses. The pension we're giving him will keep him in caviar for the rest of his life."

"In that case," said Kate as calmly as she could. "I've got some bad news for you. We've just been robbed."

It took the police three weeks to draw a blank. They went straight to Chuck Holders at his retirement cottage in the Cotswolds. But endless questioning by uniformed men and plain clothes detectives yielded nothing. Sure he had accumulated the antiques over the past twenty years. Certainly he had paid for them with the New York *Post*'s money—he could even produce the receipts.

But as far as their disposal was concerned, he simply hadn't a clue. The fancy office, like the expense account lunches, was something that went with the job. And when he kissed goodbye to the *Post,* he put the perks that went with it firmly behind him. He would no more take the office furniture than he would rob a bank.

But somebody had taken it. And both Kate and the police had a shrewd idea who it was. The finger pointed firmly in the direction of Jeremy Boyle. Why else would he have lied to Kate about Holders's non-existent arrangement to take the stuff with him? And where was he anyway?

For Jeremy Boyle had seemingly disappeared into thin air. He didn't turn up at the office the following day. And subsequent investigation revealed that he was not at his flat. The three-room apartment in Notting Hill Gate had been taken over by an Australian couple. The previous occupant had left no forwarding address.

Jeremy's father, the Hon. Timothy Boyle, could shed no light on his whereabouts either. He and his youngest son had never been particularly close and the merchant banker preferred it that way. He despised the way Jeremy earned his living. And as for his private life, well, it was better that he kept it private. He had two daughters of marriageable age. He didn't want Jeremy's sordid reputation ruining their chances.

Even the receptionist, the feeble-minded Kathleen, proved to be a dead end. Boyle had hired her from an agency and told her nothing.

Kate had been conned and she knew it. And by the

oldest trick in the book. Bright, tough Kate Kennedy, the veteran of office politics, the scourge of New York journalism, had been taken in by a cheap hustler. And she had been so overwhelmed by her new responsibilities, so concerned about throwing her weight around, that she didn't even see him coming.

She spent the next weeks in self-castigation. It didn't matter that the insurance company paid for the losses. It didn't matter that she was absolved of every scrap of blame by the *Post*. She had been taken for a fool and she couldn't forgive herself for it.

Jeremy Boyle had found her a ground floor apartment in Chelsea Cloisters, off the Kings Road. She moved out of it as soon as she could. The tiny house in Eaton Mews was a higgledy-piggledy affair but anything was better than something Boyle had found.

Her lowest point came two weeks after the robbery. A detective inspector came by the office with a photograph of Jeremy Boyle. It had been taken two days previously in Marbella. Could she positively identify it?

Kate could. And when she did, she was filled with feelings of hatred and revenge. She had rehearsed time and time again what she would say to him when she was finally face to face with him. The fact that she was never going to get that chance was carefully explained to her by the young, round-faced detective. In fact while the robbery was going on he was having lunch at the Savoy with Kate herself. No, all the evidence they had was the fact that he worked at the *Post* and he had lied to Kate about a press conference and Holders's fictitious arrangements about the furniture. But that was her word against his.

"Can't you take him in for questioning?" asked Kate desperately. "You know where he is. Surely it's a simple matter to arrest him and do a little interrogation."

The young policeman spread his hands. "If Mr. Boyle was anywhere but Spain, we could do it. But for us it's a no-go area. Britain has no extradition arrangement with that country, more's the pity. There are far bigger fish than Boyle toasting themselves in the sun over there. But we can't lay our hands on them.

"No, unless your Mr. Boyle decides to visit London there's no way we can touch him, let alone ask him any questions."

And that was that. Kate was stymied. Not only was she denied the pleasure of getting even with Jeremy, she couldn't even replace him. For she knew no one in London at all. She had no friends except Jeff Peterson, and as his archrival she could hardly call him for help with her operation. There were no contacts either. She had left New York in such a hurry that she had given herself no time at all to prepare her ground.

In the normal course of events somebody at the office would have had a friend who worked in London. Her new colleagues would have had counterparts in Europe. If she had given herself a week or two, Kate would have arrived with ten useful phone numbers and a working knowledge of whom to call if she was in a bind.

But she had well and truly burned her bridges. And now she was all alone with her pride. In the end Kate did the only thing that was open to her. She worked harder. The hell with Ted Gebler for not loving her enough. The hell with Jeremy Boyle for robbing her. The hell with the entire human race. This was the biggest chance Kate had to prove herself to the rest of the world. She wasn't going to screw it up.

She set up a schedule for herself. In the mornings she collated all the material from her European correspondents. The London news she took from Reuters or the Press Association. During the lunch hour she grabbed a sandwich at her desk and wrote a daily column.

The moment it was on the wires she moved into stage two of her day. Lining up the big interview or the in-depth report. She read every news medium she could lay her hands on. She had her stringers in Europe send them over by Air Express. She might not have had the time to write a column and do the in-depth coverage the bureau so badly needed. But if she knew what was going on she could commission it.

For the first three months of her posting Kate ran her show like a World War One fighter pilot. Every day she struggled with a hundred insoluble problems. And every day—she had no idea how—she pulled through. But the job took its toll. She ate little. Slept less. And was constantly on the alert. If she had had the time to look in a mirror during those days she might have been alarmed at what she saw. For the New York *Post*'s new bureau chief was a thin, pasty-faced woman with badly bitten fingernails and straggly hair that looked as if it was in need of a good shampoo.

When Jeff Peterson finally ran into her at an American Embassy press briefing he could hardly believe his eyes. "For heaven's sake, Kate, what have you done to yourself?" he exclaimed. He hadn't changed. He still looked like an absent-minded professor. And he still cared about her. "You haven't been ill or something, have you?"

"Of course I haven't," she said quickly. "I've just been busy."

He grabbed a glass of champagne and led her over to a chair. "I know you've been busy," he said patiently. "I read the papers. And I must say you're doing a good job. But what else has happened to you? You look like you've aged ten years. And why haven't you been in touch? I called your office a couple of times and your secretary always tells me you're tied up. What's going on?"

She put her head in her hands. "Jeff, it's a long story. And I don't even know if I should be telling you anyway."

For a moment Jeff was totally confused. This wasn't the Kate he knew at all. The girl he remembered was chic and pretty and spilling over with self-confidence. If he wasn't careful, the Kate that was sitting in front of him now would have a nervous breakdown. Maybe her new responsibility was too much for her.

"Kate," he said softly, "I think you need help. I don't know what your problems are, but whatever's gone wrong in your life has had a bad effect on you. Look, are you doing anything later on? Because if you're free I'd like to buy you dinner. Right now I think you could use a friend."

She nodded weakly. "I think you're right," she said.

They arranged to meet at the American Club in Piccadilly at 7:30 P.M. Kate had planned on going home after work to change. But as always something came up. This time it was a major scandal in the Italian movie set. The story had been covered by *International American,* Rome's English language paper. Kate spent nearly two hours haggling over the American publishing rights for the piece. And when she finally tied up the deal she was exhausted.

All she really wanted to do was go home and fall into bed, and for a moment she was tempted to call Jeff and put him off.

Then she reconsidered. She was fond of the guy. He was the first friendly face she had seen in the past three months. And now that she had found him, she didn't want to lose sight of him.

So she washed her face in the rather primitive office bathroom. Ran a comb through her hair and pulled it back into a ponytail. Then she prayed she'd get her second wind by the time she reached Piccadilly.

The moment she walked into the American Club Kate realized she should have made more effort. The huge, airy hall with its marble floor, its atmosphere of money, reminded her of a brownstone in the Seventies. The bar, furnished almost entirely with expensive leather sofas, intensified the image. She could have been back in New York. With a rush of homesickness she wished she were.

London had taken the color out of her cheeks and the bounce out of her step. She felt like somebody's country cousin. Then she caught sight of Jeff Peterson and she hoped she didn't look it. For Peterson was not alone. Sitting drinking what looked like a whisky and water was a tall, expensive-looking man with graying hair. There was something familiar about him. Then she remembered. It was the British agent who had rescued her the night she finally came face to face with Sandy Gebler. That was one party she would carry with her to the grave.

She took another look across the room. The face was definitely the same. Hard-looking. A face that was used to calling the shots. Yet she remembered a sense of humor too. She searched her mind. What was his name. Charlie. Yes, Charlie, she was sure of it now. Champagne Charlie, she thought ruefully. Except you were just the opposite. You stopped me from drinking my way to oblivion. What was it he had said? "You don't really want to go on being shown up in public by your lover's wife." Then he had taken her out to dinner.

Jeff Peterson brought her back to the present. He was on his feet, curly hair standing on end. And he was coming toward her. "So you finally got here," he said. "I'm glad, even if you are half an hour late."

"I'm sorry. There was a problem at the office. It took a while to sort it out."

Out of the corner of her eye she saw Charlie watching them. And she knew he had recognized her too. Without thinking, her hand went up to her hair. She unfastened the clip holding it back from her face and the whole mass of it swung loose around her shoulders.

It was a theatrical gesture. She knew that. A bit flashy. Not really worthy of her. Yet she was still glad she'd remembered to shampoo her hair that morning.

"Charlie," she said, "how nice to see you after all this time."

And it was nice. More than nice. She had forgotten how attractive he was. Then she pulled herself up short.

She was just recovering from an affair with a married man. She had no intention of repeating the experience.

Charlie Hamilton got to his feet. She noticed he was smiling. "Of all the people in the world," he said, "you are the very last I expected to run into. What are you doing so far from home? If that's not an impertinent question."

"Not at all, I work here. As of three months ago I've been running the European desk for the *Post.*"

Once more she noticed the warm smile. The one with the sense of humor.

"And how do you like London?" he asked.

"I like it a whole lot better since I ran into Jeff. You have no idea what problems I've had."

"You sound as if you could do with a drink." He sat down, indicating that she should do the same. Then he signaled the waiter. "If my memory serves me right, it's a glass of champagne. Or have you changed your tastes since I last saw you?"

"No," she said, looking at him hard, "I haven't changed my tastes."

Then she stopped herself again. He'll think I'm flirting, she thought. And he'd be right. She rearranged her face. "Champagne would be fine," she said, "if it's okay with Jeff."

"Of course it's okay," said Jeff. Then he looked at Kate and said, "I'd no idea you two knew each other."

"We don't really," said Kate. "We ran into each other at a play in New York. Then we just sort of lost contact. It's not difficult when you live that far away."

Then she remembered the flowers he had sent her the morning after that hazy, drunken night. Without thinking, she said, "How is your wife, Charlie? Fiona was her name, wasn't it?"

His face froze, the hard features taking on a remote quality. There was a silence, and when he spoke again, his voice had a guarded, neutral quality.

"My wife, I'm afraid, is dead," he said. "She was killed in a hunting accident the end of last year."

So that was why he didn't call, thought Kate. There I was expecting to meet the grand English lady, the childhood sweetheart. And instead of visiting New York, she was back home being buried.

"OhmyGod, I'm sorry," she said, the words coming out in a rush. "I had no idea."

Hamilton put down his drink and stood up. "Don't be embarrassed. It was rough at the time, but I'm all in one piece now . . . if you don't look too closely."

Then before she could say anything else he was walking away from the table. And out of her life. A handsome, busy man on his way to another appointment. "See you around," he said. "Enjoy your dinner."

Kate stared at Jeff, a faint smile on her face. "That's the second time in the last six months I've felt like a complete and utter idiot."

Jeff lit a cigarette and handed it to her. "Tell me about the first time."

"Jeremy Boyle was the first time," she said. "Then I thought all of London knew about it. That shyster's neat little rip-off didn't exactly go unnoticed in Fleet Street. The *Evening Standard* even ran a small item about it in their journal. I suspect it was an even bigger item around the bar in El Vino's."

So that's it, thought Jeff. That's where the problem

started. He leaned closer to her. "Tell me what happened after Boyle left. No, delete that. Tell me how you felt when Boyle took off."

She made a face. "How do you think I felt? I was completely shattered. Here I was, a new girl in London in a big new job, and suddenly the roof caves in. It wasn't easy, I can tell you."

"So why didn't you call me? You know my number. At least you know the number of the office. I was surprised not to hear from you."

The waiter came over with the half-finished bottle of champagne and topped up their glasses. For once Kate didn't stop him. She was beginning to let go and it felt good.

She took a fresh sip of her drink. "How could I call you, Jeff? We're on opposite sides of the fence now. I was sent into Europe by the *Post* to give you a run for your money. How would it have looked if I had started yelling for help my first week?"

"I see what you mean," he said, "though I can't begin to agree with it. Anyway, we'll come back to that later. Go on with your story. How did you cope, when to my knowledge you didn't go asking for help from anyone else around town?"

She looked at him. "You really want to know?"

He nodded.

"Okay, then, I'll tell you. I coped on my own. It was sheer stubbornness, I guess, but I wasn't going to let the little bastard and his cheap conman trick get the better of me."

Jeff was astonished. "You can't mean it. You're not

honestly informing me that you write a daily column and organize features without any help."

"Well, that's not strictly true. I do have a great team of stringers around Europe. I would have been lost without them."

He looked at her with something approaching awe. "But you run the show, don't you, Kate? You make all the decisions and handle all the flak from New York." He scratched his head. "I always said you were crazy. Ballsy yes, but completely out of your mind."

She laughed. "Do you mind telling me what you mean?"

"Not in the least, but I'd rather do it over dinner. I don't know about you, but I'm starving."

Now that Kate had time to think about food, she realized she hadn't eaten at all that day. It was with a certain relief that she allowed Jeff to propel her up the curving polished-wood staircase to the dining room. It was full that night. Expatriate American men and their expensively dressed wives were out in force and Kate wondered why they thronged to the place. It couldn't have been to remind themselves of home. The formal dining room with its glittering chandeliers and vast, expensive oil paintings was about as English as you could get.

Then she looked at the menu and she realized what all the fuss was about. Every favorite American dish she had ever had was there. Pecan pie, Maine lobster, soft-shelled crab, black-eyed peas. Even corned beef hash. She remembered the last time she had eaten it—at the "21" Club with Ed Kramer. And she decided to skip it. There were some old home experiences she could do without.

She turned to her companion and gave him a friendly once-over. "I can see you haven't changed. You're still carrying ten pounds of extra weight around. I always told you it was bad for your health."

"Look who's talking. Did anyone ever tell you you're starting to look like a scarecrow?" Then he stopped what he was saying. "I'm sorry, I didn't mean that. It was damned rude of me. Ever since we met again I've been going on about how terrible you're looking. You must think I've turned into a boar."

Now it was her turn to stop and think. "I don't, you know. Quite the opposite if you must know. I think you care, though I can't for the life of me imagine why."

He grinned and motioned the hovering waiter to go away. "Then you are a sillier woman than I thought. Has it ever occurred to you that I'm your friend first and your newspaper rival second? I've been meaning to talk to you about this all evening, and I'm going to get it off my chest now even if we do have to wait to order dinner.

"Look, Kate, you and I are wage slaves. We work for other people. But that doesn't mean they own us. Nor does it mean we have to believe everything they tell us. I bet before you came here Hartmann gave you some line about annihilating the competition, meaning me. Well, that's baloney. You don't have to annihilate me and I don't have to screw you into the ground in order to insure that our respective papers get good European coverage. They'll get that anyway. And they'll get it because we're both good operators who know what we're doing. Not because we want to wipe each other off the face of the earth. That kind of crap's for college kids with no self-discipline. We grew out of that years ago."

She looked at him. "Have you finished?"

"Yeah, I guess that just about wraps it up."

"Good," she said, "then maybe we can get something to eat. By the way, thanks for the lecture. I hadn't thought about it that way before. I guess I needed to hear it."

He leaned back in his chair and signaled the waiter. Then with a certain amount of relief they both ordered dinner.

But Jeff hadn't finished with her. "I think maybe it will help you if you put the Jeremy Boyle thing into perspective," he said. "It's one thing to be conned. But to be conned and not have any idea why—that's bad for the soul."

"OK," she said, "lay the whole thing out for me."

He put his soup spoon down and wiped his mouth with his napkin. "I think the first thing you have to understand," he said, "is that people like Jeremy simply don't exist in New York. Our town's full of achievers and doers. People with goals who are hell-bent on reaching them. The Jeremys of this life just aren't like that. His family must have once had goals they wanted to reach. But that was generations ago. They've arrived now. Or at least they feel they've arrived. So their offspring aren't exactly driven to go out and prove themselves."

"So you mean Jeremy really didn't want to do a job."

"That's for sure he didn't."

"So what in God's name was the little shit doing dirtying his hands working for the *Post*?"

Jeff smiled. "He had to. Our friend had a taste for

cocaine, and we all know how much that costs. I also happen to know there was no way old man Boyle was going to fund the habit, even if he knew about it. So there was nothing else to do. The boy had to work."

Kate looked at her companion. "Did he have to steal for it too?"

Jeff shrugged. "Why not? All Jeremy was interested in was the money—he wasn't particularly concerned with his professional reputation. So when he found an easier and quicker way of getting the money, he went for it."

Kate lit another cigarette. Talking about her former assistant made her nervous. Nevertheless, her curiosity was aroused. "Tell me," she asked, "was our friend Jeremy any good at what he did?"

"If you're asking if his departure damaged the *Post*'s London operation, I'm afraid I have to say it did. The little shyster had a ratlike instinct for a story. He was born with it—you don't teach that kind of thing in school."

Kate looked surprised. "Are you trying to tell me he didn't have any formal training for the job?"

"Not really. Listen, Kate, I know we Americans take our college education very seriously. You majored in journalism, didn't you?"

She nodded.

"Well, that kind of thing doesn't cut any ice over here. I'm not saying it doesn't help. Most editors, given the choice, go for a graduate. But they don't close their eyes to naturals either. Lynda Lee-Potter of the *Mail* was an actress before she went into newspapers. Anne de Courcy, the class act on the *Evening Standard*, didn't have any training, either. The woman actually taught herself everything she knows. And we're talking about a heavy-weight, Kate, not just some assistant. The British place a great value on talent. And over here all you need to make it in the newspaper business is just that. Plus a certain knowledge of the street. Jeremy had both. In fact the only real difference between you and Jeremy as professionals is that he knows the territory. And you don't."

"So what do I do about it?"

"You come to me for help. Jeremy Boyle's not the only decent reporter in Fleet Street, you know. I could name half a dozen just as clever as him and they don't put their fingers in the till either."

She started to interrupt, but he held up his hand. "Remember all that stuff about us being friends first and rivals second. I meant it, you know. Kate, I've decided to make it my business to find you a new assistant. The office doesn't have to know about it. And if a whisper of this gets out, we can both deny it. Nobody can prove anything."

"Well," she said slowly, "it would make things easier." Then as the idea took hold she broke into a broad grin. "Jeff Peterson," she said, "I don't care who you find or what they look like. I'm leaving the whole thing entirely in your hands. Just find me a decent deputy fast. I can't go on like this much longer."

11

Jeff Peterson was as good as his word. The following afternoon he called Kate at home and gave her a list of three possible candidates for the job of her assistant. He had spoken to them all that morning. They were all first class journalists. They knew the town backward and forward. And they were all interested.

Before she picked up the phone to arrange meetings, Kate looked over the list again. The favorite choice was Claud Becker. Currently an assistant editor on the *Express,* he was feeling frustrated and wanted to get back into the field. Kate could see why. Becker had a superb track record. He had covered both the Vietnam war and the Six Day war in Israel for the *Daily Mail.* The *Express* had poached him from their closest rival because they could offer him what the *Mail* was unwilling to provide.

A base in London. Becker's wife, it seemed, got bored every time he went away on a foreign assignment. And because Elaine Becker was very beautiful, her boredom inevitably led to affairs. Claud begged the *Mail* for a London position, but his superiors found him too useful overseas. In the end when the *Express,* who knew of his predicament, offered him a job as a features executive he reluctantly accepted. Now he was restless again. He didn't want another foreign job, but he did want to get back to reporting.

The other two candidates were less impressive, but each one sounded like a suitable contender for the job. Doug Freeman, the arts editor on the *Financial Times,* had formidable contacts in both the City and the entertainment world. And Alan Baker was one of the hardest working freelancers in the business.

First thing on Monday morning, Kate contacted Claud Becker at the *Express.* He sounded more than pleased to hear from her and suggested a drink at the Connaught. They set a date for that Wednesday and when Kate had written it in her calendar she leaned back and heaved a sigh of relief.

Then she picked up the phone and dialed the *Financial Times.* Her training had taught her to cover her options. No matter how firm a solution looked on paper, she knew from experience that nothing was ever certain until it was in the bag. Becker looked like the obvious choice, but who knew? Maybe the *Express* would decide to up the ante and persuade him to stay.

Doug Freeman was as affable as Claud Becker. He too was looking forward to meeting Kate and suggested a drink on Friday evening after office hours. Once more she got out her calendar and made a note of the date.

That only left Alan Baker. Unlike the other two he was surprisingly difficult to contact. Each time she called, Kate was met with an answering machine. After she had left the second message she assumed Baker was away on an assignment and would get in touch when he returned. The situation didn't worry her. Her first and second choices were lined up and ready. By the time Baker finally got in touch, she'd probably have to tell him that the position had been filled. Now that she was on the way to solving her most pressing problem Kate decided to take stock of herself. Apart from needing three years' sleep and at least another ten pounds on her frame there wasn't that much wrong with her. Nothing a good gym and a sympathetic hairdresser couldn't fix.

Kate flicked through the latest issue of *Harper's and Queen,* the classy English glossy, and had no problem finding both. The gym was in Fulham Road, five minutes by taxi away from her little mews in Belgravia. The hairdresser was off Park Lane. She could get there during her lunch hour.

She decided on the hairdresser first. It would take at least three weeks in the gym to get herself back into shape. What she was in need of was a more immediate transformation.

Three days later, looking more or less like her old self, Kate arrived at the Connaught Hotel to meet Claud Becker. The Connaught had two bars. One just as you came in, where grand old duchesses would meet each other for a pre-prandial sherry. The other was at the back of the hotel and a more serious affair altogether. It was here that she had arranged to meet Claud Becker.

The bar consisted of two large rooms stuffed full of squashy sofas and little round tables, and was the kind of place where men of power met each other to clinch million-dollar deals. Or just shoot the breeze. Kate decided to shoot the breeze first. If Claud Becker looked half as good in the flesh as he did on paper she would clinch the deal later.

Becker had arrived first and she was gratified to see that he had taken the trouble to find out what she looked like. The moment she walked through the door he started signaling to her. She crossed the room to the corner table where he was sitting. Her first surprise was that Becker was smaller than she had imagined. And considerably older.

Her second was that he was three-quarters drunk. This fact made itself apparent early on in their conversation. It wasn't that Claud Becker lurched around or made himself unpleasant in any way. It was just that he kept forgetting things. He'd be halfway through a story about Golda Meir when he'd forget what he was saying. He'd talk about the Queen's press secretary and find himself reaching for the man's name.

Kate started to feel irritable. Claud Becker wanted to work with her, didn't he? So why was he blowing the whole thing by turning up loaded? She wondered if he was nervous. She'd heard of people who were wonderful when it came to doing the job, but terrible at the interview. So she stopped talking about newspapers and asked him about himself. Maybe that would relax him.

It did. But Claud Becker relaxed was an even more

daunting prospect than Claud Becker tense and trying
to impress. For when the man was off duty he liked to
tell jokes. They were the kind of jokes a circuit comic
tells when he's on the road. A second-rate circuit comic.
Some of the jokes were so old Kate had forgotten them.
Desperately she tried to get her guest back on to newspapers, but there was no stopping him. It was as if she had
wound up a clockwork doll. There was nothing for it but
to let him go until he had run out of steam.

She leaned back in her chair and tuned out. And as
she did so, she tried to imagine what it would be like to
have this man working for her. He was certainly well-
connected. Even half-drunk he had managed to drop all
the right names. He looked the part, although with his
thinning gray hair and florid complexion, nobody could
be blamed for thinking he was the bureau chief and Kate
the assistant.

Then she thought about his track record and wondered if she could live with his jokes. She decided she
couldn't. "Mr. Becker," she said, "may I ask you a personal question?"

"Be my guest."

She paused, wondering how to phrase it. Nervously
she cleared her throat. "Do you by any chance have a
drinking problem?" There was an audible silence.
Becker frowned. "Who told you about that?" he asked.
"I had no idea Jeff Peterson knew anything about it."

Kate kept quiet. The man had verbal diarrhea. With
any luck, he'd run his course—like he did with the
jokes—and tell her the whole story. Becker didn't disappoint her. The man had been a drinker all his life. But
a drinker who could handle it, until he was sent to Viet-

nam. The horrors he saw there drove him straight to the brandy bottle, and he went on a bender which lasted until he left the paper. Then came a period of drying out in an expensive clinic, followed by the call from the *Express.*

Kate suspected that far from headhunting Becker, the *Express* had taken him on because they knew the man was desperate for a job and the paper could get him cheap. She smiled inwardly. How different people look on paper from the way they do in real life. The man would never do, of course, but how could she tell him?

In the end, she took the coward's way out and told him she had to see a couple more candidates and would be in touch.

When she finally managed to get rid of Becker, who went in for long farewells, she felt both relieved and disappointed. It was becoming clear that she wasn't going to find a deputy as easily as she had thought. Then she thought, what the hell? Becker wasn't the only fish in the sea. She was bound to find the right person soon enough.

Kate met her next candidate on Friday at 6:30 P.M. in the bar of Burke's restaurant, off Bond Street. As befitted a man about town Doug Freeman was a member of the trendy club founded by Patrick Lichfield and Doug Hayward. The dimly lit bar was set slightly above the main restaurant, giving it an air of privacy. And when Kate arrived, Freeman was the only man in the place.

Even if the bar had been full, he would have stood out. He was a tall man, somewhere in his mid-thirties with springy brown hair and a profile that reminded her of Byron. The man was devastatingly good-looking and Kate suspected he knew it.

There was something a little over-confident about

the way he ordered her a glass of champagne, without asking if it was what she wanted. The fact that it was exactly what she had in mind irritated her even more.

I must concentrate, she told herself crossly, but she found it hard. For Doug Freeman made her feel as if she was out on a date. When she asked him about his background, he told her, but in a witty, anecdotal way, as if she were some favored guest, a pretty woman to be entertained, rather than a prospective employer.

The more attractive she found him, the more irritated she became. Finally she said. "Doug, I'm pretty impressed with your track record. But there's one thing that's worrying me. How do you feel about taking orders from a woman? Because that's what you would be doing if you came and worked for the *Post*."

He leaned forward and looked at her steadily. "I don't think that's something either of us have to get excited about. I've worked with women before without being emasculated." He raised his eyebrows. "In some cases the situation's been quite the reverse."

This time the sexual innuendo was unmistakable. Damn you, she thought. You're playing with me. And I'm sitting here letting you get away with it.

Freeman didn't seem to notice the cross expression on the American girl's face. Or if he did, it didn't seem to bother him. "If you're not doing anything," he said casually, too casually, "would you like to stay on here and have dinner with me?"

For a moment Kate hesitated. Burke's had one of the most delicious displays of hors d'oeuvres she had ever seen. There was cold asparagus, a dozen different salads, every kind of seafood. Then she changed her mind. For she had a hunch that the next item on the menu would be her. She glanced down at the bottle of champagne cooling by the side of the table. *I bet he'd have me served up stewed while he was at it.*

She suppressed the desire to giggle. "I'm sorry," she said as calmly as she could, "but I do have to be somewhere else right now." Then she shook his hand, promised to be in touch and hurried out of the restaurant. *It's too bad,* she thought, as she headed toward Bond Street. *The guy's got terrific credentials. He's just the right age. And I bet he's got a way with words. But how on earth can I hire him?* She remembered the too-confident way he had assumed she drank champagne. Before they'd even met properly. *No,* she thought. *If I hire Doug Freeman, he'll be giving me orders before I know it. In and out of bed.*

She hailed a cab and gave the driver her home address. When she got back she made herself a sandwich from the leftovers she found in the fridge and settled down to watch the ten o'clock news. But the problem kept on coming back to her. *She had to have an assistant. She couldn't go on the way she was. Not if she wanted to keep her sanity. So why was it so hard to find one?*

She spent all night tossing and turning and worrying about her future. *Why the hell had she decided to take this London position? She must have been a fool. There were easier jobs in America. Come to that, she might have stayed with the job she had.* Then she thought about Ted and the way he had betrayed her. And she knew she had no other choice. Whether she liked it or not, London was her only option. *She would just have to learn to live with it. Or die with it,* she thought morosely.

*   *   *

At eight o'clock the following morning Kate was brewing up coffee and thinking about going to the gym when the phone rang. Who on earth, she thought, would call her on a Saturday morning? Apart from Jeff Peterson, who went away every weekend, she knew no one in London.

She answered the phone and a pleasant rather quiet voice announced himself to be Alan Baker. As she thought, he *had* been out of town on a story. Now he was back and was curious to meet her. Her previous experiences had made her wary. She told him to call again on Monday when she was in the office. Kate was so frightened of being disappointed for a third time that she wanted to put off the moment for as long as possible.

The voice on the end of the phone wasn't having any. Monday was impossible. He was flying to Madrid for the *Observer* on Monday. Would Miss Kennedy wait till the end of the week? Then when he had dealt with the *Observer* perhaps they could work something out. He suggested the week after next.

Kate panicked. She'd been in London for three months and had achieved nothing. There was no guarantee that she was going to get anywhere if she met Baker before he left for Spain. But she had to give it a shot. It was the only one she had.

"How free are you this weekend?" she asked cautiously.

"How free do you want me to be?"

If Doug Freeman had said it, it would have sounded pushy. But the stranger on the other end of the phone wasn't showing any urgency. He was merely being practical.

Kate came to the point. "How about lunch today?" she suggested.

"That's fine by me. Do you have anywhere particular in mind?"

Kate thought hard. Where did Londoners go for lunch on Saturday? She thought of Langan's and dismissed it. Too chic for a weekend. The Carlton Tower? Too formal. Finally she said, "To be honest, I've no idea where to take you. I guess I'm new to this town. Forgive me."

Alan Baker laughed. "There's nothing to forgive. What kind of a meal do you want? Would you feel relaxed in a bistro? Or would a fish restaurant be more to your liking? I know a place in South Kensington where you can wear jeans and still feel formal."

"Sounds the kind of thing I had in mind, if I knew it existed."

"Fine then, we're on. It's called the Poissonerie and it's on Draycott Avenue by the side of Conran's. I'll book us a table. Does one o'clock suit you?"

Kate assured him it was fine and hung up. If the guy's credentials matched his telephone manner there might be hope for her yet. She rooted out a pair of suede jeans and threw on a casual checked shirt. Cowboy boots completed the look and when she set out for South Kensington she almost felt happy.

When the waiter led her to Alan Baker's table, she wondered if he had made a mistake. Then Baker stood up and held out his hand and she knew he was the right man. Just for a moment she was surprised. For Baker was black.

There was nothing tactful about Baker's looks. He wasn't coffee-colored. His features were in no way European. He was simply and without argument the most aggressive-looking, the most beautiful, the most proud-looking black man she had seen in a long time.

He offered her a seat and she took it. Then he smiled and indicated the bottle of Muscadet in front of him.

"I'd love a glass," she said. Then she settled back in her seat and took a closer look at this latest candidate for the job as her deputy.

"I wasn't quite what you were expecting, was I?"

She grinned. "I don't know yet. You haven't told me what you can do."

"Before I tell you that, why don't I fill you in on a couple of things I don't do. First, I don't drink. Not the way Claud Becker does, anyway. Second, I don't patronize women. Or try to seduce them. My wife would kill me if she thought I did."

Kate was confused. "How on earth did you know about Doug? And Claud Becker for Christ's sake."

"Lady, you're hiring a reporter, not a stenographer. First thing I did when I heard the job was up for grabs was to find out who the competition was. And I'm impressed. It's not a bad line-up. Not bad at all."

"Something tells me it doesn't faze you."

Now it was Baker's turn to smile. "Don't get me wrong," he said, "both those guys would have done a reasonable job for you. There might have been a couple of personal complications, of course. But you're a grown-up woman. You could have handled them."

"The thing that makes me different is that I don't come with complications. What you see is what you get."

Kate started to relax. "It all sounds too good to be true," she said. "There's got to be a catch."

He spread his hands. "Look, I'm not in the business of selling myself. I've got quite enough work to be going on with. But if you're interested why don't you call up Andrew Neil at the *Sunday Times,* or Max Hastings on the *Telegraph.* They'll tell you what kind of reporter I am."

"There is an easier way," she said. "You could show me your clips."

He reached down into the bulky leather briefcase at his feet and produced a stack of Xeroxed copies. "I thought you'd never ask."

As she ploughed her way through the investigations, the political stories, the showbiz interviews, Kate began to feel a sense of relief. By the time she had finished, half an hour later, she was almost light-headed. For she knew without a shadow of a doubt that Alan Baker was her man.

She looked at him thoughtfully. "Are you quite sure you don't have some terrible secret you haven't told me about?"

He smiled and refilled both their glasses. "There is just one thing. I like to get paid for what I do. And when I say paid, I mean top rates. I'm not looking to be number one. But I said goodbye to the junior league a long time ago."

For a moment she was worried. "I couldn't go above £25,000 a year."

He signaled the waiter. "Good, because I couldn't go below it."

"How about if I threw in a £5,000 bonus at the end of the year? And let's say two hundred in expenses a week."

"I'd say, I could be persuaded."

And with that Baker ordered lunch for both of them. It was not until the waiter returned with their food and put it in front of them that Kate remembered she didn't eat oysters.

Baker started work the day after he had finished his assignment with the *Observer*. Right from the start things went in the right direction. Baker's contacts were superb, if slightly offbeat. He counted as his friends the head of the vice squad, a prominent socialist peer, Victor Lownes, *Playboy*'s recently deposed London chief, and the leader of the opposition. He also had top-level connections with powerful public relations organizations in Europe.

Kate let Baker take care of the weekly European report while she went around and met everyone. She trusted Baker with her column, just as he trusted her with his carefully cultivated contacts. Together they made a formidable team.

Three months later her conscience bothered her. Apart from dashing off a brief thank-you note she had made no effort to contact Jeff. There had simply been too much to do. And no time at all to do it in. He must think I'm a rat, she thought. She picked up the phone. There was only one way to find out.

Peterson answered the phone himself. When he

heard Kate's voice, he didn't sound the slightest bit surprised.

"I figured it would take you till nearly Easter to sort yourself out. And I was right. So how goes it? Is Alan everything he's made out to be?"

"He's terrific. So terrific. I've had my hands full just keeping up with him. I'm truly sorry I didn't call before."

"Don't be silly. I told you I didn't expect it. But now that you are on the line, I take it you're back in circulation again."

She laughed. "Sure thing. I was going to ask you to dinner. It's my turn."

"Listen, I've got a better idea. Why don't we have dinner at my place instead? You haven't met my new wife, have you?"

"Not only have I not met her, I didn't even know you got married."

"Last time we met didn't seem like the right moment to tell you about my personal life. You had other things on your mind."

"So tell me now."

"How long do you have? An hour, a day, a week maybe?"

"Just give me a synopsis. My imagination will do the rest."

"Okay. Her name is, or rather was, Louise Preston. When I met her she was a walk-on glamor girl in a Bond movie. And I knew right off she was meant for better things than posing half-naked on a film set."

"Did you tell her so?"

"I kind of got around to it on the second date. After

that the least I could do was marry the girl. I had to offer her some kind of alternative.''

''It all sounds very romantic. And not a bit like you. When do I get to meet this Louise?''

''How about next Tuesday? We're having some friends over for dinner. In fact one of them you know.''

''Who's that?'' she asked.

''Charlie Hamilton. You remember, the guy you ran into at the American Club. The one I was having a drink with.''

Kate felt her stomach flip over. Charlie Hamilton. In her mind's eye she saw the tough-guy face. The well-cut Savile Row suit. The way he walked out on her when she brought up the subject of his wife. His dead wife. I don't stand a chance with him, she thought. I don't suppose I ever did.

There was a silence. Then Jeff said, ''What's the matter, Kate? Don't tell me Charlie makes you nervous.''

Damn Jeff. Damn him for knowing her so well.

''Of course he doesn't make me nervous. Don't be ridiculous. Anyway I hardly know him.''

''Then it's settled. Come to dinner on Tuesday, let's say around eight. And I can guarantee Charlie will be more than pleased to see you.''

''You can?''

''Sure I can. He was only talking about you the other day.''

Before she could ask him anything else Jeff had hung up. She sighed. There was no point in calling him back. As with everything else in her life, she was just going to have to stick it out and see.

*   *   *

On Tuesday morning Kate realized she had nothing to wear to the Petersons' dinner. Her mind raced over the possibilities. She could cancel her lunch and raid Harrods. Impossible. It had taken her two months to pin down the American ambassador. To change the date now would be disastrous.

She could call Saint Laurent and get them to send something over to the office. No, forget that. What if what they had didn't suit her? She'd probably end up making an expensive mistake.

In the end she settled on the tried and true. A black lace dress from Bergdorf's that was guaranteed dynamite. She smiled, remembering the men who had tried to get her out of it—and the men who had succeeded. Then she dropped the smile. What the hell would I want to wear that for? she thought. It's only asking for trouble.

But she wore it all the same.

The Petersons lived in Chester Square in one of those tall, thin houses you often find in the center of London. The American ghetto, thought Kate, as she approached the green, leafy enclave. Alan Baker had told her that these few expensive acres of real estate were much favored by well-to-do Americans. Particularly when their company was paying the rent. Indeed, when the multinationals sent their top executives to London for a year or so many of them had it written into their contracts that they reside in Chester Square.

Kate could see why. The Petersons' house had the grandeur that you only find in England, combined with room sizes you normally find in New York. She thought of the tiny little drawing room in her own mews cottage and allowed herself a pang of envy.

She handed her wrap to the maid, then headed up the stairs to the main room on the first floor where the party was being held. The first person she saw was Claud Becker. With him was a middle-aged woman wearing a lot of diamonds. She had the air of someone who had once been very beautiful. Kate surmised it must be Claud's wife.

Becker was in close conversation with her host, so taking her courage in both hands Kate made her way over to them. She and Jeff embraced. Then Kate held out her hand to Becker. He took it briefly and without enthusiasm. But before he could open his mouth, Jeff offered loud congratulations. "You and Alan are quite a force to be reckoned with," he said, then turning to Claud, he added, "I hear it was a close-run thing. But in the end it turned out you were too big for the job. Isn't that right, Kate?"

She heaved a sigh of relief. Saved by the bell. "Sure," she said, smiling. "Our little operation just couldn't contain a man of Claud's experience. I was flattered that he made the time to buy me a drink."

"Think nothing of it, my dear," he said. "I feel it's something of a duty to clink glasses with visiting firemen. Improves foreign relations and all that sort of thing."

Pompous idiot, thought Kate. Am I glad I didn't have to work with you. Before she could think of something to change the conversation they were joined by a slender blonde, who looked uncomfortably like Sandy Gebler.

Jeff put his arm around her. "You haven't met Louise, have you? Kate, this is my wife. Louise, Kate Kennedy, an old colleague from New York, now my closest rival on the *Post*."

The blonde smiled. "Jeff's told me a lot about you," she said.

Across the room Kate saw Charlie Hamilton talking to a small, plump brunette. He must have said something amusing, for she threw her head back and was consumed by giggles.

"You look as if you've just seen someone you know," observed Jeff. "Shall I go and fetch him? Or can you contain yourself until dinner?"

"I don't know what you mean," said Kate stiffly. Had she been that obvious?

Louise sensed her embarrassment and came to the rescue. Taking Kate by the arm, she said, "I have a number of very serious questions to ask you, starting with the new season's fashions. Have you any idea yet where to go and buy them? Because if you don't, will you let me take you around the shops? Dinner parties and shopping are two of my favorite things."

Kate let Louise prattle on. The woman seemed to be as trivial as she looked. Yet Kate sensed a shrewdness behind the carefully applied make-up. Maybe they could be friends. The absence of Ruth had left a gap in her life. She could sure do with a sympathetic female ally.

Out of the corner of her eye she saw that Charlie Hamilton was still talking to the brunette. They seemed to be fascinated with each other. She wondered why she was there.

Things changed at dinner. Jeff had been as good as his word. Kate was seated on Hamilton's left. On his right was the once-beautiful Mrs. Becker. The brunette was down at the far end of the table.

To look at, Charlie Hamilton was every inch the English gentleman. His cufflinks bore his family crest. His tie advertised the fact that he had been educated at Harrow. His suit came from Hunstman and his shirts from Turnbull and Asser. It was only when you looked closer that you realized he didn't get his muscles from the golf course. Or the rugby field. His body had a trained look about it. And there was something knowing about his eyes that made you feel that perhaps Charlie didn't always play by the Queensbury rules.

But most people didn't question the façade he had so carefully built up. Most people he encountered in business, that is. They only found out later, when they had been thoroughly outmaneuvred, that this polite gentleman was a tiger in disguise. For Charlie had the jungle instincts of a killer.

He had inherited his nature from his father, Hon. Cecil Hamilton, who had been a fighter pilot during World War II. Normally men of his class went into the army. But Cecil Hamilton thought the army was tame. He had no wish to be an officer and a gentleman planning campaigns or hiding behind the armored safety of a tank. He wanted to be out there where the action was. So much to the disapproval of his family, he enlisted in the Royal Air Force. Charlie's father never lived to see the end of the war, or the birth of his second son. His plane went down over Berkshire, but not before he had taken three Messerschmitts and a Dornier with him.

Charlie's mother never remarried. Her life had been so disrupted by Cecil that all she wanted was a little peace and quiet to devote to her numerous charitable works and to bring up her two sons, Robert and Charlie.

Robert, Charlie's elder brother and the heir to the family fortunes, was the apple of his mother's eye. He had her determined nature and an academic turn of mind. At Oxford he studied history and classics, which provided him with a suitable background to run the family's vast estates in Leicestershire.

Charlie was his father's son, a fact which made his mother distinctly nervous. Although she had loved her husband, she was relieved when that early turbulent time of her life was over. To see Cecil live once more in the fast-maturing body of her second son unsettled her. So she did what all grand English ladies do with children they don't quite understand. She sent him away. First to prep school. Then to Harrow. And then to Sandhurst, one of the toughest military academies in the world. Sandhurst had been known to break many eager young men. But not Charlie. He thrived on it. In later life when people asked him where he learned his particular brand of ruthless courage, he would always answer, Sandhurst.

"The instructors were all such sadistic bastards," he would say, "that the only way to survive the place was to be smarter than they."

Stealthily and with considerable guile, he learned the weakness in each instructor's character. Which one was a homosexual. Which one could be bribed. Which one liked to take one too many drinks. Then he let them know that he knew.

It worked like a charm. Yes, he had a rough time like everyone else. But no one went over the line with Charlie. If any of them wanted to make one of the cadets suffer, that cadet was never Charlie. Nobody could afford to get on the wrong side of him.

The rest of his life followed the same pattern. Leaving Sandhurst he turned down his commission and went into the theater. Like his father he rejected the gentlemanly professions expected of him. And while he was treading the boards he discovered he had no talent as an actor. And no gift for directing actors. But what he did have was a way with them. Their complexities and the contradictions in their characters fascinated him. Because it was something he had been used to watching out for as a boy, he was aware of people's weaknesses. And he was sympathetic to them.

He decided to become an agent because he wanted to protect these talented, mixed-up people from the rest of the world. And when he got to know the shysters, the conmen and the wheeler dealers who largely ran the entertainment industry, he knew for sure that the artistes he represented needed his protection. His clients saw the gentle side of Charlie Hamilton. To them he was father confessor and nursemaid all rolled into one. The rest of the business saw the tiger. Many of his critics compared him to a big cat, because of his stealth. Just like in Sandhurst, Charlie knew all their guilty secrets. He knew about the skeletons in their closets. And if he had to use those secrets to get what he wanted for one of his actors, he didn't hesitate.

His clients were not the only people who saw his human side. His wife, Fiona, whom he married after he left Sandhurst, knew the real Charlie better than anyone else. A girl from his own background, she met him at a hunt ball in Northamptonshire. Fiona Grey was one of the most beautiful girls of her season. And the moment Charlie set eyes on her, he knew at once that he had to possess her.

It wasn't difficult. Fiona had a pliant nature. She was used to doing what other people expected of her. Besides, she found this tall, black-haired, powerfully built man disturbingly attractive. So when he told her of his intention to marry her, the second time they met, she put up little resistance. Her family wanted her to make a suitable marriage and nobody could say the second son of a baronet wasn't suitable.

Fiona's marriage to Charlie was everything she could have wanted. Charlie for his part was fascinated by his new wife. She was a soft, lovely creature full of secret female rituals which seemed to absorb her. The mysteries of the couturier and the masseur were beyond him. As were the intricacies of *petit point.* But he didn't try to understand them. That was her world and he indulged her in it. His world, after all, made more than enough claim on him, frequently taking him away from her side. It comforted him to know that she had her own interests.

They had little in common except their desire for each other. And before the novelty of that wore off Fiona became pregnant, giving birth to their only child, Maria—Fiona's doctors advised her against another pregnancy. The baby cemented their marriage. She gave them both something in common. Something they could talk about apart from their social life.

If Fiona's mare hadn't hurled her onto the hunting field, life would have followed this serene pattern until

Charlie's dotage. As it was he was suddenly violently widowed at thirty-nine.

In the beginning he threw himself completely into his work, rejecting all his former friends. They reminded him too much of Fiona. In his grief he was solitary.

The grief ended abruptly, joyfully, when Charlie was seduced by a Hollywood actress. To his relief, the experience left him feeling no guilt. He spent several weeks with the actress. Mainly in bed. She had very little conversation. But after that it was as if a cloud had lifted.

The world, Charlie discovered, was full of actresses and models more than willing to share his bed. He also discovered he had been missing a great deal in life. For although his lovemaking with Fiona had been satisfying and sweet it had not been inventive. Charlie discovered he was a novice between the sheets. Not for long. As with everything else in life, Charlie Hamilton was a quick study.

Since the Hollywood actress there had been several one-night stands and more than a few flings. But in all of these there was something missing.

There was no intelligence. No real companionship. It was during that time in his life that he thought about Kate. There was something about the American girl that had intrigued him. Something he had responded to. He had been tempted to pursue her. But loyalty to Fiona had gotten in the way. That and Kate's married boyfriend.

Now there was no Fiona. And no Kate either. Until quite by accident he ran into her at the American Club. And he knew he had to see her again.

He thought about calling her, then decided against it. She might still be involved with the boyfriend. In the end, he got Jeff Peterson to organize a dinner. If she wasn't interested, he'd soon find out.

Now he was sitting beside her. The next move was up to him. Casually, conversationally he asked her about her time in London. And when she started to tell him of her disastrous beginning he leaned back and let her talk. There was no mention of Ted Gebler. The affair had to be over.

Subtly, without her noticing, he probed to see if there was anyone else in her life. When it came to women, he hated hassles and dramas. Love for Charlie was a smooth pleasant journey with one inevitable ending.

Kate was surprised at how relaxed she felt. She had anticipated Hamilton would be difficult. All that business about his wife had thrown her off balance. Instead he was the same man she had met in New York. He understood the problems she had had with the *Post*. And he was very enlightening about Jeremy Boyle. Apparently he had met him once or twice on social occasions and his observations about him made her smile. She was reminded that he had a wry, almost cruel sense of humor.

After dinner, Charlie took Kate into the vast formal drawing room. Then as if he had just thought of something he turned to her. "Is your heart set on rounding off the evening here?" he asked. "Or would you find it fun to come on somewhere else with me?"

She smiled. If he thought she was going back with him to his apartment he was in for a disappointment. It was as if he had read her mind.

"I thought Annabel's would appeal to you. We can dance there as well as drink coffee and brandy."

He had scored a direct hit. Kate had learned from Alan Baker a week or so earlier that Annabel's was an experience not to be missed. It was where the upper middle class met the Middle East, Baker had said somewhat cynically. It's also where Kate Kennedy gets closer to Charlie Hamilton, she thought, taking his arm.

Out on the street a large, dark-blue Rolls-Royce pulled up in front of them. Then a chauffeur in a peaked cap got out and opened the back door. Kate got in.

So he's rich, she thought. I didn't expect that. And for the first time that evening she started to feel nervous.

The club was everything she had been led to believe. There was an atmosphere of money about the place. Here rich women put on their best dresses and went on display. But it was the not-so-rich women that held Kate's attention. You could tell who they were by their youth, their good looks and the hunger in their faces. These girls were on the hunt. Then her eyes took in the hunting ground. And she started to get really worried.

The focal point of the club, the place where the middle classes really got to grips with the Middle East, was the dance floor. It was a tiny, circular area full of whirling lights and darkness. A place to seduce and be seduced.

We can drink coffee and dance, she thought. A likely story. The thought of being close, that close, to Charlie made her feel slightly dizzy.

Mentally she took stock of herself and decided she was behaving like a teenager on her first date. Then Charlie asked her to dance. And she panicked. "I think I'd rather have a drink. If that's okay."

If he was ruffled he didn't show it. "Do you want

to drink at the bar. Or would you be happier at my table?"

My table, she thought. So you make a habit of coming here. Aloud she said, "The bar looks fun. Why don't we go there?"

And she let herself be led over to the horseshoe-shaped bar which was even darker than the dance floor. The barman, who seemed to know Charlie, started to pour out brandy.

"Will you join me in one of these? Or do you want something else?"

"Brandy would be fine."

The minute she said it she regretted it. Brandy always gave her a monumental hangover. She took the warm crystal balloon in her hands and sniffed. Just the fumes made her light-headed. Then she thought, what the hell, and threw back a large gulp.

"Steady on." The voice was concerned and slightly amused. "I don't frighten you that much, do I?"

"Of course you don't. Why should I be frightened of you?"

"Because if you weren't you'd let me dance with you."

"That's not fair."

He smiled at her. "Poor Kate. So full of illusions about what's right and what isn't. Why don't you just relax? Go with the flow?"

"And what happens after that?" For some reason she could hear her heart beating.

"That depends entirely on you."

Before she could say anything else, he took the glass

out of her hand and returned it to the bar. Then he put his arm around her waist and led her to the dance floor.

She had been right about being close to Charlie. It did make her dizzy. For a moment she thought of Ted. But only for a moment. Ted was the past and she could think of nothing but the future. The immediate future.

What happens next? she had asked. And he had told her. Now it was up to her.

Her hand had been resting lightly on his shoulder. She slid it up his neck until her fingers were buried in his hair. He responded by gently pulling her closer. Now she was aware of the feel of his body and the faint, lemony smell of his cologne. And she knew that he wanted her.

So this is how it ends, she thought. Then she laughed at herself. How could I have been so naïve? Did I really think it would be any other way?

She made no attempt to move off the floor. She knew the route she was about to take, and she wanted to prolong the moment. So she stayed pressed up against him in the semi-darkness, letting his desire print itself upon her.

When they finally parted she found she was trembling slightly all over. As if separating herself from him was too big a shock to her system.

And there was no more fencing with words. They simply talked softly and directly to each other, the talking a continuation of their dance. He asked her to come home with him. And when they got out on to the street, to her surprise she saw the first faint streaking of dawn in the sky.

How long had they been in there? Two hours? Three? Time was no longer of any consequence.

What if I don't see him again after tonight? She wondered lazily. What if I'm just another conquest? But even as she let the doubts into her mind, she knew it was too late to wonder.

For all her toughness, Kate was no match for Charlie Hamilton. First he disarmed her. Then he desired her. Then he communicated the fact. In a way she couldn't quite understand, this sequence of events had aroused her. Now nothing would stop her from seeing the scenario through to its inevitable end.

Yet while she was on the way, she allowed herself a wry smile. A private joke. I never could manage to keep this damn dress on, she thought. Serves me right.

He lived in Eaton Square in a large bachelor penthouse that seemed to be dominated by its gracious drawing room. As he led her in she registered the sporting pictures by Stubbs and Ferney. The imposing furniture. The crystal chandeliers. The long white sofas covered in silk. She registered all of it. And she discarded it.

"Just show me the way to the bedroom," she said.

He raised an eyebrow. "I thought you might like to go through the motions of being a lady."

"I'm not a lady," she said, "I'm an American. And I'm not up to doing impersonations at this hour of the morning."

She was sitting in a low easy chair in front of the fireplace. And as he crossed the room toward her, she held out her hands. He pulled her to her feet and there was a roughness about him. A brutality she hadn't seen before. And when he kissed her, there was a hunger in him that matched her own.

His hand found the zipper at the back of her dress and the black lace tumbled around her ankles.

"The bedroom," she murmured.

"Not now," he said and undid her bra.

They made love with their clothes half on. Then he picked her up and carried her into the bedroom where they tore everything else off each other and made love again.

She wanted to bury herself in this man. To sink in so deeply she would merge with him. And when the first climax came she cried out like an animal. There was nothing she could compare to this. No man had ever roused her to this point.

With Ted there had been passion and the sweetness of love. But with this man, this near stranger, there was something primeval. A hunger so primitive that when she remembered it days later it shocked her.

He did things to her she had only read about. Explored parts of her she didn't know she possessed. And afterward, when the uncontrollable need inside her was satisfied, she felt grateful.

For Charlie Hamilton had shown Kate something she had never seen before. He had shown her herself.

When she woke up the next morning the sun was streaming through the windows. She grabbed her watch from the bedside table and swore softly when she saw the time. It was midday. The lines to New York were just starting to come alive. Alan would be holding the fort all on his own.

Then she took in her surroundings and remembered

the night before. The office seemed a million miles away. Slowly she stretched, enjoying the feeling of her own body. Then for some unaccountable reason, she suddenly discovered she was starving.

She found a silk dressing gown on the back of the bathroom door, wrapped it around her and explored the rest of the apartment. There was a dining room, all silk curtains and Persian carpets, at the end of the hall. And leading off of it a large, country-style kitchen. Sitting at the table, reading the *Financial Times,* was her lover of the night before. She noticed he wore half-glasses and the sight reassured her. There was something ordinary about shortsightedness. Something human.

He looked up from the paper and grinned. "So you finally decided to join me for breakfast. About time too."

He was wearing faded jeans and no shoes and he hadn't combed his hair. Yes, he was definitely human. Clearly he put on the politeness, the slightly foppish manner with his Savile Row suits.

"Do you want eggs? Or will just toast and tea do?"

She hesitated. He probably had as much to do today as she had. And she felt shy. She had been more intimate with this man than any she had known. Yet she still didn't know him well enough to ask him what his schedule was.

He caught the uncertainty in her eyes. "I called the office an hour ago," he said, "and canceled all my appointments. So depending on you we can either have breakfast here or go out to lunch."

So it wasn't a one-night stand. That was a relief.

"Give me two minutes on the phone and I'll clear my day too." She held up her hand. "Don't move. I'll use the one in the hall."

And she was on her way, stepping lightly. Smiling to herself. The ghost of Ted had been well and truly laid. Royally laid. And now? She didn't dare think.

Maybe the man was a playboy. Maybe this was just another fling for him. Then she thought about the night before and the way he had touched her, and the future seemed unimportant.

She picked up the phone and dialed her private line. Alan picked it up on the second ring.

"That was quick," she said.

"Damn right," replied her assistant, "I've been waiting to talk to you all morning. Where the hell are you?"

"At a friend's . . ." Her voice trailed off.

"Spare me the details. I haven't got time to hear them in any case. All I need to know is are you in London? And can you reach a taxi fast?"

"Listen, what is this? The President hasn't threatened to drop in on us, has he?"

"Worse." His voice was terse. "Hughes Hartmann, our editor-in-chief, has decided to pay us a visit."

"What's so terrible about that? So Hartmann's stopping by. One of us can make ourselves free."

"It's not one of us he wants to see. It's you. Oh, and he's not dropping by, as you put it. He's in Brussels attending the EEC convention on human rights. And he wants to have dinner with you. Tonight!"

Her internal panic button started to register. It was lunchtime already. If she was to make it to Brussels she would have to move fast. "Damn," she said aloud, "damn, damn, damn. Why does he want to see me? Why now? What's all the rush about?"

"Calm down." Kate detected a note of amusement in Alan's voice. "It's not a drama, I promise you. Hartmann's already been in Brussels for three days. He happens to be free for dinner tonight. You *are* his European chief. And he sees this as a neat way of combining business with pleasure."

"Terrific," said Kate. "So I have to drop everything and run across to Brussels just because he can't find anything else to do."

"I don't think it's quite like that. But even if it was, I don't know what you're bitching about. The guy hired you, didn't he? He backed you up while you were learning about the job. And now all he wants is the chance to talk about the last six months over dinner. Pull yourself together, Kate. You'll blow it if you don't."

"Okay, enough. I can be ready in forty minutes. Make it half an hour. Where do I have to go?"

"The check-in desk at Heathrow at three. Your plane leaves just before four. And you might throw something in an overnight bag. You're booked into the Intercontinental near the airport so you can make a fast getaway in the morning."

Distracted, she ran her hands through her hair. Was there anything she needed to take from the office? Recent clips? Any confidential material she might have gathered in the past couple of weeks? She racked her brains and came up with nothing. What's happening to me? she thought.

Alan's voice crackled over the line. "There's a file on a potential scandal brewing up in the trade union movement. Oh, and Joan Collins is planning to marry Peter Holm. I finally tied it up today and he can run it exclusive any time he wants. Also there are a couple of clips you might want on Mark Thatcher. Background stuff. I've put it all in an envelope and sent it down to the airport. You can pick it up from the first-class desk when you check in."

She let her breath out slowly. "Alan, what would I do without you?"

"Go back to bed with Mr. Wonderful, I should think. You've got me to thank for saving you from all that sordid business."

He put the phone down. If only you knew, she thought.

The minute she walked into the kitchen Charlie sensed that something was wrong. Five minutes ago she had been soft, pliable. Feminine. Now there was a difference in her. Nothing about her appearance had changed. She was still wrapped in his dressing gown. Her hair was still tangled. But there was a firmness about her jaw he had never seen before. And when he looked into her eyes he knew she was already halfway out of the apartment.

"What is it?" he asked. "What happened on the phone? Did your mother die? Or did a husband you forgot to tell me about arrive home unexpectedly?"

She grinned. "Nothing so dramatic. My mother's safe and sound in Westchester. And there's no husband, I promise you. No, it's a boring work thing. My editor's in Brussels. He wants me to have dinner with him."

He looked relieved. "Oh, so that's all it is. Then you don't have any problem. Sit down and I'll make you some tea. Then we'll plan lunch. Where do you feel like going?"

"I don't think you understand," she said. "I have to be out of here in five minutes. My plane leaves for Brussels at four."

He looked incredulous. "I don't believe it. You're not going, are you?"

"Of course I'm going. What else can I do? The guy pays my salary."

"Just because he pays your salary doesn't mean he owns you, you know," Charlie said quietly. "You belong to you. Never forget that. Now if you want to go to Brussels, really want to go, that's one thing. But if you're going because someone ordered you to, then you're being silly."

She looked wretched. "You know I don't want to go. The only place I want to be right now is here. With you."

"Then tell your editor to go to hell. You don't have to jump every time he snaps his fingers."

She sighed and got up from her chair.

"I wish I was that brave. Or that sure of my future. But I'm not. I only started this job six months ago. And I haven't exactly made a brilliant success of it. Not yet anyhow. Until I've proved myself, really proved myself, then I have to go on jumping for the boss. Just like any other employee."

He looked at her in disbelief. "Didn't last night mean anything at all? Or was it just a diversion between assignments? Or should I say assignations?"

She felt suddenly cold. And with the coldness came anger. "I seem to remember having this conversation with you somewhere else. New York, wasn't it. You were making off-color remarks about career girls then.

Men like you seem to have some wonderful fantasy about women who work. Why should we be more sexy, or should I say sexually available, than old-fashioned girls who just get married and live off men? Or can't you answer that?''

"My dear, your availability in bed isn't what we're talking about. I thought it was lunch that was being discussed.''

She couldn't believe it. One moment he was all warmth and affection. The next it was politeness and manners and where shall we go for lunch. And that really got to her. This cold fish, this prig, was more interested in having his meals on time, than anything else. Last night clearly counted for nothing. Her future? Forget it. In fact forget everything if it dared to get in the way of lunch.

She pulled the silk foulard dressing gown tightly around her and turned on her heel. "Lunch," she said, "is off. So, for the record, is my availability. So you'd better find yourself another playmate. One with plenty of time to sit around in restaurants. I've got better things to do." And she stomped off into the bedroom.

It took her less than five minutes to get dressed and less than two to get out of the apartment. Her lover of the night before made no attempt to follow her, or plead with her to stay. But even if he had it would have made little difference.

Kate was in such a fury that only when she had walked around the square and into her own mews did she realize why people were looking at her with such surprise. Black lace, decolleté black lace, and three-inch heels is not something you normally see on the street at twelve-thirty in the afternoon.

In New York it had been a long winter. For Ruth, a winter filled with hospitals and convalescent homes and more hospitals. A winter filled with pain.

When she had finally gotten home from Paris and consulted her own doctor, Richard Stein, he found exactly what the French doctors had found. An infected kidney. He ordered her home to bed immediately.

Ruth was indignant. "Okay, so I've got a cold in my intestines," she protested. "There must be a pill for it. There always is."

Dr. Stein, a tall, permanently sad-looking man, looked even more distressed than normal. "Ruth, there is a pill for it. They gave it to you in Paris and it didn't work. Why don't you just go home to bed?"

Ruth knew when she was licked. She went home to

bed, put her head under the covers and waited for something to happen. She didn't have to wait long. Her mother called. The instant Phyllis Bloom was in the picture, nothing could keep her away. She arrived with food. Chopped liver, pickled herring, lokshen pudding and chicken soup. Naturally.

Ruth, who was not feeling particularly bright, felt sicker. Dr. Stein ordered her into the hospital. So when Mike called from London to see how she was, it was Phyllis Bloom who gave him the news. Ruth was in the hospital dying from a kidney.

Mike came over on the next plane. He checked into St. Andres hotel near the New York Central hospital. And there he stayed for the next six months. It was a time during which he made his presence felt. The medical staff at the hospital were subjected to a daily cross-examination. Phyllis Bloom was permitted only brief visits. And then only with Gerry, Ruth's father. And the *News* was given regular bulletins about Ruth's condition.

Ted, who had a horror of hearing anything second-hand, decided to go and visit her. It wasn't easy. As soon as he arrived, he found Mike outside Ruth's private room.

"You can't go in there," he said. "I don't want her worried."

Ted was used to handling difficult customers. "If you don't want Ruth to worry, you'll let me through. One thing I can guarantee is that the office will be on her mind."

"Listen, sunshine, Ruth's problem is whether she'll see the office again. Not when."

"And you told her that? Very comforting."

"No, of course I didn't tell her that. What do you take me for?"

Ted was about to inform him. Then he thought better of it. "Look, let me go in for five minutes, will you? I'm not going to kill her. I just want to say how we're all missing her. And how we'd cope better if she was there in person. I promise you one thing, if she doesn't think she's needed back at the ranch, it really will kill her."

Mike looked reluctant. "Okay then. But just five minutes, and go easy on her."

If Ted was shocked at what he saw when he got through the door, he didn't show it. "So you finally managed to lose weight," he said cheerfully. "It suits you."

"Who's kidding who? I look like shit and you know it. So don't try to tell me different."

Ted forced a smile. "You're sick, Ruth. Nobody looks wonderful when they're sick. Now get a grip on yourself. I've got some news that will cheer you up."

For the moment her eyes brightened. "What's that?"

"Just a small item about the fashion department. You'll be pleased to hear it's holding up in your absence. No thanks to Tracy."

"Really?" Now she was sitting up and taking an interest.

"Your little assistant is the original klutz," said Ted, pleased with her reaction. "Eight times out of ten she gets her facts wrong. And her photo-sessions. It's a good thing you're not there to see them."

Ruth looked alarmed. "So how are you coping?"

"Easy. Bill and I are buying in outside help. And

Tracy goes out to lunch a lot. It's not ideal but it keeps her out of mischief.''

"I can't wait to get back and start sorting out the mess.''

"And I can't wait for you to do that. But only when you're better. If you come back before then, Mike will have my guts for garters.''

"Mike.'' She smiled and settled back. "If it wasn't for him, I don't think I could make it through this.''

And she meant it. At thirty-five years old, after eight years of calling the shots with the opposite sex and getting away with it, Ruth finally began to understand the mechanics of loving. She learned to accept things. Pain. Being out of control. Having to depend on somebody else. It wasn't easy. There were times when she screamed out her frustration at everyone who could hear. The nurses. Her mother. And Mike. But no matter how loud she shouted, or what she shouted, Mike didn't waver. He just went on loving her. And in the end she ran out of rebellion.

Mike loved her. The fact was undeniable. He stood by her in Paris. He came over to New York and repeated the performance all over again. And now when she was feverish and fretful and not looking her best the guy was still there. There was nothing else for it but to give in to the fact. Mike Stone was hers. For as long as she wanted him to be there. In sickness and in health.

The moment she acknowledged this, a change came over her. She returned the emotion Mike gave to her. In spades. It did her soul the world of good. Her body took longer to respond. Her other kidney succumbed to the infection. So now, as well as love, Ruth had to adjust to another new experience. A dialysis machine.

Three times a week she was wheeled down to a special unit, where they attached needles to her arms and changed her blood. Ruth started to wonder how much longer she could go on living like this. But she wondered in silence. She didn't want to ask the doctors anything, for she feared they might tell her the truth. And she wasn't ready for that.

Then six months after her collapse, just as Dr. Stein had started the search for a kidney donor, Ruth's body decided life was worth living after all. She started to respond to the drugs they were giving her. It wasn't a sudden recovery. But the pain started to recede. And the color began to creep back into her cheeks.

By the spring she was able to go home in a wheelchair. And when she had been home a week or so, she was able to move around by herself. Mike came home with her and stayed.

His moving in wasn't a dramatic gesture. Ruth needed someone to look after her and he wasn't going to entrust her to some proxy nurse. So almost without knowing it, they set up housekeeping. When Phyllis Bloom asked Ruth what she was doing, her daughter simply looked at her as if she was mad.

Ruth and Mike became a couple a week after they started living together. There was no drama to that either. Ruth had been in the habit of sleeping in Mike's arms, even in the hospital. It made her feel safe.

Then one morning she woke up before Mike and discovered his erection. She took hold of it with a certain wonder.

"How long have you been keeping this from me?" she inquired as he sleepily opened his eyes.

He yawned contentedly. "Until you were ready."

At the beginning of May Ruth decided that if she was well enough to make love she was certainly well enough to go back to work. Her doctors confirmed this diagnosis. And in the second week of the month, when the town was beginning to turn on its air conditioners, Ruth went back to her job on the *News*.

The first sight to greet her eyes when she walked into her office was Tracy, her young assistant. Before she went off to Paris Ruth had noticed a change in Tracy. But it was nothing compared to this. For Tracy Reeves looked as if she had joined the cast of *Dynasty*. The role she had chosen to play was Alexis.

Her dark red hair swung around her shoulders like heavy, burnished silk. The make-up with its glossy lips and pan-cake complexion, was pure Hollywood. The clothes were all from Valentino.

Looks like Tracy's been pretty busy in those long lunch hours of hers, thought Ruth. She had a vision of the redhead taking the subway to Loehmann's in the rush hour. Then she thought, no—she's too lazy for that. Someone's buying all that designer stuff for her. Then another thought occurred to her. Maybe she's gotten a raise and she's buying it herself.

That bothered her. If Tracy had been given a raise, it meant one thing. She'd been promoted. An hour later Ruth's suspicions were confirmed.

At eleven-thirty, right after the editorial meeting, Bill Gerhaghty bustled into the office. After a perfunctory nod at Ruth, whom he had seen earlier, he made for Tracy's desk. "What have you got for us this week?" he asked.

Tracy lowered her eyes. "I think you should be asking Ruth that. Now that she's back I guess she'll be taking over again."

"Sure, sure," said Gerhaghty, "but Ruth's been back a couple of hours and she probably hasn't caught up yet. I want to know what's on the page now. There isn't much time." He looked at Ruth for confirmation. "Isn't that so?"

Ruth's first instinct was to blast him out of the room. What right had the bastard to breeze into her office and behave as if she wasn't there? But she played for time. Something was up. If she trod carefully she might pick up a few clues as to what it was.

"I admire your enthusiasm, Bill," she said, "but what's all the hurry? The first major fashion spread of the week always falls on a Thursday. Or has that changed since I've been away?"

He looked uncomfortable. "Kramer isn't exactly wild about those big picture spreads you went in for. Right now fashion news is the new hot item around here. Or didn't you know?"

Ruth knew. She had been following the paper avidly since she had been away. And the first thing she had noticed was that the fashion coverage had shrunk dramatically. It hadn't surprised her. Ted had told her Tracy didn't have the experience to take on her competitors on the *Post* and the *Times*. She knew he was buying in material to cover for her until she came back. Then she noticed something new in the paper. It was a small column on a news page entitled "Hotline on the Fashion Scene." The author was Tracy Reeves.

In essence it was a beat up of all the press hand-outs. And at first Ruth felt relieved. The *News* was maintaining a presence in fashion. A toehold almost. It was as if the paper's executives were waiting for Ruth to bring them back into the mainstream when she returned.

She started to worry when Tracy's column began to appear every day. The girl was becoming a fixture. And fixtures, she knew from experience, were very difficult to dislodge.

She decided to find out how difficult. "This fashion news," she asked tentatively, "does Ted have anything to do with it, or is it strictly your department? Up to when I was on sick leave, fashion always came under features."

Gerhaghty started to fiddle around with the knot of his tie. Ruth noticed he had dirty fingernails, and the sight didn't reassure her. Grubby hacks masterminding the department. Inexperienced assistants throwing together a second-rate column. Something was terribly wrong.

Gerhaghty cleared his throat nervously. "Actually, Ruth," he said, "fashion doesn't come under any particular department anymore."

"How come?"

"You'd better ask Kramer. After we knew you wouldn't be back for a while, he decided to pull the whole thing under his personal wing. Ted and I just take it in turns to see that the column comes in on time."

She thought for a moment, then she said, "So this fashion news is Kramer's baby?"

Gerhaghty nodded.

Ruth experienced a familiar sinking feeling. So Ted hadn't told her everything. Newspaper politics, she thought. Turn your back for one minute and the bastards stick a knife in it. I should have known, she raged silently. Nobody, not even Dorothy Parker, could be out sick for as long as I did and expect to come back and find everything as it was before.

Aloud she said, "Why don't you and Tracy go ahead and organize tomorrow's column? I'm sure you have it all planned out by now. I'm going to take a little walk."

Then she put on her sweetest smile, gave Tracy's cheek a little pinch and set off down the corridor. When she got to Ted's door, she stopped walking. Her intention had been to visit Kramer. And she would do so, but in good time. First she was going to have a few words with Ted Gebler. He owed her an explanation.

"Come in," he shouted, as she poked her head around the door. "I've been expecting you. In fact I've even penciled you in for lunch."

"Have you now?" She grinned. "What makes you think I haven't got something more pressing on my agenda?"

He came around the desk and put his arm around her. "Come off it, Ruthie, it's me you're talking to. Your most pressing task is to see Kramer. And there's no way you'd stick your neck out with the editor without dredging my mind first. Unless you've had a sudden change of style. You haven't changed your style, have you, sweetheart?"

She kept a straight face. "Do I look like I've changed my style?"

"No, that's why I booked Reuben's for twelve-thirty. I take it illness hasn't changed your appetite?"

"No way. It's pastrami on rye as usual. With cole-slaw, and gerkins. And maybe now that I'm feeling myself again, they could just tempt me with a little chopped liver to start."

Reuben's, on Second Avenue, was to connoisseurs of kosher cuisine what Maxim's was to grand gourmets. It had none of the usual hustle and bustle of a New York deli. Instead it was a dimly lit collection of booths where chicken soup and lokshen pudding were served with reverence by a succession of elderly Jewish waiters. People who ate there had the sensation of being back in their parents' front parlor. And this is what made it so popular among the Jewish population, who reveled in their childhood memories.

Ruth just liked the food. Illness had done little to alter her shape. Sure, she'd lost a great deal of excess poundage when she was at the point of no return. But that had been some months ago. As she recovered, so had her appetite.

However, at her first working lunch it wasn't just the food that attracted Ruth. It was the privacy that the booths at Reuben's afforded. She suspected that Ted had a lot to tell her. A public bar wouldn't have encouraged him to unburden himself.

She knew her hunch was right by the time the chopped liver had arrived. Ted hadn't said anything directly about Tracy. The name of Kramer had hardly been mentioned. But she knew him well enough to catch his drift. Okay, it's time to stop playing footsy," she said.

"There's something going on between my assistant and that old fart who calls himself an editor, isn't there?"

Ted sighed. "You've said it. Look, I haven't got anything concrete to go on. They're not holding hands in the elevator or anything. But they're too close for it to be reasonable anymore."

"What do you mean?"

He raised an eyebrow. "Lunch twice a week. And not at the Algonquin either. When he's with Tracy, Kramer goes in for those expensive, red plush numbers uptown. The kind of thing that costs an arm and a leg for a plate of designer food and maybe a spritzer or two."

She looked at him questioningly. "How come you know so much about that kind of scene? I thought you were behaving yourself now that Kate's gone away."

"Listen, we didn't come here to talk about my sex life. That's my problem."

He looked closed, somehow. And tougher. Ruth saw her advantage slipping away. Quickly she said, "Sorry, sorry I poked my nose. It's a bad habit of mine. Tell me more about Kramer. Knowing about it means a lot to me. We could be talking about my future at the _News_."

He shrugged. "If Tracy means business, you may be right."

Tracy meant business. She had not expected Ruth to return to the paper. Though what exactly she did expect, she didn't care to think about. Wishing somebody dead is one thing. Having it actually happen was not the kind of reality Tracy wanted to face.

In an ideal world Ruth would have gracefully disappeared into a convalescent home and never surfaced again. Maybe she might have decided to marry that photographer she was living with and devote herself to raising a family. Tracy could have lived with that. What she could not live with was Ruth, fat as ever, bursting into the department, her department, and acting as if she had never been away. That was insupportable.

There was only one thing to do. She would have to arrange for Ruth to be removed. She knew Kramer had no love for the fashion editor. She knew he much preferred her in the job. She laughed out loud. Because he much prefers me *on* the job, that's why, she thought.

The last eight months had not been without event in the life of Tracy Reeves. When Ruth was taken sick, Tracy knew with an instinct born only to politicians and opportunists that her big chance had finally come. So she went for it.

Her seduction of Ed Kramer had been swift, crude and ruthlessly effective. The flint-faced editor had gotten into the habit of calling her into his office two or three times a week to talk about the fashion business. She dreaded these occasions. For she knew that every time she went into the imposing, teak-lined office she would be subjected to a lecture of mind-blowing boredom. Kramer behaved just like a schoolmaster. Giving her books to study on the garment industry. Showing her layouts for fashion spreads. Going through sheaves upon sheaves of black and white photographs, which to Tracy all looked depressingly the same.

She knew she was being groomed for Ruth's job. And her ambition welcomed this. But there had to be an easier way of going about it than this long, tedious apprenticeship. At this rate it could take years before she was sitting in the coveted fashion editor's seat. Tracy didn't have years. So she left her panties off the next time she came to work. She had to wait around for two days with the breeze blowing up her skirt until Kramer sent for her. But when he did, she made it worth his while.

The afternoon's little teaching session, Tracy discovered, involved looking at fashion pictures. Good, she thought, that gives me every reason to sit on his desk. This was a crucial element in her plan. For how else, as she gazed at a David Bailey print, could she part those knees? How else could Ed Kramer get an undisturbed view of everything Tracy had to offer?

Kramer had no problem with his eyesight. Though he did seem to have a considerable problem with his blood pressure. He also seemed to have trouble with his breathing. And Tracy knew she was home free. One look at the naked lust on the man's face told her she could play this scene any way she chose.

She let her skirt ride up a few inches. Then she took his hand and placed it between her legs. To her surprise she found the old guy turned her on. There was something expensive and immaculate about him. Ruffling that polished surface excited her. Made her feel powerful.

She took her shoes off, then she inched one stockinged foot across an expanse of thigh until it found the hardness that told her he had a full erection.

She looked him in the eye. "Here?" she asked.

"Jesus Christ, no," he groaned. "Anyone could walk in." Then before she could say anything more he half-pulled, half-dragged her from the desk. Tracy found herself being propelled across the office. When they reached the door to his private shower room she realized what was in store.

How interesting, she thought. I've never done it standing up. Whether Kramer had or not, she didn't have long to wonder. For as soon as they were through the door, and that door was firmly closed behind them, Kramer wasted no further time.

With one hand he undid his trousers. With the other he pushed her skirt up around her waist, parted her legs and thrust himself into her.

She cried out softly as he entered her. There was no way she had expected him to be so big. And so energetic. She pushed her pelvis forward and gave herself up to the experience. This was better than looking at boring layouts. And it sure beat the hell out of discussing the garment industry.

Ed Kramer was clearly of the same opinion. For he never ever talked to her about the fashion page again. In fact he didn't talk to her at all. He avoided her eyes when he met her in the corridor. And there were times when she wondered if the whole situation hadn't been a dream. Then she remembered the way he pinched her ass the first time she went to see him in his office. And she ceased to wonder. The old guy had the hots for her. Of that she was certain. Her only mistake had been to bring him to the boil too fast. Next time she'd be more careful.

As far as Kramer was concerned there would be no next time for Tracy Reeves. That incident in his office. That disgraceful, delicious way she showed herself to him. The way it all finished in the shower room. It must simply never happen again. It was too messy somehow. Too real. It wasn't his style.

Automatically he checked himself in the mirror before going into the morning editorial meeting. His shirtsleeves were the required inch below his cuffs. His shoes were freshly glossed. Every slicked-back hair was immaculately in place. No one would ever suspect that just a couple of days ago he was fucking the ass off the office junior and enjoying every minute of it. Or would they? Maybe the girl had talked. He suppressed a shudder. It wasn't possible. She wouldn't dare. Anyway who would believe her?

But as he walked into the conference room he felt distinctly uncomfortable. A murmur, even a ripple of scandal and that puritan prick Henkel, his proprietor, would be on his neck like a ton of bricks. He sent up a silent prayer. Dear Lord, please stop that cheap little tramp from telling a living soul.

At the very moment that Kramer was fervently hoping for Tracy's silence, she was pouring out the whole story to her best friend in the world, Randy Newsome.

"Tracy, my darling," he gasped, "you're killing me with these details. It's so marvelously sordid. I hope you'll keep me posted with regular reports from under the shower . . . if you get my meaning."

Tracy looked deflated. "No dice, Rand," she said. "My aged playmate isn't playing anymore."

"Why not? From the sounds of it, you're a hot enough number. A regular turn-on if you ask me."

"That's not the point. To turn somebody on, you have to get near enough to do it. And right now Kramer won't allow me within a mile of him."

"Why not?"

She shrugged. "Scared, I suppose. The *News* has a born again Christian for a proprietor. So any fucking between consenting colleagues is a definite no-no. Kate Kennedy was practically fired for having a thing with Ted, our features chief. And that wasn't so long ago either."

"But Kramer's the boss. Surely he can do what he likes."

Tracy giggled. It was a tiny, tinkling girlish sound and as always Randy felt astonished when he heard it. Tracy had such an experienced face. Too experienced for such an innocent expression of joy. Her next words reassured him he was right. "Of course Ed Kramer can do what he likes," she said, "and he will. He just has to have the right motivation, that's all."

"And how do you propose to motivate him?"

"I'm not the one who's going to do the motivating. You are."

Right away Randy was intrigued. Maybe it could work, he thought. Stranger things have been known to happen.

Randy Newsome was one of New York's top stylists. When Coca-Cola was doing one of their beautiful-people commercials, Randy was the man they called in to design the set. If Jerry Hall was being photographed at home, she wouldn't let the cameraman in until Randy had approved her look. So it seemed the most natural thing in the world to Tracy that if she was going to stand any kind of chance with Ed Kramer, Randy was going to have to redesign her. A mousy junior fashion assistant—no matter how sexy she was—could not motivate

Ed Kramer into a risky affair. A classy, expensive-looking cover girl. That was a different story.

Randy went along with her plan for several reasons. First, he liked her. But second and most important, he didn't have anything better to do. The commissions weren't exactly pouring in. He wasn't in love. And the summer stretched ahead of him. Long, hot and very, very boring. The transformation of Tracy would give him something to occupy his time.

The first thing he did was take her to the hairdresser to have her hair dyed red.

"But I've got red hair already," she wailed.

"Not my kind of red hair," said Randy, propelling her through the door of Lily Dache. It took Kenneth most of the day to turn Tracy into Randy's kind of redhead. And at the end of it, the bright expensive color that came out of a bottle looked far more natural than the color that God had given her. It also set her back two weeks' salary.

"I want you to look upon this whole little exercise as an investment," said Randy. "You are, after all, playing for pretty high stakes."

Tracy swallowed hard and took out a bank loan. After that she did everything Randy told her without a murmur. She changed her face with blushers and shadows and expensive paint. She firmed her body at a pricey gym where they gave personal instruction. She threw out her entire wardrobe and started again at Valentino, where at least Randy managed to get her clothes at trade rates.

The whole operation took nearly a month. And absorbed all of Tracy's loan. But she jumped through every hoop with the dedication of a big game hunter stalking the most desirable prey she had ever set eyes on. For that's what Ed Kramer was. Prey. Tracy knew she had little to offer the world of journalism. Yet she wanted her place in the sun. And Ed Kramer was going to get it for her.

Kramer, who set great store by physical appearances, noted with approval the changes in Tracy. The girl certainly seemed to have taken herself in hand. In fact she was quite a looker if you liked that kind of thing. Funny that he hadn't noticed it before.

Tracy sensed Kramer's renewed interest the way a hunting dog picks up the scent of a fox. But this time she played it differently. She walked into his office demurely. With her eyes downcast. She had something very important she wanted to discuss with him, she said. Would he by any chance be free for lunch?

Kramer was on the verge of turning her down. Then his eyes strayed to her waistline. And from there to her hips. And on to her long, slim legs. Unbidden into his mind came the image of Tracy in the shower room, her short skirt hitched up all the way over those legs. He heard himself agreeing to lunch. And agreeing to lunch that very day. It was then that he knew he was sunk.

Lunch was spent in Kramer's apartment. In bed. This time it wasn't a short, frenzied session up against a wall. This time Tracy had time and space. And she made full use of both. By the early afternoon Ed Kramer had a new hobby. And Tracy had a new job.

In return for her silence and continued discretion, Tracy was promoted to fashion columnist. She got a raise in salary. And Kramer put the important fashion features, an essential ingredient of the *News,* temporarily on ice. Ruth could deal with that side of things when she got back. Kramer was having too much fun to worry about details like that.

If Tracy had anyone to thank for her blossoming affair with her editor, it was her editor's wife, Bernice.

Bernice Kramer, an imposing woman in her late forties, ran her life by her social calendar. For her this centered around horses. The Kramers had a considerable spread in the Hamptons. With stabling, of course.

There really seemed to be no point in Bernice visiting New York. The town bored her. And on the rare occasions when she did come to the city, her husband was always too busy on the newspaper to make time for an early, civilized dinner. So she simply gave up bothering to come.

Ed went out to the Hamptons every Friday after lunch and didn't return to New York until the following Monday. The break from each other during the week gave them new things to talk about. It also gave Bernice a chance to be with her beloved horses. The arrangement suited them both perfectly.

It suited Ed even better now that Tracy was in the picture. Sex with her was a revelation. The girl took it seriously. Worked so hard at it. In the past when he had indulged in the odd daliance with one of his wife's socialite friends, he had been the one who had to make all the effort. And it tired him. He preferred to expend his energy on the newspaper. Now he could have his cake and eat it too. For with Tracy, sex didn't sap his strength. In fact it gave him renewed vigor. The creature knew so many new ways to turn him on. She covered his cock with whipped cream and licked it all off. She dressed up like a whore in a bordello. She let him take her in every position imaginable. The dear girl was so inventive. So enthusiastic. Nothing was too much trouble.

Visions of Tracy, naked except for a lacy black garter belt and high-heeled tart's shoes spun through Kramer's mind as he arrived at his exclusive pied-à-terre on the East side. He had given her the front door keys four months previously. She had become a habit with him now. He liked her to be there when he came home later after a long day at the paper. He wondered what she had in store for him that evening.

As he got into the elevator he could feel the beginnings of a hard on. And when he finally made it to his front door he knew he was going to fuck her there and then. Whatever she was wearing. Or wasn't.

Tracy answered the door in the demure black knit dress she had worn to the office that day. Around her neck was a single string of pearls. She was wearing sensible flat pumps on her feet. And she looked the way she felt. As if she meant business.

Kramer felt his erection subside. Tracy looked so fierce. So unwelcoming. What the hell was the matter? He walked through into the drawing room and made straight for the drinks cabinet. "What are you drinking, darling?" he called.

"A Perrier. No ice. No lemon." Her voice was flat and hard. It was worse than he thought.

He filled a heavy, cut-crystal glass with Bourbon and water and walked over to the fire. "Okay," he said evenly, "what is it that you want?"

On the rare occasions that Tracy felt any irritation

with her lot, she used sex as a bargaining point. Kramer didn't blame her for it. How could he? They both knew it was her only asset. Her trump card. The kid sure didn't have any other talent to fall back on.

"What I want," said Tracy, who had played this game before, "is something I don't think you'll be able to deliver."

Kramer took a swig of his drink. "Let me be the judge of that."

Tracy pouted. It was a well-rehearsed pout. She had glossed her lips specially for it. Kramer admired the effect.

"Well, don't keep me in suspense. Tell me what you've set your little heart on and I'll do my best to give it to you."

She held the pout for a minute longer. Then she said, "I wonder if you will?"

Kramer lost his patience. It was ten o'clock already. He hadn't eaten dinner and he was tired. Maybe he was getting too old for this kind of thing.

"Look, Tracy," he said through clenched teeth, "just give me the story, will you? I haven't got all night. And nor have you if you continue to get on my nerves."

She retaliated by bursting into tears. Kramer knew when he was beaten. Putting his drink down he crossed the room and took her in his arms.

"There, there," he said. "I didn't mean to upset you. But I can't help you either if you don't tell me what's bugging you."

In the end after much smoothing and patting and the addition of a big glass of restorative brandy, Tracy told Ed what was on her mind. He was aghast. "You can't mean it," he said. "Ruth is probably the most talented fashion journalist in New York. If I let her go my reputation would be in tatters. To say nothing of the *News*."

Tracy started sobbing again. "What you really mean is I'm not good enough," she spluttered. "I've been slaving away all these months producing a column. And for what? For you to throw it away the minute the great Ruth deigns to do you a favor and come back to work."

"Come on, baby, it's not like that and you know it. Ruth's been very sick. There was a time when we all wondered if she was going to make it at all. So coming back to work hasn't exactly been in the favors department. Now has it?"

"I suppose not." Tracy was calmer now. Too many tears would only ruin her make-up. And then Ed wouldn't be in the mood to give her anything, let alone her own way. And her own way she was going to get.

"Look," she said, "what do you need Ruth for? I've been acting fashion editor for the past eight months now. And I've done a good job. Everybody says so. Ask Bill Gerhaghty, he'll tell you how the readers lap up my stuff."

I bet he will, thought Kramer. Bill Gerhaghty will tell me anything if he thinks it's what I want to hear. Since I've been backing this dumb kid for nearly a year now, he'll probably tell me she deserves the Pulitzer prize.

Aloud he said, "I don't need Bill to tell me how good you are. I can see that with my own eyes. That little column of yours is first rate. Great stuff. And what's more, I'm not going to let it go."

He saw the faint glimmer of a smile and experienced

a feeling of relief. Kramer had handled tougher characters than Tracy in his long career. He'd make her see reason.

She threw her arms around his neck. "That's what I've been telling you all along. My column's popular. It's the new hot item. You really don't need Ruth anymore."

Kramer went to the bar and poured himself another bourbon and water. It was going to be a longer night than he thought. When he returned to the fireside, he had his senior editor's expression on. The one that was guaranteed to instill fear and respect into the hearts of his subordinates.

"Tracy," he said, "I admire your enthusiasm. But I think there's something you've forgotten. And I don't blame you for it. You never liked putting together a big fashion spread, did you? You know—collections of fall clothes, or spring clothes or any damn clothes that are going to make our readers drool, then rush out to the stores to buy. Our advertisers depend on that kind of coverage. And your column, excellent though it is, simply doesn't deliver that."

"But, Ed," she wailed, "you never told me that was what you wanted. I know how to do a spread like that with my eyes closed. All you had to do was ask me."

Sure, he thought grimly. And it would look as if you'd done it with your eyes closed. He cleared his throat. "Ruth came to see me today," he said, "and we had a very useful conversation. Very useful."

"Oh, yes," said Tracy, some of the hardness coming back into her voice, "and what did you both decide? During this useful conversation."

"Only good things," he said, gently raising his hand

to her cheek. "First of all, I want you to stop worrying about your column. Ruth loves it as much as I do. We all love it."

This wasn't strictly true. What Ruth had to say about Tracy's column was unrepeatable, but she doesn't have to know that. Not at this minute at any rate.

"Second of all," he went on, "I think you work quite hard enough without having to do spreads as well. So I told Ruth that was what I wanted her to do. Just spreads. Nothing else."

Tracy looked at him from under her eyelashes. Who does he think he's kidding? she thought. "So Ruth goes on calling the shots in the fashion department," she said, "and I just continue to write my column."

He smiled. "Sure, honey. What else?"

"I'll tell you what else," she said. "If Ruth goes on calling the shots in the department she does it without me. I haven't taken orders from that fat cow in eight months. And I'm not about to start doing so again. I don't care how talented she is."

"Now, Tracy, be reasonable."

She set her jaw. "No, you be reasonable. I'm prepared to work every hour of every day. And night," she added. "But if I'm putting in the hours, I want to be fashion editor. Or else."

"Or else what?" he said softly.

"Or else you don't see me again. In the office. Or here either. Do I make myself clear?"

"My dear, you make yourself very clear." He was about to add, so pack your bags and hand in your resignation. Then he stopped himself. Kramer had a soft spot for Tracy, for all her simple-mindedness, her avarice and her undoubted laziness. The girl had ambition. True, she didn't have too much talent, but she made up for it by sheer determination. Who else would have gone to the trouble of turning themselves from an ordinary-looking kid into this head-turner. And for him. She did it to please him. He felt his erection returning.

What had Ruth ever done for him? he thought uncharitably. Sure, she did her job. And a good one. That was unarguable. But she did it in spite of him. Not because of him. And when he raised any objection to what she did, all he got was her lip. That at least he could do without. He wondered if he could do without the other things she provided. And for that he had no answer.

What Kramer needed, he reflected, was time. Time to find out how replaceable Ruth really was. Time to find out if there was anyone else on the staff who could do her job. And do it with discretion. Another queen bee he didn't need. He came to a decision. If there was a way of getting rid of Ruth without the paper or his reputation suffering, he would do it. But for a while, anyhow, he had to get Tracy out of the way. If there was any suspicion that he was favoring his mistress, that he even had a mistress, his puritanical proprieter would be down on him like a ton of bricks.

No, he couldn't risk that. Tracy had to go away for a while. But where. Then he had a brainstorm. "Darling," he said, "how do you feel about paying a little visit to the South of France? For the paper, of course."

Tracy looked confused. "I didn't know there was any kind of fashion event going on down there."

"There isn't. But for the next couple of weeks I don't want you to work on fashion. I want you to cover the Cannes Film Festival. Do you think you could do that?"

Her eyes shone. The idea of sun, sand and bronzed movie stars appealed to her no end. Satisfying an old man exhausted a girl. She could do with some time off to play.

Then she pulled herself up sharp. Was he trying to buy her off by putting her on general features? If so, it was still no deal. She had set her heart on being fashion editor. And fashion editor she was going to be. "I don't know if I'm all that interested in Cannes," she said guardedly. "It's not going to alter the Ruth situation any, is it?"

"That's where you're wrong. The Ruth situation could alter quite dramatically during your absence. But I need to be free and clear to alter it. With you around, there are just too many distractions."

The penny dropped. And as it did, Tracy's heart lifted. She'd gotten her own way after all. The old fart was going to give Ruth the heave-ho, but he wanted to look kosher while he was doing it. She could understand that.

Then she thought about the next two weeks in Cannes and she felt even better. Today had been the biggest gamble of her life. And it had paid off. Slowly she walked into the bedroom. "I think it's time," she said, "that I got out of these dreary office clothes. Don't you, darling?"

Kramer sighed. Tracy was nothing if not predictable.

The carousel at Nice airport was congested at the best of times. During the film festival it was a mob scene. Movie moguls and their retinues jostled with starlets who fought it out with publicists, gofers, journalists and hangers-on.

It reminded Kate of Grand Central at rush hour. Clinging to her wire trolley she looked with a certain desperation at the bobbing heads between her and the moving belt that promised to bear her luggage.

She had left London for Nice that morning, and she wished she hadn't. For she had nothing definite lined up. Kate liked to organize her schedule in advance. Running the bureau made it almost a necessity, for she didn't have the time to waste on maybes. Either a story stood up or it didn't. And if it didn't, she moved on to something else without moving from her desk.

The Cannes Film Festival didn't work that way. If you wanted a story, you came down and took your chances along with everybody else. There were no promises and no guarantees.

How did I get myself into this? she thought crossly, as she caught sight of the bags trundling out of the conveyer. A large man built like a bear thrust himself in front of her, momentarily winding her. This is lunacy, she thought. I should have known better.

The Festival had caught Kate's interest a month previously when she discovered that Paramount had submitted the new David O'Neill film as the American entry. Movies starring David O'Neill were guaranteed box office. Mass-market stuff. But this one was different.

For starters, the subject matter had little in common with the usual O'Neill scenario. The Irish actor went in for swashbuckling roles. He was at his best as the brawling, hard-drinking macho man. The kind of hero who ate the leading lady for breakfast and came back for a second course. He had had a string of hits with titles like *Jungle Jim* and *The Don Hits Back.* Money-making epics with plenty of action and little for the mind.

O'Neill's new film did not fit into this mold. Titled *The Last Goodbye,* it was a chronicle of the final months in the life of an AIDS victim. O'Neill took the title role of a promiscuous homosexual facing his final judgment. There had been a few TV movies dealing with the subject, but Hollywood hadn't put its big bucks behind the killer disease. Until now. And now not only was there big money riding on the film, there was a big reputation as well. If O'Neill was anything less than brilliant in *The*

Last Goodbye, he was going to have a problem getting anymore work.

As soon as she could, Kate called Paramount and asked to see a preview of the film. They turned her down. Previews were being shown at Cannes. And Cannes only. If she was interested in *The Last Goodbye* she would have to make the journey to the South of France. Undeterred, Kate got on to her New York office. Could they rustle up a print? Again the answer was no. The best they could come up with was Phil Danvers, the film critic, who had managed to sneak a look at the movie in Los Angeles.

When Phil came on the line, Kate knew she had to make the journey to Cannes. For he was ecstatic. "The guy turned in the kind of performance I would have expected of Richard Dreyfuss, or maybe even Olivier in his early days. It's the best thing he's ever done. When the titles came up I wanted to cry, and coming from me that's a big admission. When you see four movies a week, you don't have too much left in the way of emotion."

"Okay, Phil, I'll take your word for it," said Kate. "How do I get to see this O'Neill?"

"Rogers and Cowan handle his publicity, though they're being obstructive at the moment. They won't let anyone near O'Neill until the film gets its first screening. The guy isn't even posing for pictures."

"What about Paramount? Aren't they lining up interviews?"

"Once again, no dice. Everyone seems to be waiting for the critics' reaction before the guy will open his mouth."

Kate sighed, "Come on, Phil, there must be some way of getting to him. Even if we can't have a talk in advance, surely we can set a date at the festival. I'd be prepared to go down myself."

"Judging from the atmosphere around here, I think you'll be going down there anyway. I hear the *News* is sending somebody from New York. And *Time* and *Newsweek* will both have stringers on the spot."

"Okay, I get the picture. But surely there must be something one of us can do to make sure we bring the story home first."

There was a long silence and for a moment Kate worried that she'd lost the connection. Then Phil's voice came crackling back on the line. "There is one chance. But it's a long shot. David O'Neill has an agent. A British guy who works out of London. Name of Hamilton. Charlie Hamilton. Does that mean anything to you?"

Now it was Kate's turn to be silent. Damn it, why hadn't she thought of it before? The first time she'd met Charlie had been in New York at a David O'Neill opening night. He'd even told her he represented the actor.

"Phil, I think I've met the guy," said Kate tautly. "I'll see what I can do at my end."

When she put down the phone she knew it was hopeless. There was no way in the whole world she could pick up the phone to Charlie. Not after the last time she saw him. It had been weeks now and she hadn't heard a word from him. There had been no apologies. No flowers. No nothing. At first she had been surprised. Then hurt. And finally she had been disappointed.

The man was nothing better than a playboy. The kind of man who saw women as convenient extensions of himself. Things could be fine with Charlie Hamilton if you fell in with his plans. But heaven help you if you had plans of your own. The Charlie Hamiltons of this world couldn't tolerate that. Maybe it was too much of a threat to them. Or too much trouble.

Either way Kate wasn't interested in finding out. She had only just recovered from one man. She didn't need another to complicate her life. So instead of calling Charlie, she called Jeffrey Lane in Rogers and Cowan's London office and asked to be put on the list for the David O'Neill interview.

If the actor decided to talk, she had as good a chance as anyone else of getting the story. It was the best she could do until she got to the Festival. Once she was there she would make her own plans.

Nevertheless, when she finally rescued her bags from the crowded conveyor belt and struggled through the crowd to find a taxi, she began to doubt it. The only other time she had visited France had been seven months ago when she went to cover the Paris collections. But if the collections were frenzied, this was ten times worse. Pushing and shoving she could understand. She'd lived with that all her life in Manhattan. But this crowd hysteria was something else. There was a frightening undercurrent to it. A feeling of incipient violence, as if any minute you expected someone to pull a knife or a gun and bludgeon their way through to get a bag or a taxi or simply a breath of air.

With a certain relief she found herself in the taxi line. It wouldn't be long now until she checked into her hotel.

Her secretary had booked Kate into the Majestic, one of a dozen or more identical ice-cream palaces on the Croisette. The Majestic had three bars, two restaurants, several conference rooms where receptions were held almost continuously during the Festival, and a terrace out front where journalists who were on the hunt for starlets who were on the lookout for producers drank their aperitifs. The Majestic, like all the other five-star hotels, had its own beach where you could hire umbrellas and beach mats for the price of lunch anywhere else. And if you could still afford to eat, the beach even boasted its own restaurant.

When Kate arrived, hot and dusty from the airport, the beach was the last place she wanted to be. Instead she took the elevator up to her room and paid off the porter who followed with her bags. Then she kicked off her shoes and flung herself onto the vast, white canopied bed.

Outside her window Cannes shimmered in the heat. It reminded her of a Van Gogh painting. Bright primary colors, blues and golds and whites flung together in the crude unmistakable pattern that told you you were in the South of France. Nowhere else in the world looked that way, or could. She fell asleep while the Midi burned itself into her unconscious mind.

Half a mile along the Croisette, in the Presidential suite of the Carlton, David O'Neill was making an early start on the cocktail hour. The Cannes Film Festival was a place to drink. And a place to enjoy a woman. He amended that. Enjoy women. As many women as you could. After all, somebody else was picking up the price tag, weren't they.

Despite the fact that his career in films had made him a millionaire many times over, David O'Neill was a careful man. Like all Irishmen, he was firmly rooted in his past. His boyhood in County Wicklow was still more real to him that the life he lived nowadays in his mansion in Beverly Hills.

It was this sense of reality that had decided him to accept the part of Kevin McDonald, the doomed AIDS victim in *The Last Goodbye.*

O'Neill's background was the classical theater. Ten years in rep and five in the Royal Shakespeare Company had made him a good actor. A solid actor. Unfortunately it had made him very little else. Despite his undoubted gifts, he was virtually unknown outside the West End stage. His wife, Gwen, another good, solid actor, was forced to go on working instead of setting up a real home and having the children they both longed for. For the couple, like all gifted, struggling artists, had very little money.

Then came a supporting part in a TV series. A flashy, rather vulgar character, O'Neill was later to say. What he didn't add was that vulgarity was in style that year. Just as O'Neill's flaxen-haired, blue-eyed looks were. It didn't take long for William Morris's talent scout to recognize his potential.

Six weeks later, thanks to the Morris office, O'Neill had landed a supporting part in a spaghetti Western. The theatrical demands of the part were far below O'Neill's capabilities. He did it, in fact, while learning his lines for the lead in *Look Back in Anger.* The production was due to be staged at the Royal Court the following spring.

David O'Neill never made it to the Royal Court. After the spaghetti Western he was offered the lead in *Forever and a Day,* a romantic comedy with swashbuckling overtones. It was the kind of part Errol Flynn used to specialize in. All it required was the ability to look good in fight sequences. And in profile. O'Neill turned it down flat.

Then William Morris told him how much the studio was offering him to do the film. It was more than he had earned in his entire career as an actor. More than he was ever likely to earn again. He reconsidered.

Three movies later he was still reconsidering. By then he and Gwen had moved to Los Angeles and Gwen was pregnant with their first child. When she told him the news there was no going back. The work he was doing was dross. He knew that. But it was highly paid dross. It meant he and Gwen could have the kind of home he had only read about in *Photoplay.* And of course there was the baby to think of.

Gwen had a second child before she decided to go back to the theater. Unlike her husband, who had now become a megastar, she was still a respected actress. Broadway welcomed her with open arms.

To say the O'Neills grew apart during David's Hollywood years was an oversimplification. They had always been a working couple, so there was no reason for their careers to divide them. What separated them was more obvious, yet more complex.

David liked women. He always had. When he and Gwen were in separate productions, he usually had a run-of-play affair with his leading lady. It was one of the perks of the job. Gwen understood that. Just as she understood that he would never leave her.

David was a good Catholic, and like many Catholics he believed there were women you married, women worthy to be the mother of your children. And there were tarts. He also believed there was a place for both kinds of women in his life.

If David hadn't become famous, Gwen would have probably gone along with her husband's madonna whore complex. As it was, she became increasingly irritated with seeing him all over the scandal sheets with yet another bimbo in tow. It was demeaning. She was, after all, a respected actress. A force to be reckoned with. David was making her look silly. So she got even. She had an affair with a boy nearly half her age. An actor she met at a party. She did it to put David in his place. What she didn't expect was to fall in love. But that's what happened. A casual fling, intended as a slight to her husband, ended up as the grandest passion of her life.

At the age of thirty-eight, David O'Neill found himself divorced and discarded for a boy of twenty. It did little for his self-esteem. And even less for his image. He attempted to put both to rights by bedding every available and unavailable woman who caught his eye. The unavailable ones were best. The thrill of the chase, the hard-won conquest did something to redress the balance.

Then it got boring. David O'Neill was far too bright and too lazy to devote the rest of his life to venging himself on a permanent girlfriend for when he was between films. During the run of a film, as in his theater days, he liked to be free for whatever came along. On his last film that was very little.

The Last Goodbye, for obvious reasons, had an all-male cast. Even the continuity girl was a lesbian. As he mixed his second martini of the day David cursed his decision to ditch Fawn Gray, his bedmate for the past nine months.

Fawn, a Beverly Hills socialite, might not have been all that bright. But she was very female. And very, very obliging. Which is more than you could say for anyone else he had shared his professional life with for the last six months. Not that life had been a sexual wilderness. He had made do with the odd bar girl and the wives of a couple of his old friends. But it was hardly enough. What he needed right now was someone gorgeous. Not one of the available girls you found hanging around this kind of bunfeast. But someone special. Someone with a bit of class. A touch of magic. And that, he knew from long experience, was not found very easily.

He leafed through the dozens of party invitations scattered on the Italian marble coffee table. Grace Robbins was organizing a party on her yacht. That might be worth a look. Minda Feliciano was having one of her exclusive cocktail do's. Another distinct possibility. Then there was always the big bash at the casino to launch the Festival. Real actresses went to that one. Real socialites too. He wouldn't have to fight off the groupies there.

Moodily he took another slug of his martini. The thought of hunting for another floozie made him feel tired. He'd just finished the most demanding acting job of his life. He had nothing left to give to the flowers and champagne routine. Yet he knew he was going to have to summon up the effort. Somehow.

He poured himself another gin. Maybe it would put him in the mood.

*　　*　　*

Tracy didn't need gin to get her moving. In fact she didn't need anything, except the lights, the music and the fantastic, crazy atmosphere of the best club she had been to in her entire life. Louis Brown's Studio 51.

When Randy's friend had taken her there she hadn't known what to expect. But then what could she expect from a friend of Randy's?

She had suspected her friend dabbled in drugs for a long time. But she didn't have any complaints. The guy had changed her life, hadn't he? She remembered the first time he took her to the hairdresser and told her to spend two weeks' salary getting a tint. She'd complained at the time, but it had been worth it. Now it was her turn to return the compliment. Randy had asked her to deliver a little package to a friend of his while she was at the Festival. And she had obliged. Now she was off the hook and she was relieved.

Right from the start she hadn't liked this thin, washed-out-looking character who was escorting her. There was something dirty about him. Unwashed, sort of. She shuddered. You would have thought the British aristocracy would have taken better care of themselves.

The guy—Jeremy was his name—turned out to be even more boring than he looked. She had agreed to have dinner with him more for Randy's sake than anything else. And she had nearly fallen asleep listening to him rave on about the films that were showing at the Festival. There she was, dying for some gossip about Princess Stephanie and her latest boyfriend, and all she got was a load of rubbish about some AIDS extravaganza.

Well, it wouldn't do at all, and she told him so.

What Tracy Reeves was after, was a bit of action.

Not meaningless gossip about films she had no intention of going to see. She demanded to be taken to a club. Not any old club. But a hot one. The hottest club in town if he could find it.

The moment she walked into the cavernous night-spot Tracy knew she had found what she was looking for. A hundred tiny round tables were placed around the biggest, grooviest dance floor she had ever seen. Spangled signs, some of them in neon, glittered over the top of it. The whole area seemed to be made of silver. And on it, as if floating on some exotic ice rink, were some very funky-looking guys. Their jeans fitted where they touched.

Most of their shirts were unbuttoned to their waists. Those of them who were wearing shirts, and not sexy, next-to-nothing little vests, that was. They all seemed to be somewhere around her age. Or younger. And best of all, nobody seemed to be dancing with anybody in particular. The floor was just a huge, heaving mass of boys and girls. Grooving, dancing, having fun. It was definitely too good to miss.

She left her escort at the bar as soon as she decently could. Then she hurled herself into the fray. And there she had remained for the past hour. Bopping herself into oblivion.

Stupid little slut, thought Jeremy Boyle, ordering his fourth large whisky and water of the night. The things he did for friendship. If Randy hadn't made his supply of very pure, very good cocaine possible, he would have ditched her there and then. But he couldn't. He had promised the American stylist he'd look after this flaky little protégée of his. See she had a good time and met the right people. And he was duty bound to do just that.

To his relief he spotted a couple of old friends making for the bar. Don Black of the *Star* and Steve Keegan of the *Sun*. They had to be here for the Festival. He waved and indicated his glass. They were over like a shot. And not for the drink either. They both knew how well-connected Jeremy was. How gossipy he was. How useful he could be. Especially now that he wasn't in competition with them anymore.

The three converged like old friends at a coffee klatch. There was catching up to be done. Records to set straight.

"What in hell's name are you doing here, old fruit?" asked Don, a portly, balding man in his late thirties. "The word was that the fuzz were after you to help them in their inquiries, as the saying goes."

Jeremy put on his best world-weary smile. "How very tiresome of them. Everyone knows there's no way I can be of any help to anyone—least of all the law. They're not exactly the top of my pops."

Steve, thin and seedy in a Burton suit, chipped in: "Feeling guilty about running off with the office nick-nacks are we?"

"Look," said Jeremy, who was getting bored with the game. "I didn't run off with the office nick-nacks, as you put it. But there's no way I'm going to spend the next few years of my life trying to convince you, or the police for that matter, of my innocence."

"So you legged it off to sunny Spain," said Don, feeding his considerable bulk with a steak sandwich, "where nobody can ask you anything on account of there being no extradition policy."

"Right first time," said Jeremy.

Don finished his sandwich. Then he said, "So why are you risking your neck in Cannes? It only needs one person to point the finger and the gendarmes will be on to you like a pack of wolves."

Jeremy went into his world-weary smile routine for the second time. "Don't tell me anybody at this bunfeast could be bothered to nail me. They're all too busy getting pissed and fiddling their expenses to worry about yours truly."

Steve, who had been ogling the girls, suddenly paid attention to what Jeremy was saying. "I'll tell you one person down here who'd give her all to put you behind bars," he said, "and that's your ex-colleague, Kate Kennedy. She's holed up at the Majestic trying to get the big interview with David O'Neill. But she just might take a bit of time off from the project if she saw a chance of fixing you."

"Then I'll make a note to stay clear of the Majestic bar and the David O'Neill press conferences," said Jeremy patiently. "I don't think that'll be too big a sacrifice."

"I still think you're taking a risk," said Steve, but he was interrupted by the arrival of Tracy, flushed and shiny from the dance floor. Any worries about his friend flew out of his mind. The sight of the redhead made him look even more like a ferret than he usually did. "I don't think we've met," he said.

Keeping a straight face, Jeremy made the introductions.

"So you're the Tracy Reeves everyone's talking about," Steve improvised, "what are you working on?"

Her boobs alone were worthy of page three. He wondered what his chances were of getting his hands on them.

Her answer convinced him that his chances were slim. "I'm working on getting that tall, French guy over there to walk me home," she said. "Is there anything else here to work on?"

"Not a lot," said Don Black. "Unless somebody here manages to pull off an interview with the great David O'Neill."

Tracy pulled a face. "Who in God's name is interested in that? He's playing a gay who's dying of AIDS or something, isn't he? I can't see the story in that."

Both tabloid journalists exchanged glances. The chick might be good-looking, but she was certainly no heavy-weight in the brains department. Unless she was kidding of course.

Steve tested the water. "O'Neill's a very big name," he said cautiously.

Tracy snorted into her drink. A night at the disco had robbed her of all her carefully acquired gloss. Now she was a kid from Minneapolis. From the wrong side of the tracks. And she didn't give a damn. "To me the name isn't wonderful," she said, "unless you like corny caper films."

"But that's just the point," said Steve as patiently as he could. "This star of corny capers, as you call them, has suddenly turned himself into an actor. A real actor too. My guess is he'll win an Oscar for this new film of his."

"So he wins an Oscar for playing a dying queen," said Tracy. "Who cares?"

Jeremy decided the moment had come to wise Tracy up. He owed Randy that much. "Kate Kennedy cares," he said softly. "The *Post* sent her here especially to get a big interview with him. An exclusive interview. And if you don't beat her to it, you just could be in trouble."

If he had struck her in the face, she couldn't have sobered up faster. This was all she needed. She'd worked this hard. She'd come this far. And now, just when everything she had always wanted was in her sights, she was in danger of blowing it.

Damn Kate Kennedy, she thought. Damn the bitch to hell. She wasn't going to get away with it. Tracy would find a way of getting to David O'Neill. If it was the last thing she did.

Nobody answered Kate's calls. And when she finally turned up at the production office, nobody wanted to talk to her. Everyone surrounding David O'Neill, from his publicity men to his producer, was giving out one message and one message only. No comment.

Kate was stumped. She had run into this situation just once before. In Hollywood. A well-known actress was divorcing her husband and citing his boyfriend as the other party. Then it was no comment in a big way. And Kate could understand it. This situation was beyond her.

The Last Goodbye had got ten raves from the critics on its Cannes showing. David O'Neill was the hottest name in town. Any town right now. And the man wasn't saying a word. She wished she'd made more of an effort to talk to him at his first-night party all that time ago in New York. She wished she hadn't quarreled with Charlie Hamilton. There were times when she wished she hadn't involved herself in this whole ridiculous circus. But she had. And she decided to make the best of it.

The best thing she could do under the circumstances was to team up with Doug Freeman. She had run into the oversexed *Financial Times* correspondent in the lobby of her hotel. She was on her way out to see a film so she hadn't seen him coming. And before she could duck and run she found herself exchanging greetings and small talk.

At a second glance Freeman wasn't as overpowering as she remembered. He was still handsome in a flashy sort of way. Nobody could take that away from him. But some of the aggression had gone and she guessed that now that she wasn't a potential employer he didn't have to prove anything.

She discovered something else. She wasn't the only one getting the bum's rush from David O'Neill. As well as Freeman, an entire outside broadcast unit from the BBC was drawing a blank. And none of them was enjoying it.

"We're all meeting for dinner tonight to find out if there isn't some way out of this mess. Do you want to join?"

In any other situation Kate wouldn't have considered it. She recalled the last time Freeman had asked her to dinner. And the sexual invitation that went with it. This time it was different. There was a group of them. He couldn't proposition her in front of witnesses.

When they got to the restaurant Kate found more

witnesses than she bargained for. For sitting at the far end of the barn-like room was David O'Neill himself. With him were Jeffrey Lane of Rogers and Cowan, Alan Leigh, the film's producer, and Charlie Hamilton. The four men were clearly talking about the picture, for they had formed themselves into a tight huddle and seemed oblivious to anyone else.

Kate felt both relieved and irritated. She had little desire to renew her friendship with Hamilton. But, Goddamn it, at least the man might have acknowledged her existence. She picked up the menu and tried to relax.

Les Trois Canards, high up in the hills, above Vence, was world-famous for its cuisine. It didn't do badly with its prices either. Which was just as well, for the customers certainly weren't paying a thousand francs a head for the decor. The restaurant—like many in that part of the world—was a rustic affair. There were flagstones on the floor. The tables were of bleached pine, covered somewhat haphazardly with checked cloths. And the place was lit by storm lamps and candles which spluttered and dribbled from their holders on the stone walls. Anyone who hadn't been told that Les Trois Canards was the chic place to be seen could easily have mistaken it for the kitchens of some vast château. Kate, who was still coming to terms with European style, felt ridiculously overdressed in a black velvet dinner dress.

It was only when she looked around her that she began to feel better. Every woman there would have looked totally at home in Maxim's. Or the Ritz.

Gold bracelets circled naked arms, bronzed by the sun. Diamonds glittered discreetly in tanned cleavages. The air was heavy with the scent of Joy.

Kate put her menu aside. The intricacy of the dishes confused her. She longed for a grilled steak and a plain green salad. She wondered if Doug would think she was a barbarian if she ordered just that. She was about to ask him, when a hush fell over the other diners. Every eye seemed to be fastened on the entranceway. And Kate could see why. Standing there was the most spectacular girl.

In contrast to the other women there she had only the palest of tans, which made her seem fragile. Ethereal almost. The effect was set off by her bright red hair which fell in soft waves about her shoulders. She wore no jewelry. Not even a simple gold eternity ring. And her dress was stark in its simplicity.

To Kate it seemed as if she was wearing a white silk shift. But to call it a shift would have been to do it an injustice. The dress was so cunningly seamed, so cleverly cut that it made the girl look as if she had the body of a goddess.

As she walked into the restaurant, there was a collective sigh as everyone let out their breath. From Kate there was a gasp. For she realized that she had seen this girl somewhere before. As she approached their table Kate remembered with a terrible clarity exactly where she had seen her. In Ruth's office at the *News*. What on earth is Tracy Reeves doing here? she wondered. Then she caught sight of the man who was escorting her to a table in the corner. And she froze. It was Jeremy Boyle.

Kate felt slightly faint. Tracy Reeves and Jeremy Boyle, her two least favorite people, were sitting together on the opposite side of the room whispering together like conspirators.

The weather was still and warm. The air was filled with the tinkle of trivial conversation. Kate felt no desire to call the local gendarmerie, despite Steve's dire predictions. Yet the hairs at the back of her neck stood on end and a still, small voice deep inside her said that something would happen tonight that would alter the course of the entire Festival.

Uneasily she reached up and massaged her neck. Doug looked concerned. "Is anything wrong?" he asked. "You look as if a bomb was about to fall."

She smiled wanly and took a sip of her wine. "Everything's fine," she replied. "It's me. I'm just being a bit silly. Take no notice."

The conversation at the table returned to normal. One of the men from the BBC started talking about the forthcoming opera season. José Peres was threatening to boycott Covent Garden in favor of the Coliseum. Everyone had their favorite story about the Spanish tenor. And by the end of the evening Kate felt almost relaxed. Almost. Somewhere at the back of her mind was the faint sound of warning bells. They wouldn't go away.

Then the hush that had fallen once before that evening returned to the restaurant. For the beautiful redhead was on the move again. This time she was on her own. And she was walking toward David O'Neill's table.

In places where celebrities dined there were unwritten rules. The celebrities were left to their own devices. Nobody asked for an autograph, not even the waiter. Nobody greeted the famous person, unless he or she was a friend. And nobody in their right mind would ever have dreamed of barging in on what was after all, a private party.

That night Tracy broke every rule in the book. With devastating effect.

"She'll never get away with it," muttered Doug under his breath. "O'Neill's an old hand at this kind of thing. He'll turn her away before she gets the chance to sit down."

But he was wrong. As Tracy approached, David O'Neill broke off his conversation, got to his feet and motioned her to join him. Then he called a waiter. A bottle of champagne and an extra chair appeared as if by magic.

Kate couldn't believe her eyes. The Irish actor seemed entranced by Tracy. The looks passed between them left her in no doubt that this could be the start of something. A big something.

Doug groaned and put his head in his hands.

"Well, that kisses goodbye to any interview we might have been dreaming of. That little tart's got the situation all sewn up. We might as well call it a day and go home now."

Half an hour later Tracy got to her feet and returned to her table. Doug could stand it no longer. He marched over to her table and demanded to know what was going on. "Do we read your exclusive interview in tomorrow morning's paper?" he asked nastily.

Tracy opened her eyes very wide. "Don't be silly," she said. "I need longer than twenty minutes for the kind of interview I'm after."

"And when, pray, will David O'Neill grant you the kind of time you need?"

She gave him her sweetest smile, with just a touch of acid. "Tomorrow might. Over dinner in his suite."

She paused. "You can tell your friend Kate Kennedy to buy a copy of the *News* on Friday morning. She'll read everything she needs to know about David O'Neill right there. Under my byline."

The following morning Kate packed her bags. Slowly. The hangover from the night before dictated her movements. The night before. She grinned, ruefully remembering.

I should be thoroughly ashamed of myself, she thought. Yet she didn't feel ashamed. Getting loaded and laid should have made her feel sordid. But it didn't. It had had a strangely cleansing effect. Like the cauterizing of a wound.

When Tracy and Jeremy had swaggered out of Les Trois Canards she had been mortified. And she wasn't alone. Doug Freeman and the rest of the group shared her sentiments. For what had happened made a mockery of everything they believed to be true. Talent, hard work, a certain tenacity, all counted for nothing. They had to, when sex, and pretty obvious sex at that, was a deciding factor in the way their living was earned. When they left the restaurant the BBC men went back to their hotel. They had an early camera call in the morning and they needed their sleep. For Kate and Doug there was nothing that demanded their attention. Few stars of any note had attended the Festival that year. Doug had seen all the films worth seeing. And Kate had missed the one story she'd come down for. So they decided to get drunk.

It wasn't a spoken decision. Nobody said, let's hit the nearest bar and blow our minds apart. It was something that just happened. When the boys from the BBC had said their goodbyes the pair of them found themselves standing in the hotel lobby. Neither of them wanted to go to bed. To do that would have meant being alone. Alone with a sense of failure. There were better ways to end an evening.

Doug suggested a visit to the casino and it seemed the perfect distraction. There was a grandeur about the white and gilt edifice at the end of the Croisette. The marble floors, the crystal chandeliers, the dinner-jacketed croupiers, all suggested that this was a place where you could throw your money around with dignity. Kate threw her money around. First at roulette, where she lost some of it. Then at blackjack where she lost all of it. It didn't make her feel dignified. It just made her angry.

She felt everything she had had been taken away from her. Her professional standing, her money. Even Charlie Hamilton had failed to recognize her. There seemed little else to salvage. She headed for the bar. Doug had beaten her to it. He'd been cleaned out twenty minutes earlier and was on his second whisky. Courtesy of American Express.

Kate signaled the bartender. When he came she ordered a vodka stinger. Kate turned to this concoction of iced vodka and white crème de menthe the way other women turn to a box of chocolates. It provided comfort. And that was something she could use.

By one o'clock that morning, Kate was well and truly consoled. Both by the stingers and Doug Freeman, who had turned out to be surprisingly companionable. The chauvinism that had irritated her when they first met was no longer on display. Well, he's hardly the handsome hero of the day, thought Kate. Then she laughed at herself. I'm not exactly the leading lady either.

She had expected him to flirt, and when he didn't she felt both relieved and disappointed. This is silly, she thought. I'm not looking for an adventure.

She tried to concentrate on what Doug was saying and found it surprisingly easy. His years around the entertainment business had given him an elegant cynicism. He had traveled the world for the *Financial Times*. By way of Beverly Hills. And he had had his fair share of bizarre experiences. As he talked about them, he re-lived them in his mind's eye. She could see it amused him.

Kate remembered the last time Doug had told her about his life. Then he focused on her, using the anecdotes as a prelude to courtship. Now he told the stories for their own sake. And once more she was dismayed that she wasn't the center of his attention.

She regarded the Byronic profile from underneath her eyelashes. What if I do want an adventure? She thought. The idea didn't alarm her anymore. And she wondered somewhat hazily if the vodka stingers weren't warping her judgment. She decided she didn't care. The words of an old refrain went around in her mind.

It's the wrong time and the wrong place. Though your face is charming, it's the wrong face . . .

Briefly she thought of Charlie Hamilton in the restaurant that night. Serious. Withdrawn. Indifferent.

It's not his face, but it's such a charming face, that if some night you're free . . .

She expected him to make his move when they got back to the hotel. And she was right. After they had collected their keys he turned to her and said casually, as if he was suggesting afternoon tea, "Why don't we go to bed?"

I can't say how happy I am that we met. I'm strangely attracted to you . . .

If she had been sober, she probably would have been insulted by his arrogance. But she wasn't sober. And in some kind of perverse way the idea of going to bed with Doug excited her. She wondered how impenetrable that glossy surface was. Something in her, something she had never acknowledged before, wanted to break through the charming veneer. Smash it into tiny pieces.

There's someone I'm trying so hard to forget. Aren't you trying to forget someone too . . . ?

She led the way to the elevator. "Doug Freeman," she said, "I thought you'd never ask."

It all started rather mechanically. She noted with a certain fascination that he hung his suit up neatly before coming to bed. He has to be a bachelor, she thought. He's too used to looking after himself to be anything else. Then she saw his body, broad and tautly muscled, and she stopped thinking about his marital status.

To say they made love would have been to sentimentalize the act. For just beneath the passion there was a cruelty about what they were doing to each other. For Kate, it was as if all the anger and frustration of the past twenty-four hours was finally finding expression. She clawed, rather than caressed, his body.

And when he entered her, she bit him on the top of his shoulder, her teeth drawing blood. It only increased his excitement.

He thrust into her like a bull, pulling her legs high

above his neck. She responded with her own frenzy. And the two of them writhed and flailed and beat the demons out of their souls. Kate climaxed before Doug, her body wracked with long shudders. And at the end of it, he burst inside her, his anger finally matching hers.

Then they slept, deeply and peacefully, and as friends. For it was as if they had come through a battle, each healing the other's wounds when the fighting was over.

In the morning they were easy together. He made love to her again, but it lacked the conviction of the night before. It was a kind of politeness on his part. He had found her in his bed and he felt it was expected of him.

She did not stay for breakfast. Her mind was already too busy with the day ahead of her. There were planes to be booked, suitcases to be packed. She wondered how early she could call America.

When she got to her room, she called the desk and asked them to book her on the midday flight to London. Five minutes later the phone rang. That was quick, she thought. But it wasn't the concierge as she expected, it was Rogers and Cowan. Somebody called Alastair Riley came on the line and inquired if she was still interested in doing an interview with David O'Neill.

It took Kate several seconds to register what he was saying. Then she reacted. Fast. When was Mr. O'Neill thinking of giving his interview, she inquired. Because if it wasn't today, she wasn't interested.

Riley went to find out. Five minutes later, having consulted with Jeffrey Lane who was masterminding the project, he was back. "If you can be ready in an hour," he told her, "David O'Neill will expect you in his suite."

She did a rapid calculation. She would be with O'Neill by 11:30. If the interview took an hour and it took another hour to knock it into shape she could have the whole thing on the telex before the end of lunch. That gave the New York office, which was five hours behind her, all day to process it into Thursday's paper.

Then she thought about Tracy. The girl would be interviewing over dinner. Or after dinner. That still meant she could have her story in New York around seven-thirty their time. It would catch the later editions. She sighed. She wouldn't beat Tracy, but at least she would be level with her. And with any luck she'd get a better interview.

"Are you still there, Alastair?" she asked. "Fine, then tell David O'Neill I'll be knocking on the door of his suite at the Carlton at the appointed time. Oh, and tell him I'll be looking forward to it."

Then she hung up. It was only after she put down the phone that she remembered something. Tracy had told Doug last night to look out for Friday's paper. Not tomorrow's. The lazy bitch, she thought. She's so confident of getting the exclusive that she isn't bothering to file her story till the morning.

She smiled to herself as she turned on the shower. At least Tracy will have one consolation when she sees I've beaten her to the O'Neill story, she thought. She can always tell her grandchildren she once went to bed with a famous movie star.

The interview went surprisingly well. Kate had expected the Irish star to be as shy as he was reclusive. But she was wrong. He was in fine spirits, pouring lethal martinis and answering every question she asked him.

At the end of an hour she had the whole story of his lowly beginnings in the legitimate theater and his need to get back to it. The commercial movies had been a way of allowing Gwen, his ex-wife, to give up work and bear his children. Now that he had money in the bank and no wife to worry about he could do what he wanted to do in the first place. Act.

It was the perfect explanation for his taking on the controversial part in *The Last Goodbye*. And filling it so magnificently.

As she hurried out of the Carlton Kate felt elated. The interview she had on her tape recorder was exactly what her readers wanted. In the past O'Neill had given interviews about the breakdown of his marriage. But he had never spoken about his driving force. His need to express himself as an artiste.

She couldn't wait to get to her room and knock the thing into shape. But before she did, she paid a visit to the bar. There she purchased a bottle of their best champagne. A vintage Bollinger '74. Jeffrey Lane had moved mountains for her. The least she could do was say thank you.

An hour later, her story safely on the wire, she rang the airport and got herself a seat on the last plane out that day. As she was finishing packing she heard the phone. It's probably Doug, she thought, wanting dinner. She had half-agreed that morning to pay a return visit to the casino with him. This time to eat.

I'll tell him to set up something when we're back

in London, she decided as she hurried into the next room. But it wasn't Doug calling. It was Jeffrey Lane.

"Darling," he said, "a million thanks for the fizz. Such premier quality too. But I can't say I'm worth it."

She laughed. "After everything you did for me I'd say you were more than worth it."

"But you're so wrong. I didn't lift a finger to help you any more than any other journalist down here. The man you should be sending presents to is David O'Neill's agent, Charlie Hamilton.

"You didn't tell me you knew him, Kate?"

She hesitated. "I don't know him. Not well, anyway."

"You could have fooled me. The moment he saw you in that restaurant last night you were the main topic of conversation. I got the feeling that if he had known you were going to be in town he would have set something up beforehand. I nearly came over to get you, you know that?"

"What kept you?"

"What do you think? Come on, Kate, you saw it yourself. The moment that little trollop from the *News* sashayed over, David didn't want to know about anything else. It took Charlie half the night to convince him to see you at all. He had a hard time, I can tell you. It was only when he told our prima donna that you were the most influential member of the New York showbiz contingent, that he agreed.

"Our Charlie really put his neck on the line. Nobody tells David O'Neill what to do. If he'd caught him in a different mood, Charlie could have found himself without his biggest client."

Kate couldn't believe it. That chauvinist, that man who didn't give a damn about her career, was sticking his neck out to help her. What was he thinking of? "Jeffrey," she said cautiously, "are you sure you didn't dream this? I mean, why would Hamilton want to help me?"

"I dunno. Maybe he's got the hots for you. Listen, love, I've got to fly. There's a call on the other line. Give my regards to Charlie. He's in room 198 at the Carlton. And remember, love is never having to say you're sorry."

Then he hung up.

Now what did he mean by that? Kate thought. And then she grinned. Did Charlie make it that obvious? Despite herself, she felt flattered. More than that, excited. Her encounter with the Englishman had meant more to her than she cared to admit. Even to herself. She had suspected he was out of her league when they first met in New York. And when he told her he was married, she was more than a little relieved. There was nothing she could have done about him. Not with Ted in her life.

Then they had met again, in a different time. A different place. And something had happened.

For a moment she was back in his grand, old-fashioned apartment in Eaton Square. Her stomach turned over. She knew exactly what had happened with her and Charlie Hamilton. She picked up the phone. Room 198 at the Carlton, she thought. Why not? You only live once.

She had to hang on five minutes before the hotel answered. Five minutes of mounting anxiety and wondering if she was doing the right thing. Finally she got through.

"Bonjour Hotel Carlton," said the operator.

Kate decided to speak in English. At their prices, they could afford to understand the language. "Would you put me through to room 198?" she asked. "Mr. Charlie Hamilton."

There was silence. Then there followed a clicking sound. The voice of the operator came back on the line. *"Monsieur Hamilton n'est pas là. Voulez-vous parler avec la réception? Peut-être laisser un message?"*

"Thank you, but no," she said firmly, putting down the receiver. Her French wasn't up to leaving messages. And the Carlton weren't up to employing linguists on their exchange that season. Even at their prices.

She finished packing, and scribbled a note to Doug telling him she was returning to London, and canceling their dinner date.

Then she rang for a porter to collect her bags and made her way down the hotel corridor to the elevator. She pressed the call button and glanced at her watch. There was just an hour before her plane left. So intent was she on making her connection that she didn't hear the phone ringing in the room she had just left. If she had, she would have had quite enough time to retrace her footsteps and answer it. For Charlie Hamilton held on to the receiver in his room at the Carlton for a full five minutes before slamming it down in frustration.

Kate's story on David O'Neill caused a stir in Cannes that year. Everyone present agreed it was the best media event to come out of the Festival. Doug Freeman read it with admiration and just a touch of envy. Jeremy Boyle glanced at it in frank surprise. And Tracy couldn't believe what had happened.

She had just emerged from the shower in David O'Neill's suite at the Carlton when she saw it. There was a pile of copies of the *Post* on the marble coffee table at the bottom of the bed and, clad in just a fluffy white bath towel, she made her way over to it. When she saw the front page, she wished she hadn't. For under the masthead was a postage-stamp sized picture of the man she had just spent the night with. The words accompanying the photograph left her in no doubt about what she would find if she turned to the arts section. "David O'Neill talks about his controversial new role in *The Last Goodbye.* Turn to page 24 for Kate Kennedy's exclusive report from the Cannes Festival."

Outside in the late morning sunshine David O'Neill sat with his feet up on the breakfast table, demolishing the last of the croissants and checking through his quotes.

He nodded with satisfaction. Kate Kennedy had caught his meaning exactly. Charlie had been right about the girl. He looked up to see that Tracy had managed to find a copy of the story. She seemed to get less joy from it than he did. Her face was contorted with rage. And in the bright morning light that mysteriously pale skin of hers looked a little pasty.

"Are you feeling okay?" he asked solicitously, pouring her what was left of the coffee. "You look as if something's bothering you."

"You bet something's bothering me," she said through clenched teeth, "why didn't you tell me you were giving an interview to Kate Kennedy?"

David did his best to look composed. He had known there would be trouble this morning. That was why he had let her sleep in so late. Now the time of reckoning had come.

"I didn't tell you, you silly girl, because you didn't ask me. Anyway I thought it was my body you were interested in."

For a moment she was stopped in her tracks. But only for a moment. "Oh, David," she wailed, "I was interested, really I was. But I have a living to earn as well. How can I do that when you two-time me with that bitch, Kate Kennedy?"

"None of us gets everything they want," David replied. "Not all the time, anyway. This morning Kate got her story. And you got me. I'm not such a terrible consolation prize, am I?"

He could have saved his breath. Tracy was like a child who'd lost her lollipop. Her bright hair, wet from the shower, was starting to dry in unattractive little wisps. And she was crying.

David cursed inwardly. Why did this always happen to him? He'd find a glorious, glossy girl. The possibilities would seem infinite. So he'd take her to bed and explore possibilities. But no matter what happened during the night, the morning was always the same. He'd wake up to find the gloss had worn off and he was landed with a spoiled kid. He sighed. It was time to get rid of her. He looked at his watch. "Love, I've got to run. My agent wants to see me for lunch at Cap d'Antibes. If I don't leave now, I'll be late."

Tracy sat up with a start. Things weren't going the way she'd expected. David O'Neill was meant to be on his knees begging for forgiveness, not getting the hell out. This scenario she didn't understand.

Swiftly she removed her bath towel—the only thing between her and complete nudity. Then she stopped crying. "What are you doing after lunch?" she asked.

But David O'Neill had seen it all before. "I'm packing," he said tersely. "A friend of mine, a very old friend of mine, died in Los Angeles. I have to fly over there to attend his funeral."

She grabbed the towel, and with it the last shreds of her dignity. "Are you saying you want me out of here?"

"That's about the size of it. You may have all the time in the world, but it's not the same for poor Cy Goldberg. His life ran out yesterday. And if I'm not on a plane and out of here this afternoon, I won't be able to say goodbye to him."

With that he grabbed his jacket and was out of the door before Tracy could protest.

As David O'Neill was walking away from Tracy, a man in a dark suit and a snap brim hat was walking toward a table at the Martinez where Jeremy Boyle was sitting. From his wallet he produced his identification. Then he sat down.

"What the hell is this?" protested Jeremy, who was more than a little woozy from all the Pernod he had consumed.

"The name is Delon," said the stranger, "Inspector Delon of the Cannes Sûreté. I think it would be wise if you came with me to the bureau. *Doucement.*"

"But I don't understand." Jeremy was gabbling now. "You can't do this. You have no authority."

"That's where you are wrong, Monsieur. I have my own authority. And I have the authority of Scotland Yard. They want you, I think, for questioning about a robbery."

Despite the heat and his drink-fuddled brain, the truth of the situation started to filter through to Jeremy. He stood up. "I don't know anything about any robbery," he said. "Who told you I did?"

"We had a visit last night from a young woman. She was on her way to the casino and she called in to tell us she had seen you. Her story seemed a little farfetched. But she was so very angry, I was intrigued.

"I called London this morning. They confirmed everything she told me. So all I had to do was find you."

He produced a pair of handcuffs, one of which he attached to Jeremy's wrist, the other to his own. "It wasn't much of a manhunt," said the French policeman mournfully. "You English are so snobbish about where you take your aperitifs. It has to be a terrace by one of these expensive hotels. Or Les Routiers on the Croisette. Now if you had been a Frenchman or even a Corsican it would have been a different story . . ."

For the duration of the hot, dreary walk to the police station Inspector Delon treated Jeremy to a dissertation on the drinking habits of his countrymen. When he was finally marched into one of the cells with the door closed in his face it seemed like a blessed relief.

14

"**B**ut I don't understand," said Sandy, her voice full of tears. "Why can't you come out to Los Angeles?"

"Because Kramer won't hear of it," said Ted for the tenth time. "And Ed Kramer is all that stands between this rapidly growing family and Poverty Row."

They had been arguing all night about something that should have been so simple. Her father had died and she needed Ted, her husband, to come with her to the funeral. It shouldn't have seemed too much to ask. But apparently it was.

When Ted had told his editor he was taking the best part of a week off to go to his father-in-law's funeral, all hell broke loose. Bill Gerhaghty was on vacation. Ruth was still too busy getting back on her feet again, and even Tracy, the dingbat who covered for her, was away at the

Cannes Film Festival. If Ted went off for a week Kramer would be left with a disorganized rabble of writers, none of whom could be expected to deputize for the features editor. So he panicked. If Ted took the week off, he threatened, his job just might not be waiting for him when he came back.

Ted suspected that he was bluffing. These were the hysterical ravings of a man he had long suspected was too small for the job of running a New York newspaper. But he didn't want to put it to the test. Sophie was still a baby. And the boys seemed to be growing out of their clothes every time he looked at them. No, Sandy would have to bury her father without him. It wasn't as if she would be alone on the occasion. As well as her suffocating family, half the film community of Los Angeles would be turning out to say goodbye to Cy Goldberg. So he set his jaw and hardened his heart. He was staying in New York and that was the end of the discussion.

Sandy knew when she was beaten. It was something she'd had a lot of time to get used to. Though if anyone had told her a year ago that things would have turned out this way, she would have laughed and called them a liar. She looked back to the night in The Palm. The night she had told Ted she was expecting their third baby. How different it had been then. In her mind's eye she could still see her husband's face. He seemed surprised. Stunned almost. But afterward when he had recovered from the news, she was convinced at long last that their marriage stood a chance.

"I won't see Kate again," he had promised her. "It's over. All I want now is you . . . and our children."

And she had believed him. What wife wouldn't? How was she to know he was going to change?

Bit by bit she remembered the way things had been with Ted. If he had turned his back on her there and then, it might have been easier. At least she would have known where she stood. But he didn't.

It started with the silences. Up to then they had always had things to talk about. The boys' schooling. What the plans were for the weekend. Where they were going to go on vacation. Now he didn't seem interested anymore. When she tried to talk to him, he seemed to be somewhere else. Then one day he was.

Instead of having a drink when he came home and talking about the day as he used to, Ted retreated into his study. There was always some lame excuse for the disappearances. Problems at the office. Papers he had to go over at the end of the day.

But on the occasions when she poked her head around the study door, Ted didn't look busy at all. All he seemed to be doing was nursing a martini and staring into space.

In the beginning she tried to involve him in her life. The children's lives. But it was like talking to a dead man. He ate, he drank, he even made love. But when she looked into his eyes, she couldn't find anyone she knew.

For the first time since they were married, she began to feel alone. And it scared her. Even when Ted was having the affair with Kate, it hadn't been like this. At least he gave part of himself to his family. Now there was nothing.

She hardly recognized this new man as the one she had married. The one she had promised to love forever.

Something had happened to change him. And she suspected it was in some way connected to Kate Kennedy. She had to find out. So she plucked up her courage and called the only friend she and Ted had in common. She called Ruth.

Ruth was not displeased to hear from Sandy. At least she was real. Since her illness Ruth's view of the world had undergone a change. Now her life was not just filled with people. It was filled with two kinds of people. There were the ones she worked with. The photographers, the models, the stylists, and the majority of her colleagues. And there were the real people. Mike was real. Her mother was real. And so was Sandy Gebler, née Goldberg.

While she was feeling vulnerable, Ruth preferred the company of real people. They were more restful. So she invited Sandy over for lunch. "It's high time you came over and visited the sick," she told her. "That is, if you're not feeling too sick yourself."

She had heard of Sandy's latest pregnancy from Ted. Somebody else had told her about Kate's departure. But there was no doubt in her mind that the two were connected. Yet she didn't pass judgment. She wasn't feeling well enough. Anyway, despite her loyalty to Kate, she had a sneaking admiration for Sandy. And a sympathy. The last few months couldn't have been easy.

Sandy was bigger than she expected. More pregnant-looking. And impending motherhood seemed to suit her. Her skin had a healthy rosy look to it. Her hair fairly glistened. And her eyes looked even bigger and bluer than they usually did. Yet there was an unhappiness about her that seemed strangely out of place. Ruth made a mental note to ask Sandy how she was getting on with Ted. But not right now. Right now she was too busy telling Sandy about her own life.

"How did you meet him?" asked Sandy, who had heard through the grapevine that Ruth Bloom had a live-in lover.

"In Paris, on an assignment," said Ruth, "and I can tell you it was lust at first sight. For him anyway. I was a little turned off men at that point in my life."

"But you got over it," said Sandy, who loved a happy ending.

"Luckily," said Ruth, "for both our sakes."

"What about marriage?"

Ruth pulled a face. "I never liked the idea when I was well. Now that I'm sick, it appeals even less. No, living together suits us both. Incidentally, while we're on the subject of relationships, how are you and Ted getting along? He always seems a bit tense when he comes to see me. I can't figure out whether it's the office or his home life that's putting him on edge."

Ruth wasn't strictly telling the truth. She knew exactly what was bugging Ted. Every time he came to visit, he'd talk endlessly about Kate. Wondering where it all went wrong. Harking back to times past. Blaming himself for driving her away. But she didn't want to tell Sandy any of this. Not unless she had to. So she listened to Sandy's version of the last few months. She saw through the other woman's eyes the retreats into the study, the long silent dinners, the lovemaking without love. At the end of it, Ruth knew what she was going to say to Sandy. What she had to say.

"I suppose you know that Kate's left New York. For

good, I mean." Then she looked at Sandy and realized that she hadn't known. She decided to go on. "Look, Kate left for London the moment she heard you were pregnant. I know you probably don't want to hear this, but I think she behaved decently. She loved Ted, but she knew you needed him more. So she just cut out. She didn't say goodbye to anyone. Not even me."

She paused. "You can imagine the effect this had on Ted. Giving up a girlfriend is one thing. But having the girl give up on you is something else. His pride was hurt, and he felt he'd failed in some way."

Sandy looked desperate. "What can I do about it? How can I help? I guessed it was something to do with Kate and, believe me, I've done everything I know to take his mind off it."

Ruth took the blonde girl's hand and squeezed it. "Stop trying too hard, honey. He'll come out of it. Men always do. Right now, if you come on too strong, you'll only remind him of what's bugging him.

"No, if I were you I'd stop pushing. Give Ted a bit of space to heal himself. You'll see, if you give him some time to wallow in his disappointment, he'll come back to normal. And Sandy, next time you're feeling low, keep this in mind. When Ted does get back to himself, you know you'll have him one hundred percent. Kate Kennedy's gone for all time."

Sandy took the piece of knowledge Ruth had given her and hugged it to herself. There was consolation in it. And the promise of a brighter future.

Then the baby came and she stopped thinking about Ted. To Sandy's delight, her latest arrival turned out to be a little girl. She called her Sophie, after Ted's mother.

She didn't check to see if the gesture had pleased her husband. She was far too involved with her daughter to worry about the existence of any other human being. Sophie wasn't her first child, yet she was different from the other two. And not just because of her sex. Right from the start, the twins had had each other. Of course they loved her. She was their mother, wasn't she? But they didn't need her in the same way Sophie did. Sophie was all alone. Eight years separated her from her brothers. Her father was curiously uninterested in her, almost as if she had been an accident instead of a blessing. All she had was Sandy. And Sandy was there for her.

It was as if the child had filled a void in her life. For Sandy was a woman who needed, more than anything, to love and be loved. When Ted had drawn away from her, she had been alone. Now she wasn't anymore. Now there was Sophie.

Ruth's advice turned out to be a blind alley. Ted never did get back to himself. Or if he did, then he didn't get back to Sandy. In the end, she ran out of patience. She had feelings too and they needed to be considered.

She went out and bought a new kitten. Their cat, Tiger, had died a few months earlier. She started seeing more of Martha Ward, her neighbor. She involved herself in coffee mornings and baby talk with the other young mothers in the neighborhood. She started to make a life for herself. A life without Ted.

Then on the last Tuesday in May, her father died suddenly of a heart attack. The event shocked her. It grieved her. But worse than any of those things, it made her feel alone again.

She needed her husband. And she needed him bad.

This was not a wound that could be healed with Cona coffee and a new kitten. So she reached for Ted. She held out her hands across the rift that divided them and asked for peace. And he failed her again. How silly she had been to think he'd do anything else.

With a sense of great weariness she made arrangements for her children. She might have to go to a funeral but she didn't want them to be touched by her sadness. They were too young, too innocent to know about life's troubles. The time for that would come soon enough.

Ted's parents offered to take care of the boys. Martha Ward took Sophie in. She felt good about that. Martha was one of the few people left whom she trusted.

Then she packed her good black suit and a couple of pairs of jeans and set off for the airport. She had never felt so isolated in the whole of her life.

As Ted predicted, half the movie colony turned out on Forest Lawn to say goodbye to Cy Goldberg. Because it was a Jewish funeral there were no flowers, no wreaths and few people wore black—the color not being mandatory on these occasions. Instead the crowd of mourners gathered around the graveside in drab, dull colors which matched their expressions.

David O'Neill, who clung to his own traditions, wore black for the occasion. A smart morning suit, made by Huntsman of London, a crisp white shirt and a black silk tie. He also carried a hip flask full of brandy in his trouser pocket. The Irish favored a stiff drink after a burial. He didn't know what the Jews did, but he was leaving nothing to chance.

After he had deposited his handful of earth on the

coffin, he'd take a belt from the flask then head off to Murphy's in downtown L.A. to say a proper goodbye to his friend. Cy would have wanted it that way.

As he stood in line waiting to pay his last respects, he wondered where his chauffeur had gone. He had given the man strict instructions to pick him up in forty minutes. That would just give him time to say goodbye to Cy and pump the hands of the agents, producers and fellow thespians who regarded this kind of event as a social occasion. Because his arrival in Los Angeles had been unexpected, his regular driver was away on vacation. And for the life of him, David could not remember a single thing about the guy who was standing in for him—except that he was stocky and middle-aged.

The description fitted a good seventy percent of the assembled multitude and David scanned every face in the crowd in an attempt at recognition.

For a moment his eyes stopped. There was a face he recognized, though it was a damn sight too good-looking to be his chauffeur's. It was also female.

What was her name? Suzie? Sharon? No, that wasn't it. His mind went back to where he first met her. It was New York, he remembered. A first-night play. And then he knew. Of course it was Cy's daughter, Sandy. He remembered how surprised he had been to discover that she had grown up to be such a good-looking woman. He also remembered, with a touch of regret, that she had a husband.

Nevertheless when he had done what was expected of him, he made his way across to her. A man had to pay his respects to the family. It was only proper.

Sandy looked both pleased and surprised to see him.

And when he looked at her his heart turned over with pity. The death of her father had clearly taken it out of her. She was so thin. In New York she had been voluptuous. Stacked. Now she was all skin and bone. And the way she was wearing her hair, drawn back into the nape of her neck. It didn't suit her at all.

"How's that husband of yours?" he asked, in an attempt to be jovial. "The one with the deadly right hook. Should I run for cover when I see him coming?"

She smiled and he was relieved to see that bereavement hadn't done anything to her face. Even without the paint and powder she was still one hell of a looker.

"He's not here," was all she said, "so you can stop looking worried."

For a moment he was surprised. "Why isn't he here? You didn't get divorced since I last saw you?"

Again she gave him the Cinderella smile. "No," she said. "Nothing as drastic as that. Ted's just been a little busy lately. Extra responsibilities at the office. You know the kind of thing."

You bet I know the kind of thing, he thought grimly. It's probably big and busty and answers to the name of bimbo. He felt the rage boil up inside of him. What kind of jerk was this guy she married?

"Well, I wouldn't let any wife of mine go to her father's funeral on her own," he said gruffly. "It wouldn't matter how busy I was."

She was silent for a long time, and for a moment he thought she was going to cry. Then she pulled herself together and looked at him steadily. "No, I don't think you would," she said. He was about to ask her what she was doing later on, when an older woman with the same blonde hair as Sandy's came over. He recognized Freda Goldberg from years ago and offered his condolences. She thanked him, and the thanks came out as an automatic response. She'd heard the same speech too many times that day.

"We're having a few people over for tea and honey cake. The usual kind of thing," said Sandy awkwardly. "You're welcome if you want to come."

David considered. He'd been to this kind of thing before. The family would be sitting down in a semi-circle. All the mirrors would be draped in black. And there would be speeches and reminiscences about the dead man.

Then he thought about the long bar with the brass rail at Murphy's. They wouldn't be serving tea there; it would be good solid bourbon with steak sandwiches, not honey cake. He suddenly realized he was famished. Then he looked at Sandy. Pale and thin and grieving for her father on her own.

"Lead me to it," he said. "I couldn't think of anything I'd like better than a cup of tea."

The things he did for women.

On a clear day, from his table at Spago, David O'Neill could see the whole of Hollywood spread out in front of him. Acre upon acre of swimming pools and armored glass twinkling their invitation to all the good times money could buy.

Today was not a clear day. But David had more than enough in his line of vision. For sitting opposite him, picking at her dish of crudités, was Jerry Adams.

To look at, you could see right away that she was

either an actress or a model. And you would be right on both counts. For at various times in her short career she had been both. In between men. They always came first on her list of priorities. Jerry didn't waste her time, her youth and her forty-inch bustline on just anyone. The men she dated had to be rich. And they had to provide. Tickets on the Concorde, emeralds from Boucheron, private beaches on private islands.

Jerry was a commodity with a sell-by date. For she knew that by the time she reached thirty the goods would be past their best. She was twenty-two. There were eight years to go.

David knew all this about his newest companion, and he felt relatively safe. Eight years gave him plenty of leeway. She wouldn't start getting anxious about her future until she was at least twenty-five. And by then he would be ancient history.

He leaned forward and urged her to try the caviar. It wasn't a specialty of the house. Pizza was Spago's forte. But David knew better than to suggest it.

They had met three days previously at a party in Bel Air. Cy Goldberg's funeral had left a sour taste. The death of his old friend, coupled with the troubles of that daughter of his, had depressed him. He needed a lift. Something to remind him that he was rich and celebrated and attractive to women.

Then he had met Jerry and he knew he had found what he was looking for. She was a tall girl, Latin-looking, with jet-black hair which she wore piled up in a chignon. Not a neat, Grace Kelly chignon, but a big messy, wispy concoction which looked as if it might tumble around her bare shoulders at the slightest provocation. She had a tiny waist which was accentuated by her ridiculously tight dress. And her heels were so high that David had felt she could topple over at any moment. He had had an insane desire to ravish her on the spot. But he didn't.

He had contained himself until the party was over. Then he had ravished her in the comfort of his house on the beach. It was a less exhilarating experience than her appearance had led him to expect. Not that she was in any way inept. Quite the reverse. And that was the problem. Where he had imagined abandon there was a practiced professionalism. It wasn't that the girl was a whore. Not in the true sense, anyway. But there was a premeditated quality about the way she gave herself to him.

It started with the way she took her clothes off. Most women he had known had let him undress them. Or if not, they might have undone a button or two. Left a zipper open.

Not Jerry. For Jerry, getting undressed in front of a man was a production not unlike a burlesque show. At first it was fun. Her hair came tumbling down, just as he knew it would. The dress came off rather like unpeeling a banana. Then just as he thought she would kick her shoes off and let him do the rest, she shooed him away.

For the next twenty minutes Jerry Adams paraded around his bedroom in her high heels and lacy black garter belt as if she had played the scenario a thousand times before. It should have been exciting. Her breasts were the size of melons and seemed to have a life of their own. She wasn't wearing panties. Yet David was reminded of a centerfold in *Playboy.* And when she finally settled back on his bed, parted her legs and smiled prettily, he felt he could have been anyone. Anyone who could pick up the bill at Boucheron or buy her a first-class airline ticket.

Jerry Adams didn't make him feel attractive, that was for sure. But she made him feel rich and celebrated. Given his needs of the moment, two out of three wasn't a bad batting average.

He was brought back to the present by the arrival of the caviar. Spago certainly knew how to present it. The black fish eggs were resting in a crystal bowl which was positioned right in the center of an ice sculpture. The sculpture was in the shape of a swan. He wondered idly whether the swan would melt before Jerry had had time to finish eating the caviar. Not that he could be bothered to watch her. There was something about her hunger, her greed, that he found vaguely obscene.

His eyes wandered around the restaurant. It was filling up fast, he noticed. And he knew from experience that soon the lines would start forming. Spago was the only restuarant he knew of where well-known people with big bucks would line up for a table. He had seen them passing hundred-dollar bills to the waiters for special treatment. But it didn't stop them from standing in line. In a fashionable watering hole where everyone can afford the price of a bribe, everyone waits.

His eyes took in agents making deals with casting directors. Actors, like himself, resting between pictures. Girls on the town. His gaze stopped at a couple at the far end of the restaurant. He recognized Mel Cohen, one of the last of the old-time directors. He had been Dietrich's lover way back when, or so rumor had it. Right now he looked as if he had other plans in mind. He took in the blonde sitting across from him, expecting a standard-issue bimbo. And he looked again.

For the girl with Mel was no bimbo. The girl was Sandy Gebler, Cy Goldberg's daughter. David guessed Mel was offering condolences; he and Cy had been close. And just for a moment, he wished he were sitting across from Sandy.

He noticed with approval that she was eating a pizza. He also noticed that she was looking considerably better than when they had last met, four days ago. There was life in the saucer-blue eyes now. And she had obviously washed her hair that morning. There was something clean about Sandy. Wholesome. He wondered if she went through the striptease routine to turn on her husband and instantly despised himself.

Women like Sandy, nice women with children, didn't go in for that kind of cheap trick. She probably wouldn't know where to start, he thought. And for an instant he was reminded of Gwen.

David hadn't thought about his wife, his ex-wife for years. Not since the divorce. Now the memories came flooding back. He had been happy then. He had had a home to go to. And a wife who knew how to make him comfortable. Even the kids didn't get on his nerves. In a way it was nice having them around. They went with the territory.

He looked across at Jerry, who was finishing up the remains of the caviar. The girl was chasing the last few black specks across the plate with her finger. Then she put it in her mouth and sucked the end of it.

He looked at her with mounting despair. Half the men in the city would go crazy for this piece and all I can do is feel sad, he thought. He pulled himself together.

"Is the striptease your only routine?" he asked her. "Or do you know others?"

It was dark in the house on Malibu beach and David was alone. For that he was grateful. Licking his wounds was something he preferred to do without an audience. He got up and made himself a drink. A vodka straight with a handful of ice and a squeeze of lemon. To hell with the vermouth.

The first mouthful tasted good and he ambled over to the porch and switched on the lights. Now that he was outside he could smell the ocean and feel the cool of the evening on his skin. Maybe he would live after all.

He sat down by the bar and as he did so he saw the earring. It was fashioned like all the Cartier jewels that season. Little pavé diamonds set in gold. And he knew it belonged to the girl. He would have to get it back to her. Maybe a messenger service, or his secretary would oblige. There was no way he wanted to meet her again.

He reflected on what had happened after Spago's. They had gone back to the house by way of Saint Laurent on Rodeo Drive. Jerry had seen a suit she liked the look of and David picked up the tab without her having to ask. The girl had promised to take him to paradise that afternoon and he figured a little extra incentive wouldn't do her any harm.

He was right. The minute they got back she went into action. And he couldn't help thinking there was something indecent about her willingness to please. For it had nothing to do with desire. She didn't find him handsome, or at least she hadn't said so. She hardly even listened to what he said half the time. No, he had done something for her and now it was her turn.

He remembered the price of the suit from Saint Laurent, and gritted his teeth. This had better be good, he thought. It was. It was more than good. It was superlative. Though where she learned the trick with the cold cream and the hot water he could only guess.

He was lost in admiration. At least his eyes and his mind were impressed. The rest of his body failed to respond. So Jerry changed tack. She moved to the swimming pool where she demonstrated her talents under water. That didn't work either.

David started to get irritated. What am I trying to prove? he wondered. Then he looked at the softness of his flesh and he knew. For the first time in his life he actually felt embarrassed. He went over to the poolhouse and grabbed a terrycloth robe. Once he was covered he felt better. Then he looked around for the girl. She was nowhere to be seen.

With something like relief he made himself a drink. Maybe she had taken the hint and gone home? Anybody else would. Anybody but Jerry Adams. For Jerry was intent on giving value for money, whatever the setbacks.

Five minutes later she was back. Stark naked except for a liberal covering of baby oil and a pair of long black boots. She fixed him with a look of pure determination. "Have I got something for you."

Something snapped. Later David realized it was probably his patience. He put his drink down on the bar and got to his feet.

"Have you any idea how bloody ridiculous you look?"

She was startled. "What do you mean, ridiculous? Men go crazy for this."

David O'Neill did go crazy. But not in the way she had intended. He walked over to her, grabbed her by the hand and propelled her toward the bedroom. Then, still keeping hold of her hand, he pointed toward the chair where her clothes were lying. "I want you in those and out of here. Fast. And when I say fast, I mean five minutes. Do you hear?"

Jerry heard. She was dressed and on her way before he had finished his drink. She took the designer suit with her.

He smiled, remembering. The kid had guts. He couldn't fault her there. No, if anyone was at fault, it was him. A wave of self-pity rose up to meet him. With an effort he shrugged it off. This was no time for *mea culpa*.

Something had to be done. Something to get him back to normal. As the word normal came into his mind, so did a vision of Sandy Gebler. Clean, wholesome Sandy Gebler. As normal as apple pie.

Maybe that's what I need, he thought. Maybe I've been rutting around for too long. He made himself another drink, took a deep breath of the salty night air and thought about it. The idea intrigued him. David O'Neill and the girl next door. He thought about Gwen. Why not? He'd been that route before and it hadn't been so terrible. He'd never had any problems getting a hard on for his wife.

And that decided him. From now on there would be no more exotic routines. No more black leather boots.

No more underwater sports. He went inside for his address book. The sooner he called Sandy Gebler the better.

When David called and offered to drive her to the beach, Sandy grabbed at the chance to get away for an afternoon. She'd forgotten how warm the sun was in California. It was a different kind of warm from New York, which was harsh and scorching. Here it was gentler. And when she felt the sand under her feet and smelled the dampness of the sea, she knew she had come home.

All her early life, Sandy had been the archetypal California girl. Blonde, tanned and freaked out on health food and exercise. She was at the bottom of every class in school because she was too busy surfing and skateboarding. She was the first among her friends to go vegetarian. And if she could have had her face lifted at seventeen she would have done so.

Her only problem was that she had no problems. Other girls—her friends—had psychotherapists, and nutritionists. She longed to emulate them. But how could she? She was happy and beautiful.

Her ten years in New York had eroded both those qualities. But now she was back, and in the space of one short afternoon she was starting to feel more like the girl she had left behind.

Then the sun started to go down. And with the dusk came reality. She must go and see her mother. She had to call her children in New York. David didn't press her. Which was unusual for him. He didn't normally listen to excuses from women, particularly when they interfered with his plans. But he listened to Sandy. For some reason that he couldn't quite fathom, he didn't want her to find him inconsiderate. He put it down to a temporary delusion brought on by the sun.

They went to the beach the next afternoon. And the afternoon after that. On the third day she discovered that David had a house there. "Why didn't you tell me?" she chided. "It would have been more comfortable lying on a deck. We could have had something to drink. Maybe I might have made you a sandwich."

He looked embarrassed. "I didn't think it was very proper. What with you being a married woman and all."

"Proper is a state of mind," she said. "If you'd wanted to you could have had your wicked way with me just as easily on the beach."

"What, in all this sand?" he protested. "Out in public? I've got my reputation to think of, you know."

Sandy looked at him. It was the kind of look only a very grown-up woman knows how to transmit. It told him who she was and what she wanted from him. Exactly. For the first time in his life, David was completely confused. "Are you sure?" he asked.

"Only if you want the same things that I do," she replied. "Otherwise the answer's no."

He held out his hand and helped her up. Then he picked up the beach towels and the tote bags. "I live five minutes away," he said. "Two minutes if we run."

They ran all the way to David O'Neill's house on the edge of the sea. As fast as their legs would carry them.

It was Friday morning and Ted was in a hurry. He had been pushed all week—ever since Sandy had left for the Coast.

The problem was Kramer. Something was bugging him, and when the editor had something on his mind everyone near him suffered. Which meant Ted suffered. And Bill Gerhaghty suffered.

The Irishman had gotten the third degree over lunch two days ago. Today it was Ted's turn, which was why he was in a hurry. The first priority was to find a clean shirt. Irritably he riffled through his closet for a suitable choice. There wasn't one. There was the gray denim which he used to do the garden in on Saturdays. And there was one with pale blue checks and a detachable collar. Both of them were dogs.

Sandy, Sandy, he muttered under his breath, where are you when I need you? For the first time since her departure he began to actively miss his wife. It wasn't just for her clean shirts either. The weekend was looming up and he needed someone to share it with. Normally when Sandy was there they'd drive out to the market together and do the weekly shopping. On the way back they'd stop off and grab a burger. Then they'd unload the car, grab the kids and the whole family would go swimming. On Sunday there'd be a picnic or a barbecue with friends.

As weekends went, they were pretty unremarkable. But after the kind of week he had in the office they were exactly what he needed to recharge his batteries. How else was he expected to cope with a monster like Ed Kramer? He thought of calling Sandy and asking her what he was supposed to do about a decent shirt. Then he thought better of it. He remembered the way she had looked when she left to bury her father and he felt like a bastard.

She had looked so defeated, so on her own. And he

asked himself for the hundredth time that week why he had allowed Kramer to get away with it. Why hadn't he simply stood up to the man and insisted on taking the time out to go with Sandy? It would have been the decent thing to do. In the short run, anyway, it would have made Sandy happy. But in his heart of hearts, Ted wasn't all that interested in the short run. What concerned him, what kept him awake at night, was the long run. And the long run wasn't about family funerals and the minutiae of married life. The long run was about Ted's future on the *News*.

Depending on the way the cards fell, it could be a very big future indeed. For there was a job vacancy. The deputy editor's job. And Ted was directly in line for it. Unfortunately so was Bill Gerhaghty. The two men had been fighting for the number two position on the paper ever since Bill Boroughs, who had had the job for fifteen years, died suddenly. All it would take was for one of them to give Kramer a push in the right direction. A major scoop would do it. So would solving a pressing problem. So would finding the right goddamn shirt to wear to lunch. Ted was beginning to feel desperate. The old bastard was so fussy about how people looked, anyone would think he was running a beauty contest instead of a newspaper. In the end Ted decided on the blue checked shirt. He could always send his secretary out to Bloomingdale's for a white one when he got into the office.

The moment he sat down to lunch, Ted sensed he was in for a rough ride. Whatever was bugging Kramer was making him irritable. So far he had taken out his temper on the wine steward (his Manhattan was the wrong strength), and it looked as if the waiter was in for it next. Kramer wanted a turbot, a plain poached turbot, and the restaurant couldn't oblige that day.

"Why do I come here?" he asked the terrified flunkey. "Why do I spend a fortune of the *New*'s money in here three times a week, when you can't even give me something decent to eat?"

Sole was suggested. Plaice was proferred. Even halibut was put up in place of the elusive turbot. But they wouldn't do. In the end Kramer called the maître d', who was more accommodating. Of course he could supply a poached turbot, if Mr. Kramer was prepared to wait a few minutes. Ted had visions of the chef being sent out to scour the restaurant kitchens of New York City until he came back with the offending fish. He squared his shoulders. It was bound to be his turn next.

But he was wrong, for the moment anyway. Kramer, mollified by his victory over the "21" 's kitchen staff, was prepared to be charming. So while the mood lasted, Ted brought up the subject of the deputy editor's job. He met with a blank wall. He even asked Kramer straight out whether he was in the running. He got waved aside. The man simply wasn't interested in the running of the paper that day. He wanted to talk about the fashion department.

So that's what's bugging him, thought Ted. I'd better humor the klutz. As patiently as he could, he listened to Kramer's evaluation of the fashion coverage. There was nothing new in it. The *News* needed fashion spreads, because the advertisers expected them. And because the competition provided them.

Finally over the second round of drinks Ted turned

to Kramer. "I don't see what the problem is," he said. "Ruth takes care of all that. Now that she's back on track, surely our worries are over."

Kramer looked cunning. "She's back on track now," he said, "but what if it doesn't last? What if she has a relapse? It's been known to happen. Then where would we be?"

Ted felt distinctly confused. What the hell was Kramer driving at? "Look," he said, "I think you're making a problem where one doesn't exist. Ruth's a hundred percent. Her doctor can vouch for it. She's as likely to have a relapse as I'm likely to go under a truck."

"That's what you think," said Kramer. "I'm not so convinced. So bear with me and let's just float around one or two ideas of what we might do if, let's say, Ruth wasn't around."

The trouble that had been hovering on the edge of Ted's consciousness finally took form. So that was the reason for the lunch. Kramer didn't want to talk about promoting him. Kramer wanted to talk about getting rid of Ruth.

With an ease born of long practice Ted tuned into the situation. "How do you see Tracy in the job?" he asked. At this stage, there was no point in being subtle.

Kramer was equally direct. "I don't," he said shortly. "Don't get me wrong, Tracy's a good kid. Great potential, but she hasn't got the experience we're looking for."

Ted was relieved. Tracy might be appetizing, but the old trouper hadn't completely lost his marbles. Not yet anyway. "What about hiring someone from one of the fashion magazines?" he suggested, testing the water.

"I have the names of a couple of hotshots who'd be ripe and ready for a move."

To his surprise, Kramer turned down the idea out of hand. "I don't want to take anyone else on board at present," he said. "I don't have the budget. Anyway it would cause too much disruption."

"No, Tracy wouldn't be happy working for anyone else," said Ted, catching on fast. "I mean since she's been virtually running the department in Ruth's absence."

"Quite," said Kramer. Then he added somewhat unnecessarily, "I'm glad you understand."

I bet you are, thought Ted grimly. Though why I should waste my time making allowances for your whims and fancies, I have no idea. Unbidden, Kate came into his mind. How different it all might have been if Kramer had understood instead of flying into a panic. He looked at the polished, aging executive sitting across the table and fought down the urge to strangle him. Since he had started taking an interest in Tracy, there had been no talk of the proprietor's morality clause. We are all equal, he thought, recalling his George Orwell. Only some of us are more equal than others. Enjoy your little redhead, Ed. Enjoy her all you can. Because some day I'm going to make you regret you ever set eyes on her.

Aloud he said, "Have you sounded Bill out about the problem?"

Kramer nodded.

"Was he any help?"

"Not really. He came up with a couple of names who could do the job. But that isn't the solution I'm looking for."

Ted looked thoughtful. "I think I know of a way,"

he said, "but why don't we order lunch first and then I'll tell you about it."

Ted knew that ordering lunch at "21" was a ritual that could take at least ten minutes. If the wine steward was slow it could take even longer. He watched Kramer signaling frantically for service. The least he could do was make the bastard sweat before he got him off the hook.

Ted's plan was simple, it was cheap and, most important of all, it made no difference whatever to Tracy. If anything it complemented her.

His idea was to throw the fashion pages open to the women who dictated style. The editors of the fashion bibles. So one week Elinor Green of *Vogue* would offer her interpretation of the autumn look. The next, Betty McQueen of *Fashion* would tell the readers how to look like a million on a tight budget. The beauty of the scheme was that each magazine got a free plug in the *News*, which meant a major boost to their circulation. And the paper had at its disposal the top talent in a specialized market.

Kramer went for the idea with the fervor of a drowning man clutching at a life raft. This was exactly what he had been looking for. It provided him with the perfect excuse to get rid of Ruth. Even she couldn't compete with an assortment of the best fashion brains in New York.

It also meant that he could promote Tracy to fashion editor without running the risk of her ever actually doing the job.

When the lunch dishes were cleared away, Kramer summoned the head waiter. Then he turned to Ted. "I think this calls for a celebration," he said. "Will you join me in an Armagnac? Henri assures me the restaurant has a supply of the finest you'll find anywhere.''

Ted swallowed hard. His brilliant scheme had put him points ahead of Gerhaghty in the race for the deputy editorship. It had also shot Ruth's career down in flames.

He nodded and allowed the black-jacketed flunkey to pour him a generous measure of the brandy of Napoleon. But as he raised his glass, he couldn't quite meet Kramer's eyes. There was no sentiment in business. There was no love in business. And now it seemed there was no friendship in it either.

Sandy lay very still in a large white marble bath shaped like a shell. The steam from the water carried with it the scent of Joy. And on the raised tile border stood two glasses and a bottle of Krug, chilled and open.

Her eyes traveled over the gold mosaic tiles, imported from Rome. The fluffy white carpet. The Portault bath towels. Then she closed her eyes and froze the scene in her head. It was her last day in California. Her last afternoon in David's beach house. She wanted to make sure she carried a mental photograph of it with her when she went back home.

"What are you doing lying there with your eyes closed?" asked David as he stepped out of the shower. "You look like a corpse."

"Shut up," said Sandy amiably. "Can't you see I'm recording this scene for posterity?"

David was flummoxed. "What on earth for? It's not the Sistine Chapel, you know."

"It is to me," she said firmly. "It's one of the few

places where I've been truly happy. I want to remember it always.''

He went over to the bath, put his hands around her waist and hauled her into a sitting position. She was so surprised that her eyes instantly flew open. So did her mouth.

''That's better,'' said David, ''now at least I have your full attention. What's all this about recording the inside of my bathroom for posterity? It has a very final ring to it. I don't like it at all.''

Sandy reached over to the iced Krug and poured herself a glass. The bubbles fizzed up her nose, making it tingle, so instead of looking serious she merely looked off balance. Like a kitten who has had its tail tweaked.

''Look,'' she said, making an effort to pull herself together, ''this has all been wonderful. Like a great, fabulous vacation. But you know and I know that it can't go on. Be sensible, darling.''

''Why should I be sensible. Where is it written that David O'Neill has to behave like a sober citizen, and wave fondly goodbye to the most beautiful blonde in the world.''

''Try to be serious,'' she said patiently. ''Aside from being blonde and, in your eyes, beautiful, there are a number of other considerations, starting with my husband.''

David took the bottle and topped up her glass. Sandy was very sexy when she got a little high.

''I don't think that's all that serious,'' he said. ''From what you tell me about him, the guy's either away working or off screwing somewhere. If I started visiting New

York every now and then, I don't expect he'd even notice."

She put down her glass. "Is that what you propose to do? Fly in, *en route* to wherever movie stars go, for a quick fuck in the afternoon. Well, you can just forget it. It sounds as tacky as hell."

He tangled his fingers into the long blonde hair and smoothed it out of her face. "Hey, calm down, will you? I wasn't suggesting anything tacky—unless of course you call what we've been doing for the past few days tacky."

She looked at him suspiciously. "Then what are you suggesting?"

"Do you want the whole picture? Or just part of it?"

She started to smile. "Tell me the whole megillah. I have an hour or so before my plane leaves."

He grabbed a thick white towel from the heated rail and handed it to her. "Then get out of the tub, woman, and come back to bed. I'm not spilling my guts out to a mermaid." Deftly she wrapped two hundred dollars' worth of terrycloth around her. Then with her wet hair trailing down her back she followed him into the bedroom. "What is it that's so important that you have to drag me out of the bath?"

"Just a little matter of your name," he said lazily. "Gebler's okay for now, but I don't think you should hang on to it for too long."

Sandy was mystified. "You want me to start calling myself Goldberg?" she said. "How would the children feel?"

"I don't think Goldberg's such a wonderful idea, either. It's too Jewish. No, I think a name with a nice Irish ring would suit you better. Something like O'Neill.

Sandy O'Neill. Mrs. Sandy O'Neill. What do you think?''

She sat down on the bed. Speechless. It didn't last for long.

"What about Ted?" she asked desperately. "What about the children? It's all such a shock. They'll go out of their minds."

He put his arms around her. "Nobody's going out of their minds. Not even you." He ran his hand across her cheek. "You're such a silly girl," he said. "Why do you think I offered to come and visit you in New York? It's certainly not for the occasional interlude in bed. I can get that anywhere. What I want from you is much more serious. And because it's so serious I don't expect you to make up your mind in five minutes.

"I think we should talk it through first. Get you used to the idea. I just thought it would be easier in New York." He grinned. "But if you want to come out to the beach, I suppose I can always take a plane."

She sighed. "David, David," she said, "why are you doing this to me? Why are you doing this to us? Can't we just leave things the way they were? It would be so much simpler. We could avoid so much pain."

He looked at her, exasperated now. "You still don't understand, do you?" he said. "I love you. And I think you love me. If that's going to ruffle a few feathers, it's just too bad. It's something we're going to have to learn to live with."

There were twenty messages waiting for Kate when she got back to her office in Vogue House. Only two of them caught her attention.

The first was from Hughes Hartmann in New York congratulating her on the O'Neill exclusive. She felt good about that. It was the first story of any significance she had filed from Europe and she knew she had made a breakthrough. The other message she took note of was from Doug Freeman. He wanted to take her out to dinner.

Under normal circumstances she would have called him right back and set a date. But now she wasn't so sure. The reappearance of Charlie Hamilton had thrown her off balance. If she met him again, she knew she would be lost. But what about him? Had he committed himself, or was he playing some sophisticated game?

She decided to put everything on hold for a week. By then the heat and passion of the Cannes Film Festival would be a memory—the English summer would see to that. Kate concentrated her whole attention on the bureau. Long conversations with Alan Baker convinced her of something she had suspected for a long time. Europe was a territory full of untapped potential. The mistake every bureau chief seemed to make was to devote all their energies to writing a record of the week's events.

It's not necessary, she thought. Alan writes a very professional column. Why take it away from him? She decided to let him go on doing it and concentrate her attention on the really big stories.

Princess Caroline of Monaco was rumored to be pregnant again. She went through her clippings. There was nothing interesting on her new husband. But her first husband, Philippe Junot, still had plenty of mileage. An interview with him would make world headlines. She put him at the top of her list.

Then she looked at the English royals. Princess Michael was overtaking the Duchess of Kent in the popularity stakes. From the corner of the file a picture caught her eyes. It was of the American porn star, Koo Stark. Was she still seeing Prince Andrew? Kate made another note.

By the end of the week she had chronicled and researched every potential major story on her turf. She had enough to keep her busy for the next twelve months. Even if she pulled off only twenty percent of what she had set out to do, she would have more than justified her existence.

So immersed was she in what she was doing that it

took a second call from Doug Freeman to jerk her back
to the present. It had been nearly two weeks and she still
hadn't done anything about Charlie Hamilton. Half of
her hoped he would try and make contact but she knew
she was being unrealistic. He'd made the first move. It
was up to her now.

She signaled to her secretary to hold Doug's call,
then instructed the girl to tell him she was in a meeting.
She would call back the minute she was free.

She picked up her private line and dialed Charlie's
office. The time for playing games was over. For a moment, when Charlie's secretary answered the phone, she
felt nervous. Then she pulled herself together. I'm Kate
Kennedy, she reminded herself, head of the New York
Post's London bureau, not some teenager with a crush.

She gave her name and full title to the girl on the
other end of the line. But it didn't make her feel any better. When Charlie's secretary told her he wasn't there,
her doubts about calling him returned.

This is silly, she thought. She asked when he would
be in the office. The girl didn't know. Mr. Hamilton was
out of the country.

"When will he be in London?" Kate asked, exasperated. His secretary didn't appear to know that either. The
most Kate could get out of her was that he was tying up
a film deal in California and if she wanted to leave her
number she could get a message to him. Kate told her
to forget it. It wasn't anything urgent. Then she put the
phone down in defeat. If her New York editor had asked
her to get an exclusive interview with the President of
France, she could have done it. If he had wanted an audience with the Pope, she could have arranged that too.

But to get a simple message of thanks to a British showbiz agent, that was beyond her capabilities.

She shook her head. They had been so close, she and Charlie. So close to falling in love, yet something always got in the way. First it was her job. Now it was his. She wondered if they would ever meet again. Or if they would go on missing each other for the rest of their lives.

There was an empty feeling in the pit of her stomach as she considered the prospect. Then she got a hold on herself. The best cure for a man, she remembered from some old Hollywood movie, was another man. Well, if Mae West could do it, so could she. She picked up the telephone again and called Doug Freeman. He might not make her heart beat any faster, but she liked the guy. And after the hard work of the last two weeks she needed someone to relax with.

When Doug roared into Kate's mews at eight o'clock the following evening she had no idea what to expect. A glance at his open-neck shirt and sporty looking XJ6 reassured her that at least it wouldn't be a repetition of their first dinner. And she realized why Burke's Club had irritated her so much. It was the kind of restaurant the jet set went to when they were slumming. You needed money to go there. Or a generous expense account. A man of around her age, on her kind of salary wouldn't go there with a friend. Even a girlfriend. That's why I felt so ill-at-ease with him, she thought. The whole setup was phony.

There was nothing phony about the place he took her to that night. It was a tiny Greek restaurant, just off Queensway. The neighborhood reminded Kate of Little Italy or Chinatown. There was an easy, cosmopolitan air about it. People came here to enjoy themselves, she realized, as they whizzed past first a skating rink, then a casino.

When they got to the Greka, Doug got a tumultuous welcome. The cashier came out from behind the desk and pumped his hand. The waiter put down the bottle of retsina he was carrying and hugged him like a brother. Even the cook, a weatherbeaten old man in a checked apron, poked his head out of the kitchen door and yelled his greetings.

"Come here a lot?" asked Kate, grinning, when they were finally allowed to sit down.

"Only with friends," he said. "Who else would understand?"

After that it was easy. They simply took up where they left off in Cannes.

Kate was eager to know what had happened to Jeremy Boyle, and Doug supplied the details with the relish of a born gossip. He told her everything from his incarceration in the Cannes police station to his eventual deportation twenty-four hours later. "You can imagine Jeremy screamed bloody murder all over the place. He demanded to see his lawyer. Insisted it was his right. But it didn't get him all that far with the French police. He had to get this side of the Channel before anyone took him seriously."

"Then what happened?" asked Kate, fascinated.

"The family went into action, of course. Jeremy might have been a drop-out and a disgrace, but he was still a Boyle. They didn't want too much shit thrown at the family reputation. So Clifford Gee was pressed into service. That particular firm of solicitors has been getting generations of Boyles out of the mire, and I must say they did well by Jeremy.

"He got out on a bail of £50,000. And I imagine old man Boyle spent another twenty grand in bribes all over the place to keep it out of the papers. Though I don't rate his chances too highly when they finally set a court date. You don't keep that kind of thing quiet forever."

As the food arrived, Kate pondered the fate of Jeremy Boyle. He had had it coming, of course. There was a limit to the amount of lying and cheating anyone could do before it caught up with them. No, she thought, as she contemplated the taramaslata, the aubergine dip, the fat black olive. I'm not sorry about what happened to you. I'm just sorry it had to be me who finally called the cops. Then she put the whole episode out of her mind and concentrated on her dinner.

She began to understand why Doug liked the place so much. Not only did the Greka provide a feast for its favorite customers, it also treated them like part of the family. A bewildering variety of drinks kept arriving at their table—ouzo, retsina and a strange Greek brandy which tasted deceptively mild and had a kick like a horse.

Kate sipped at the wine and drank a lot of Perrier. There was no point in letting alcohol warp her judgment the second time around.

Doug called for the bill. And when it came he looked at her thoughtfully. "You are coming back with me, Kate," he said.

She considered all the excuses. She was tired. Tomorrow was a busy day. She wasn't in the mood. Then she thought, what's the point? He's fun, he's attractive, and it's not as if we haven't been to bed together already. So because she needed a friend, Kate went back to Doug Freeman's flat.

He lived nearby in a large, modern, concrete block. The lobby with its fountains and violently patterned carpet reminded her of a four-star hotel. The apartment itself had the same soulless quality. As far as Doug Freeman was concerned, this was a stopping place rather than a home. The furniture was modern, low and obviously expensive. But everything from the carpets to the curtains was of a uniform beige color that suggested he put little thought into his surroundings. I bet he doesn't spend too much time here, Kate observed, as he crossed the room bearing a bottle of Hine and a couple of glasses. He started to pour the drink when she held up her hand. "I can't face the idea of a hangover," she said. "Why don't we just go to bed?"

So they did. And thus began the most aimiable, most convenient affair of her life.

16

Something was up. Ruth knew it without being told, yet she couldn't put her finger on the problem.

The whole thing had started with her secretary. The girl who looked after the feature writers was out sick and the chief stenographer couldn't spare anyone to fill the gap. So Ruth's girl Friday, Brett, was pressed into service. Her new duties, she was informed first thing on Monday morning, included looking after Ruth plus the other writers. The other writers were to take precedence—after all, there were more of them.

Ruth discovered the new arrangement when she got into the office. All her phones were ringing and nobody was picking them up. Five minutes later a red-faced Brett dashed into the department and explained what was happening.

The fashion editor hit the ceiling. First with Brett who burst into tears. Then with the general manager who seemed oddly unmoved about Ruth's lack of help. Finally with Ted who looked embarrassed.

"I could manage if Tracy was here," Ruth said in desperation, "but with her away in Cannes, I'm tied hand and foot to the office. How does anyone expect me to get this week's fashion spread together if I can't even get to see the clothes?"

"Have them sent in," said Ted. "You don't have to hike around the showrooms."

"What about the photography?" she demanded. "You're not going to suggest I organize the session by remote control."

"That depends on which photographer you use," he replied. "If you lean on somebody you trust, somebody who knows how your mind works, then you could probably get away with not being there. Just for this once."

It all sounded very reasonable. Ruth had to admit that. But it was almost too reasonable. Why wasn't Ted jumping up and down at the injustice of it? He normally didn't like any department he controlled having to make do. Yet here he was calmly extolling the virtues of second best.

She decided not to have an argument about it. There were other things that needed her energy, starting with the spread.

Her nerve endings jangled for the second time two days later when she looked at the flat plan. Before it went into print, every newspaper was mocked up in miniature, the whole package looking like a thin magazine made entirely of blank paper. On the blank pages was sketched the space allocated for each story together with the ads, which filled the rest of the available column inches. And the ads were what frayed Ruth's temper.

Normally her spread went over two pages, the ads taking bite-sized chunks out of each side. Ruth lived with the ads. She had to; they were the reason her page was there in the first place. But that day she knew she could live with them no longer. For the ads weren't just biting at the spread. They looked as if they had eaten it for breakfast. Out of a dizzying collection of what looked like every retail store in Manhattan, she was left just half a page for her swimwear feature.

For the second time that week she stormed into Ted's office. "What the hell's going on?" she demanded.

Ted looked up from his desk. Ruth was standing in front of him, hair awry, face flushed, absolutely shaking with rage. Oh Christ, he thought, it's started. "You're asking me about the spread," he said as calmly as he could.

"I'm not asking you about the state of your health," she yelled, "though if you can't give me a straight answer this time, I'd start worrying about it."

"Ruthie, come down off the ceiling, and start thinking about *your* health for a change. Mine I can take care of. But yours bothers me."

And because he really did care about Ruth he decided to level with her. He walked across his office and closed the door that connected him with the rest of his department. Then he went to the liquor cabinet and got out a bottle of Scotch and some ice. It was five o'clock, the start of the happy hour. Or the unhappy hour, depending on who you were.

He poured the drink into two glasses. Ruth looked at him as if he were mad. They'd known each other since high school and he'd only seen her drink alcohol once—and that was at her brother's bar mitzvah. Why was Ted suddenly pushing Scotch at her?

Then she understood. He was going to tell her something she didn't want to hear. Something so bad that she needed a drink to steady her nerves. Or he did. She took a sip out of her glass. "Okay, Ted, get it over with. Tell me the worst."

He made a face. "I can't do that," he said. "That's up to Kramer."

She jiggled the ice cubes around in her glass, a habit she had when she was nervous. "Listen," she said, "if our editor hates the fashion this week, he doesn't have to tell me in person. Not at first, anyway. You can fill me in on the broad outline. He can give me the details later."

"Ruth, it's not the fashion." His voice had a flat, dead quality she hadn't heard before. She took another sip of her drink.

"It's my secretary then. You're taking her away and giving me a temp."

He smacked his glass down on the desk. There were times when he hated this business. "Ruth, it's not your secretary. It's not the fashion. I've seen the fashion, the fashion's fine. The problem lies with Kramer, you've got to see him and have it out."

"So that's what it's all about," she said. "Why didn't you tell me instead of beating around the bush? It's finished, isn't it? The job, I mean. He wants me out."

She paused, then said, "Tell me, Ted, how much longer do I have?"

He finished his drink in one long gulp. Then he reached for the bottle and poured himself another.

Ruth nodded. "It looks to me," she observed, "like it's more a matter of days than a matter of weeks. How long have you known?"

"Not long," he said shortly, then he said, "Oh God, Ruth, I'm sorry. I would have told you sooner if I could have . . ."

"But it was more than your future was worth," she finished for him.

She stood up. "I'm not blaming you, Ted," she said, "you've got a wife and family to support. I've got less to lose. And there's always Mike to look after me until I find something else."

She balanced her half-finished drink on the edge of his desk. "Thanks for that," she said, "and for breaking the news gently. I always could rely on you to look after my interests."

When she got back to her office Ruth called Kramer's secretary and told her she wanted to see him as soon as possible. The girl told her to hold on while she had a word with her boss. Then she came back on the line. "He'll see you in half an hour," she told Ruth. "Is that okay with you?"

Ruth said yes, then she took a key out of her bag and unlocked a drawer at the top of her desk. In it she kept the private correspondence she didn't want even her secretary to see. There were letters from former boyfriends. Confidential payments to freelancers. There was also a copy of her contract.

For the next half hour she studied it in detail, going over every clause. When the time was up she folded the document and put it in her purse. Then she put on fresh lipstick, ran her hand through her tangled curls and headed down the corridor. It was showtime.

Kramer was standing up when she came into his office. His arms were folded and there was a closed expression on his face.

He looks like he's expecting trouble, thought Ruth grimly. I wonder if he knows how much.

"To what do I owe this visit?" he asked, motioning her to sit down. "It's a little past your going home time, isn't it?"

"Yes," she said pleasantly, "but I wouldn't be too happy going home if I thought things weren't altogether right."

The hard, flinty face didn't change expression. "What do you think isn't right?" he asked her.

"A couple of minor details," she replied. "My secretary—or rather the absence of my secretary. The way you screwed up the fashion page this week. Oh, and your choice of a new fashion editor. Tracy is far too inexperienced to do my job. She'll fall flat on her face with the first major assignment you give her. Just like she did in the South of France."

For a moment she thought she saw fear in his eyes. Then he covered it, the closed, hard expression returning to his face. So I guessed right, she thought. Score the first ten points to Ruth Bloom.

Kramer refused to be goaded. When it came to playing games he was an older hand than she was. "What do you want?" was all he asked. Then he opened his top drawer and took out a large white document, which Ruth recognized as her contract.

"So, we seem to have the same reading material," she said, keeping her voice steady. "How do you interpret clause five?"

"The same way the company lawyer interprets it," he replied. "We're offering you half of what it says on the page. You took off too much time this year to be entitled to any more."

Ruth gasped. Surely she couldn't be hearing right. She'd been sick this year. She'd been at death's door this year. And the lousy bastards were making her pay for that. Literally.

She asked for a glass of water. Play for time, Ruth, she told herself. You guessed right the first time, go on with the guessing game. It's the only chance you've got.

Her mind raced while Kramer crossed to the bar and got her a glass. Her memory called on everything she knew about the man. He drank lightly. He was careful about the way he looked in public. His wife was—what was his wife's name? Bernice. That was it. She lived in the Hamptons, reared horses or something.

Then she remembered a lunch she had had with Ted when she'd just gotten back to work. They'd gone to Reuben's because Ted had something private to say to her. Of course, Tracy was the clue to it all, why hadn't she thought of it before? So that's why Kramer gave her the column. And my job as well, by the looks of it.

She took the glass of water he proffered, and put it down on the table in front of her. Then she said, "Does Bernice know about Tracy? Or do you keep that sort of thing secret from your wife?"

He sat down sharply and the overstuffed leather chair let out a little hiss of surprise.

"I don't know what you're talking about," he said, "but it sounds like cheap, street-corner gossip to me."

"I don't think there's anything cheap about it," said Ruth, "at least not the way I heard it. Lunch at some of those uptown eating places you've been taking her to costs the best part of a week's salary."

"What uptown restaurants?" His face had gone an unpleasant shade of red. Mottled, sort of. For the first time she realized how old he was.

"Lutece," she said, playing a hunch, "and a couple of others. Let's not go into details."

He grabbed her glass of water and took a gulp. When he looked at her again, his color had gone more or less back to normal. "I think you're making a big deal out of nothing. How many times do I see you sneak off to lunch with Ted? If every female journalist who had lunch with one of our executives was screwing him, they'd all be called Kate Kennedy."

It was a cheap crack and he knew it. Ruth knew he knew it and she leaned back, satisfied. She'd rattled him and he was starting to make mistakes. She decided to press her advantage. "I always thought that was Tracy's game," she said softly. "A couple of the guys told me she'd do anything to get her own way."

"Who said that?" he shouted. "Tell me their names. I demand to know their names."

"We're not getting jealous, are we?" said Ruth, starting to enjoy things. "I thought you were a sophisticated man, Ed. Surely you didn't imagine you had sole visiting rights on my nymphomaniac ex-assistant."

He sat stock still. And for a while the silence between them shimmered with tension. Then he got to his feet. "You can't prove anything," he said. "Or can you?"

"No," said Ruth, "and I won't even try. As long as you honor clause five of my contract."

"You bitch," he said, "you fat, ungrateful, dirty-minded bitch. That's blackmail."

She smiled the smile that made her look like a cheerleader. "You bet it's blackmail," she said. "What exactly are you going to do about it?"

He walked across to his desk and picked up the contract. "Let me look at this again," he said gruffly. "Then I'll have a word with the lawyer. I'm pretty sure we can work something out."

"Good," said Ruth, getting out of her chair. "I'm pretty sure we can too. I'll be in my office as usual when you want to talk to me."

Kramer stared hard at Ruth's broad, retreating back. I'd no idea she even suspected, he thought. The sooner I get rid of her the better. Before she has anything more concrete to go on.

Mike had a tough day in the studio. The society beauty whose portrait he'd been commissioned to do turned out not to be so beautiful. The fact was, she was a dog. And it had taken the make-up and the hairdresser an hour longer than he'd allowed for, to get her into some kind of shape. At the end of it she'd been passable. When his assistant had finished lighting her, she was almost attractive. The rest was up to Mike.

It had taken him two hours, concentrating hard, to get the effect he wanted. The spoiled bitch he'd been photographing hadn't been any help either. All she could do was moan about the time. If she'd known it was going to take so long she'd have canceled her cocktail party. What was he doing anyway, fiddling around with all those cameras? Surely taking a snapshot was a simple affair?

With an effort born of experience Mike had kept his mouth shut. Until the last shot was in the can. Then he let her have it. "Sorry if I kept you," he told her cheerfully, "but the fault was on your side, rather than mine."

She looked surprised. "How come? I turned up on time, didn't I?"

"Sweetheart, with a face like yours you could turn up two hours early and we'd still be working late. I'm a photographer, not a magician."

Then he hefted his camera bag over his shoulder and walked out of the studio. The Long Island Kellys would probably never speak to him again, even though they were destined to love the pictures. Maybe, he thought, with a beatific smile on his face, I'll be banned from the entire length of the East Coast of America.

He was still grinning when he climbed into his Chevrolet sports car. The notion that he would never have to take another picture of a rich, spoiled woman ever again cheered him up. As he turned onto the highway and headed for home he thought once again about George Perry's offer. And he was tempted. Who wouldn't be? he thought. A partnership in one of New York's most prestigious design companies was an offer he was finding hard to refuse. He would have to give up taking pictures, of course. And there was a lot he needed to learn about layout and the whole business of running a company. Which was why he was hesitating.

He turned his car into the garage underneath the apartment block on Second Avenue. He'd talk the whole thing over with Ruth, he decided. He could always count on her to put a problem in perspective.

"Ruth," he yelled as he pushed open the front door. There was no reply. Funny, he thought, it's nearly half past eight. She's usually home hours before this.

Ruth was home. But due to the fact that her mouth was full at the time, she wasn't communicating the fact. Mike found her in the kitchen, surrounded by the contents of the fridge. She'd managed to eat almost everything they had in the apartment, including a fresh delivery of groceries which had only arrived that morning. Now she was starting on the freezer. Something had to be terribly wrong.

He went up to her and removed a half-eaten chicken drumstick from her fingers. "Why don't you try talking about it instead?" he suggested.

"Okay, okay, eat yourself to death. See if I care. But it won't solve anything, you know. Even if you polish off the entire contents of the fridge. Even if I go out and get some Chinese takeout and really finish the job, you're still going to have to deal with whatever it is that's driving you crazy."

She looked at him. "You win," she said. "Let's go into the other room and I'll tell you all about it."

She looked with distaste at the half-open packages of cookies, the bones of the chicken carcass, the remains of the French cheeses, the empty pizza container. "I'll clean up the devastation later," she promised, "when I'm feeling stronger."

He put his arm around her and led her through to

the warm, wooden-floored center of the apartment.
Aside from the Persian carpet, Ruth's pride and joy, all
the furniture in this main room was his. Over the years
he'd built up a collection of exquisite modern pieces
Ruth could never have afforded. The leather sofa from
Milan, the perspex and glass bookcases he'd had specially
made by a designer friend in San Francisco, the dramatic
lighting by Rotoflex, all transformed Ruth's main room
into a very expensive backdrop. The perfect setting for
two of the most successful media people in Manhattan.

Right now, Ruth felt unequal to all this splendor.
Despite her talent and all her connections, she had just
been fired as brutally as a bored housewife would dismiss the hired help. And that's exactly how Kramer had
made her feel. Like somebody's inefficient hired help.
Unimportant and certainly unworthy to sit on thousands
of dollars' worth of leather sofa.

She told Mike what had happened at the office, spar-
ing him none of the details. After nearly an hour of hearing about Tracy's treachery, Kramer's peccadilloes and
Ted's suspected involvement in all this, Mike leaned back
and shook his head.

"It seems to me, you're well out of it, my love.
Somebody with your talent shouldn't have to come into
contact with rubbish like that. There's an old saying in
my business—if you hang around with shit, you eventually get contaminated by it. Looks like you got out just
in time."

She sighed. "I guess you're right. The problem is,
what do I do now?"

"Come on, that's never been a serious worry for
you. I know at least half a dozen glossy fashion bibles

who'll be calling you non-stop the minute the news gets out you're quitting the paper. The only problem you'll have, my love, is which one you'll grant your very expensive favors.''

She put her head on his shoulder. "Has it occurred to you," she asked, "that I might not want to take on another job in the fashion jungle? The last couple of weeks have robbed me of quite a few of my illusions. You know, I really believed that if you had talent, or at least an eye for style, you could make it in my business. Now I know that's a crock of shit. No matter who you are, you could be a budding Helen Gurley Brown, it doesn't matter. You're only as good as your employer thinks you are.''

Mike sat her up and looked at her sternly. "I think you've got this whole thing out of proportion. Just because some no-talent shithead wants to promote his girlfriend, you don't suddenly cease to exist. What about your readers? They must know the difference between good and bad. Credit them with some intelligence, for God's sake.''

She made a face. "What do you expect them to do? Write in and complain they don't see my column any more? Stop buying the paper? Don't be silly. Sure, a few of them will miss me. Or rather they'll miss the page. But not enough to make any difference.

"You seem to have forgotten, Mike. I was out sick for over six months and I didn't notice the circulation of the *News* dropping dramatically because I was away. No, Tracy Reeves, bad as she is, will make a passable fashion editor. And you can be sure Kramer will underpin her inexperience by buying in stuff from free-lancers."

"Okay," said Mike, "I accept that the *News* behaved badly and will doubtless get away with it. But why does that stop you from wanting to get another job somewhere else?"

She looked at him with the beginnings of exasperation. "You haven't been listening to a word I've been saying. If I take another job, I'll be in the same bind as I was the last time. Forget my talent, forget my experience, forget my reputation even. I'll be a hired hand, the same as any other. And the moment it no longer suits the guys who call the shots to have me around, they'll push me out. Just the way they did at the *News*."

"So what's the answer? Or is there one?"

She thought for a moment. Then she said, "Right now, I don't know. I guess I could raise the money to start my own magazine. Though to be honest I really don't have the business expertise. And I'm not interested enough in the money markets to go out and get it. I could look around for an editorship. There's nothing going on in the nationals at the moment but I guess I could probably swing it with one of the trades. At least that way I'd be the one who called the shots."

She grinned. "I suppose I could always retire and live off you. How do you feel about raising fat babies in the middle of Manhattan?"

He stood up and went over to the liquor cabinet behind the bar. Then he came back to the sofa with a bottle of Californian champagne and two glasses. "So you've finally decided to become a Jewish mother," he said. "About time too. At least you can depend on yours truly not to push you out if I don't like the color of the baby's eyes."

He pulled the cork out of the chilled bottle. "A little replica of you," he said softly. "Do you think she'll have your curly hair and your big appetite? Because if she does I'm going to have to think about earning more money."

"You mean you like the idea?"

"Like it? It's the first thing you've come up with today that makes any sense at all. No, correct that. The first thing since I met you. Darling, it's a wonderful idea, why on earth didn't you think of it before?"

"Because I didn't plan on giving up my job. Also you didn't mention that you wanted to marry me."

He looked astonished. "I don't want to marry. I never did. The whole notion of permanence and houses in the suburbs gives me the willies. You know that. We've talked about it often enough. But that doesn't mean I don't want to live with you for the rest of my life. I think you know that too. So how about it, Ruth? What do you say to a family?"

She poured out the champagne and handed him his glass. "I'll think about it," she said. "I agree you're not perfect husband material. You're not even Jewish. But are you going to make a suitable father? That's what I want to know. I'm not exactly crazy about you running all over the world taking pictures while I bring up our family. It could get very lonely."

For the first time since he got home that night Mike relaxed. He knew he could rely on Ruth to solve a problem, no matter how complicated. "Listen to me," he said, "there's a guy I want you to meet. He's called George

Perry and he runs a design studio. He's got something in mind that could just solve all our problems.''

He's bound to yell at me, thought Tracy, as the yellow cab sped along the highway, eating up the miles between Kennedy and the Big Apple. Shortening the distance between Tracy Reeves and Ed Kramer's temper.

Cannes had been a disaster, there was no getting away from it. Kate Kennedy had seen to that. Her and that slimy lecher, David O'Neill. Like all born survivors, Tracy had her own recipe for coping with defeat. And the first move on the long flight back was to blame somebody else.

Now she had apportioned the blame, all she had to do was to rearrange the facts, and tell her version of those facts to anyone who would listen.

Tracy's version went like this. Kate had done a deal with David O'Neill's organization well before the film festival. Tracy strongly suspected money had changed hands, for when she tried valiantly to get the story, she met with a blank wall. She even stormed the star's table in an expensive French restaurant (she must remember to put in a large bill for this). But it was to no avail. David O'Neill refused to give her an interview. In the end she took matters into her own hands. With the help of Jeremy Boyle, a well-known socialite, she found out where O'Neill was staying and went up to his suite.

At this point in the story Tracy got stuck. Should she stay with the general flow and admit she spent the night there? If she did that, she could always say O'Neill forced his attentions on her. Or should she lie and confess that after one drink O'Neill stuck to his guns and sent her packing?

The latter course had a lot going for it. Tracy emerged from the encounter with her reputation intact. Her reputation as a woman that was. Her reputation as a journalist she didn't like to think about.

So she didn't. Instead she headed for the woman's room at the *News,* where she flicked a comb through her hair and applied fresh lipstick. Then she pointed herself in the direction of Kramer's office. Best to get it over with, she thought, then I can ask him about what's really on my mind. Ruth's job.

But Tracy didn't get off the hook as easily as she expected. Kramer was irritated with the way events had gone in the South of France. When he had finished hearing Tracy's story he was more than just irritated. He was hopping mad. "You don't mean to tell me," he said, "you actually sat down and had a drink with O'Neill. Not just in a restaurant—but in his hotel room as well."

"Yes, but it wasn't any good. He didn't want to do the interview."

Kramer's eyes were colder than usual. He kept his voice low. "Exactly how long did you spend with the man? If that isn't a personal question?"

"About ten minutes . . . why?" What the hell was the old goat driving at?

"Why, she asks me. I'll tell you why. Because if you spent ten minutes with this Hollywood hero, then you'd have been able to file some kind of story. Even if he'd recited the telephone directory."

Tracy was close to tears. "But I told you, Ed. David had promised the whole caboodle to Kate Kennedy.

They'd done a deal together, before the Festival even started."

"Listen, you stupid girl. What Kate Kennedy arranged with David O'Neill is no concern of mine. He could have promised to marry her and I still wouldn't be interested. What bothers me is the way you handled the situation.

"You told me with your own lips that you spent ten minutes with David O'Neill. You even shared a drink together, two drinks, if you count the one in his room. So why didn't you make something of the conversation? You could have asked a couple of questions. Put a few words in his mouth. Hell, you could have made up a couple of quotes. It's been done before. If you had kept the story bland and given the film a plug he wouldn't have denied anything."

Tracy was speechless. Kramer had called her bluff and she had no defense. What could she say? *David promised me the story. I went to bed with him on the understanding that it was all mine. It wasn't her fault that the treacherous bastard double-crossed her at the last minute.*

"I'm sorry I blew it," she said in a small voice. "I didn't mean it. Honestly I didn't."

She was wearing what she had traveled in from France. Faded blue jeans and a tee shirt several sizes too big for her. She might have been some street urchin had it not been for her hair. She had had it styled at Carita before she left and it fell in sleek, glossy waves around her shoulders. It had an expensive, almost impossible perfection that told the world that she was female and she was fun. Far too much fun to do without, Kramer knew.

He sighed and for umpteenth time, he wondered if he wasn't behaving like a fool.

"Why don't you go home, Tracy?" he said to her as kindly as he could. "Take a bath, take a nap, get over your jet lag. Then when you're feeling better we'll talk."

She looked worried. "What do we have to talk about?" she asked suspiciously. "You're not going to kick me out are you?"

"Not this time," he said tightly, "but I'm tempted."

Tracy made it to the door as fast as she could. This was not a time to push her luck. On her way out she decided to wander through the fashion department. She knew better than to ask Kramer what had happened to Ruth, but that didn't mean she couldn't conduct her own investigation.

When she walked through the door she wondered where the fire was. For Ruth's office and the outer office looked as if they had been hit by a minor explosion. Filing cabinets stood with their drawers hanging open. Half the files were stacked on the floor and the other half were sitting in large plastic bags. Brett was hunched behind her typewriter sorting through huge piles of correspondence.

Tracy sauntered over to her. "What the hell's going on?" she asked.

Brett looked up from what she was doing. When she saw it was Tracy, she gave her an old-fashioned look. "Come on, Tracy, that's a stupid question coming from you. I would have thought you'd know exactly what was going on."

Tracy's over-made-up face started to come alive. Somewhere a light was dawning. "I've been away, dummy, or didn't you notice?" she said irritably. She rifled through the letters which threatened to obliterate the desk, then she looked up. "It seems to me that somebody's moving out though."

"Of course somebody's moving out," said Brett. "Ruth's moving out. And if I were you I wouldn't bother to go in and say any fond farewells. She may just throw her typewriter at you."

For the second time that day, Tracy beat it. Good things coming her way. She didn't want to buck the trend.

That night Kramer didn't call Tracy. He assumed she knew by now that she'd gotten the job she wanted. So he worked late at the paper. Went home alone. And spent a sleepless night knowing that Tracy could be sharing his bed if he bothered to pick up the telephone.

The next morning he arrived early and waited for her to make her entrance. He didn't have too long a wait. At ten o'clock his secretary rang through and announced that Tracy Reeves was in his outer office and wanted to see him.

He told the girl to show Miss Reeves in at ten-thirty. It wouldn't hurt to make her wait half an hour. By that time some of the arrogance might have worn off.

He should have known better. He could have kept the redhead waiting all day and her self-confidence wouldn't have suffered one iota. Jesus Christ, he marveled as she walked through the door. The woman even looks the part.

The way Tracy looked that day could best be described as early Joan Crawford. She had on a fitted black suit with a velvet collar that fashion editors always seem to wear in the movies and never in real life. She was covered in gold jewelry. And over one eye was tilted a tiny black pillbox with a view.

He threw his head back and roared with laughter. Tracy was priceless. You had to hand it to her, she certainly knew where she was going.

She looked injured. "What's so funny?" she asked.

"You," he spluttered. "I haven't even told you I'm giving you the job yet and already you've come prepared."

For a moment she looked doubtful. "I am getting it, aren't I?" she said.

He considered playing with her. With a little guile he could spin out the proceedings for another half hour. Then he thought, what the hell? She's a sparky kid. She knows how to make a man feel like a man. Why put her through it? So he nodded his head and told her yes.

The effect was instantaneous. She squealed, she gushed, delight and thanks falling over each other in an effort to convey her pleasure. Then she ran around to his side of the desk and threw her arms around his neck. "You darling, darling man," she breathed, "how can I ever thank you?"

He smiled and disentangled her. "You can cut the drama for a start. Anybody could walk in here. Then what would they think?"

She pouted. "I don't care what anyone thinks. This is the best thing that ever happened to me. Why shouldn't I be pleased?" She paused. "Anyway," she

said, "it's only half past ten. No one would come to see
you till at least eleven."

He raised an eyebrow. "How did you know I'd be
in?"

"Because I knew you wanted to see me. And I know
you well enough to know you couldn't hold out till after
the editorial meeting."

Slowly, with a certain amount of care, she took her
tiny, ridiculous hat off and put it on the side of his desk.
Then, before he could stop her, she unlooked her slim,
black skirt and let it fall to her ankles.

In her moment of victory, Tracy had left nothing to
chance. Kramer noticed with a certain fascination that
her stockings were held up by a lacey garter belt.

"For pity's sake, Tracy," he said. But it was pointless
to protest. She was already unbuttoning the fitted fashion
editor's jacket. With a sinking heart he saw that she
wasn't wearing a bra. The need to have just one firm,
juicy breast in his mouth was too much.

He sunk to his knees in front of her. The perfume
she wore was exotic and expensive and quickened his
senses. Blindly he reached for her, his mouth circling the
full, rosy nipple. For five minutes he feasted on her. First
her breasts, then as his tongue traveled down towards her
navel he tugged gently at her panties. He always liked
to leave the best till last.

Tracy squirmed and wriggled and finally parted her
legs. Kramer had made her wait for half an hour outside
his office. Five minutes was the very least she could deny
him before she let him put his tongue inside her.

Finally Kramer got to his feet and started to unzip
his pants. But Tracy put out a restraining hand. "There

are better places than the floor," she said. Then she walked on her thin, high heels over to his imposing teak and chromium desk. She ran her hands lovingly over the polished leather that covered its surface. Later that day that leather top would have the proofs and galleys of tomorrow's newspaper scattered over it. Now it was hers to do whatever she liked on. Her own personal playground. Gingerly she sat on the edge, testing it for stability. Then when she was satisfied that it would hold her weight and more, she swung her legs up on to it.

Kramer caught on fast. Swiftly crossing the room he spreadeagled her across his desktop. Then he pulled his pants down and took her where she lay.

At that precise moment the door to his office swung open and Ted Gebler walked in.

They all saw each other at the same time. And everyone stopped what they were doing. Ted stopped walking. Tracy stopped thrusting. Kramer froze completely. Then he thawed.

Two seconds later he was on his feet and pulling up his pants. Then he took Ted by the arm and led him to the outer office. Before he closed the door on her, he turned to Tracy.

"Get your things on," he snapped, "then get the hell out. I don't want to see you in this office, or in this building. Do you understand me?"

Tracy understood. She got her clothes on at the speed of light. Then she opened the back door of Kramer's office and took his private elevator to the street.

At a moment like this, there was no way she was going to face Ted Gebler or Ed Kramer or the rest of the office.

*　　*　　*

Tracy didn't know it at the time, but there was no way she was going to face Ted Gebler, Ed Kramer or the *Daily News* ever again. This was decided over lunch at the "21" Club later that day by Ted Gebler, drinking dry martinis, and Ed Kramer, drinking mineral water. Ed had had enough intoxication for one lifetime. From now on sobriety was the name of the game. And survival. Which was why he was having lunch with Ted Gebler and promising Tracy's instant dismissal. "It was an aberration," he said somewhat shakily. "A terrible mistake. But then you understand that kind of thing. You went through it yourself not so long ago."

Ted closed his face. Ed Kramer wasn't going to get off the hook this easily. He and Kate might have been having an affair, but no one could prove it. And no one had caught them in the act. The Tracy Reeves business was a horse of a different color. It was time to tell Ed Kramer the facts of life.

By the time coffee was served the expensively suited editor was more than willing to do a deal. Any deal Ted had in mind, so long as he kept his mouth shut.

Ted ordered a brandy, accepted a cigar from the hovering flunkey, and made his pitch. His requests were simple and specific. He wanted the deputy editor's job over and above Bill Gerhaghty. And he wanted the appointment to be effective from that day. He also wanted one more thing. He wanted Ruth to be brought back as fashion editor.

Kramer pursed his mouth into a thin line and regarded the ambitious young man facing him over the starched linen tablecloth. Lunch today had confirmed everything he had suspected about Ted Gebler. He was tough. He was completely without scruples. And in about eighteen months' time he would probably be making a pitch for the editor's seat.

In the normal course of events Kramer would have sat on Ted and promoted someone stronger than Gerhaghty to keep him in line. But now it was too late. Things were no longer normal and never would be again. He braced himself for the years to come when he would have to live with his head permanently looking over his shoulder. It was not an attractive prospect.

There was a short silence, then he said, "Are you absolutely sure about Ruth? I was due to instruct the accounting department to send her her severance pay this week. I suspect at this stage of the game that's the only thing she'll want out of the *News*."

"I don't think either of us is in a position to guess what Ruth wants from the *News*. Who knows? When she hears that Tracy has resigned she could be interested in having her old job back."

Kramer sighed. "I'll let you handle that one. As deputy editor you are responsible for heads of departments. With my approval, of course."

Ted took in a lungful of cigar smoke and coughed. Then he pulled himself together. In his new job he was going to have to get used to expensive cigars and restaurants like the "21" Club. He looked at Kramer. "And do I have your approval? About Ruth, I mean?"

Kramer spread his hands, palms upward. "Sure," he said. "If she wants her job back who am I to stand in her way?" Then he looked at the younger man through half-closed eyes. The effect was surprisingly lethal. "I've got a little suggestion for you," he said. "One you might take seriously."

He leaned back in his chair. "You've had an easy ride today. A very easy ride, and I've been in no position to make it otherwise. But don't think you've got it made."

Ted leaned forward. "Why not?" he said.

"I'll tell you why not," said Kramer. "I promoted you today because you threatened to blow the whistle on me to our proprietor. That's fair enough. But if you're ever tempted to use what you know about me again I'll can you tomorrow. I don't mind going down. I've been in this game long enough to know the rules. But if I go down, then you go down right along with me."

He looked up and signaled the waiter for the check. Then he signed it, stood up, and without waiting for Ted walked swiftly out of the restaurant.

Ted looked after Kramer with increasing respect. He'd win in the end. He knew that. He was younger and stronger and versed in the ways of the jungle. But he had to take his hat off to the old man. Kramer sure knew how to give him a run for his money.

T he best way to describe how Doug Freeman made love was to say it was incredibly well-mannered. He knew what pleased a woman and he did his best to give a good account of himself. Kate was flattered at the trouble he took, and wished quite desperately that it had moved her. But the truth was that she was neither shaken, nor stirred.

What they did with their bodies was in a way an extension of their conversation. Relaxed and lacking in passion. If their lovemaking did anything, it brought them closer as friends. And for that, Kate was thankful.

She had a few intimates in her adopted city. Alan Baker was a lively lunchtime companion, but after office hours he devoted all his time to his wife and children out in the suburbs of Berkshire. There was the occasional invitation to Sunday lunch, just as there was from the Petersons. But joining other people's family weekends only reminded her of her solitary state.

Doug Freeman changed all that. He had a wide circle of friends, most of them, like him, either single or divorced. The closest any of his friends got to marriage was living with their partner. But there were no happy families and that suited Kate. Just as Doug himself suited her. There were no serious intentions and no declarations of love. But there were no jealous rows either. If Doug did something that irritated her Kate told him so. And vice versa. Everything between them was straight and clear and understood.

As the weeks turned into months, Kate began to learn more about this intelligent, considerate man she had gotten involved with. She discovered his surface gloss went only skin deep and had been carefully applied to hide who he really was. For Doug Freeman was ashamed of his background. When Kate discovered why, she was sharply reminded of the difference between England and America. Doug Freeman was born to a life of poverty in the Midlands.

In the States no one would have given a damn about his past. What mattered was his present. But in this old, class-conscious society, the rules were different. Here you were judged by where you came from, and so Doug always took pains to conceal the fact that his father had worked as a laborer on a building site. When Doug was just four years old, his father was killed in an industrial accident, leaving his mother to bring up Doug and his two sisters on social security. She didn't enjoy it. And a year later she ran off with a traveling salesman. None of them ever saw her again.

The council and the social workers did what they could. They succeeded in persuading a distant aunt to take in the girls. But no one wanted to know about Doug. In the end, he was brought up in a children's home.

If God had been neglectful in some ways he had been kind in others. For he had given Doug Freeman two gifts: intelligence and good looks. His intelligence took him to the top of every class he attended. In the end it won him a scholarship which took him out of the orphanage and into college.

He graduated from Bristol with a first-class honors degree and found little trouble getting apprenticed to the Manchester office of a national newspaper. His good looks got him to Fleet Street. He was spotted by his proprietor's wife during a tour of the provinces. A week later he was transferred to the London office of the *Gazette*. A week after that he found himself getting better acquainted with the woman who had effected his transfer.

To say Doug Freeman slept his way to the top would have been unfair. Any man as bright and determined as Doug would have made it. The proprietor's wife merely hastened the process.

The affair ended a year after it began and Doug started looking around for another job. His humble start in life had made him streetwise. He knew when the writing was on the wall before anyone took out a pencil.

Luckily for Doug, the *Financial Times* was looking for a film critic when he was looking for an out from the *Gazette*. Within days he had crossed the street.

Doug Freeman remained at the *Financial Times* from

that moment on, graduating from film critic to showbiz columnist and finally to arts editor. The glamor of the job combined with the stability of the paper suited his temperament. He'd been approached once or twice by other papers. And he'd been tempted to move on. But whenever he got a definite offer the *Financial Times* always matched it. Had Kate offered him the deputy's job on the *Post,* the *Financial Times* would have probably behaved in exactly the same way, leaving Doug richer and Kate thwarted.

As it was, Doug and Kate got together in an entirely different way. And the arrangement suited them better.

As summer gave way to autumn, the affair began to take on a set pattern. They would spend every weekend together, alternating between Doug's rather austere apartment in Bayswater and Kate's cozy mews cottage. During the week, they'd spend a couple of nights together, but neither of them left any personal belongings behind. Kate sensed that Doug was the kind of man who needed a certain amount of privacy. And she was glad. She had not the slightest impulse to move in on him. Her work was proving too demanding for any closer involvement. And when she set off one Friday evening in November to meet her lover at the BBC, she felt for the first time in her life that she was actually having her cake and eating it too.

The Corporation was holding a party to launch its Christmas schedule, and the plan was to have a quick drink at the reception before going on to dinner at the Petersons'.

Kate was wearing one of the new, calf-length skirts that were fashionable that season, a tweed hacking jacket and flat boots. She had let her hair grow halfway down her back, because Doug liked it that way. And as she caught sight of her reflection in the plate glass lobby of the BBC she felt as if she had shed ten years since she arrived from New York. Her mirror image was younger, softer, more female. She smiled as she pressed the button of the elevator that would take her to the penthouse suite.

How deceptive appearances are, she thought. Here I am looking for all the world like Alice in Wonderland, yet I've never felt stronger in my whole life. Jeremy Boyle wouldn't have stood a chance with me now. I'd have eaten him for breakfast. Him and anyone else who tried to push me around.

When the elevator reached the ground floor where she was standing, it was empty. She got into it quickly without looking behind her. She never trusted the machines, particularly in England, so she didn't notice the other passenger who followed in close behind her. Only when she turned around did she realize that she was face to face with Charlie Hamilton.

Charlie acted with the kind of decisiveness that had made him famous as a negotiator on both sides of the Atlantic. He pressed the stop button, jamming the elevator between the first and second floors. Then keeping his finger on the control panel, he leaned over and kissed Kate full on the mouth.

The elevator stayed where it was for ten minutes. Then it started to move again. Downward.

When they reached the lobby Charlie, his arm firmly around Kate now, ushered her into the street. They were nearly intercepted twice. Once by a producer who seemed to have an urgent message for Charlie. And once by Doug, who had just arrived for the party.

As far as Charlie was concerned, they simply didn't exist. Kate started to protest, then changed her mind. For the first time in her life, she was not in control. She had no idea what was going to happen in the next five minutes, or the next five days.

All she knew was that Charlie was back in her life again. She wasn't alone anymore. She remembered the look on Doug's face as they had pushed past him. Poor Doug. Poor, make-do man, keeping the bed warm until the man I really wanted came back to me. There would be a lot of apologizing to do. But later.

She hugged closer to Charlie. Don't leave me again, she thought. I couldn't handle losing you a second time.

It was raining when they got outside and, without consulting her, Charlie bundled her into the last taxi in line, giving the driver an address in Clifford Street.

"Where are you taking me?" she asked. "If that's not a rude question."

"For dinner, of course," he said. "Don't you ever look at your watch?"

She sighed. "How silly of me, I should have known. Stock markets can crash, presidents can be assassinated, but Charlie Hamilton always has to have his meals on time."

He looked amused. "That really got under your skin, didn't it?"

"Of course it did. I don't like being taken for granted. Anyway my work is important to me. I'd been doing it an awful long time before I met you."

He squeezed her hand. "I realized that. Why do you

think I pushed David O'Neill into seeing you in Cannes. Not that I got any thanks for it."

"But I did try to thank you."

"I didn't notice."

Once more she sighed. "Look, I tried calling your room as soon as the publicity office told me you were responsible for the interview. But there was no answer. I tried to leave a message, but no one spoke English. Then I was late for my plane, so I decided to leave it till I got back to England."

"And you couldn't get me, because I was in the States," he finished for her. "Dear Kate, what a mess we've got ourselves into. All I ever wanted was a simple love affair. Nothing dramatic. I don't see myself playing Chekov or Shakespeare. So what happens? We both end up in the *Comedy of Errors*."

She hugged him. "I like the *Comedy of Errors*. It has a happy ending."

The cab drew up outside a tall, narrow, corner house with a plain black door. Charlie paid off the driver and rang the bell. Almost immediately a butler in full regalia answered it.

They went through into a small, tiled hall, the main feature of which was an ornate, curving wooden staircase. Everything around her was polished wood or brass and the whole place had an air of antiquity that made her think of Victorian England. Victorian England just two minutes from Bond Street, London's most expensive shopping thoroughfare. It could never have happened in Manhattan.

"Where exactly are we?" she asked in a small voice.

He put his arm around her. "Only my club," he

said. "I didn't know of anywhere else where we wouldn't have to make a reservation for dinner. Come on, I'll take you up to the bar, you look as if you could do with a drink."

It was as if she had walked into another world. Sure, she had heard about English gentleman's clubs, but for all her experience of the world Kate had very little idea of what they were really like. The room at the top of the staircase with its paneled walls, roaring log fire and oil paintings of grand old ancestors was like something out of Hogarth.

In the corner a couple of elderly men were playing backgammon, and past them through an archway was a smaller brighter room with tables in it and a bar. The bar was deserted, which suited Kate. She had taken quite enough on board that evening without having to deal with the conversation of strangers. Particularly as she had a strong suspicion that she wouldn't understand a word anyone was saying.

She was suddenly, uncomfortably, aware that the man who was standing beside her, ordering drinks, organizing dinner, was almost a complete stranger himself. She saw him looking at her, amused. "You look as if you're suffering from a severe dose of culture shock," he observed. "Don't worry, the first hundred years are the worst. After that you soon get the hang of it."

Kate allowed herself to be led through to a half-empty dining room. Friday night, Charlie explained to her, was a quiet one in the club. Most of the members had left town for their country estates.

They sat down at a table by an open fire. And then she recalled something about the English she no longer even thought about. They didn't heat their rooms properly. She was aware that her left leg which was near the fire was far too hot. The rest of her was decidedly chilly.

In a strange way it evened the score. The club might be able to run to grand old sporting pictures. The mahogany was probably antique and priceless. But they still couldn't get it together to put in decent central heating.

Now that she was no longer frightened by her surroundings she started to listen to what Charlie was saying. He was telling her about the trip he had just made to California and the deal he tied up.

When Charlie talked about the film business, he came alive. And as he did so, the cluttered, old-fashioned room faded into the background. All Kate could see were the characters he was telling her about. The actors with their fragile egos. The studio heads who were more interested in the bottom line than the talent they employed. And, at the center of it all, the negotiation. This was the part that Charlie loved. The reason he was there.

As he told her the details of the financial battle he had just been through she started to warm to him. This man, this hustler, was someone she could understand. Then the waitress came up to the table with their dinner, and once more the room swam into focus.

He looked at her anxiously. "Is something the matter?"

"Not really. I just feel a little out of place."

"Come on, you can do better than that."

"OK, I'll be straight with you. When you talk about America and about the things you do, I can handle it. But this . . . these chandeliers, the oriental carpets, the way you talk to the help—like they're old family retainers or something. That doesn't make sense to me at all. It's like you're a different person, and I don't know if it's somebody I'm ever going to know."

"Aren't you selling yourself short? I thought your family came from Westchester, not the Bronx."

"The distance between Westchester and the British aristocracy is still halfway around the world."

"And when we made love," he asked, "how far did it seem then?"

She met his eyes. "Hardly any distance at all."

"In that case," he said, putting down his fork, "I think it's time we went home."

They spent the weekend at his apartment in Eaton Square. If she had been with Doug, she would have gone home for a change of underwear, cream to take her make-up off, or just a pair of blue jeans. Now she did without, for she needed nothing. She washed her face with his soap. Her hair with his shampoo. When she was cold she put on one of his dressing gowns. When she was hungry she raided his fridge. For the first time since she had turned her back on New York City she was happy.

They made love most of the weekend. And in between making love they talked. He told her about his first wife, Fiona. She told him about Ted. In a way she needed to. As if by talking about Ted she would somehow purge his memory.

"I didn't expect you to be untouched by experience," was all he said. "At your age, it would have seemed rather eccentric."

"But do you expect me to love you?"

"Yes. Without some kind of commitment this kind of thing can be very tawdry. I know. I've been there."

She smiled, thinking of Doug. "Not so much tawdry, as empty. Meaningless. But love . . . that's a very big word."

He stroked her hair. "Try affection then. Or maybe concern. They're good feelings if you're not ready for the other one."

"But I want to love you, dammit. It just seems so impossible."

"What's impossible? Me, or the places I visit?"

She pulled a face. "The places, I suppose. That club you took me to last night. It's a whole world away from me. I'd never fit in there, even if I wanted to."

There was an edge to his voice. "I didn't invite you to fit in," he said. "I merely asked you to take a look. It may seem stuffy and old-fashioned to you, Kate, but that world I showed you last night is the one I grew up in. You talk grandly about fitting in with me. What you don't know is that I'm the one who'd done the fitting in. All my bloody life. What do you think it's like for a grand young Englishman struggling to make his way in a world where people earn their living? Your world, Kate. When you've got the sort of accent I had, it's almost impossible.

"I told you I started life as an actor in the English provinces. In those days I didn't talk like normal people. Every time I walked into a pub and asked for a pint of beer, people pissed themselves with laughter. But I survived it. I eventually got accepted . . . eventually. It didn't happen overnight."

She looked at him with the beginning of understanding. "I'm sorry," she said. "I had no idea. I was so busy worrying about myself I didn't even think about you. Forgive me if I was rude about your background."

He put his arms round her and held her close. "You weren't rude, darling. Just defensive. It'll get easier, you'll see."

Charlie was wrong. Things didn't get easier. They became more difficult. But once Kate had made up her mind to love, there was no stopping her. A sane woman would have drawn the line at what Charlie Hamilton expected. For what he wanted, what he felt entitled to, was a carbon copy of his first wife. Kate had lost all sense of reality, so she didn't walk out on him. Instead she let things ride.

Fiona had been a cordon bleu cook, so Charlie imagined that Kate would be in the habit of whipping up gracious little dinner parties. Or even sumptuous feasts for two. He was disappointed.

In the summer Fiona had played tennis and in winter she hunted. She had done both superbly. The only physical activity Kate had time for was an hour's work-out in the gym. And she had her hands full keeping that up more than three times a week.

In the space of a few short weeks Charlie discovered that Kate had no patience for embroidery. No interest in antique procelain. And always dropped her clothes off at the laundry. Furthermore she expected him to do the same.

He was thrown into confusion. The Englishman had never known a woman who didn't exist solely to please a man. This independence of Kate's was a whole new experience.

Kate, for her part, was equally perplexed. In the world where she worked, women were men's equals. She had never been expected to come in second. Not by her father. Not by her three brothers. Certainly not by any of her lovers. Even Ted helped her make dinner on the rare occasions when they ate together. Now here was this man expecting a handmaiden as well as a lover. It couldn't last. But it did.

Despite the surprises, the misunderstandings, the constant fights, Charlie and Kate stayed glued together as closely as Siamese twins. For when all was said and done, they needed each other. Neither of them could figure out why, but the fact remained that if one of them went away, even for one night, the other pined.

I guess it must be love, thought Kate, as she wrestled with the intricacies of a *boeuf bourgignon*. If it wasn't you wouldn't find me within two miles of a kitchen stove, let alone living with one.

For in everything but name they were living together. During the week, she stayed in Charlie's apartment while making brief forays to Eaton Mews to pick up a change of clothes or a grand dress if they were going out in the evening. On the weekends, Charlie lived out of a suitcase in her tiny, higgledy-piggledy mews cottage.

One Friday morning, after six months of this, Charlie woke up early, hauled Kate out of bed and bundled her into the front of his dark blue Rolls-Royce. Then without a word of explanation he drove around to her house. Once in the kitchen, he made them both a cup of coffee.

"Now," said Kate irritably, "would you mind telling me what all this is about? If you've decided to throw me out, why the hell don't you pick a more civilized hour?"

"I'm not throwing you out, Kate," he said patiently, "or if I am, then I'm throwing myself out too. What I'm trying to do is rationalize our lives."

"Come to the point," she said crossly. "I haven't got all morning."

"Okay," he said, "you asked for it. What I want you to do is move in with me. Permanently."

She was aghast. Seeing her stricken expression, he put his arm around her. "Look, I'm not asking you to marry me. Not yet anyway. All I'm asking is that we stop living like gypsies and start behaving like two grown-up people. Everyone knows we're sleeping together. The Petersons. Your office. My office. Even your ex-boyfriend, for Christ's sake. So is it too much to ask you to be organized about it?"

She thought for a moment. "I suppose when you put it that way, it doesn't sound unreasonable." She was silent for another minute or two. Then she said, "Look, I'll keep this house and I'll leave a couple of things here. Then if one of us changes our mind, I can always move back in."

He was exasperated. "You haven't moved out yet, and already you're talking about leaving me. Darling, I'm sorry if you think I've pushed you into this. I didn't mean to. What I'm trying to say is that I love you and I want to be with you. I don't want to see you running off every five minutes to get your hairdryer or a clean pair of panties. It unsettles me. I hate it."

A look of dawning relief came over her face. She put down her coffee cup, stood up and took him by the hand. "Follow me," she said. Then she led him up the winding, narrow flight of stairs to the top bedroom. In the corner stood a stack of trunks and suitcases she had brought with her from New York. "If you'll help me carry all this downstairs," she said, "I'll start packing."

He looked bemused. "This is all very sudden, my love. What changed your mind?"

"Just one thing. One simple thing, without which I would have stayed firmly rooted here, instead of just paying the rent and leaving it empty."

He looked even more confused. "I'm not with you," he said.

"Then you don't listen to yourself, do you? Have you any idea what you just said to me, Charlie Hamilton? You told me you loved me. I've been slaving over a hot stove for six months to hear you admit it."

He took her in his arms and put her down gently on the narrow, truckle bed under the eaves. Then slowly, with infinite care, he undressed her. Then he made love to her.

After what seemed like hours she finally lay still and spent. He was the first one to speak. "You don't have to say it all the time to mean it, you know."

The only thing he never talked about was the girl. Kate had seen pictures of her. There was a silver-framed photograph on the piano in the main drawing room. Yet another on the kitchen dresser. And when they were going through some vacation pictures she saw her again. Tall and slender with a mass of dark hair and a look of the British aristocracy.

Kate suspected she was some lost love of Charlie's,

and for a while she avoided talking about her. Then one day, when she caught him staring at the sad, dark girl in the silver frame, she decided enough was enough.

"Who is she?" she asked. She met with silence. Exasperated, she said, "Look it's apparent to me that you once loved her. So will you stop the mystery and tell me once and for all who the hell she is."

"I didn't once love her," said Charlie. "I still do. I suppose I always will."

It was worse than she had thought. Slowly she said, "At least tell me what her name is. And how you know her. We can work out how this affects me later on."

He came across the room and took her hand. "Darling, I'm sorry. I didn't realize it was upsetting you. Look, she's no threat to you. She's no threat to anyone, that's the problem. If more people cared about her she wouldn't be in the mess she's in today."

"You still haven't told me who she is."

"Her name is Maria. Maria Hamilton. She's my daughter."

"Charlie, I had no idea you had a daughter. Why didn't you tell me about her before?"

He looked sad. "There seemed to be no need. She's a long way away. In good hands, or so I thought. Now I'm not so sure."

"Where the hell is she? And why on earth did you send her away in the first place? I thought you told me a minute ago you loved her."

"And so I do. But I couldn't cope with her. Maria had a very special problem. I didn't want to risk it coming back. So when Fiona died I sent her to school in Switzerland. She's been there for nearly two years."

"And now something's gone wrong." She looked at him closely. "I'm right, aren't I?"

He sighed. "Yes, Kate, you're right. Though what I'm going to do about it, I simply don't know."

"Look, suppose you tell me about Maria from the beginning. All about her. Don't leave out any of the details. Then maybe I can help you get things clearer in your mind. I don't pretend to know anything about teenage girls, except I was one myself once. So at least I know how it feels."

"Darling, do you really want to hear it? It's a hell of a burden."

"Yes, I really want to hear it. I won't give you any peace until I get to the bottom of this mystery. So you'd better prepare yourself for a long siege."

It was early in the evening when Charlie started to describe his daughter and the forces that had formed her. By the time he had finished it was past midnight and neither of them had bothered to stop for supper. It was not a story that encouraged an appetite.

The first thing that went wrong in Maria's life was that she wasn't born a boy. Fiona had longed for a son. And when her prayers were answered with a girl, she was less than pleased.

Most mothers love their babies whatever their sex. Fiona was different. Because she was a placid, rather acquiescent woman she had little control over her life. Her father had made most of her decisions. And when she married, she allowed her husband to do the same. There was only one area in which Fiona was powerful, and that was in her own home. She decided what kind of chintz would cover the windows and the sofas. She chose the menu for every meal. And when it came to babies, Fiona's word was law.

From the moment she was born, Maria had had the effrontery to defy her mother's wishes. Apart from being a girl, there were other things that were not exactly right. The way she looked, for a start. As Maria grew into a toddler, it became apparent that she was not going to take after Fiona. She had none of her feminine grace. There was no delicacy about her. Instead, Maria was a stocky child with long strong limbs and a voice that could wake the dead.

When Maria cried at night, she not only woke the nanny, she woke the housekeeper, the cook, Fiona and usually Charlie as well. On these occasions Charlie would beg his wife to go to her. But Fiona refused. When children cried in the night, it was the nanny's job to comfort them. Everyone knew that.

Unfortunately, nobody had informed Maria of this fact. So when her mother failed to come when she called for her she just went on crying. She cried away most of her girlhood. For try as she might, there was simply no way she could please her mother. The arts of flower arranging, tapestry, even dancing, eluded her. She was too big and ungainly for such pursuits.

Not that Maria wasn't good at things. She was just good at the wrong things. She had inherited her father's mind as well as his looks and she was always the head of the class in arithmetic and chemistry. She was a wonderful swimmer, had the fastest serve in her year and ran everyone off their feet on the hockey field.

If her mother frowned at these achievements, her father applauded them. She was his daughter all right.

Down to a tee. He was proud of her and he showed it. But it was never enough. From an early age, Maria had set herself the impossible task of making her mother love her. If it killed her, she would make Fiona take notice. It nearly did.

By the time she was adolescent, Maria finally caught on to the fact that to succeed in her mother's eyes she would have to look like her mother. Her hair would never be fair like Fiona's, that she knew. At twelve, she was too young to have her face altered through plastic surgery, that she knew too. But there was one thing she could do. She could be thin. All she had to do was stop eating.

It took Maria three months to starve her strong, healthy five feet six inch frame to eighty-four pounds. Then her mother noticed her, but not in the way she wanted. She was packed off to a Harley Street specialist, made to feel like a freak and told to eat up or else. Maria's weight dropped to seventy pounds. It was then that she was admitted into the hospital. The next two years were spent in and out of clinics. Being stuffed full of food to get her to the right weight. Fasting when she was let out so she could look like the skeleton she perceived to be perfection.

Ironically Maria's life was saved by her mother's death. For when Fiona died two great obstacles were removed from Maria's path. She no longer needed to make her mother notice her. She wasn't there anymore. And she no longer needed to emulate her either. Her place was taken by other role models. Her gym teacher, her grandmother, an actress her father was being seen around with. Fortunately for Maria, none of them was thin. Within three months of her mother's demise, her weight returned to normal.

When Charlie's mother, Maria's grandmother, suggested a Swiss finishing school he agreed to the plan with relief. She was off the danger list. She looked like a human being again. Maybe in Switzerland she would learn some of the female graces Fiona had failed to teach her. She would have liked that, his beloved, misguided dead wife.

So he wrote out the vast check that was needed for his daughter's further education. Trusted his mother to look after her during vacations. And stopped worrying. Until the smart Swiss finishing school called to tell Charlie that his daughter was pregnant. She had to leave immediately.

"So that's what all the fuss is about," said Kate. "Now I understand. Poor girl. She must be in a hell of a state being thrown out of school and being pregnant. What are you going to do about her?"

He shrugged. "Talk to my mother, I suppose. Mary's close to the girl. As close as anyone can be—she's a spikey little thing. I daresay she'll decide what to do in the end." He sounded resigned.

"Am I allowed to be involved in this family drama?" Kate asked. "Or would it be easier if you and your mother hammered it out between you?"

Charlie looked at her with some surprise. "I didn't think you'd be that interested. It's all rather sordid, after all. I would have thought you'd have given it a wide berth."

Now it was Kate's turn to register surprise. "There are times when I think you really don't know me at all.

What's so sordid about Maria? She had a rough childhood. From the sound of it, her mother didn't give a Goddamn about her. And now the kid's gone and gotten herself knocked up. It's happened to all of us you know. Even me. Only I was lucky. My mother loved me, so I pulled through the experience."

For the first time that evening, Charlie put his glass down. "I don't believe you," he said, "why didn't you ever tell me about this?"

"Look, I wasn't trying to conceal anything from you. I just didn't think the fact I once had an illegal abortion when I was a junior reporter was going to make any difference to our relationship. After all I'm hardly a virgin. And anyway, wasn't my experience of the world something you found rather attractive? Or have I gone and ruined everything by confessing all?"

"No, it's not that." Charlie was confused. "It's just not something I expected of you."

Kate laughed without much humor. "You mean nice Catholic girls don't go in for abortions. Or do you mean nice Catholic girls don't go in for getting pregnant? Or maybe it's the nice girl syndrome that worries you. Listen, Charlie, any girl whether she's a hooker or a nun, can get pregnant so long as she goes to bed with a guy. The fact that she loves the guy. The fact that he loves her. The fact that it's the first time for both of them doesn't matter. None of it matters. What counts is that they had sex. And they weren't careful about not making babies. What really pisses me off about this whole thing is that the girls who get pregnant usually turn out to be innocents. In my experience it's the good time girls who never get pregnant. They're far too wised-up about the pill or the IUD or whatever form of contraception they prefer.

"No, it's nice girls like me, or nice girls like your daughter, who get the babies and the rotten reputations. Or didn't you know?"

He went over to where she sat on the big white sofa and put his arms around her. "Will you promise me one thing?" he asked.

"What's that?"

"Will you repeat all that to my mother when we go up and see her tomorrow?"

Kate stiffened. "If it will help her understand the situation. And if it will help Maria. I think she's the most important person around here right now."

Mary Hamilton was a chilly lady with a sense of tradition. Anyone looking at her hairdo would have known that. For it wasn't so much a hairdo as an edifice. Dyed blue, teased and laquered within an inch of its life, it reminded Kate a little of the Eiffel Tower.

She and Charlie had driven down that day for what she thought would be an informal lunch. Her first sighting of Mary Hamilton soon destroyed that illusion. Here was a lady who was playing it by the book.

When they went into the dining room Kate knew her hunch was right. For Charlie's mother had left nothing to chance. The shining mahogany dining table was magnificently set. Row upon row of silver cutlery was lined up on either side of the plates. Kate was confronted by not one, but three crystal drinking glasses and it was hard to figure out what should go in them. If I pour mineral water into the claret glass she might never ask me back, Kate panicked.

As if the table didn't have enough on it already, what with the soup plates, the side plates, the silver dishes containing salt and what Kate imagined to be mustard, Charlie's mother had added some little touches of her own. There was an array of silver ducks which would have served as a centerpiece if it weren't for the flower arrangement. This was Mary's *coup de grâce.* A giant array of spring daffodils, it was placed in such a way that Kate wasn't able to see Charlie at all. She could see everyone else and they could see her, but the man she loved was concealed from her.

Despite herself, Kate was unnerved. As a reporter she had been in any number of bizarre situations. But this one made them all seem ordinary.

Mary Hamilton wasn't alone at her formal table. With her was her oldest son and Charlie's brother, Robert—the twelfth baronet and owner of the stately pile they were sitting in. Also present was Robert's wife, Charlotte. They could have both stepped straight out of the pages of the *Tatler.* Robert, thin and rather stooping, with silvery blond hair and a rather weatherbeaten face, bore no resemblance to his brother whatever. In his corduroy trousers and tweed hacking jacket he managed to make Charlie look out of place. There was nothing wrong with the cut of Charlie's suit, but somehow the dark gray flannel he had thrown on so hurriedly that morning looked wrong in the country. The minute the butler had shown them into the drawing room before lunch, Kate had realized that. And she wondered if somehow Robert hadn't done it on purpose. Charlie had always been the rebel. And now that his daughter was in trouble it was as if his entire family was conspiring to put him in his place.

Kate pulled herself together. It was an uncharitable thought. I'm imagining things, she told herself. The place is getting to me. She concentrated her attention on Charlotte. She was the least fearsome of Charlie's family and judging from her conversation the most empty-headed. A chubby redhead with an almost transluscent complexion, she seemed fixated on two subjects: the weather and the goings on of a number of characters with improbable names like Snee, Duff and Boofy. Kate did her best to concentrate on the weather. Charlotte's gang sounded as if they came straight out of the Muppets.

Talk about the weather lasted until the cheese came around. Then the family wanted to get down to the business of the day. Maria. With an effort, Kate concentrated on what Mary was saying and tried not to notice what the butler was pouring in her glass. She hadn't seen a bottle of Perrier since she had arrived and it bothered her. Like most Americans she liked an aperitif, but rarely drank alcohol with her meals. If she didn't have a glass of water soon, she could easily end up roaring drunk.

Then she heard what Mary had on her mind and stopped worrying about the Perrier. Maybe another drink wasn't such a bad idea after all.

What Mary Hamilton had to say was brutal and to the point. Maria was no good, her actions had proved that. And for girls like her there was only one solution. She must have an abortion—an expensive, discreet abortion. Then she must be sent to live in the country with her family until a suitable husband could be found for her. As long as Charlie was prepared to settle a sizable amount of money on his daughter Mary was willing to come up with a list of candidates.

Kate was dumbfounded. The whole discourse was like something out of the Middle Ages. "You can't do that," she said. The words were out of her mouth before she could stop them. Suddenly Kate found she was the center of everyone's attention. Robert gazed myopically at her with watery blue yes. Charlotte opened her mouth and closed it like a Dutch doll. And Mary turned to her, an icy smile on her lips.

"Tell me, my dear," she said. "Why can't I organize Maria's life? She is, after all, my granddaughter."

Kate felt her face go hot, then she took a sip of her wine. Well, here goes, she thought. Keeping her voice even she said, "Look, Maria might be your granddaughter. I'm not disputing that. But she's also sixteen years old and a woman. I mean, she's a thinking, feeling human being. You can't just go and sell her off to the highest bidder. She may not even want to get married for God's sake."

Mary drew her breath in. "What Maria wants or doesn't want is no longer of any importance. She forfeited her right to choose when she got herself into her present difficulties."

"You mean Maria ceased to have any rights as a human being the moment she got pregnant? That's ludicrous. I simply don't believe it."

There was a silence in the dining room. And the absence of sound was more audible than if the butler had come in and dropped a tray of drinks on the carpet. Finally it was Charlie who broke the spell. "I think all Kate meant," he said gently, "was that we should discuss my daughter's future like a family, rather than make any rash decisions." He turned to his brother. "What do you think about the situation, old boy? Surely it's not as bad as all that. This is 1986 after all. Maria's not the only girl in her circle to get into trouble."

Robert was flummoxed. If the truth be told he agreed with his brother. And with Kate. But he couldn't afford to get on the wrong side of his mother. There was a high price to be paid for defying Mary Hamilton, for she not only controlled her family but also had a good deal of influence over most of the other families in the country. In her straight-backed dotage, Mary had the kind of respectability that is the equivalent of power in more commercial communities.

So in the end the twelfth baronet went for the soft option. "I'm inclined to go along with Mother," he said. "I know what year it is, Charlie, but we do have certain standards to maintain. If this family can't play by the rules and set a good example, then where would anyone be?"

"By anyone," said Kate, a steely note in her voice, "I take it you're referring to tradesmen and lesser mortals without titles and grand family trees."

"Come off it," interrupted Charlotte. "You're not calling us prejudiced, are you?"

Kate smiled and looked at the closed, inbred faces around her. Then her eyes strayed to the walls where she met the same faces in the family portraits. Every eye, real and painted, stared at her with irritation. "I actually think I am," she said pleasantly. Then she leaned forward and moved the cut-glass vase of daffodils to one side. For the first time during the interminable lunch she was able to get an uninterrupted view of the man she loved. With a certain relief she saw he was smiling.

"Look," she said, her confidence returning, "I know you have standards, and I respect them. And if you're able to live up to those standards I'm sure they can be a great source of security and reassurance. But what if you can't? What if you're screwed up and misunderstood like Maria? Is it really necessary to sacrifice her on the altar of your standards, just because appearances would suffer if you didn't? It's a bit harsh, isn't it? Doesn't a sixteen-year-old girl deserve better than that?"

Mary Hamilton stood up. Totally ignoring Kate, she rang for the butler. He appeared almost instantly and Kate wondered if he hadn't been crouched behind the door the whole time listening to their conversation. "Your ladyship?" he said.

"Coffee," she said. "And Boyson, we'll be taking it in the drawing room."

With that she left the table like a battleship under full steam. Robert and Charlotte followed like two attending destroyers, Kate waited behind for Charlie. "What now?" she whispered. "Is it pistols at dawn? Or will your mother just slip a lethal dose of arsenic in my coffee?"

He came and put his arm around her. "I'll tell you what," he said, "if you promise not to drink anymore, I'll do something that could save your life. And my inheritance," he added.

"What's that?" she asked.

"I'll get you out of this house and into the car in ten minutes flat. Then we can talk about Maria properly."

She planted a kiss on his cheek.

"You've got yourself a deal," she said.

They talked about Maria for most of the two-hour drive home on the highway. And both of them agreed an arranged marriage was out of the question.

"What Maria needs," said Kate, "is time and somebody to talk to. Somebody who really understands her problems. Maybe you should think about the possibility of therapy—she sure sounds as if she could use it."

Charlie lit a cigarette and passed it to Kate. "Maybe you're right," he said, "but I don't much like the idea of paying someone to look into my daughter's head. Surely there's another way. I wonder if an older woman, someone who's been around a bit, could help her."

Kate puffed on the cigarette, inhaling the strong, acrid, smoke.

"We don't know any older women," she said, "unless you're thinking of your mother. And I hardly think she's going to be a great help in this situation."

Then she turned to him. "I've got an idea," she said. "What about an older man?"

"Sorry," he replied, "I don't follow you."

"Okay, I'll spell it out. The older man I was thinking of was you. You are her father, for Christ's sake. You do love each other, surely the two of you can work it out together."

Charlie was quiet for a moment. Then he shook his head. "It won't work," he said. "I wish it would, but Maria and I have never been close enough for the kind of discussion you have in mind. No, it has to be another woman. Don't worry, Kate, I'll think of somebody."

They said nothing for the next fifteen minutes. Then as they left the highway and headed into the suburbs of North London, Kate started to talk. "You don't have to think of somebody to talk to Maria," she said, "I'll do it myself. I guess I've been kicked around enough to know about the world."

"I can't ask you to do that," he said. "You've taken me on. You even tried to sort out my bone-headed family. But I can't wish Maria on you. That would be too much to ask."

"Then who will you wish her on?" asked Kate angrily. "Some do-gooder who doesn't give a damn about you or your daughter? You know who you remind me of right now? My mother. Only being Catholic, she'd probably come up with some worthy nun. Listen, both of you have it all wrong. The only person who can help a girl who is in as much trouble as your daughter is someone who genuinely cares. I care because I love you. And I think, if we give it time, I could come to love Maria too."

They argued it out until they reached Eaton Square. Finally Charlie stopped the car outside their house and leaned against the wheel. "You mean what you say about taking on Maria, don't you?"

"Sure I mean it. She can even come and live with us for a while until she gets on her feet. The girl needs some kind of security."

He sighed. "Clearly this is my day for doing deals with you."

She looked curious. "You want to make some kind of deal about Maria. Is that it?"

He nodded.

"Okay, I'll listen. I'll agree to anything you have in mind as long as it's reasonable."

He smiled. "It's reasonable, my love. The way I see it, there's only one way I could possibly allow you to take on the responsibility of my daughter. As my wife. What do you say, Kate? Are you willing to give it a try?"

She leaned back in her seat and folded her arms. "That's not a deal," she said, "that's a proposal."

"Okay, so it's a proposal." He was impatient now. "Well, what do you say to it? You still haven't given me an answer."

Kate smiled and all the tension and frustration of the day went out of her. "The answer's yes, you silly bastard," she said softly. "I'd love to be your wife. It's the best deal anyone ever offered me."

Maria came home a week later. An abortion had already been arranged for her. So instead of going to Charlie's apartment she went straight to Abbot's Clinic in Maida Vale. Once there she checked in and refused to see anybody until the operation had been completed.

Kate's first sight of the girl who was to be her stepdaughter was in the private ward of an abortion clinic. It was nothing to write home about.

The dark, lustrous hair in the photographs was lank and unkempt. Her skin was pasty, almost puffy-looking. And the face was not so much sad as empty. Kate couldn't wait to get her home. Once she was back where they could look after her properly they might stand a chance of getting her back to normal. Whatever normal was.

In a few weeks, Kate started to find out. For Maria turned out to be less of a problem than she had expected.

She was a fastidious, rather vain girl, who seemed to spend most of her mornings in the bathroom. Kate didn't begrudge her the time. After her experience Maria needed all the help she could get to bring her back to the human race.

In the beginning Kate provided her with the little luxuries that every woman hoards in the bottom of her closet. Bath oil from Floris. The Estée Lauder skin care products she was going to use when she got around to it. Chanel's newest fragrance. The pure silk nightdresses still in their packages that she bought in Henri Bendel when she was last in New York.

Maria accepted everything and said thank you politely. The way she'd been taught in finishing school. Slowly her appearance began to improve. Her skin began to take on the kind of see-through, luminous look that only English girls seem to possess. She started to put on weight. And the moment her hair began to look like hair again, Kate sent her off to Michael at Leonard's, who had been taking care of her since she came to the city.

In three months, Maria started to look like a normal sixteen-year-old. A normal sixteen-year-old from the upper-middle classes, that is. She went in for silk scarves with horse brasses and pieces of saddlery all over them. Her hair was habitually fastened back with a wide velvet bandeau. And she wore the kind of low-heeled Gucci shoes that had shiny gilt chains across the front of them.

When Maria returned to the human race she finally found her tongue. At first she started talking about her time in Switzerland. Kate would come home to find her deep in conversation with her father about off-piste skiing and bobsled racing at St. Moritz.

Kate welcomed this new development. Once Maria opened the lines of communication, she could be reached. And once she could be reached, she could be helped.

Then came the first setback. Her grandmother sent for her. Kate put her foot down. The girl was coming along just fine. She didn't need Mary Hamilton to ruin all her patient nurturing. In the end it was Maria who decided what should happen next. For she had come across a letter from her grandmother in Charlie's study.

"Why does Granny want to see me?" she asked over dinner that night.

"She probably wants to lecture you on what a wicked girl you've been in Switzerland," said Charlie as gently as he could.

"Oh dear, I knew I'd have to face the music sooner or later."

"You don't have to face anything you don't feel like facing," said Kate angrily. "All you did was get pregnant. You didn't commit any kind of crime."

The girl took a forkful of food and chewed on it thoughtfully. She didn't look troubled. Quite the reverse. She looked rather docile, and Kate was reminded somewhat uncharitably of a cow out to pasture.

Finally Maria spoke. "I know I didn't do anything wrong in your eyes, Kate. But you've got to understand, it's different for Granny. She's not used to that kind of behavior. It must have been a terrible shock for her."

Kate was visibly surprised. "So what do you plan to do about your grandma?"

"Go up and see her, of course. I'll explain everything to her. And she'll rant and rave and want me to go and live in the country. Then I'll apologize nicely. Which will calm things down a bit."

Kate put her glass of water down. She couldn't believe what she was hearing. "When you've apologized," she asked, "what will you do then?"

"Promise to help in the stables, I should think. She knows that always keeps me out of trouble. If I go up there every other weekend to start with, you won't hear any more complaints from Granny." She turned to Charlie and fixed him with her clear, rather protuberant blue eyes. "I promise you, Daddy, you won't get a peep out of her once we've had our little talk." Then she folded her napkin neatly, asked to be excused from the table, and went to her room.

Just for a moment Kate had a wild urge to run after the girl, bring her back and tell her the facts of life. Loud and clear. The way she saw them.

She fought to control herself. I can't protect Maria from everything, she thought. Anyway she's going to have to face Mary Hamilton sooner or later. She's better off going to the country and facing her now. No doubt, I'll be the one to pick up the pieces afterward, she thought grimly.

But Kate was in for another surprise. Maria came back from the country full of smiles. Granny had been angelic, she said. And very understanding. Oh, and she'd arranged to go up there the following weekend because the local hunt was meeting at the house.

Kate never did have the close, heart-to-heart talk she'd planned with Maria. Somehow something always seemed to get in the way. Her future stepdaughter had made contact with a second cousin who lived nearby in

Ovington Square, behind Harrods. The cousin turned out to be a girl, Olivia, of around Maria's age. And the two seemed to have a lot of secrets to share. Kate would come upon them whispering in the drawing room. Or devouring the contents of the fridge. It was this that formed the basis of their first serious row.

Kate had invited the Petersons, Hughes Hartmann, her editor-in-chief and his wife, and a Hollywood film director friend of Charlie's for dinner one Friday evening. The day before, she had been to Fortnum's during her lunch hour and loaded up with smoked Scotch salmon, strawberries out of season and a rack of lamb. She knew she had spent far too much money but she considered it was worth it. The food would take hardly any time to prepare and her guests would be impressed as well as well fed.

The art of entertaining is not in the preparation, she thought a trifle smugly. It's in the buying. She caught a taxi back to the apartment and deposited everything in the fridge. Then, still feeling pleased with herself, she went back to the office.

Kate didn't get home till late that evening. There had been a rail crisis outside Paris and her French stringer, Bernard Brochand, had taken his time getting the story together and putting it on the telex. When she finally got in, she was exhausted. The sound of loud giggles coming from the kitchen did nothing to improve her mood.

I bet she's got that damned Olivia staying for supper, thought Kate. If I have to spend another evening listening to tales from the polo ground, I swear I'll scream bloody murder. Nowadays she couldn't even rely on Charlie to switch the conversation to anything more interesting. He seemed fascinated with all things equestrian, and would spend hours with the girls, talking about the finer points of cubbing and the art of jumping while riding sidesaddle. This was something his mother had mastered as a girl and he made it sound equivalent to taking an honors degree in the humanities.

Wearily she hung her coat up and made her way to the kitchen. It was then that she saw what Maria was preparing for supper. Scotch smoked salmon. A rack of English lamb. Followed by strawberries out of season. Everything was neatly set out on plates and Olivia had thoughtfully squeezed lemon on the salmon.

Kate let out a cry of anguish. "Thát was my dinner party for tomorrow night, for Heaven's sake! What do you think you're doing with it?"

Maria smiled her sweet grown-ups-don't-understand smile. "You didn't tell me about any dinner party. I thought you'd bought all this for tonight. I did tell you Olivia was coming."

Kate took a deep breath. "Maria, if you'd bothered to look, you would have seen that I'd bought enough food for eight people. There are only four of us tonight. Surely whatever intelligence there is in that empty little head of yours would tell you the stuff in the fridge wasn't for tonight."

Maria went bright pink and ran over to her father who was standing rather uncertainly in front of a pile of freshly washed strawberries. "That's not fair," she screamed. "Daddy, tell Kate she's not being fair. If she had meant the lamb to be for a party, she should have left a note by it."

Kate turned to Charlie. "Since when do I have to start leaving notes in my own kitchen?"

"Kate, try to be reasonable . . . the child isn't a mind reader. How was she to know?"

"I've said it once, for God's sake. By thinking. Though I'm beginning to doubt whether she's capable of anything quite as advanced as rational thought."

Maria let out a scream. "You bitch. Just because you've got some high-powered job in the press I suppose you think you know everything. Well, let me tell you something. You know fuck all about anything. You dress like a tart. Your table manners are all over the place. And Granny told me you actually smoke in the dining room. Daddy would be better off without you. We all would. So why don't you do yourself a favor and go back to New York where you belong?"

There was a long silence while they all held their breaths. Finally Kate spoke up. "So that's what you really think of me, is it?"

Charlie hurried over to her. "The girl didn't mean it, Kate." He looked imploringly at his daughter. "You didn't, did you, Maria? Things just got out of hand. We all say things we don't mean, when we're upset."

Maria shuffled her feet. Then she looked at Kate. "I'm sorry," she said. "I didn't mean it about the way you dress. Or your table manners. It's just that you're different from the rest of us. But then Americans are different from us. Daddy told me so only the other day . . ."

Her mother came over to help her choose her wedding dress. It was something Kate knew she was perfectly capable of doing on her own. But as the date for her marriage drew closer, she felt she needed an ally.

Not that she lacked for wellwishers. There was Maria, who was sticking out her neck to be helpful. Alan Baker, who constantly shooed her out of the office to have her teeth checked, her hair trimmed, her passport renewed. Even Mary Hamilton unbent and sent her a wedding gift—an old-fashioned dress ring Charlie's father had given her on their tenth anniversary.

Yet still she felt as if she was on her own. Of course there was Charlie, but he was the bridegroom. No, she needed someone close. Someone American. Someone from her team. So she sent for her mother.

When Anne Kennedy arrived she checked into the Waldorf, an old-fashioned hotel in the city. Kate had wanted her to stay in the apartment, but Anne refused. "You've got quite enough to do without running around after me," was all she said. And she refused to be budged.

In a way Kate was grateful. Despite all their efforts to be friends, she and Maria remained at loggerheads. Increasingly she resented the way the girl monopolized her father. She used any and every excuse to involve Charlie in topics of conversation Kate had no interest in.

Kate had a vision of her mother sitting blank-faced while Maria and Charlie went over the finer points of the Trooping of the Color. No, she was better off at the Waldorf. Sometimes it was safer to be alone than to be surrounded by people who bored you stiff.

When she had lunch with her mother at Harrods the following day, she noticed that Anne looked worried. "Is everything okay at the Waldorf?" she asked. "You look as if something's on your mind."

"There is, and it's not the Waldorf."

"Then what is it?"

"Kate, darling, it's you. Look, I know I shouldn't say this, but are you quite sure you're doing the right thing by marrying this man? I know he's charming and the perfect gentleman. When I set eyes on him at the airport, I realized that. But is it enough? You're going to spend the rest of your life with him, child. Are you sure he'll be giving you the future you want?"

Kate was concerned. "Mother, whatever brought this on? I've been living with Charlie for nearly a year now. If I had any real doubts, surely I'd know about them by now."

"Kate Kennedy, it's me you're talking to. Not one of your chic new friends. I know what makes you happy. Really happy, and I'm not sure that Charlie does."

Nor am I, thought Kate. But it's too late to turn back now. Unbidden into her mind came a memory of Ted. He was sitting behind his desk in the features department and all around him was chaos. At his elbow was a half-eaten roast beef sandwich and a bottle of beer. In front of him was a stack of page proofs. And lining up to see him were Bernard Glen and Tracy Reeves.

What struck her about the Ted in her mind's eye was his enjoyment of the situation. For he was yelling and screaming and carrying on at the top of his voice like a prize fighter. Only in New York, she thought. Over here we lock away lunatics like you. Out of nowhere she was filled with a fierce longing for the chaos and disruption of her home. If it hadn't been for Ted, she thought, I could have been back there now. Instead of in this wilderness. With a man who knows nothing at all about me. A man who is about to become my husband.

Damn you, Ted, she thought. Damn you for making me love you. Damn you to hell . . .

Her thoughts were interrupted by her mother, who was looking at her anxiously. "Kate," she said, "you're crying. I was right. Something is the matter."

The most important day in Sandy's life fell on Thursday, a week before Easter. Because there was no getting out of it, she spent it the way she had been spending it for the last eight years. She did the weekly wash. Lionel and Thomas's football shorts, little Sophie's rompers, Ted's never-ending pile of shirts, all sat waiting for her in the laundry basket.

I wonder, she thought, if they ever imagine what happens between the moment they dump them on the floor and the moment they find them on their shelves clean and puffed up and ready to put on again. She sighed and started to load the machine. Never mind, she thought, I won't be doing too many more washes where I'm going.

For Sandy had finally made up her mind. After nearly a year of snatched afternoons with David O'Neill, flights to the coast on the pretext of seeing her family. After over a year of pretending she was married to Ted when they hardly even talked anymore, she had had enough. That crazy fling in the sun right after her father's funeral hadn't been so crazy after all. What she and David had for each other had survived separation. She smiled. There was no getting rid of the man.

In her thirties, when most women have grown wise to love, Sandy had only just discovered it. What she had had with Ted wasn't love at all, she realized. It was too one-sided for that. A man who loved you, really loved you, didn't need any convincing. He was sold on you without you having to get pregnant, or work your fingers to the bone making a home out of nothing. He just wanted you because you were you.

She had been suspicious at first. She'd read about David's reputation with women and she imagined she was just another blonde. Replaceable. Interchangeable. It had taken him a long time to convince her otherwise. But his persistence had succeeded. Heavens, the man even wanted her with her children! He wouldn't hear of it any other way. He had to be crazy. Or in love. Sandy decided on the latter and made her plans accordingly.

Now the point of no return had come. Tonight over dinner she would tell Ted their marriage was over. If she had to she would tell him about David, but she hated the idea. It would be so much cleaner, so much nicer for the children, if she could just pack up and go home to her mother while the lawyers sorted out the details. There was time enough for Ted and the rest of the world to know about David. Her first task was to break free.

She prepared the dinner with her usual attention to detail. Roast lamb with rosemary, jacket potatoes, string beans. Then when everything was ready to go in the oven, she looked at her watch. It was time to round up the children. The twins were no problem. The ever-reliable Martha had agreed to have them spend the night. She had even gone along with Sandy's lie that she and Ted wanted a special private celebration.

The last time Ted and I went in for anything like that, she thought ruefully, was over two months ago. And then he was drunk from an office party. Still, Martha didn't have to know. Nobody had to know except for her and Ted and maybe the kids when the dust had settled. The kids, she thought with something like panic. What on earth am I going to do about Sophie? It was too much to ask Martha to have her spend the night as well.

Sophie was going through a difficult phase at that time. Sandy's normally placid, angelic, little girl was becoming fretful and erratic. As if something in her unconscious mind had picked up the disturbances in her home and was reacting to them.

Sandy went out into the garden and found her daughter teasing the cat to the point of torture. She picked up the unfortunate feline and carried him inside to his favorite chair. Then she dealt with Sophie.

The slap was short and sharp and landed square on her rosy pink cheek. It was followed by a loud wail. "That's for being cruel to Oscar. Now maybe you know how he felt."

But Sophie was too young to understand why her mother was being so unreasonable. She wailed even harder. In the end Sandy put her to bed early. Divorce or no divorce, Sophie was in no state to be farmed out. Poor baby, she thought, I'll make it up to you the moment we get away. You see if I don't.

She was just getting into the bath when the phone rang. It was Ted. There was some kind of celebration at the office and he was going to be late. Did she mind waiting on dinner?

Sandy did. She had spent the best part of a week nerving herself up for tonight. She had even gone and told David she was finally having it out with her husband. How could he be late?

"Try to keep the party as short as you can," she said tightly. "I have something important to say to you when you get home. And it won't keep."

Ted put down the phone with a familiar sinking feeling in the pit of his tomach. Sandy was pregnant again. He knew it. Why else would she demand that he came home on time? They didn't have that much to talk about nowadays.

He stayed on later at the party than he intended. Part of it was nerves. He wasn't looking forward to hearing Sandy's news. Three mouths to feed was tough enough, but four? That kisses goodbye to the extra money from my promotion, he thought. At the rate his family was growing he would have to oust Kramer sooner than he planned.

He turned to the bartender and ordered himself another bourbon and water. Then he raised his glass in a toast to the woman the party was in honor of, Ruth. They were celebrating the impending arrival of her first baby. Her's and Mike Stone's. It's got to be the time of the year, he thought moodily. What was it about the winter months that made women so fertile?

While he propped up the bar, Ted did his best to count his blessings. Ruth had to be at the top of the list. Fashion editors that good were hard to find. Not that it had been easy persuading her to come back to the paper after Tracy had been fired. He thought back to the long evening he had spent at her apartment. At first she had been quite adamant. As far as she was concerned newspapers and everyone on them were a crock of shit. She wanted nothing more to do with journalism.

She had started to soften a little when he told her about Tracy's dismissal. Particularly when he said it was on the grounds of talent—or, in her case, lack of it. It was a lie of course, but what else could he say? Anyway it seemed to do the trick. Ruth's confidence in the system seemed to have been restored. After that it had taken a few encouraging words from Mike. The promise of a raise in salary and Ruth was back on the payroll. Only it wasn't as simple as that. Life never was. Six months after going back to work Ruth walked into his office, bright as a button, and announced that she was pregnant.

His first reaction was to calculate how much time she needed for maternity leave. Spring was a busy time of the year for the fashion department. All the advertising for the new year needed support. What the hell was she doing getting pregnant at a time like this?

But he put a good face on it. There was no point in antagonizing her. Not in her present mood. So he took up a collection and reserved the downstairs room in O'Henry's. And here they were drinking to the fact that he was about to lose his fashion editor for the next three months.

It was no good, he thought, no matter how much whisky he consumed, his mood wasn't going to get any better. So he paid the bill and started to make tracks for home. Better face the music and get it over with.

He got back around nine-thirty. The lamb was overdone. The potatoes were reduced to a mush. And his wife was looking as ruined as the dinner. What on earth was the matter? Usually when Sandy got pregnant, she bloomed. He made an effort to be nice to her. "I'll go around the corner and buy some champagne," he said. "I've a feeling we'll be needing it tonight."

Sandy looked at him as if he had lost his mind. Did her husband know something she didn't? And if he did, what was there to celebrate?

She shook her head. "I think a dry martini would be a better idea. Under the circumstances."

Ted looked confused. "But you never drink hard liquor when you're pregnant." Then he grinned. "Well, not in my experience, anyway."

Sandy did her best to control her voice. "Who said anything about me being pregnant?"

"Come on, darling, it was pretty obvious. First you insist I come home early from the office. Then you announce you have something important to tell me. What else could it be?"

Sandy collapsed into the nearest armchair and took a hold on her drink. There's no point in beating about the bush, she thought. The time for home-cooked meals and polite conversation is over. I'd better tell him and get it over with.

She took a strong pull on her martini. "I want a divorce," she said.

Ted looked puzzled. "Did I hear you right? Are you saying you want out of this marriage?"

"That's what I'm saying," she said.

"But that doesn't make any sense. Between us we've got three children and a mortgage to maintain. Why on earth would you want such a thing?"

She started to feel angry. Any other husband would have been wounded. Or at the very least screaming mad. All Ted could do was look worried and talk about the price of school lunches.

"Maybe you haven't noticed," she said, "but our marriage hasn't exactly been functioning for a while. A very long while. And while we're at it," she added, getting it all out, "it's a kinda big assumption you made about me being pregnant. How in God's name can I get pregnant from a husband who doesn't make love to me unless he's blind drunk? It takes a lot of loving to make a baby. Or maybe you don't remember?"

He walked across to the bar area and made himself a drink. Then he came back to where she was sitting and took her roughly by the arm. "Sandy," he said, "what is all this about? It's coming up on eight years since we've been married. You've never complained before—except once, and I did something about that. So why do you suddenly want out?" His face took on a hard, suspicious look. "There isn't somebody else, is there?"

She pulled away from him. It was an instinctive gesture. The man gripping her so painfully above the elbow was beginning to look like a stranger. For some unaccountable reason she felt scared of him. Things definitely weren't going as she had planned.

"Why would there be anyone else?" she said weakly. "Stamford isn't exactly humming with action. And even if it was, when would I have the time?"

She was protesting too much and she knew it. Damn you, Ted, she thought. No matter how far away from you I get, you can always see through me.

He let go of her arm and sat down on the sofa opposite her. "I think it's time you told me what's going on," he said softly. Then he looked at her face, white and terrified, and he made an attempt to smile. "Look, I'm not going to eat you, Sandy, I promise. Maybe you're right, maybe I haven't been as good a husband as I should have been. But if I don't know what's happening in my own house, how can you expect me to make any sense of the situation?"

"Nothing happened in the house," she said. "Absolutely nothing. I swear to that."

"Then where?" he asked her.

She thought of stalling. Then she thought, the hell with it. He'll find out in the end, why not tell him now? "Los Angeles," she said in a small voice. "Mostly Los Angeles. There have been times in New York too. But not often. Like I said, I don't have all that much time to spare away from the children."

He looked at her coldly. "So you considered the children. That's very generous of you. Very generous indeed. And have you told them about this . . . affair?"

She shook her head. "I told nobody. I thought I owed you that much. Now all I want to do is go. I don't want any discussions. Or any recriminations. It's too late for that." She looked at him. "Do you want to know something? It was too late even before I met David."

The moment she mentioned his name, she regretted it. For she knew that Ted knew exactly who she was talking about. Serves me right, she thought, for trying to make him jealous in the first place. What a shame he'll never know we were play-acting. That the real thing didn't even start until a good year afterward.

Ted put his head in his hands. "I guess I know when I'm licked. What match am I for David O'Neill, a Hollywood star? Or should I say stud?"

"You can say whatever you like," she said, "it's not going to change the way I feel. About him. Or about you. It's over, Ted. It's been over for a very long time. Why don't we just give it a decent burial and call it quits?"

He held his hand out. "You win," he said. "But just clear up one thing for me, will you? Did Kate have anything to do with this? I mean, if she hadn't come along would you have stopped loving me?"

She hesitated, then reached in her bag for a pack of cigarettes. Ted stared at her in surprise. Sandy had never been a smoker. Then he sighed. There seemed to be a hell of a lot of things he didn't know about his wife.

She lit a cigarette, inexpertly, fumbling slightly. Then she said: "Kate didn't make me stop loving you. I was willing to go on with things in spite of her. No, Kate didn't make me stop loving you at all. *You* made me stop loving you. I don't suppose you remember now, but when she left town you as good as sat shiva for her. For months on end you walked around the house with a long face, mourning for this big lost love of yours."

She looked at him hard, trying to communicate the

pain that had been stored up in her for so long. "Do you have any idea how lonely it is to live with a man who belongs to someone else? Oh, there's no denying that you were there in body. You even lent me that body from time to time. But you didn't convince me, you know. I knew I'd lost you. Even then. I guess in the end I ran out of patience waiting for you to come back to me. To tell the truth, I really didn't believe you would."

He was staring at the floor, concentrating on a point somewhere between his feet. And for the first time since they started the conversation, Sandy realized her husband couldn't meet her eyes.

"So it was that obvious, was it? I had no idea. I always imagined I managed to keep the whole thing to myself." Finally, after what seemed like a long time, he looked up. "Forgive me, Sandy," he said. "I didn't know I hurt you so much. I never intended to. I thought, given time, the whole thing would blow over and we'd eventually work things out."

"You might have told me instead of keeping me guessing. If we could have just talked about it." She put her drink down. "What's the point of 'if'? Play that game and you end up with, if I hadn't got pregnant, if you hadn't stood by me. If you hadn't met Kate. We can't change our lives, Ted. All the iffing in the world can't do that. All we can do is try not to blame each other too much for what happened. And try to repair the damage."

Almost as if on cue, the air was split by the piercing scream of their youngest child. Instinctively Sandy got up and went to her. Minutes later she reappeared with Sophie in her arms. "What is it, sweetie?" she murmured. "Bad dreams?"

Sophie snuggled up to her mother and mumbled something unintelligible. Sandy smoothed her hair. "It's a dream, silly. That's all. Just a dream." She blew at an imaginary obstacle somewhere above the little girl's head. "See, it's all gone now. There's nothing to be frightened of anymore."

Just for a moment, Ted felt a pang of envy toward his daughter. She'll always be there for you when you wake up in the night, he thought. But what about me? What happens if I have a bad dream and need someone to chase it away for me? And the realization that he was going to lose his wife finally hit him. He had never really valued her before. The fantasy had always been Kate. Bright, beautiful, unattainable Kate. If I had met them both at the same time, he thought, I wonder which one of them I would have chosen. But he hadn't. And now he had neither.

He went into the kitchen and made a pot of coffee and some sandwiches while Sandy put Sophie back to bed. Sandy was right. There wasn't too much they could do for each other now, except repair the damage. The lawyers would sort out who got the house and where the furniture went. He imagined she wouldn't want too much in the way of maintenance with David O'Neill in the picture. But that still left the question of the children. He didn't want some Beverly Hills shyster deciding how many times he could visit them.

He and Sandy talked over the question of their three children until the early hours of the morning. And when they finally made their decisions, they did so as friends. Ted could see his children as often as he wanted. He could take them away every year for a vacation. And every other year for Christmas. It wasn't ideal, but it was the best they could do.

Before they called it a night, Sandy turned to Ted. "There's one final thing I think you should know," she said. "Call it a goodbye present if you like, but I think I should tell you, your friend Kate Kennedy is getting married."

He felt as if someone had hit him in the face. In an evening full of surprises, this was the final irony. "Is it anyone I know?"

"I don't think so. The guy's name is Hamilton, Charlie Hamilton. He's some kind of theatrical agent."

"Is she in love with him?" Suddenly it was important to know.

Sandy shrugged. "I don't have the faintest idea. Though if you ask me, it could be a rebound affair. It happens to a lot of women." Me included, she thought. Aloud she said, "Why don't you find out, Ted? London's not that far away. Though if I were you I'd get a move on. The girl's getting married the day after tomorrow. You don't have that much time to change her mind."

She frowned. The only disadvantage to loving David O'Neill was that the guy who handled his career was the same guy that Kate Kennedy was planning to marry. The thought of meeting Charlie Hamilton and his new wife appalled her. She'd had quite enough of the skinny broad for one lifetime.

She hoped against hope that Ted would be in time to knock Charlie Hamilton out of the running.

Epilogue

The man had been traveling for a long time. He had come across land and flown over sea. He had fought his way through the hustle of airports and braved the rush-hour traffic on two continents. Now at last he had reached his destination.

In front of him stood Kate Kennedy in navy flannel trousers and a turtleneck sweater. She looked untidy and slightly pink in the face, as if someone had woken her from a deep sleep. She did not look like a bride on her wedding day.

"Why are you here?" she asked him. It was as if they had only finished speaking the day before yesterday.

"I heard you were getting married," he said. "I came as soon as I could." Then looking at her disheveled appearance he asked, "You are getting married, aren't you?"

She smiled. "That was the plan, but it's early in the morning. I'm not due at the church till four-thirty, so I haven't started getting ready yet."

Then she looked at the man she had once loved, travel-stained and weary in his camelhair overcoat. "Look," she said, "why don't you come in for a moment? You look as if you could use a cup of coffee."

He walked into her bow-fronted drawing room with its higgledy piggledy furniture and worn leather sofa. She saw the look on his face and laughed. "Most of the time I don't live here. So it isn't a palace. Staying here last night seemed traditional."

He didn't say anything. He didn't have to. It was obvious where she lived and it wasn't something he wanted to think about. He didn't have time.

"Sandy and I are getting divorced," he said abruptly. "The marriage didn't work out after all. In spite of the baby."

"I'm sorry," she said softly. "Is that why you're here?"

"No," he replied. "Even if we were together, I'd still be here. When I knew you were getting married I had to come."

She looked at him and it was as if all their years of loving were suddenly back with them in the room. And there was no need for words. She crossed to where he sat and held out her hands. He took them and she led him up the winding stairway and into the room where she had slept the night before. The bed was still undone and the pillows were rumpled and disturbed.

As they got undressed, his eyes didn't leave her face. Then they were together and all the longing and the needing that they had both put aside finally found expression. Their bodies fitted together, the way they had always done. As if they had been created for each other. And just like the first time, they wasted no time on preliminaries. Their need was too urgent.

Being inside her was like coming home. A sweet, hot home he would never leave again. They climaxed together quickly the first time. After that they resumed their old rhythm. And it was like the beat of the sea on the shore. Timeless and unending.

The bright sunlight streaming through the attic window woke him. With a start he looked at his watch. It was already past noon. Kate had a date at four-thirty. A date to marry another man.

He shook her gently. "Wake up, chicken, you've got a big day ahead of you."

She smiled and stretched. "What's so big about it?"

"Maybe this is a bad time to remind you, but you did mention that you were going to a wedding this afternoon."

"Oh, that." She looked worried. "What the hell am I going to do about it?"

"What do you want to do?"

"Ted, you should know me well enough not to have to ask that question. What do you think I want to do? I want to be with you, you klutz. I always did."

"I know, but I wanted to hear you say it. Now all you have to do is dispose of this Charlie Hamilton character you're meant to be getting hitched to. You can't just pack your bags and walk away from him, you know. The guy deserves some kind of explanation."

Charlie. For a moment she experienced a pang of regret. It had been good while it lasted. Very good.

But it couldn't go on forever. She should have known that from the start. From the moment he took her to that stuffy English club of his. It was as if he was introducing her to a whole new lifestyle. A lifestyle that she could never, would never, fit into.

And that daughter of his. She made a wry face. Maria might have been a royal pain, but at least she laid it on the line. "Americans are different from us," she had said. "Daddy told me so only the other day."

What a pity Daddy didn't explain it to me too, Kate thought. We could have saved an awful lot of misunderstanding.

Now she was going to have to set the record straight. Once and for all. She dreaded the prospect. She reached over to the alarm by her bed. It was nearly one. Charlie would be having lunch at the apartment with Maria and Olivia. The maids of honor.

A thought struck her. "What plane are you booked back on, Ted?"

"The five-thirty. Why?"

"I was just wondering if we had enough time to book an extra ticket."

He reached across to where his jacket was lying. From the pocket he extracted a package. In it there were two tickets to New York. First class.

She smiled. "That was presuming a lot. What if I'd told you that I wasn't interested? That I was going ahead with my wedding plans?"

"Then I would have wasted the money. Either way

it didn't seem like the biggest risk I've ever taken. I was gambling on my life, Kate. Both our lives."

She thought ahead to the future. In a city where she belonged. With a man she belonged to. And for the first time in years she felt free. And very sure. What she had to say to Charlie wasn't going to be so difficult after all.

Trudi Pacter has been chronicling the lives of the rich and infamous for the past twenty years. A former Fleet Street Women's Editor, she currently divides her time between London, New York, and her family's estate in Leicestershire. She is married to Baronet Sir Nigel Seely.